FROM THE PAGES OF
THE RISE OF SILAS LAPHAM

"I guess you wouldn't want my life without the money."   (page 3)

"If the girls are going to keep on living in Boston and marry here, I presume we ought to try to get them into society, some way; or ought to do something."   (page 27)

"There is nothing really to be ashamed of in mineral paint. People go into all sorts of things."   (page 62)

He deferred to his business superior with the sense of discipline which is innate in the apparently insubordinate American nature. If Corey could hardly have helped feeling the social difference between Lapham and himself, in his presence he silenced his traditions, and showed him all the respect that he could have exacted from any of his clerks.   (page 103)

"If society took in all the people of right ideas and good sense, it would expand beyond the calling capacity of its most active members. Even your mother's social conscientiousness could not compass it. Society is a very different sort of thing from good sense and right ideas. It is based upon them, of course, but the airy, graceful, winning superstructure which we all know demands different qualities."   (page 129)

What harm could giving the dinner possibly do them? They might ask any or all of their acquaintance without disadvantage to themselves; but it would be perfectly easy to give the dinner just the character they chose, and still flatter the ignorance of the Laphams.   (page 161)

Lapham put his napkin into his collar too, and then, seeing that no one but Bellingham did it, became alarmed and took it out again slyly.

He never had wine on his table at home, and on principle he was a prohibitionist; but now he did not know just what to do about the glasses at the right of his plate.   (page 178)

"I really suppose that you can't put a more popular thing than self-sacrifice into a novel. We do like to see people suffering sublimely."
                                                              (page 184)

"I was the only one that wasn't a gentleman there!"   (page 196)

"There is something you have got to bear. It's a mistake we've all made. He don't care anything for you. He never did. He told Pen so last night. He cares for her."   (page 228)

She began to bewail herself, and to sob convulsively: "Oh, Silas! Oh, Silas!" Heaven knows in what measure the passion of her soul was mixed with pride in her husband's honesty, relief from an apprehended struggle, and pity for him.   (page 262)

The morning papers brought the report of the fire, and the conjectured loss. The reporters somehow found out the fact that the loss fell entirely upon Lapham; they lighted up the hackneyed character of their statements with the picturesque interest of the coincidence that the policy had expired only the week before; heaven knows how they knew it.   (page 296)

"Why are you so particular? When you drove me out of the business you were not so very particular."   (page 310)

It is certain that our manners and customs go for more in life than our qualities. The price that we pay for civilization is the fine yet impassable differentiation of these. Perhaps we pay too much; but it will not be possible to persuade those who have the difference in their favor that this is so.   (page 337)

THE RISE OF
SILAS LAPHAM

William Dean Howells

WITH AN INTRODUCTION AND
NOTES BY MORRIS DICKSTEIN

GEORGE STADE
CONSULTING EDITORIAL DIRECTOR

BARNES & NOBLE CLASSICS
NEW YORK

ЛВ

BARNES & NOBLE CLASSICS
NEW YORK

Published by Barnes & Noble Books
122 Fifth Avenue
New York, NY 10011

www.barnesandnoble.com/classics

The Rise of Silas Lapham was serialized in *Century* magazine in 1884
and 1885 and first published in one volume in 1885.

Published in 2007 by Barnes & Noble Classics in paperback with a new Introduction,
Notes, Biography, Chronology, Inspired By, Comments & Questions,
and For Further Reading.

Introduction, Notes, and For Further Reading
Copyright © 2007 by Morris Dickstein.

Note on William Dean Howells, The World of William Dean Howells and *The Rise of
Silas Lapham*, Inspired by *The Rise of Silas Lapham*, and Comments & Questions
Copyright © 2007 by Barnes & Noble, Inc.

The Rise of Silas Lapham
ISBN-10: 1-59308-287-8
ISBN-13: 978-1-59308-287-1
LC Control Number 2005937674

Produced and published in conjunction with:
Fine Creative Media, Inc.
322 Eighth Avenue
New York, NY 10001

Michael J. Fine, President and Publisher

Printed in the United States of America

QM

1 3 5 7 9 10 8 6 4 2

FIRST PRINTING

WILLIAM DEAN HOWELLS

Novelist, essayist, critic, and editor William Dean Howells was born on March 1, 1837, in Martins Ferry, Ohio. His parents, Mary Dean and William Cooper Howells, were printers and publishers of a small newspaper whose editorials reflected their liberal politics. In the early years of young Will's life, his family moved frequently, living briefly in the Ohio cities of Hamilton, Dayton, Columbus, Ashtabula, and Jefferson, and for a year in the utopian community of Eureka Mills. Largely self-educated, Will was a precocious reader who taught himself several languages. Although he had little formal schooling, the family publication offered him an early apprenticeship as a typesetter, proofreader, and editor; at nineteen, he put his experience to use as a journalist.

From the state capital, Columbus, Howells sent weekly dispatches on the legislature to the *Cincinnati Gazette* before joining the *Ohio State Journal*, a partisan newspaper for the fledgling Republican Party. He also published several poems, stories, and reviews in the *Atlantic Monthly* and other magazines. In 1859 Howells was tapped by the Republicans to write a campaign biography of their candidate, Abraham Lincoln. After Lincoln's victory, Howells's contributions were acknowledged with an appointment as U.S. consul in Venice. Before departing, he traveled to New England, where he met such leading literary figures as Nathaniel Hawthorne, Ralph Waldo Emerson, Henry Wadsworth Longfellow, and James Russell Lowell, the influential editor of the *Atlantic Monthly*.

While the American Civil War raged, Howells made his home in Italy, writing sketches and articles about Venice that were first published in magazines and later revised to be included in *Venetian Life* (1866) and *Italian Journeys* (1867). Following the war, he returned with his wife, Elinor, and their infant daughter and was soon hired as an assistant editor at the *Atlantic Monthly*. The family settled in Boston, where Howells became a friend of novelist Henry James, whose reputation Howells helped to establish. In 1871 he was promoted to chief editor of the *Atlantic Monthly*, a post he held for ten years, during which time he initiated a cross-Atlantic dispute on the merits of a new literary style: realism.

Howells was not only a practitioner of realism but also its preeminent American champion. It was in this style that he wrote his most enduring novels, *A Modern Instance* (1882) and *The Rise of Silas Lapham* (1885). In 1886 he began to write—for *Harper's* magazine, one of the country's most influential periodicals—a column called "The Editor's Study," supporting realism through critical reviews in which he defended its emphasis on accurate representations of life in the middle and lower classes.

Following *The Rise of Silas Lapham*, Howells turned his pen to the cause of social justice. His increasing political involvement and consciousness of class struggles are reflected in his novels *Annie Kilburn* (1889) and *A Hazard of New Fortunes* (1890), among others. Meanwhile, in his monthly columns he advocated for authors he admired, including Mark Twain, Sarah Orne Jewett, Stephen Crane, and Emily Dickinson. Prolific until the end of his long life, Howells continued writing memoirs, travel narratives, criticism, novels, and short stories, including *A Boy's Town* (1890), *The Landlord at Lion's Head* (1897), *Literary Friends and Acquaintances* (1900), *The Leatherwood God* (1916), and his last novel, *The Vacation of the Kelwyns* (1920). Howells was so influential in literary matters that he was known as the "dean of American letters"; in 1908 he was elected the first president of the American Academy of Arts and Letters. William Dean Howells died on May 11, 1920, in New York City.

TABLE OF CONTENTS

THE WORLD OF WILLIAM DEAN HOWELLS
AND THE RISE OF SILAS LAPHAM

1837 On March 1 William Dean Howells is born in Martinsville (now Martins Ferry), Ohio. His father, William Cooper Howells, is a printer and publisher whose liberal politics often place him at odds with the community.

1840 The Howells family moves to Hamilton, Ohio, where William Howells owns and edits a newspaper, the *Hamilton Intelligencer*. The family also publishes a Swedenborgian newspaper, *The Retina*.

1843 Novelist Henry James is born. The U.S. Congress commissions Samuel Morse to build the first telegraph from Washington, D.C., to Baltimore, Maryland.

1849 The Howells sell the *Intelligencer*. They move to Dayton, Ohio, where they try unsuccessfully to start a new paper.

1850 The Howells family tries to establish a utopian community in the countryside at Eureka Mills, near Xenia, Ohio. Nathaniel Hawthorne, one of Howells's heroes, publishes *The Scarlet Letter*. American philosopher Ralph Waldo Emerson publishes *Representative Men*.

1851 Herman Melville publishes *Moby-Dick*.

1851– The utopian experiment at Eureka Mills fails, and the family
1852 moves to Columbus, then Ashtabula, before settling in Jefferson, Ohio.

1852 Russian author Ivan Turgenev, greatly admired by Howells, publishes *A Sportsman's Sketches*.

1857 Howells works briefly as a correspondent for the *Cincinnati Gazette*.

1858 While living in Columbus, Howells begins writing a literary column for the *Ohio State Journal* called "News and Humors of the Mail." Oliver Wendell Holmes publishes *The Autocrat of the Breakfast-Table*.

1859 Karl Marx publishes *Zur Kritik der politischen ökonomie* (Critique of Political Economy).

1860 With poet John James Piatt, Howells publishes *Poems of Two Friends.* The *Atlantic Monthly* publishes Howells's poem "Andenken." During Abraham Lincoln's bid for the U.S. presidency, Howells's campaign biography, *Lives and Speeches of Abraham Lincoln and Hannibal Hamlin*, is published. In August he travels to New England, where he meets the major literary figures of the day, including Nathaniel Hawthorne, Ralph Waldo Emerson, James Russell Lowell, and Henry Wadsworth Longfellow. Lincoln is elected president.

1861 For his service in President Lincoln's campaign, Howells is appointed American consul in Venice, Italy. The American Civil War begins.

1862 William Dean Howells and Elinor Mead are married on Christmas eve.

1865 The American Civil War ends. President Lincoln is assassinated. Howells returns from Venice, arriving in September in New York City, where he works for the magazine *The Nation* as a commentator and critic.

1866 Howells becomes assistant editor for the *Atlantic Monthly*, in which he publishes the first of many book reviews. He moves to Boston, where he begins a friendship with author Henry James. *Venetian Life*, a book of articles and sketches he had written in Venice, is published.

1867 He publishes *Italian Journeys*, a second collection of material written in Italy.

1871 Howells is promoted to editor at the *Atlantic Monthly*. American authors Theodore Dreiser and Stephen Crane are born.

1872 Howells publishes his first novel, *Their Wedding Journey*, about a honeymoon trip in the American Northeast.

1873 Howells's novel *A Chance Acquaintance*, a social comedy, is published.

1875 Howells publishes *A Foregone Conclusion*, a novel that depicts the conflict between American and Italian manners.

1876 Mark Twain publishes *The Adventures of Tom Sawyer*.

1877 Showing clear signs of Howells's influence, Henry James's *The American* is published. In France, Émile Zola publishes *L'Assommoir*.

1878 Russian writer Leo Tolstoy, an important influence on Howells, publishes *Anna Karenina*.

1879 Howells refines his distinctly American novel of manners in *The Lady of the Aroostook*. Henry James publishes *Daisy Miller*.

1881 Howells resigns the editorship of the *Atlantic Monthly*. He publishes *Doctor Breen's Practice*, the story of a woman doctor's struggle for acceptance in the field of medicine. Henry James publishes *The Portrait of a Lady*.

1882 After a serious illness, Howells travels to Europe, visiting England, Switzerland, and Italy. *A Modern Instance*, one of his best novels, is published. Henry Wadsworth Longfellow dies.

1884 *The Rise of Silas Lapham* begins serial publication in the *Century*. Mark Twain's *The Adventures of Huckleberry Finn* is published in England; American publication follows in 1885.

1885 *The Rise of Silas Lapham*, considered Howells's best novel, is published in book form. Zola's *Germinal* is published.

1886 Howells begins writing a monthly column, "The Editor's Study," in *Harper's New Monthly Magazine*. He also publishes the unsentimental love story *Indian Summer*, which was originally serialized in *Harper's*. The American Federation of Labor is founded.

1887 Howells publishes another novel, *The Minister's Charge*.

1889 Howells publishes *Annie Kilburn*, a novel that addresses the problems of labor. Mark Twain publishes *A Connecticut Yankee in King Arthur's Court*. North Dakota, South Dakota, Montana, and Washington become states.

1890 *A Boy's Town*, a reminiscence of Howells's youth in Ohio, and *A Hazard of New Fortunes*, an urban novel, are published. Tolstoy publishes *The Kreutzer Sonata*. Henrik Ibsen's play *Hedda Gabler* is produced. American philosopher William James, Henry James's brother, publishes *The Principles of Psychology*.

1891 Howells publishes *Criticism and Fiction*, a collection of critical essays. Melville dies.

1892 The last "Editor's Study" piece appears. Howells briefly assumes editorship of *Cosmopolitan*. He publishes *The Quality of Mercy*, a politically charged novel. American poet Walt Whitman dies. Iron and steel workers strike the Carnegie Steel Company.

1893 *My Year in a Log Cabin*, a memoir of the Howells family's stay at the utopian community Eureka Mills, is published.

1895   Stephen Crane publishes the Civil War novel The Red Badge of Courage. William Cooper Howells dies.

1897   Another novel, The Landlord at Lion's Head, is published.

1898   Henry James publishes The Turn of the Screw.

1899   Ernest Hemingway is born.

1900   Howells publishes a memoir, Literary Friends and Acquaintances, about his journey to New England forty years earlier. He begins to write the "Editor's Easy Chair" column for Harper's Monthly. American novelist Theodore Dreiser publishes Sister Carrie. Stephen Crane dies.

1904   Howells publishes a tragic novel, The Son of Royal Langbrith. Oxford University awards Howells an honorary degree. American writer O. Henry publishes Cabbages and Kings. Theodore Roosevelt is elected president of the United States.

1907   Howells publishes the utopian novel Through the Eye of the Needle. English author Rudyard Kipling wins the Nobel Prize in Literature.

1908   Howells is elected first president of the American Academy of Arts and Letters.

1909   He is a founding sponsor of the National Association for the Advancement of Colored People.

1910   Elinor Howells, Mark Twain, and Leo Tolstoy die. Howells publishes a tender, eulogizing memoir, My Mark Twain.

1913   New Leaf Mills, a fictionalized memoir of his family's stay at Eureka Mills, and Familiar Spanish Travels, drawn from Howells's experiences abroad, are published. American poet Robert Frost publishes A Boy's Will.

1914   World War I begins in Europe.

1916   The Leatherwood God, the last novel published in Howells's lifetime, and Years of My Youth, a memoir, are published. Henry James dies. Irish author James Joyce publishes A Portrait of the Artist as a Young Man.

1917   The Bolshevik Revolution takes place in Russia; Vladimir Lenin is appointed chief commissar.

1918   World War I ends. H. L. Mencken publishes In Defense of Women. American writer Henry Adams dies.

1919   Lillian Sabine adapts The Rise of Silas Lapham for the stage. Sherwood Anderson publishes Winesburg, Ohio, a collection of interrelated stories. H. L. Mencken publishes *The American Language*. Pulitzer Prizes are awarded to Carl Sandburg for *Corn Huskers* and Booth Tarkington for *The Magnificent Ambersons*.

1920   The last "Editor's Easy Chair" column is published. On May 11 William Dean Howells dies of pneumonia in New York City. A final novel, *The Vacation of the Kelwyns*, is published posthumously.

INTRODUCTION

Readers and critics have often expressed nostalgia for the kind of social novel that went out of fashion with the coming of modernism in the early decades of the twentieth century. The journalist Tom Wolfe, for example, complained about the disappearance of the novelist as social observer and tried to fill the breach first with what he called the New Journalism, using some of the techniques of fiction, then with novels of his own. It's not hard to understand why social novels gradually lost their hold on the modern imagination, though they long remained a staple of popular fiction. Many serious writers felt that society had grown too complex, too elusive—even too freakish—for any novelist to grasp as a whole. A close observation of manners had once seemed like a key to the social map, including the real distributions of class and power. But by the early twentieth century, the mores of social intercourse, like the relations between the classes, were proving harder to read or were simply breaking down under new egalitarian pressures. Increased education and upward mobility made class lines more porous. Moreover, the wars of the twentieth century, the new weapons of annihilation, the growth of totalitarian dictatorship, and the descent into outright genocide made older techniques for decoding social relations look irrelevant. The darker shadings of the thriller, of existentialism, or of the new Freudian psychology seemed like a better match for the writers' bleak outlook on the world. Masters of unease like Dostoevsky and Kafka, with their profound sense of blockage and frustration, spoke to twentieth-century readers more deeply than Balzac or Trollope, who were so adept at laying bare the mechanisms of class, power, and personal ambitions in their time.

For American writers these issues played out somewhat differently. Henry James had long argued that the United States, as a relatively new society, lacked the density of institutions and manners to nourish the novelist. He himself left for Europe to seek out such a society but instead found his best material in the clash between the new world and the old, without feeling entirely at home in either one. Another exile, D. H. Lawrence, followed James in the 1920s by arguing that the great American classics were all obsessive myths, metaphysical adventure stories, or boys' books, and he read them as no one had done before—with a psychological grasp that made them surprisingly compatible with modernism. Certainly Hawthorne's fables of sin and self-torment, Poe's Gothic melodramas, and Melville's wrestling with ultimate questions could be seen as prescient anticipations of the literature of extremity of the twentieth century, just as Whitman and Emerson foreshadowed the radical self-absorption typical of the modern age.

In the footsteps of James and Lawrence, critics like Lionel Trilling, Leslie Fiedler, and Richard Chase argued that the romance rather than the novel was central to American fiction; the major American realists and social novelists who had emerged in the decades after the Civil War were at best marginal to that tradition. By the 1940s and 1950s, in the aftermath of war and the Holocaust, when the modernist outlook was at the peak of its influence, the prestige of realist writers like William Dean Howells, Theodore Dreiser, Stephen Crane, and Frank Norris sank to a low ebb, while Howells's friend and contemporary, Henry James, was rediscovered and lionized as yet another forerunner of modernism.

If James was highly valued where Howells and Dreiser were dismissed, this was partly because of the rigor of James's writing and his exacting sense of form. The nineteenth-century novel was often a loose construction, a mixture of melodrama, descriptive writing, disguised autobiography, history, and social criticism. For James, such novels were well represented by the "loose baggy monsters" of Tolstoy and Dostoevsky, books he saw as ambitious but relatively formless. But both James and Howells were drawn to the "craftsmanship" of French fiction, especially in the work of Flaubert, Daudet, Zola, and Ivan Turgenev, the Russian writer living in Paris. James believed that fiction could be a vehicle of high art, and saw art itself as life-giving. Like Flaubert, James brought a severe aesthetic conscience to fiction. Instead of relying on an omniscient narrator—a puppet master putting characters through their paces—he presented the world through the eyes of the characters themselves. Like a dramatist he set out to show rather than tell, building the action through scene and dialogue instead of summary narration. James's formal discipline, his commitment to art within a popular genre, strongly appealed to the New Critics, who reached the zenith of their authority in the 1940s and 1950s. James's links to modernism could be found in his growing emphasis on consciousness over action. Even an early novel like The Portrait of a Lady (1881) turns upon a scene of awareness, of pure motionless *seeing*, as he later called it, when the heroine, simply reflecting at the fireside, comes to understand her husband's connection to another woman. By the time of The Ambassadors or The Golden Bowl twenty years later, the tentacles of consciousness had multiplied and expanded; Proust's long novel about memory has nothing on these books.

William Dean Howells too was influenced by the exacting craftsmanship of the French. Like James he would fail as a playwright yet preferred the give and take of dialogue and the life-like portrayal of character to elaborate plotting. "He hates a 'story,' " James wrote about him in 1886. "Mr. Howells hates an artificial fable and a dé-nouement that is pressed into the service; he likes things to occur as they occur in life, where the manner of a great many of them is not to occur at all" (quoted in The Rise of Silas Lapham, edited by Don L. Cook, p. 494; see "For Further Reading"). "The plot is the last thing for which I care," Howells wrote to his publisher. "In whatever I do I try to make the faithful study of character and the dramatic treatment of incident my hold upon the reader" (quoted in A Modern Instance, edited by William Gibson, p. vii). But Howells's aesthetic discipline is much more lax than James's or Flaubert's; he writes rapidly, with silver-tongued fluency, as attentive to the needs of the market as to the exigencies of art. With the instinct of a canny businessman, he is always mindful of the taste of editors and readers. Howells hates popular fiction for its falsity and sentimentality yet is determined to make his own kind of fiction popular. Though his best books turn on dramatic encounters between genuinely convincing characters, he freely supplies his own commentary on the social history surrounding their lives and the tangled motives underlying their behavior. His books are dotted with trenchant observations about social change. In his first major novel, A Modern Instance (1882), he reports shrewdly on the state of journalism, the transformation of religious feelings, the emotional economy of marriage, and the new independence of the younger generation from parental authority.

"I would be ashamed to write a novel that did not distinctly mean something, or that did not show that I had felt strongly about it," he told his publisher as he was writing the book (quoted in *A Modern Instance*, p. vii).

Howells's social register was so finely tuned, his irony so telling, that these insights still reverberate more than a century later. Of one small town in New England, a region once imbued by Puritanism, he writes:

> Religion there had largely ceased to be a fact of spiritual experience, and the visible church flourished on condition of providing for the social needs of the community. It was practically held that the salvation of one's soul must not be made too depressing, or the young people would have nothing to do with it. Professors of the sternest creeds temporized with sinners, and did what might be done to win them to heaven by helping them to have a good time here (*A Modern Instance*, p. 18).

Such remarks could have come from an essay, or from the travel books that made Howells's reputation before he began writing fiction. Yet every character in the novel is marked (and ultimately warped) by his relation to religion, from the stubborn anti-clericalism of the heroine's father to the moral slackness of her wayward husband and the bitter turn toward a stark Calvinism of her would-be lover, whose rectitude impels him to rescue her without allowing him to marry her, even after the death of her husband.

Howells's cutting irony extends to the characters themselves. Describing the carriage of a wealthy but philanthropic woman, he writes:

> It was a very handsome equipage, and was in keeping with all the outward belongings of Miss Kingsbury, who mingled a sense of duty and a love of luxury in her life in very exact proportions. When her *coupé* was not standing before some of the wretchedest doors in the city, it was waiting at the finest; and Clara's days were divided between the extremes of squalor and of fashion (*A Modern Instance*, p. 178).

This is no mere exposure of radical chic or the hypocrisy of the rich; Clara is as benevolent as she is self-indulgent. She's only a minor figure, but in a late scene we see her with her new husband, sympathetically discussing the plight of the main characters over a lavish breakfast. Clara Kingsbury is less a character than a social type, not taken over from other novels but sketched from life. Like the protagonist of *A Modern Instance*, the journalist Bartley Hubbard, she reappears briefly in *The Rise of Silas Lapham*, published three years later in 1885. Other characters from *Silas Lapham* surface in Howell's next novel, *The Minister's Charge* (1887). For the New Critics, characters exist only as verbal formations in the works in which they appear. But to Howells they belong to a larger peopled world outside the novel; by revisiting them from book to book he projects an illusion of their ongoing lives beyond the glimpses we get in any one story. The casual weave of Howells's fiction, the dips into authorial commentary, the subplots that often seem clumsily managed, his attraction to social types over idiosyncratic individuals, all tell us that social observation, not storytelling, was the main motive for his fiction. His theory of the novel focused on rounded characters in plausible settings, people who would behave and feel as they might in life. He made it clear that a novel was an intensified selection, a simplification, of the actual world. But unlike many novelists, Howells was less interested in creating a world of his own than in illuminating the life around us, offering a lively record of places, people, professions, institutions. The first kind of fiction he described as romance, full of sentimental fantasy and wish-fulfillment. The second kind he labeled realism, and he spent a large part of his career campaigning for its acceptance, promoting many other authors in the process. "Let fiction cease to lie about life; let it portray men and women as they are," he wrote praising the work of his closest friend, Mark Twain. "Let it speak the dialect, the language, that most Americans know—the language of unaffected people everywhere" (Goodman and Dawson, *William Dean Howells: A Writer's Life*, p. 150).

Howells was close to James and close to Twain, who had little or no interest in each other, but these last comments reveal a less likely kinship—with Walt Whitman. Howells read Whitman early but saw Whitman's sexual themes all too clearly; he always remained ambivalent about him in print. In a review of the 1860 edition of *Leaves*

of *Grass*, the young Howells said "he has told too much. The secrets of
the soul may be whispered to the world but the secrets of the body
should be decently hid. Walt Whitman exults to blab them" (Cady, *W.
D. Howells as Critic*, p. 14). But a word like "blab" shows Howells's lin-
guistic affinity for Whitman, for he too, like Twain, was drawn to
colloquial speech, allowing literature to "speak the dialect, the language, that most Americans know." Despite his reticence about sex,
which was part of his sense of what the literary market would bear,
Howells was one of the great democrats of American literature. While
the realists who followed him would often focus on large economic
institutions and dramatic differences of class and power, Howells always placed his emphasis on the ordinary, the commonplace, even
the uneventful. Like March, who is the point-of-view character in
Howells's great city novel, *A Hazard of New Fortunes* (1890), Howells was
a walker in the city, a flaneur; he could describe the urban flow or
the mass of humanity on a ferry boat as vividly as Whitman. "The
novelist who could interpret the common feelings of commonplace
people would have the answer to 'the riddle of the painful earth' on
his tongue," says one character in *The Rise of Silas Lapham* (p. 189).

His work could also be as ambiguously autobiographical as
Whitman's. March and his wife, who had served as the main characters in Howells's first novel, *Their Wedding Journey* (1872), were mildly
satirical versions of William and Elinor Howells, as most readers easily understood. Many of the marriages in Howells's novels had a similar biographical basis, including the much darker relationship of
couples like the mismatched Hubbards in *A Modern Instance*. Other
novelists turned to marriage as an arena of romance, passion, bore-
dom, transgression, even a sense of entrapment. Adultery—passion
as transgression and betrayal, the lure of the forbidden—was woven
into the warp and woof of nineteenth-century fiction. Howells
focused instead on the routine of marriage, the mundane clash of
stubborn wills, opposing personalities, and quicksilver emotions
that come into play in managing a household, balancing work and
leisure, bringing up children. Howells focuses on the disparity between the sexes, the small daily compromises, the subtle variations of
moral feeling of the kind that bedevil the Laphams. His women are active, tough-minded figures; their way of thinking puzzles and chal-
lenges the men who live with them. "The silken texture of the marriage

tie bears a daily strain of wrong and insult to which no other human relation can be subjected without lesion," he writes early in *The Rise of Silas Lapham*. "Two people by no means reckless of each other's rights and feelings, but even tender of them for the most part, may tear at each other's heart-strings in this sacred bond with perfect impunity" (p. 45). Howells writes less about love than about compatibility and negotiation. For him marriage was a society in miniature, perhaps sacred in origin, a daily expression of the same stresses and bonds. He felt that the chemistry within a single family, or the subtle vibrations between two families, could reveal as much about the larger world as the huge social canvases of Dickens or Balzac. Howells transferred Whitman's demotic realism and truculent individualism into the realm of family life.

In his own way Howells was as restless as Whitman, an unquiet spirit changing homes frequently, traveling widely, but always remaining the detached observer of people and places. When he converted to Christian socialism in the late 1880s under the influence of Tolstoy and publicly protested the unjust execution of anarchists for the Haymarket bombing of 1886, he came closer to Whitman's radically democratic politics as well. Reverend Sewell, his spokesman in *The Minister's Charge*, concludes the novel with a sermon on "complicity" that sums up Howells's own new outlook. He envisions an order in which

> no one for good or for evil, for sorrow or joy, for sickness or health, stood apart from his fellows, but each was bound to the highest and the lowest by ties that centered in the hand of God. No man, he said, sinned or suffered to himself alone; his error and his pain darkened and afflicted men who never heard of his name. . . . Let no one shrink from such a burden, or seek to rid himself of it. Rather let him bind it fast upon his neck, and rejoice in it (*The Minister's Charge*, edited by Don L. Cook, p. 309).

Here the silken ties of marriage, with their divine purpose, are extended to humanity in general.

Long before this conversion, Howells had always been a solid Western democrat. He was born in 1837 in Martinsville (later Martins Ferry), Ohio, into a Free Soil family, strongly anti-slavery. His father,

William Cooper Howells, edited a series of local newspapers, which involved him deeply in politics. As an egalitarian and a follower of Swedenborg, the Swedish mystic, he briefly established a utopian commune with his brothers. He pulled up stakes and moved the family repeatedly, but his entrepreneurial schemes generally failed, and despite his Micawberish optimism he had difficulty providing support for his wife and eight children. As a result Howells went to work early and was largely self-taught; the future writer read voluminously and would teach himself five foreign languages. Describing the privileged background of his friend James in an 1882 essay, Howells wrote: "There are none of those early struggles with poverty, which render the lives of so many distinguished Americans monotonous reading, to record in his case: the cabin hearth-fire did not light him to the youthful pursuit of literature; he had from the start all those advantages which, when they go too far, become limitations" (Cady, *W. D. Howells as Critic*, p. 64).

In his own case it was indeed "the cabin hearth-fire" by which he schooled himself while he was apprenticed as a printer and typesetter, and then worked as a journalist and newspaper editor. Howells began sending poems to a leading Boston journal, the *Atlantic Monthly*, in the late 1850s, when its politics were radical Republican. On a trip east in 1860 he was well received by the grandees of New England literature, including Lowell, Longfellow, Holmes, and Emerson, whom he revered; their patronage would shape his early career. He quickly wrote a campaign biography of Abraham Lincoln later that year and gained a political appointment as American consul in Venice, where he spent the whole Civil War period. During the war he married Elinor Mead, a Vermont girl whose family was well connected. (A cousin, Rutherford B. Hayes, later became president; her brother, William Rutherford Mead, would become a partner in the famous architectural firm of McKim, Mead, and White.) Howells's friend Twain later remarked that both of them had married up.

After the war the couple returned to Boston where Howells became first the assistant editor (1866–1871), then the editor (1871–1881) of the *Atlantic*. In short, Howells was a rising young man: Both in his marriage and his work life, he merged seamlessly with New England tradition in culture, religion, and politics. Yet even at the heart of the Boston and Cambridge establishment, he never entirely lost the discomfort of the country boy who made good in the big city. This may help explain his long friendship with the raw westerner Twain and the expatriate James (whose travels, like his, had also made them citizens of the world). When he left the *Atlantic* in 1881 to throw himself on the market, to make his living entirely as a writer, this stress of the newcomer, the social climber, which he knew at first hand, would become one of his most important themes.

The United States in the 1880s, when Howells, Twain, and James did much of their greatest work, was a nation in transition if not upheaval. It was being convulsed by waves of immigration, industrial growth, political and labor unrest, booming westward expansion, and the inexorable flow of young people from rural areas to burgeoning cities. A cascade of books, newspapers, and new illustrated magazines supplied news, culture, and entertainment to an expanding population. Howells traced the effects of this new journalism in *A Modern Instance*, which he completed and serialized soon after leaving the editorship of the *Atlantic*, and he took account of the vogue of novel-reading in *The Rise of Silas Lapham*. Both books center on the lives of country people (like Howells himself) who were making their way in the big city. Both are set in Boston, where the new arrivals encounter an established elite. Money, like a universal solvent, challenged pedigree as a source of social status. "The suddenly rich are on a level with any of us nowadays," says Bromfield Corey in *Silas Lapham*. "Money buys position at once. . . . It is the romance, the poetry of our age" (p. 59). This social mobility, so classically American, was also the theme of a vastly popular success literature that Howells at once imitates, parodies, and contradicts in *The Rise of Silas Lapham*. The title itself alludes ironically to biographies of the famous and successful. For its time, the book became the definitive American portrait of the self-made man.

This literature took many different forms: inspirational lectures and sermons such as the "Acres of Diamonds," which Russell H. Conwell delivered more than 6,000 times; autobiographies of swashbuckling entrepreneurs who had risen from poverty and obscurity by dint of their own exertions; self-help handbooks and journalistic profiles of businessmen and captains of industry; and especially Horatio Alger novels that plotted the rise of country boys from rags to respectability and served as tour guides to the mysteries of city life.

(*The Minister's Charge* is directly based on the Alger model.) In the opening chapter of *The Rise of Silas Lapham*, Bartley Hubbard, the journalist resurrected from *A Modern Instance*, interviews Lapham, a wealthy paint manufacturer, as part of a series of articles on "Solid Men of Boston." Laphams's rural roots (like those of Elinor Howells) are in Vermont, where the high-quality paint is produced. There Lapham's father had discovered a mineral mine, but only the son had the skill and will to bring it to market. (Howells's father, after all, had failed as an editor and writer, just where the son would shine.) Readers of *A Modern Instance* will recall Bartley Hubbard's sarcastic temper and questionable integrity from the earlier novel. He encourages Lapham to boast about his triumphs and then mocks him—and the paper's readers as well—with a hyperbolic profile that sends up the clichés of the genre, a lampoon he's sure his unpolished subject will be too thick to grasp. But it beautifully serves the purposes of the novel, since it fills in details of Lapham's background and his present life while exposing the reader directly to his own gruff, colloquial voice. Like the Time-style newsreel at the beginning of Orson Welles's *Citizen Kane* (a later takeoff on a success story), this prologue affords us an overview of Lapham's career while exposing the superficiality of journalism compared to the sharper insight of fiction.

The genuine excellence of the paint and his own drive and determination have made Lapham a very rich man. He and his strong-willed wife, Persis (whose name he puts on his premium grade of paint), have lived for twelve years in a comfortable house in Boston's South End with their two daughters, not realizing that the neighborhood is no longer fashionable. But at a resort the previous summer, Mrs. Lapham and her girls have gotten to know the blue-blooded Coreys, coming in contact with Boston society as they've never done before. (In two brief passages dropped from the serial version, the Laphams debate whether property values suffered when wealthy Jews moved into their neighborhood.) To improve his daughters' prospects and their own social standing, Lapham is building a new house on filled-in new land on "the water side" of Beacon Street, where Howells himself would soon have a home. The interplay of money, status, and taste would be reflected in the building of this house. The fate of the house would parallel the rise and fall of Lapham's fortune.

The Rise of Silas Lapham was the first important novel about an American businessman and one of the few to this day that treats this figure with sympathy rather than savagery. Though Lapham was a Civil War officer, he is no hero—Howells had an aversion to heroes and heroines; for him they belonged to the unreal world of romance—but a bluff, coarse, strong-willed, fundamentally honest man who grows morally as his business and fortune decline. There is a Christian parable at the heart of the novel, that a man must lose his life in order to save it; the "rise" of the title is the reverse of the material rise at the center of most popular success literature. The novel plays repeatedly on what a "rise" means and what wealth or prosperity can do or undo. We learn of the Laphams that "they lived richly to themselves, not because they were selfish, but because they did not know how to do otherwise" (pp. 24–25). When Silas married his wife "it had been a rise in life for him" (p. 45), as it had been for Howells, but facing a moral crisis early on in his business, a choice between personal ethics and business ethics, "Lapham could not rise to it" (p. 46). Under his wife's influence, he spends the rest of the novel quietly making up for this early lapse.

Besides the business plot, however, there is a marriage plot reminiscent of one of Howells's favorite writers, Jane Austen. At the same summer resort, the Coreys' son Tom has met the Lapham daughters and eventually he falls in love with one of them—not the pretty one, as everybody assumes, but the serious one. To complicate matters further, he wants to do something with his life; the entrepreneurial genes of his grandfather, who made the family pile, have reasserted themselves in him, much to the amusement of his patrician father, Bromfield, a dilettantish painter who sees no reason why any Corey should have to work for a living. Tom is entranced with the romance of business, the adventure of seeking out new markets. He sees work as a way of finding his place in the world. Even his father admits to Lapham that his son is drawn to business "for the love of it" (p. 132). When Tom goes to work for Lapham, and when the Coreys feel obliged to invite the Laphams to a large dinner party, for which they are ill prepared, the business plot and the social plot of the novel are deliciously intertwined. The core of the novel can be found in the interplay between business success and social acceptance, but also between worldly prosperity and intrinsic moral character. As

Mrs. Lapham realizes well before her husband, "it isn't what you've got, and it isn't what you've done exactly. It's what you are" (p. 112). Deploying but also subverting the strategies of success writing, Howells offers us different angles on Lapham's business life by picturing its relationship to his moral life, his home life, and his social life. The Rise of Silas Lapham turns success literature inside out by questioning what real success entails.

If Howells was attracted to the realism of the French writers by their honesty and craftsmanship, he was also drawn to the work of Austen, Hawthorne, and George Eliot as moral fables rich in character. In his controversial essay on James in 1882, he saw his friend (and, by extension, himself) as the vanguard of a new school of American realists that "derives from Hawthorne and George Eliot rather than any others," but also "largely influenced by French fiction in form" (Goodman and Dawson, p. 230). Each of these writers had an impact on how Howells handled the story of the Laphams and the Coreys. A midwesterner with Quaker roots, Howells was comfortable with the New England tradition in which Puritanism was secularized into moral conscience. In The Scarlet Letter and in many of his best stories, Hawthorne had extracted contemporary themes from the stresses in Puritan culture. Sewell, Howells's surrogate in Silas Lapham, mocks sentimental fiction for its unrealistic and obtuse idealization of self-sacrifice. Yet when Penelope Lapham realizes that Tom Corey loves her, not her beautiful sister, she is determined not to profit from her sister's loss, even though she loves him in return. And he stoically abides by her wishes until she relents.

Consulted by the Laphams, Sewell advises instead an "economy of pain," an act of rational choice inflicting the least suffering on the smallest number of people. Lapham himself makes a great sacrifice by preparing to let his business go under rather than take advantage of distant investors who can afford the loss, though at the last moment the decision is taken out of his hands. As he spends a sleepless night trying to decide what to do, his wife sees him in biblical terms as Jacob wrestling with the angel. For Mrs. Lapham, who has always served as her husband's ethical beacon, prosperity has taken control of their lives and separated them from who they are. Once deeply involved in her husband's work as well as the running of their home, she senses helplessly that money has rendered her useless. "It is the curse of prosperity that it takes work away from us, and shuts that door to hope and health of spirit. In this house, where everything had come to be done for her, she had no tasks to interpose between her and her despair" (p. 216). From her point of view, grounded in her Puritan background, Lapham's earlier success had been tainted by how he bought his partner out of the business, much the way other Gilded Age millionaires had consolidated their fortunes. At the end the Laphams return to Vermont contentedly to begin anew. Wealth, if it comes again, can only come to the next generation; their youth and energy will build on a clear moral foundation. Howells frames a realism of character and setting within a Hawthorne-style allegory.

The influence of Austen and Eliot can best be seen in the way the novel centers on marriage. The courtship plot, here involving two marriageable daughters—one attractive but empty-headed, the other witty, satiric, and intelligent—is certainly indebted to Austen, especially to Pride and Prejudice. In the spirit of Austen's serious social comedy, Howells brings on a small cast of characters to show, ultimately, how different classes and temperaments can be reconciled. When the Laphams and the Coreys first get together, there seems to be no way that Bromfield Corey's exquisite refinement and his wife's snobbery can ever be comfortable with Mrs. Lapham's homespun honesty and her husband's social maladroitness, which makes him seem like a coarse braggart. But for Howells, character can trump class and even blood relationships; marriage is, in any case, a form of crossover. Penelope Lapham, an avid reader with a satiric cast of mind, is more like Bromfield Corey than like her own father. And the enterprising Tom Corey, who plans to use his knowledge of languages to open up foreign markets, has some of the spirit of the young Lapham. "In spite of his syntax I rather liked him," says Tom after first meeting him (p. 60). "I confess that I 'took to' Colonel Lapham from the moment I saw him," he tells his father. "He looked as if he 'meant business,' and I mean business too" (p. 62). He picks up Lapham's colloquial speech as he will venture into his business.

Tom's father, Bromfield, who once tried to live the life of the artist in Italy, has few active ventures of his own; now, back in Boston, he takes an amused, spectatorial view of the world. Bromfield is Howells's version of the ironic Mr. Bennet in Pride and Prejudice, for whom family life and his fretting wife's concerns are a never-ending source of diversion. After Bromfield pays a dutiful call on Lapham in his office, Lapham's face (in Howells's words) reveals "the struggle of stalwart achievement not to feel flattered at the notice of sterile elegance, not to be sneakingly glad of its amiability, but to stand up and look at it with eyes on the same level" (p. 135). By setting off "stalwart achievement" against "sterile elegance," Howells avows his own middle-class sympathies, his deeply felt egalitarianism, and his capacity to identify with the feelings of the outsider. Tom, in turn, inherited from his mother "the traits of practicality and common sense in which he bordered upon the commonplace" (p. 119), that terrain so important to Howells's fiction. We're told that "no man ever had a son less like him than Bromfield Corey. If Tom Corey had ever said a witty thing, no one could remember it; and yet the father had never said a witty thing to a more sympathetic listener than his own son" (p. 119). Howells looks to the younger generation as a way of bridging the conflicts between new money, amassed in and through industry, and old money, indolent, elegantly refined, but now suffering from a "shrinkage in values," in more senses than one. If the Laphams and the Coreys can never actually come to like each other, their social differences can at least be overcome in their children.

The dissonance between the two families comes through best in the celebrated dinner scene in which Lapham, unused to drinking wine with dinner, grows tipsy and begins bragging about his success, his paint, his war record, just the way he had done with Bartley Hubbard. As the gentlemen around him grow silent and Tom Corey looks away in embarrassment, Lapham gradually makes a fool of himself. As a deeply inbred society, a network of cousins, Boston is a treacherous field for an outsider, as Howells himself had been—and inwardly remained. Howells's feelings are well divided between the values of country people like the Laphams and the genteel culture of the New Englanders with whom he had cast his lot. (A few years after *Silas Lapham* he would move to New York, when it had replaced Boston as the nation's literary center.) By projecting a union between the younger Laphams and Corey, Howells was reconciling not only parts of himself but also practical achievement with good taste, wholesome morality with art and civilization. This reassurance appealed to several generations of readers. The cultural critics of a later generation, such as Van Wyck Brooks in *America's Coming-of-Age* (1915), would tear this synthesis apart or find it beyond them.

Before Lapham disgraces himself at dinner the conversation turns to the reading of novels, a theme running through the book almost as an internal commentary on it. Tom had already asked the Lapham girls if they'd read George Eliot's *Middlemarch*, which had appeared not long before. George Eliot's searching emotional intelligence and moral realism reverberate in *Silas Lapham*, especially in Howells's subtle treatment of the marriages of the older Laphams and Coreys. During the dinner party they discuss a different kind of book, a popular sentimental novel called *Tears, Idle Tears*, after Tennyson's famous poem, one of the stories "that go for our heart-strings," playing on themes of self-sacrifice by "old-fashioned heroes and heroines." Speaking for Howells, who would make this a cornerstone of his criticism as well as his fiction, Sewell finds such books noxious. He praises novelists who "painted life as it is, and human feelings in their true proportion and relation" (p. 185), just what Howells admired in Austen, Eliot, and Henry James, three key figures in what the critic F. R. Leavis later called the Great Tradition.

The serious aftermath of the Coreys' dinner party is even more dramatic than the party itself. First Lapham, in the sober light of the next day, upbraids himself with an abject apology to Tom Corey, his subordinate. Until now he was proud to have a young Corey, full of energy and ambition, working under him, training for a career in business that validates his own. Now he offers to let Tom go, "because you're a gentleman, and I'm not, and it ain't right I should be over you" (p. 197). Tom finds the older man's self-accusation unseemly. "It's enough, more than enough, for you to have mentioned the matter to me, and I think it's unbecoming in me to hear you" (p. 197). Despite his still unspoken love for Lapham's daughter and his liking for the man himself, Tom, though an instinctive democrat, reverts to the values and manners of his class. When Lapham says, truthfully enough, "I've disgusted you," Tom feels "a repressed shudder for the abasement which he had seen," and leaves the office.

> He thought of him the night before in the company of those
> ladies and gentlemen, and he quivered in resentment of his

vulgar, braggart, uncouth nature. He recognized his own allegiance to the exclusiveness to which he was born and bred, as
a man perceives his duty to his country when her rights are invaded. . . . Amidst the stings and flashes of his wounded pride,
all the social traditions, all the habits of feeling, which he had
silenced more and more by force of will during the past months,
asserted their natural sway, and he rioted in his contempt of the
offensive boor, who was even more offensive in his shame than
in his trespass. He said to himself that he was a Corey, as if that
were somewhat (p. 198).

No sooner does he shrink back in horror than he talks himself
out of his own revulsion. If Lapham, though hardly given to second
thoughts, has his moment of Puritan self-examination, his dark night
of the soul, then this is Tom's. He thinks of the social traditions, the
breeding, that set him up to feel offended. He thinks of the Lapham
daughter he loves and the father he admires and understands. He
wonders how much he and his own family have contributed to the
man's mortification: by staging a dinner at which he would not
know how to behave, by serving him wine he was not accustomed
to drink, and finally by failing to sympathize with his remorse, "not
recognizing that Lapham's humiliation came from the sense of
wrong, which he had helped to accumulate upon him by superfinely
standing aloof and refusing to touch him" (p. 199).

This scene of clashing values and manners—and the moment of
self-examination that follows—make up the heart of the novel. (Middlemarch shows a similar balance between an outer and inner action,

behavior and reflection.) Tom's recoil from Lapham shows how
much he is a creature of his class and upbringing—proper Boston,
which, as T. S. Eliot once said, was "refined beyond the point of civilization." It reflects Howells's understanding as a novelist that "social
traditions" and "habits of feeling" are instilled in us at a very early
age. But Howells also sees us as moral agents, potentially free beings
capable of self-correction, something Tom will do here, as nearly all
the Laphams and Coreys do before the end of the novel.

This ability to change, to examine and moderate the prejudices
they inherited, is what distinguishes them from the minor characters like the villainous Rogers, whom Lapham forced out of his

business—his financial dealings will trigger Lapham's downfall—
and the hapless Zerrilla Dewey, married to a drunken sailor, whom
Lapham supports because her father saved his life during the Civil
War. Such characters serve as bit players in the protagonists' moral
drama, and they remain fixed in their simple supporting roles. The
popularity of *The Rise of Silas Lapham*, on which Howells's reputation
long rested, may stem from the uncommon mixture of satire and
sympathy directed at characters like Lapham and Bromfield Corey.
This novelistic empathy is something Tom himself briefly loses but
soon recovers. Paying a call on the Laphams to apologize to the father, instead he blurts out his love to the daughter. His parents,
though somewhat at cross purposes with each other—Mrs. Corey is
often perplexed by the man her husband has become—extend themselves as well: They accept his choice of a spouse though it will cost
them some awkward social moments. This compromise, so funda-
mental to the spirit of comedy, is part of Howells's theme of reconciliation. Society is changing because, in America at least, each generation
shapes its own values; social differences can be bridged, newcomers
acculturated. In *A Modern Instance*, Howells had pushed these conflicts
to the breaking point and alienated some readers; in *Silas Lapham* they
are overcome by good will, character, and moral choice.

Bromfield's cynical but penetrating wit, "full of the triumph the
spectator of his species feels in signal exhibitions of human nature"
(p. 251), aligns him with the ironists in the book rather than the practical moralists like his son. Howells calls this joshing manner "drollery,"
and it belongs not only to Bromfield and Penelope, two characters
with a strong satirical bent, but to Howells's narrator in many novels, which were attacked for their detachment but also praised for
their humorous treatment of human foibles. Writing about "the verbal drollery of many of his people," his friend James described one
character as "so irrepressibly and happily facetious as to make one
wonder whether the author is not prompting him a little." An anonymous review in *The Nation* expressed misgivings about "the quick,
subtle, mocking spirit of the author, flashing in a phrase or comparison," giving us a "literal, merciless representation" of his main characters (*Silas Lapham*, edited by Don L. Cook, p. 400).

The light, ironic cast of Howells's fiction offended some readers,
but Howells himself saw its limits. If Bromfield could be described as

the "spectator of his species," so could most novelists. But Bromfield is a likable man and a keen observer behind his mocking manner, and there is a streak of disappointment, even self-loathing, in his amused, disengaged wit. Like Silas, he's a more complicated character than he first seems. The really dark side of this ironic attitude could be found in Bartley Hubbard, the journalist who cares deeply for no one and nothing. The Rise of Silas Lapham builds on Bartley's cliché-ridden newspaper profile but infuses its subject with a novelist's understanding. Yet many years later Howells said that he had "drawn Bartley Hubbard, the false scoundrel, from himself " (Goodman and Dawson, p. 235). Certainly he drew the figure from his background as a journalist, as he drew Silas Lapham from his own early struggle for social acceptance and economic security. In the end, Howells's shrewd management of his career made him not only self-sufficient but wealthy.

But Howells's very success left him with misgivings, which influenced the shape of Silas Lapham. Boston may have accepted him, but he never fully accepted Boston. He grew rich but fretted in his letters about why he should be so comfortable when others went hungry. In waging his lonely crusade to spare the convicted anarchists in 1887, and later protesting their "civic murder" (Goodman and Dawson, p. 292), he attracted fierce condemnation and risked a position that had taken him so long to establish. The political turbulence of these years was reflected in his most ambitious novel, A Hazard of New Fortunes, in which March, an editor modeled on Howells himself, loses his job for refusing to fire an old German-born anarchist, a Civil War veteran whose radical talk gave offense to the magazine's owner. This man, Dryfoos, a crude, nouveau-riche industrialist from the provinces, is a curdled version of Lapham, with two marriageable daughters but also an idealistic son who breaks with his father's values. For this newly rich family, things do not go well. The daughters find no suitor in Boston, where a self-absorbed artist toys with their affections, and the saintly son, like the German anarchist, dies as a bystander to a bitter labor conflict. Stricken with remorse, Dryfoos does his best to make amends, overseeing the funeral of the old anarchist, restoring the magazine to its editor, acting in his son's Christian spirit. But unlike Silas he can't go home again. "We can't go back!" he shouts at his wife. "There's no farm anymore to go back to.

The fields is full of gas wells and oil wells and hell holes generally;
the house is tore down and the barn's goin'—." (*A Hazard of New Fortunes*, p. 201). Instead he packs his daughters off to Europe, where
rich American families can usually find eligible men.

The *Rise of Silas Lapham* is far less intransigent than this later novel,
which is played out in a spacious and strikingly modern New York
setting embracing immigrants, anarchists, strikers, artists, religious
idealists and reformers, and even a die-hard southerner who opposes
capitalism with benign memories of feudalism. Yet *Silas Lapham* could
also have been called "A Hazard of New Fortunes," and when
Lapham tries to raise money to save his business, he discovers bitterly
that he has no friends, even among those he had helped or befriended. He learns that the competitive pressures of capitalism,
which had fueled his success in business, can conflict sharply with
personal ethics. In a Christian spirit he finally determines to be hon-
orable rather than successful, a conclusion that endeared the novel to
generations of readers but left realism in the dust. With the young
Tom and in Lapham himself, Howells had identified with the romance of business, the adventure of the entrepreneur. But in the
end, foreshadowing his later novels, he delivers a stern judgment
on capitalism while retaining his faith in the moral agency of the
individual.

Though *A Modern Instance* and *A Hazard of New Fortunes* are more modern novels, more unyielding in their vision, *The Rise of Silas Lapham*
broke new ground with its study of social mobility and its portrait
of a crucial new American type. Sinclair Lewis dismissed Howells as
a maiden aunt in his Nobel Prize acceptance speech, yet the com-
pound of mockery and affection in his portrayal of the archetypal
booster, George Babbitt, would have been unthinkable without Silas
Lapham. ("Make Lapham vulgar but not sordid," Howells wrote in
his notebook as he was writing the novel [Cady, *The Road to Realism*,
p. 231]). On the personal side, *A Modern Instance* was the first serious
treatment of divorce in American fiction, but *Silas Lapham* is just as subtle in its portrayal of the quotidian dynamics of marriage, with its
underlying tensions and unspoken understandings.

As a critic Howells went out on a limb to sponsor the work of
the emerging young realists of the 1890s, including Stephen Crane,
Hamlin Garland, Abraham Cahan, Paul Laurence Dunbar, and Frank

Norris, but the wry, cultivated spirit of his fiction scarcely resembled theirs. In *Silas Lapham* he struck a moment of equilibrium between his early novels of manners and his later social novels. *A Hazard of New Fortunes* looks forward to the strike novel (including the last part of Dreiser's *Sister Carrie*), the American political novel, and the great urban novels of the twentieth century. Yet *Silas Lapham*, despite its gentler tone and smaller cast, provided the template not just for the business novel but for six decades of serious novels of manners, from Edith Wharton and F. Scott Fitzgerald to J. P. Marquand and John O'Hara. (Wharton rebuked Sinclair Lewis for his attack on Howells, whose work, she said, had made his possible.) These were all writers concerned with how social mobility was woven into the fabric of American life. Like Howells they were social reporters fascinated by the clash of temperaments, ambitions, manners, and class. Howells, with his keen eye and ear, his droll, sarcastic humor, his combination of sardonic detachment and sympathetic identification, gave them some of the tools they needed to turn the ongoing drama of American life into meaningful stories.

Morris Dickstein is Distinguished Professor of English at the Graduate Center of the City University of New York, where he teaches courses in literature, film, and American cultural history. He is a senior fellow of the Center for the Humanities, which he founded in 1993. His books include a study of the 1960s, *Gates of Eden* (1977), which was nominated for the National Book Critics Circle Award in criticism; *Double Agent: The Critic and Society* (1992); and *Leopards in the Temple* (2002), a widely reviewed social history of postwar American fiction. His latest book is a collection of essays, *A Mirror in the Roadway: Literature and the Real World* (Princeton, 2005). He is completing a cultural history of the United States in the 1930s.

THE RISE OF
SILAS LAPHAM

I

When Bartley Hubbard went to interview Silas Lapham for the "Solid Men of Boston" series, which he undertook to finish up in "The Events," after he replaced their original projector on that newspaper, Lapham received him in his private office by previous appointment.

"Walk right in!" he called out to the journalist, whom he caught sight of through the door of the counting-room.

He did not rise from the desk at which he was writing, but he gave Bartley his left hand for welcome, and he rolled his large head in the direction of a vacant chair. "Sit down! I'll be with you in just half a minute."

"Take your time," said Bartley, with the ease he instantly felt. "I'm in no hurry." He took a note-book from his pocket, laid it on his knee, and began to sharpen a pencil.

"There!" Lapham pounded with his great hairy fist on the envelope he had been addressing. "William!" he called out, and he handed the letter to a boy who came to get it. "I want that to go right away. Well, sir," he continued, wheeling round in his leather-cushioned swivel-chair, and facing Bartley, seated so near that their knees almost touched, "so you want my life, death, and Christian sufferings, do you, young man?"

"That's what I'm after," said Bartley. "Your money or your life."

"I guess you wouldn't want my life without the money," said Lapham, as if he were willing to prolong these moments of preparation.

"Take 'em both," Bartley suggested. "Don't want your money without your life, if you come to that. But you're just one million times more interesting to the public than if you hadn't a dollar; and you know that as well as I do, Mr. Lapham. There's no use beating about the bush."

"No," said Lapham, somewhat absently. He put out his huge foot and pushed the ground-glass door shut between his little den and the book-keepers, in their larger den outside.

"In personal appearance," wrote Bartley in the sketch for which he now studied his subject, while he waited patiently for him to continue, "Silas Lapham is a fine type of the successful American. He has a square, bold chin, only partially concealed by the short, reddish-gray beard, growing to the edges of his firmly closing lips. His nose is short and straight; his forehead good, but broad rather than high; his eyes blue, and with a light in them that is kindly or sharp according to his mood. He is of medium height, and fills an average arm-chair with a solid bulk, which, on the day of our interview, was unpretentiously clad in a business suit of blue serge. His head droops somewhat from a short neck, which does not trouble itself to rise far from a pair of massive shoulders."

"I don't know as I know just where you want me to begin," said Lapham.

"Might begin with your birth; that's where most of us begin," replied Bartley.

A gleam of humorous appreciation shot into Lapham's blue eyes.

"I didn't know whether you wanted me to go quite so far back as that," he said. "But there's no disgrace in having been born, and I was born in the State of Vermont, pretty well up under the Canada line—so well up, in fact, that I came very near being an adoptive citizen; for I was bound to be an American of *some* sort, from the word Go! That was about—well, let me see!—pretty near sixty years ago: this is '75, and that was '20. Well, say I'm fifty-five years old; and I've *lived* 'em, too; not an hour of waste time about *me*, anywheres! I was born on a farm, and——"

"Worked in the fields summers and went to school winters: regulation thing?" Bartley cut in.

"Regulation thing," said Lapham, accepting this irreverent version of his history somewhat dryly.

"Parents poor, of course," suggested the journalist. "Any barefoot business? Early deprivations of any kind, that would encourage the youthful reader to go and do likewise? Orphan myself, you know," said Bartley, with a smile of cynical good comradery.

Lapham looked at him silently, and then said with quiet self-respect, "I guess if you see these things as a joke, my life won't interest you."

"Oh, yes, it will," returned Bartley, unabashed. "You'll see; it'll come out all right." And in fact it did so, in the interview which Bartley printed.

"Mr. Lapham," he wrote, "passed rapidly over the story of his early life, its poverty and its hardships, sweetened, however, by the recollections of a devoted mother, and a father who, if somewhat her inferior in education, was no less ambitious for the advancement of his children. They were quiet, unpretentious people, religious, after the fashion of that time, and of sterling morality, and they taught their children the simple virtues of the Old Testament and Poor Richard's Almanac."*

Bartley could not deny himself this gibe; but he trusted to Lapham's unliterary habit of mind for his security in making it, and most other people would consider it sincere reporter's rhetoric.

"You know," he explained to Lapham, "that we have to look at all these facts as material, and we get the habit of classifying them. Sometimes a leading question will draw out a whole line of facts that a man himself would never think of." He went on to put several queries, and it was from Lapham's answers that he generalized the history of his childhood. "Mr. Lapham, although he did not dwell on his boyish trials and struggles, spoke of them with deep feeling and an abiding sense of their reality." This was what he added in the interview, and by the time he had got Lapham past the period where risen Americans are all pathetically alike in their narrow circumstances, their sufferings, and their aspirations, he had beguiled him into forgetfulness of the check he had received, and had him talking again in perfect enjoyment of his autobiography.

"Yes, sir," said Lapham, in a strain which Bartley was careful not to interrupt again, "a man never sees all that his mother has been to him till it's too late to let her know that he sees it. Why, my mother—" he stopped. "It gives me a lump in the throat," he said apologetically, with an attempt at a laugh. Then he went on: "She was a little, frail thing, not bigger than a good-sized intermediate schoolgirl; but she did the whole work of a family of boys, and boarded the hired men besides. She cooked, swept, washed, ironed, made and mended from daylight till dark—and from dark till daylight, I was going to say; for I don't know how she got any time for sleep. But I suppose she did. She got time to go to church, and to teach us to read the Bible, and to misunderstand it in the old way. She was *good*.

---

*Benjamin Franklin's popular compilation of practical wisdom; it became the bible of self-improvement.

But it ain't her on her knees in church that comes back to me so
much like the sight of an angel, as her on her knees before me at
night, washing my poor, dirty little feet, that I'd run bare in all day,
and making me decent for bed. There were six of us boys; it seems
to me we were all of a size; and she was just so careful with all of us.
I can feel her hands on my feet yet!" Bartley looked at Lapham's No.
10 boots and softly whistled through his teeth. "We were patched all
over; but we wa'n't ragged. I don't know how she got through it. She
didn't seem to think it was anything; and I guess it was no more than
my father expected of her. He worked like a horse in doors and out—
up at daylight, feeding the stock, and groaning round all day with his
rheumatism, but not stopping."

Bartley hid a yawn over his note-book, and probably, if he could
have spoken his mind, he would have suggested to Lapham that he
was not there for the purpose of interviewing his ancestry. But Bartley had learned to practice a patience with his victims which he did
not always feel, and to feign an interest in their digressions till he
could bring them up with a round turn.

"I tell you," said Lapham, jabbing the point of his penknife into
the writing-pad on the desk before him, "when I hear women com-
plaining nowadays that their lives are stunted and empty, I want to
tell 'em about my mother's life. I could paint it out for 'em."

Bartley saw his opportunity at the word paint, and cut in. "And
you say, Mr. Lapham, that you discovered this mineral paint on the
old farm yourself?"

Lapham acquiesced in the return to business. "I didn't discover
it," he said, scrupulously. "My father found it one day, in a hole made
by a tree blowing down. There it was, laying loose in the pit, and
sticking to the roots that had pulled up a big cake of dirt with 'em.
I don't know what give him the idea that there was money in it, but
he did think so from the start. I guess, if they'd had the word in those
days, they'd considered him pretty much of a crank about it. He was
trying as long as he lived to get that paint introduced; but he couldn't
make it go. The country was so poor they couldn't paint their houses
with anything; and father hadn't any facilities. It got to be a kind of
joke with us; and I guess that paint-mine did as much as any one
thing to make us boys clear out as soon as we got old enough. All my
brothers went West and took up land; but I hung on to New England,

and I hung on to the old farm, not because the paint-mine was on it, but because the old house was—and the graves. Well," said Lapham, as if unwilling to give himself too much credit, "there wouldn't been any market for it, anyway. You can go through that part of the State and buy more farms than you can shake a stick at for less money than it cost to build the barns on 'em. Of course, it's turned out a good thing. I keep the old house up in good shape, and we spend a month or so there every summer. M'wife kind of likes it, and the girls. Pretty place; sightly all round it. I've got a force of men at work there the whole time, and I've got a man and his wife in the house. Had a family meeting there last year; the whole connection from out West. There!" Lapham rose from his seat and took down a large warped, unframed photograph from the top of his desk, passing his hand over it, and then blowing vigorously upon it, to clear it of the dust. "There we are, all of us."

"I don't need to look twice at you," said Bartley, putting his finger on one of the heads.

"Well, that's Bill," said Lapham, with a gratified laugh. "He's about as brainy as any of us, I guess. He's one of their leading lawyers, out Dubuque way; been judge of the Common Pleas once or twice. That's his son—just graduated at Yale—alongside of my youngest girl. Good-looking chap, ain't he?"

"She's a good-looking chap," said Bartley, with prompt irreverence. He hastened to add, at the frown which gathered between Lapham's eyes, "What a beautiful creature she is! What a lovely, refined, sensitive face! And she looks good, too."

"She is good," said the father, relenting.

"And, after all, that's about the best thing in a woman," said the potential reprobate. "If my wife wasn't good enough to keep both of us straight, I don't know what would become of me."

"My other daughter," said Lapham, indicating a girl with eyes that showed large, and a face of singular gravity. "Mis' Lapham," he continued, touching his wife's effigy with his little finger. "My brother Willard and his family—farm at Kankakee. Hazard Lapham and his wife—Baptist preacher in Kansas. Jim and his three girls—milling business at Minneapolis. Ben and his family—practicing medicine in Fort Wayne."

The figures were clustered in an irregular group in front of an

old farm-house, whose original ugliness had been smartened up with
a coat of Lapham's own paint and heightened with an incongruous piazza. The photographer had not been able to conceal the fact that they
were all decent, honest-looking, sensible people, with a very fair share
of beauty among the young girls; some of these were extremely pretty,
in fact. He had put them into awkward and constrained attitudes, of
course; and they all looked as if they had the instrument of torture
which photographers call a head-rest under their occiputs. Here and
there an elderly lady's face was a mere blur; and some of the younger
children had twitched themselves into wavering shadows, and might
have passed for spirit-photographs of their own little ghosts. It was the
standard family-group photograph, in which most Americans have fig-
ured at some time or other; and Lapham exhibited a just satisfaction in
it. "I presume," he mused aloud, as he put it back on top of his desk,
"that we sha'n't soon get together again, all of us."

"And you say," suggested Bartley, "that you staid right along on
the old place, when the rest cleared out West?"

"No-o-o-o," said Lapham, with a long, loud drawl; "I cleared
out West too, first off. Went to Texas. Texas was all the cry in those
days. But I got enough of the Lone Star in about three months, and I
come back with the idea that Vermont was good enough for me."

"Fatted calf business?" queried Bartley, with his pencil poised
above his note-book.

"I presume they were glad to see me," said Lapham, with dignity.
"Mother," he added gently, "died that winter, and I staid on with father. I buried him in the spring; and then I came down to a little place
called Lumberville, and picked up what jobs I could get. I worked
round at the saw-mills, and I was ostler* awhile at the hotel—I always
did like a good horse. Well, I wa'n't exactly a college graduate, and I went
to school odd times. I got to driving the stage after while, and by and
by I bought the stage and run the business myself. Then I hired the
tavern-stand, and—well, to make a long story short, then I got married. Yes," said Lapham, with pride, "I married the schoolteacher. We
did pretty well with the hotel, and my wife she was always at me to
paint up. Well, I put it off, and put it off, as a man will, till one day I
give in, and says I, 'Well, let's paint up. Why, Pert,'—m'wife's name's

---

*Stableman.

Persis,—'I've got a whole paint-mine out on the farm. Let's go out and look at it.' So we drove out. I'd let the place for seventy-five dollars a year to a shif'less kind of a Kanuck* that had come down that way; and I'd hated to see the house with him in it; but we drove out one Saturday afternoon, and we brought back about a bushel of the stuff in the buggy-seat, and I tried it crude, and I tried it burnt; and I liked it. M'wife she liked it, too. There wa'n't any painter by trade in the village, and I mixed it myself. Well, sir, that tavern's got that coat of paint on it yet, and it hain't ever had any other, and I don't know's it ever will. Well, you know, I felt as if it was a kind of a harumscarum† experiment, all the while; and I presume I shouldn't have tried it, but I kind of liked to do it because father'd always set so much store by his paint-mine. And when I'd got the first coat on,"—Lapham called it cut,—"I presume I must have set as much as half an hour, looking at it and thinking how he would have enjoyed it. I've had my share of luck in this world, and I aint a-going to complain on my own account, but I've noticed that most things get along too late for most people. It made me feel bad, and it took all the pride out my success with the paint, thinking of father. Seemed to me I might 'a' taken more interest in it when he was by to see; but we've got to live and learn. Well, I called my wife out,—I'd tried it on the back of the house, you know,—and she left her dishes,—I can remember she came out with her sleeves rolled up and set down alongside of me on the trestle,—and says I, 'What do you think, Persis?' And says she, 'Well, you hain't got a paint-mine, Silas Lapham; you've got a gold-mine.' She always was just so enthusiastic about things. Well, it was just after two or three boats had burnt up out West, and a lot of lives lost, and there was a great cry about non-inflammable paint, and I guess that was what was in her mind. 'Well, I guess it ain't any gold-mine, Persis,' says I; 'but I guess it is a paint-mine. I'm going to have it analyzed, and if it turns out what I think it is, I'm going to work it. And if father hadn't had such a long name, I should call it the Nehemiah Lapham Mineral Paint. But, any rate, every barrel of it, and every keg, and every bottle, and every package, big or little, has got to have the initials and figures N. L. f. 1835, S. L. t. 1855, on it. Father found it in 1835, and I tried it in 1855.' "

---

*Derogatory term for a Canadian, usually a French Canadian.
†Reckless; irresponsible.

" 'S. T.—1860—X.' business," said Bartley.

"Yes," said Lapham, "but I hadn't heard of Plantation Bitters*
then, and I hadn't seen any of the fellow's labels. I set to work and I
got a man down from Boston; and I carried him out to the farm, and
he analyzed it—made a regular job of it. Well, sir, we built a kiln, and
we kept a lot of that paint-ore red-hot for forty-eight hours; kept the
Kanuck and his family up, firing. The presence of iron in the ore
showed with the magnet from the start; and when he came to test
it, he found out that it contained about seventy-five per cent. of the
peroxide of iron."

Lapham pronounced the scientific phrases with a sort of reverent satisfaction, as if awed through his pride by a little lingering uncertainty as to what peroxide was. He accented it as if it were
purr-ox-*eyed*; and Bartley had to get him to spell it.

"Well, and what then?" he asked, when he had made a note of
the percentage.

"What then?" echoed Lapham. "Well, then, the fellow set down
and told me, 'You've got a paint here,' says he, 'that's going to drive
every other mineral paint out of the market. Why,' says he, 'it'll drive
'em right into the Back Bay!'[1] Of course, I didn't know what the Back
Bay was then; but I begun to open my eyes; thought I'd had 'em
open before, but I guess I hadn't. Says he, 'That paint has got hy-
draulic cement in it, and it can stand fire and water and acids'; he
named over a lot of things. Says he, 'It'll mix easily with linseed oil,
whether you want to use it boiled or raw; and it ain't a-going to
crack nor fade any; and it ain't a-going to scale. When you've got
your arrangements for burning it properly, you're going to have a
paint that will stand like the everlasting hills, in every climate under
the sun.' Then he went into a lot of particulars, and I begun to think
he was drawing a long bow, and meant to make his bill accordingly.
So I kept pretty cool; but the fellow's bill didn't amount to anything
hardly—said I might pay him after I got going; young chap, and
pretty easy; but every word he said was gospel. Well, I ain't a-going
to brag up my paint; I don't suppose you came here to hear me
blow——"

*Popular patent medicine for digestive troubles; its label gave the date of its
discovery.

"Oh, yes, I did," said Bartley. "That's what I want. Tell all there is to tell, and I can boil it down afterward. A man can't make a greater mistake with a reporter than to hold back anything out of modesty. It may be the very thing we want to know. What we want is the whole truth, and more; we've got so much modesty of our own that we can temper almost any statement."

Lapham looked as if he did not quite like this tone, and he resumed a little more quietly. "Oh, there isn't really very much more to say about the paint itself. But you can use it for almost anything where a paint is wanted, inside or out. It'll prevent decay, and it'll stop it, after it's begun, in tin or iron. You can paint the inside of a cistern or a bath-tub with it, and water won't hurt it; and you can paint a steam-boiler with it, and heat won't. You can cover a brick wall with it, or a railroad car, or the deck of a steam-boat, and you can't do a better thing for either."

"Never tried it on the human conscience, I suppose," suggested Bartley.

"No, sir," replied Lapham, gravely. "I guess you want to keep that as free from paint as you can, if you want much use of it. I never cared to try any of it on mine." Lapham suddenly lifted his bulk up out of his swivel-chair, and led the way out into the wareroom beyond the office partitions, where rows and ranks of casks, barrels, and kegs stretched dimly back to the rear of the building, and diffused an honest, clean, wholesome smell of oil and paint. They were labeled and branded as containing each so many pounds of Lapham's Mineral Paint, and each bore the mystic devices, N. L. f. 1835—S. L. t. 1855. "There!" said Lapham, kicking one of the largest casks with the toe of his boot, "that's about our biggest package; and here," he added, laying his hand affectionately on the head of a very small keg, as if it were the head of a child, which it resembled in size, "this is the smallest. We used to put the paint on the market dry, but now we grind every ounce of it in oil—very best quality of linseed oil—and warrant it. We find it gives more satisfaction. Now, come back to the office, and I'll show you our fancy brands."

It was very cool and pleasant in that dim wareroom, with the rafters showing overhead in a cloudy perspective, and darkening away into the perpetual twilight at the rear of the building; and Bartley had found an agreeable seat on the head of a half-barrel of the paint, which he was reluctant to leave. But he rose and followed the vigorous lead of Lapham back to the office, where the sun of a long summer afternoon was just beginning to glare in at the window. On shelves opposite Lapham's desk were tin cans of various sizes, arranged in tapering cylinders, and showing, in a pattern diminishing toward the top, the same label borne by the casks and barrels in the ware-room. Lapham merely waved his hand toward these; but when Bartley, after a comprehensive glance at them, gave his whole attention to a row of clean, smooth jars, where different tints of the paint showed through flawless glass, Lapham smiled and waited in pleased expectation.

"Hello!" said Bartley. "That's pretty!"

"Yes," assented Lapham, "it is rather nice. It's our latest thing, and we find it takes with customers first-rate. Look here!" he said, taking down one of the jars, and pointing to the first line of the label.

Bartley read, "THE PERSIS BRAND," and then he looked at Lapham and smiled.

"After *her*, of course," said Lapham. "Got it up and put the first of it on the market her last birthday. She was pleased."

"I should think she might have been," said Bartley, while he made a note of the appearance of the jars.

"I don't know about your mentioning it in your interview," said Lapham, dubiously.

"That's going into the interview, Mr. Lapham, if nothing else does. Got a wife myself, and I know just how you feel." It was in the dawn of Bartley's prosperity on the "Boston Events," before his troubles with Marcia had seriously begun.[2]

"Is that so?" said Lapham, recognizing with a smile another of the vast majority of married Americans; a few underrate their wives, but the rest think them supernal in intelligence and capability. "Well," he added, "we must see about that. Where'd you say you lived?"

"We don't live; we board. Mrs. Nash, 13 Canary Place."

"Well, we've all got to commence that way," suggested Lapham, consolingly.

"Yes; but we've about got to the end of our string. I expect to be under a roof of my own on Clover street before long. I suppose," said Bartley, returning to business, "that you didn't let the grass grow under your feet much after you found out what was in your paint-mine?"

"No, sir," answered Lapham, withdrawing his eyes from a long stare at Bartley, in which he had been seeing himself a young man again, in the first days of his married life. "I went right back to Lumberville and sold out everything, and put all I could rake and scrape together into paint. And Mis' Lapham was with me every time. No hang back about her. I tell you she was a *woman!*"

Bartley laughed. "That's the sort most of us marry."

"No, we don't," said Lapham. "Most of us marry silly little girls grown up to *look* like women."

"Well, I guess that's about so," assented Bartley, as if upon second thought.

"If it hadn't been for her," resumed Lapham, "the paint wouldn't have come to anything. I used to tell her it wa'n't the seventy-five per cent. of purr-ox-eyed of iron in the *ore* that made that paint go; it was the seventy-five per cent. of purr-ox-eyed of iron in *her*."

"Good!" cried Bartley. "I'll tell Marcia that."

"In less'n six months there wa'n't a board-fence, nor a bridge-girder, nor a dead wall, nor a barn, nor a face of rock in that whole region that didn't have 'Lapham's Mineral Paint—Specimen' on it in the three colors we begun by making." Bartley had taken his seat on the window-sill, and Lapham, standing before him, now put up his huge foot close to Bartley's thigh; neither of them minded that.

"I've heard a good deal of talk about that S. T.—1860—X. man, and the stove-blacking man, and the kidney-cure man, because they advertised in that way; and I've read articles about it in the papers; but I don't see where the joke comes in, exactly. So long as the people that own the barns and fences don't object, I don't see what the public has got to do with it. And I never saw anything so very sacred about a big rock, along a river or in a pasture that it wouldn't do to put mineral paint on it in three colors. I wish some of the people that talk about the landscape, and *write* about it, had to bu'st one of them rocks *out* of the landscape with powder, or dig a hole to bury it in, as we used to have to do up on the farm; I guess they'd sing a little different tune about the profanation of scenery. There ain't any man enjoys a sightly bit of nature—a smooth piece of interval, with half a dozen good-sized wine-glass elms in it—more than I do. But I ain't a-going to stand up for every big ugly rock I come across, as if we were all a set of dumn

Druids.* I say the landscape was made for man, and not man for
the landscape."

"Yes," said Bartley, carelessly; "it was made for the stove-polish
man and the kidney-cure man."

"It was made for any man that knows how to use it," Lapham returned, insensible to Bartley's irony. "Let 'em go and live with nature
in the winter, up there along the Canada line, and I guess they'll get
enough of her for one while. Well—where was I?"

"Decorating the landscape," said Bartley.

"Yes, sir; I started right there at Lumberville, and it give the place
a start, too. You won't find it on the map now; and you won't find it
in the gazetteer. I give a pretty good lump of money to build a town-
hall, about five years back, and the first meeting they held in it they
voted to change the name,—Lumberville wa'n't a name,—and it's
Lapham now."

"Isn't it somewhere up in that region that they get the old Brandon red?" asked Bartley.

"We're about ninety miles from Brandon. The Brandon's a good
paint," said Lapham, conscientiously. "Like to show you round up at
our place some odd time, if you get off."

"Thanks. I should like it first-rate. Works there?"

"Yes; Works there. Well, sir, just about the time I got started, the
war broke out; and it knocked my paint higher than a kite. The thing
dropped perfectly dead. I presume that if I'd had any sort of influence, I might have got it into government hands, for gun-carriages
and army-wagons, and may be on board government vessels. But I
hadn't, and we had to face the music. I was about broken-hearted,
but m'wife she looked at it another way. 'I guess it's a providence,'
says she. 'Silas, I guess you've got a country that's worth fighting for.
Any rate, you better go out and give it a chance.' Well, sir, I went. I
knew she meant business. It might kill her to have me go, but it
would kill her sure if I staid. She was one of that kind. I went. Her
last words was, 'I'll look after the paint, Si.' We hadn't but just one
little girl then,—boy'd died,—and Mis' Lapham's mother was livin'
with us; and I knew if times did anyways come up again, m'wife'd

know just what to do. So I went. I got through; and you can call me Colonel, if you want to. Feel there!" Lapham took Bartley's thumb and forefinger and put them on a bunch in his leg, just above the knee. "Anything hard?"

"Ball?"

Lapham nodded. "Gettysburg. That's my thermometer. If it wa'n't for that, I shouldn't know enough to come in when it rains."

Bartley laughed at a joke which betrayed some evidences of wear. "And when you came back, you took hold of the paint and rushed it."

"I took hold of the paint and rushed it—all I could," said Lapham, with less satisfaction than he had hitherto shown in his autobiography. "But I found that I had got back to another world. The day of small things was past, and I don't suppose it will ever come again in this country. My wife was at me all the time to take a partner—somebody with capital; but I couldn't seem to bear the idea. That paint was like my own blood to me. To have anybody else concerned in it was like— well, I don't know what. I saw it was the thing to do; but I tried to fight it off, and I tried to joke it off. I used to say, 'Why didn't you take a partner yourself, Persis, while I was away?' And she'd say, 'Well, if you hadn't come back, I should, Si.' Always did like a joke about as well as any woman I ever saw. Well, I had to come to it. I took a partner." Lapham dropped the bold blue eyes with which he had been till now staring into Bartley's face, and the reporter knew that here was a place for asterisks in his interview, if interviews were faithful. "He had money enough," continued Lapham, with a suppressed sigh; "but he didn't know anything about paint. We hung on together for a year or two. And then we quit."

"And he had the experience," suggested Bartley, with companionable ease.

"I had some of the experience too," said Lapham, with a scowl; and Bartley divined, through the freemasonry of all who have sore places in their memories, that this was a point which he must not touch again.

"And since that, I suppose, you've played it alone."

"I've played it alone."

"You must ship some of this paint of yours to foreign countries, Colonel?" suggested Bartley, putting on a professional air.

"We ship it to all parts of the world. It goes to South America, lots of it. It goes to Australia, and it goes to India, and it goes to China, and it goes to the Cape of Good Hope. It'll stand any climate. Of course, we don't export these fancy brands much. They're for home use. But we're introducing them elsewhere. Here." Lapham pulled open a drawer, and showed Bartley a lot of labels in different languages—Spanish, French, German, and Italian. "We expect to do a good business in all those countries. We've got our agencies in Cadiz now, and in Paris, and in Hamburg, and in Leghorn. It's a thing that's bound to make its way. Yes, sir. Wherever a man has got a ship, or a bridge, or a dock, or a house, or a car, or a fence, or a pig-pen, anywhere in God's universe, to paint, that's the paint for him, and he's bound to find it out sooner or later. You pass a ton of that paint dry through a blast-furnace, and you'll get a quarter of a ton of pig-iron. I believe in my paint. I believe it's a blessing to the world. When folks come in, and kind of smell round, and ask me what I mix it with, I always say, 'Well, in the first place, I mix it with Faith, and after that I grind it up with the best quality of boiled linseed oil that money will buy.' "

Lapham took out his watch and looked at it, and Bartley perceived that his audience was drawing to a close. " 'F you ever want to run down and take a look at our Works, pass you over the road,"—he called it rud,—"and it sha'n't cost you a cent."

"Well, may be I shall, sometime," said Bartley. "Good afternoon, Colonel."

"Good afternoon. Or—hold on! My horse down there yet, William?" he called to the young man in the counting-room, who had taken his letter at the beginning of the interview. "Oh! All right!" he added, in response to something the young man said. "Can't I set you down somewhere, Mr. Hubbard? I've got my horse at the door, and I can drop you on my way home. I'm going to take Mis' Lapham to look at a house I'm driving piles for, down on the New Land."

"Don't care if I do," said Bartley.

Lapham put on a straw hat, gathered up some papers lying on his desk, pulled down its rolling cover, turned the key in it, and gave the papers to an extremely handsome young woman at one of the desks in the outer office. She was stylishly dressed, as Bartley saw, and her smooth, yellow hair was sculpturesquely waved over a low, white forehead. "Here," said Lapham, with the same prompt, gruff kindness that he had used in addressing the young man, "I want you should put these in shape, and give me a type-writer copy tomorrow."

"What an uncommonly pretty girl!" said Bartley, as they descended the rough stairway and found their way out to the street, past the dangling rope of a block and tackle wandering up into the cavernous darkness overhead.

"She does her work," said Lapham, shortly.

Bartley mounted to the left side of the open buggy standing at the curb-stone, and Lapham, gathering up the hitching-weight, slid it under the buggy-seat and mounted beside him.

"No chance to speed a horse here, of course," said Lapham, while the horse with a spirited gentleness picked her way, with a high, long action, over the pavement of the street. The streets were all narrow, and most of them crooked, in that quarter of the town; but at the end of one the spars of a vessel penciled themselves delicately against the cool blue of the afternoon sky. The air was full of a smell pleasantly compounded of oakum, of leather, and of oil. It was not the busy season, and they met only two or three trucks heavily straggling toward the wharf with their long string teams; but the cobble-stones of the pavement were worn with the dint of ponderous wheels, and discolored with iron-rust from them; here and there, in wandering streaks over its surface, was the gray stain of the salt water with which the street had been sprinkled.

After an interval of some minutes, which both men spent in looking round the dashboard from opposite sides to watch the stride of the horse, Bartley said, with a light sigh, "I had a colt once down in Maine that stepped just like that mare."

"Well!" said Lapham, sympathetically recognizing the bond that this fact created between them. "Well, now, I tell you what you do. You let me come for you 'most any afternoon, now, and take you out over the Milldam, and speed this mare a little. I'd like to show you what this mare can do. Yes, I would."

"All right," answered Bartley; "I'll let you know my first day off."

"Good," cried Lapham.

"Kentucky?" queried Bartley.

"No, sir. I don't ride behind anything but Vermont; never did.

Touch of Morgan, of course; but you can't have much Morgan in a horse if you want speed. Hambletonian* mostly. Where'd you say you wanted to get out?"

"I guess you may put me down at the 'Events' office, just round the corner here. I've got to write up this interview while it's fresh."

"All right," said Lapham, impersonally assenting to Bartley's use of him as material.

He had not much to complain of in Bartley's treatment, unless it was the strain of extravagant compliment which it involved. But the flattery was mainly for the paint, whose virtues Lapham did not believe could be overstated, and himself and his history had been treated with as much respect as Bartley was capable of showing any one. He made a very picturesque thing of the discovery of the paint-mine. "Deep in the heart of the virgin forests of Vermont, far up toward the line of the Canadian snows, on a desolate mountain-side, where an autumnal storm had done its wild work, and the great trees, strewn hither and thither, bore witness to its violence, Nehemiah Lapham discovered, just forty years ago, the mineral which the alchemy of his son's enterprise and energy has transmuted into solid ingots of the most precious of metals. The colossal fortune of Colonel Silas Lapham lay at the bottom of a hole which an uprooted tree had dug for him, and which for many years remained a paint-mine of no more appreciable value than a soap-mine."

Here Bartley had not been able to forego another grin; but he compensated for it by the high reverence with which he spoke of Colonel Lapham's record during the war of the rebellion, and of the motives which impelled him to turn aside from an enterprise in which his whole heart was engaged and take part in the struggle. "The Colonel bears imbedded in the muscle of his right leg a little memento of the period in the shape of a minie-ball, which he jocularly referred to as his thermometer, and which relieves him from the necessity of reading 'The Probabilities' in his morning paper. This saves him just so much time; and for a man who, as he said, has not a moment of waste time on him anywhere, five minutes a day are something in the course of a year. Simple, clear, bold, and straightforward in mind and action, Colonel Silas Lapham, with a prompt

---

*Morgan and Hambletonian are two desirable breeds of trotting horses.

comprehensiveness and a never-failing business sagacity, is, in the best sense of that much-abused term, one of nature's noblemen, to the last inch of his five eleven and a half. His life affords an example of single-minded application and unwavering perseverance which our young business men would do well to emulate. There is nothing showy or meretricious about the man. He believes in mineral paint, and he puts his heart and soul into it. He makes it a religion; though we would not imply that it is his religion. Colonel Lapham is a regular attendant at the Rev. Dr. Langworthy's church. He subscribes liberally to the Associated Charities, and no good object or worthy public enterprise fails to receive his support. He is not now actively in politics, and his paint is not partisan; but it is an open secret that he is, and always has been, a stanch Republican. Without violating the sanctities of private life, we cannot speak fully of various details which came out in the free and unembarrassed interview which Colonel Lapham accorded our representative. But we may say that the success of which he is justly proud he is also proud to attribute in great measure to the sympathy and energy of his wife—one of those women who, in whatever walk of life, seem born to honor the name of American Woman, and to redeem it from the national reproach of Daisy Millerism.[3] Of Colonel Lapham's family, we will simply add that it consists of two young lady daughters.

"The subject of this very inadequate sketch is building a house on the water side of Beacon street, after designs by one of our leading architectural firms, which, when complete, will be one of the finest ornaments of that exclusive avenue. It will, we believe, be ready for the occupancy of the family sometime in the spring."

When Bartley had finished his article, which he did with a good deal of inward derision, he went home to Marcia, still smiling over the thought of Lapham, whose burly simplicity had peculiarly amused him.

"He regularly turned himself inside out to me," he said, as he sat describing his interview to Marcia.

"Then I know you could make something nice out of it," said his wife; "and that will please Mr. Witherby."

"Oh, yes, I've done pretty well; but I couldn't let myself loose on him the way I wanted to. Confound the limitations of decency, anyway! I should like to have told just what Colonel Lapham thought of landscape advertising in Colonel Lapham's own words. I'll tell you one thing, Marsh: he had a girl there at one of the desks that you wouldn't let me have within gunshot of my office. Pretty? It aint any name for it!" Marcia's eyes began to blaze, and Bartley broke out into a laugh, in which he arrested himself at sight of a formidable parcel in the corner of the room.

"Hello! What's that?"

"Why, I don't know what it is," replied Marcia, tremulously. "A man brought it just before you came in, and I didn't like to open it."

"Think it was some kind of infernal machine?" asked Bartley, getting down on his knees to examine the package. "Mrs. B. Hubbard, heigh?" He cut the heavy hemp string with his penknife. "We must look into this thing. I should like to know who's sending packages to Mrs. Hubbard in my absence." He unfolded the wrappings of paper, growing softer and finer inward, and presently pulled out a hand-some square glass jar, through which a crimson mass showed richly. "The Persis Brand!" he yelled. "I knew it!"

"Oh, what is it, Bartley?" quavered Marcia. Then, courageously drawing a little nearer: "Is it some kind of jam?" she implored.

"Jam? No!" roared Bartley. "It's paint! It's mineral paint—Lapham's paint!"

"Paint?" echoed Marcia, as she stood over him while he stripped their wrappings from the jars which showed the dark blue, dark green, light brown, dark brown, and black, with the dark crimson, forming the gamut of color of the Lapham paint. "Don't tell me it's paint that I can use, Bartley!"

"Well, I shouldn't advise you to use much of it—all at once," replied her husband. "But it's paint that you can use in moderation."

Marcia cast her arms round his neck and kissed him. "O Bartley, I think I'm the happiest girl in the world! I was just wondering what I should do. There are places in that Clover street house that need touching up so dreadfully. I shall be very careful. You needn't be afraid I shall overdo. But this just saves my life. Did you buy it, Bartley? You know we couldn't afford it, and you oughtn't to have done it! And what does the Persis Brand mean?"

"Buy it?" cried Bartley. "No! The old fool's sent it to you as a present. You'd better wait for the facts before you pitch into me for extravagance, Marcia. Persis is the name of his wife; and he named it after her because it's his finest brand. You'll see it in my interview. Put it on the market her last birthday for a surprise to her."

"What old fool?" faltered Marcia.

"Why, Lapham—the mineral paint man."

"Oh, what a good man!" sighed Marcia from the bottom of her soul. "Bartley! you *won't* make fun of him, as you do of some of those people? *Will* you?"

"Nothing that *he'll* ever find out," said Bartley, getting up and brushing off the carpet-lint from his knees.

II

After dropping Bartley Hubbard at the "Events" building, Lapham drove on down Washington street to Nankeen Square at the South End, where he had lived ever since the mistaken movement of society in that direction ceased. He had not built, but had bought very cheap of a terrified gentleman of good extraction who discovered too late that the South End was not the thing, and who in the eagerness of his flight to the Back Bay threw in his carpets and shades for almost nothing. Mrs. Lapham was even better satisfied with their bargain than the Colonel himself, and they had lived in Nankeen Square for twelve years. They had seen the saplings planted in the pretty oval round which the houses were built flourish up into sturdy young trees, and their two little girls in the same period had grown into young ladies; the Colonel's tough frame had expanded into the bulk which Bartley's interview indicated; and Mrs. Lapham, while keeping a more youthful outline, showed the sharp print of the crow's-foot at the corners of her motherly eyes, and certain slight creases in her wholesome cheeks. The fact that they lived in an unfashionable neighborhood was something that they had never been made to feel to their personal disadvantage, and they had hardly known it till the summer before this story opens, when Mrs. Lapham and her daughter Irene had met some other Bostonians far from Boston, who made it memorable. They were people whom chance had brought for the time under a singular obligation to the Lapham ladies, and they were gratefully recognizant of it. They had ventured— a mother and two daughters—as far as a rather wild little Canadian watering-place on the St. Lawrence, below Quebec, and had arrived some days before their son and brother was expected to join them. Two of their trunks had gone astray, and on the night of their arrival the mother was taken violently ill. Mrs. Lapham came to their help, with her skill as nurse, and with the abundance of her own and her daughter's wardrobe, and a profuse, single-hearted kindness. When a doctor could be got at, he said that but for Mrs. Lapham's timely care, the lady would hardly have lived. He was a very effusive little Frenchman, and fancied he was saying something very pleasant to everybody.

A certain intimacy inevitably followed, and when the son came he was even more grateful than the others. Mrs. Lapham could not quite understand why he should be as attentive to her as to Irene; but she compared him with other young men about the place, and thought him nicer than any of them. She had not the means of a wider comparison; for in Boston, with all her husband's prosperity, they had not had a social life. Their first years there were given to careful getting on Lapham's part, and careful saving on his wife's. Suddenly the money began to come so abundantly that she need not save; and then they did not know what to do with it. A certain amount could be spent on horses, and Lapham spent it; his wife spent on rich and rather ugly clothes and a luxury of household appointments. Lapham had not yet reached the picture-buying stage of the rich man's development, but they decorated their house with the costliest and most abominable frescoes; they went upon journeys, and lavished upon cars and hotels; they gave with both hands to their church and to all the charities it brought them acquainted with; but they did not know how to spend on society. Up to a certain period Mrs. Lapham had the ladies of her neighborhood in to tea, as her mother had done in the country in her younger days. Lapham's idea of hospitality was still to bring a heavy-buying customer home to pot-luck; neither of them imagined dinners.

Their two girls had gone to the public schools, where they had not got on as fast as some of the other girls; so that they were a year behind in graduating from the grammar-school, where Lapham thought that they had got education enough. His wife was of a different mind; she would have liked them to go to some private school for their finishing. But Irene did not care for study; she preferred housekeeping, and both the sisters were afraid of being snubbed by the other girls, who were of a different sort from the girls of the grammar-school; these were mostly from the parks and squares, like themselves. It ended in their going part of a year. But the elder had an odd taste of her own for reading, and she took some private lessons, and read books out of the circulating library; the whole family were amazed at the number she read, and rather proud of it.

They were not girls who embroidered or abandoned themselves to needle-work. Irene spent her abundant leisure in shopping for herself and her mother, of whom both daughters made a kind of idol, buying her caps and laces out of their pin-money, and getting her dresses far beyond her capacity to wear. Irene dressed herself very stylishly, and spent hours on her toilet every day. Her sister had a simpler taste, and, if she had done altogether as she liked, might even have slighted dress. They all three took long naps every day, and sat hours together minutely discussing what they saw out of the window. In her self-guided search for self-improvement, the elder sister went to many church lectures on a vast variety of secular subjects, and usually came home with a comic account of them, and that made more matter of talk for the whole family. She could make fun of nearly everything; Irene complained that she scared away the young men whom they got acquainted with at the dancing-school sociables. They were, perhaps, not the wisest young men.

The girls had learned to dance at Papanti's;* but they had not belonged to the private classes. They did not even know of them, and a great gulf divided them from those who did. Their father did not like company, except such as came informally in their way; and their mother had remained too rustic to know how to attract it in the sophisticated city fashion. None of them had grasped the idea of European travel; but they had gone about to mountain and seaside resorts, the mother and the two girls, where they witnessed the spectacle which such resorts present throughout New England, of multitudes of girls, lovely, accomplished, exquisitely dressed, humbly glad of the presence of any sort of young man; but the Laphams had no skill or courage to make themselves noticed, far less courted by the solitary invalid, or clergyman, or artist. They lurked helplessly about in the hotel parlors, looking on and not knowing how to put themselves forward. Perhaps they did not care a great deal to do so. They had not a conceit of themselves, but a sort of content in their own ways that one may notice in certain families. The very strength of their mutual affection was a barrier to worldly knowledge; they dressed for one another; they equipped their house for their own satisfaction; they lived richly to themselves,

*Dancing school, established by an exiled Italian, for proper young Bostonians.

not because they were selfish, but because they did not know how
to do otherwise. The elder daughter did not care for society, apparently. The younger, who was but three years younger, was not
yet quite old enough to be ambitious of it. With all her wonderful
beauty, she had an innocence almost vegetable. When her beauty,
which in its immaturity was crude and harsh, suddenly ripened,
she bloomed and glowed with the unconsciousness of a flower; she
not merely did not feel herself admired, but hardly knew herself
discovered. If she dressed well, perhaps too well, it was because she
had the instinct of dress; but till she met this young man who was
so nice to her at Baie St. Joan, she had scarcely lived a detached, individual life, so wholly had she depended on her mother and her
sister for her opinions, almost her sensations. She took account of
everything he did and said, pondering it, and trying to make out
exactly what he meant, to the inflection of a syllable, the slightest
movement or gesture. In this way she began for the first time to
form ideas which she had not derived from her family, and they
were none the less her own because they were often mistaken.

Some of the things that he partly said, partly looked, she reported to her mother, and they talked them over, as they did everything relating to these new acquaintances, and wrought them into
the novel point of view which they were acquiring.[4] When Mrs.
Lapham returned home, she submitted all the accumulated facts of
the case, and all her own conjectures, to her husband, and canvassed
them anew.

At first he was disposed to regard the whole affair as of small importance, and she had to insist a little beyond her own convictions in
order to counteract his indifference.

"Well, I can tell you," she said, "that if you think they were not
the nicest people you ever saw, you're mightily mistaken. They had
about the best manners; and they had been everywhere, and knew
everything. I declare it made me feel as if we had always lived in the
backwoods. I don't know but the mother and the daughters would
have let you feel so a little, if they'd showed out all they thought; but
they never did; and the son—well, I can't express it, Silas! But that
young man had about perfect ways."

"Seem struck up on Irene?" asked the Colonel.

"How can I tell? He seemed just about as much struck up on me. Anyway, he paid me as much attention as he did her. Perhaps it's more the way, now, to notice the mother than it used to be."

Lapham ventured no conjecture, but asked, as he had asked already, who the people were.

Mrs. Lapham repeated their name. Lapham nodded his head. "Do you know them? What business is he in?"

"I guess he ain't in anything," said Lapham.

"They were very nice," said Mrs. Lapham, impartially.

"Well, they'd ought to be," returned the Colonel. "Never done anything else."

"They didn't seem stuck up," urged his wife.

"They'd no need to—with you. I could buy him and sell him, twice over."

This answer satisfied Mrs. Lapham rather with the fact than with her husband. "Well, I guess I wouldn't brag, Silas," she said.

In the winter the ladies of this family, who returned to town very late, came to call on Mrs. Lapham. They were again very polite. But the mother let drop, in apology for their calling almost at nightfall, that the coachman had not known the way exactly.

"Nearly all our friends are on the New Land or on the Hill."*

There was a barb in this that rankled after the ladies had gone; and on comparing notes with her daughter, Mrs. Lapham found that a barb had been left to rankle in her mind also.

"They said they had never been in this part of the town before."

Upon a strict search of her memory, Irene could not report that the fact had been stated with anything like insinuation, but it was that which gave it a more penetrating effect.

"Oh, well, of course," said Lapham, to whom these facts were referred. "Those sort of people haven't got much business up our way, and they don't come. It's a fair thing all round. We don't trouble the Hill or the New Land much."

"We know where they are," suggested his wife, thoughtfully.

"Yes," assented the Colonel. "I know where they are. I've got a lot of land over on the Back Bay."

---

*Back Bay and Beacon Hill, fashionable residential areas of Boston.

"You have?" eagerly demanded his wife.

"Want me to build on it?" he asked in reply, with a quizzical smile. "I guess we can get along here for a while."

This was at night. In the morning Mrs. Lapham said:

"I suppose we ought to do the best we can for the children, in every way."

"I supposed we always had," replied her husband.

"Yes, we have, according to our light."

"Have you got some new light?"

"I don't know as it's light. But if the girls are going to keep on living in Boston and marry here, I presume we ought to try to get them into society, some way; or ought to do something."

"Well, who's ever done more for their children than we have?" demanded Lapham, with a pang at the thought that he could possibly have been outdone. "Don't they have everything they want? Don't they dress just as you say? Don't you go everywhere with 'em? Is there ever anything going on that's worth while that they don't see it or hear it? I don't know what you mean. Why don't you get them into society? There's money enough!"

"There's got to be something besides money, I guess," said Mrs. Lapham, with a hopeless sigh. "I presume we didn't go to work just the right way about their schooling. We ought to have got them into some school where they'd have got acquainted with city girls—girls who could help them along. Nearly everybody at Miss Smillie's was from somewhere else."

"Well, it's pretty late to think about that now," grumbled Lapham.

"And we've always gone our own way, and not looked out for the future. We ought to have gone out more, and had people come to the house. Nobody comes."

"Well, is that my fault? I guess nobody ever makes people welcomer."

"We ought to have invited company more."

"Why don't you do it now? If it's for the girls, I don't care if you have the house full all the while."

Mrs. Lapham was forced to a confession full of humiliation. "I don't know who to ask."

"Well, you can't expect me to tell you."

"No; we're both country people, and we've kept our country ways, and we don't, either of us, know what to do. You've had to work so hard, and your luck was so long coming, and then it came with such a rush, that we haven't had any chance to learn what to do with it. It's just the same with Irene's looks; I didn't expect she was ever going to have any, she *was* such a plain child, and, all at once, she's blazed out this way. As long as it was Pen that didn't seem to care for society, I didn't give much mind to it. But I can see it's going to be different with Irene. I don't believe but what we're in the wrong neighborhood."

"Well," said the Colonel, "there aint a prettier lot on the Back Bay than mine. It's on the water side of Beacon, and it's twenty-eight feet wide and a hundred and fifty deep. Let's build on it."

Mrs. Lapham was silent awhile. "No," she said finally; "we've always got along well enough here, and I guess we better stay."

At breakfast she said, casually: "Girls, how would you like to have your father build on the New Land?"

The girls said they did not know. It was more convenient to the horse-cars where they were.

Mrs. Lapham stole a look of relief at her husband, and nothing more was said of the matter.

The mother of the family who had called upon Mrs. Lapham brought her husband's cards, and when Mrs. Lapham returned the visit she was in some trouble about the proper form of acknowledging the civility. The Colonel had no card but a business card, which advertised the principal depot and the several agencies of the mineral paint; and Mrs. Lapham doubted, till she wished to goodness that she had never seen nor heard of those people, whether to ignore her husband in the transaction altogether, or to write his name on her own card. She decided finally upon this measure, and she had the relief of not finding the family at home. As far as she could judge, Irene seemed to suffer a little disappointment from the fact.

For several months there was no communication between the families. Then there came to Nankeen Square a lithographed circular from the people on the Hill, signed in ink by the mother, and affording Mrs. Lapham an opportunity to subscribe for a charity of undeniable merit and acceptability. She submitted it to her husband, who promptly drew a check for five hundred dollars.

She tore it in two. "I will take a check for a hundred, Silas," she said.

"Why?" he asked, looking up guiltily at her.

"Because a hundred is enough; and I don't want to show off before them."

"Oh, I thought may be you did. Well, Pert," he added, having satisfied human nature by the preliminary thrust, "I guess you're about right. When do you want I should begin to build on Beacon street?" He handed her the new check, where she stood over him, and then leaned back in his chair and looked up at her.

"I don't want you should begin at all. What do you mean, Silas?" She rested against the side of his desk.

"Well, I don't know as I mean anything. But shouldn't you like to build? Everybody builds, at least once in a life-time."

"Where is your lot? They say it's unhealthy over there."[5]

Up to a certain point in their prosperity Mrs. Lapham had kept strict account of all her husband's affairs; but as they expanded, and ceased to be of the retail nature with which women successfully grapple, the intimate knowledge of them made her nervous. There was a period in which she felt that they were being ruined, but the crash had not come; and, since his great success, she had abandoned herself to a blind confidence in her husband's judgment, which she had hitherto felt needed her revision. He came and went, day by day, unquestioned. He bought and sold and got gain. She knew that he would tell her if ever things went wrong, and he knew that she would ask him whenever she was anxious.

"It ain't unhealthy where I've bought," said Lapham, rather enjoying her insinuation. "I looked after that when I was trading; and I guess it's about as healthy on the Back Bay as it is here, anyway. I got that lot for you, Pert; I thought you'd want to build on the Back Bay some day."

"Pshaw!" said Mrs. Lapham, deeply pleased inwardly, but not going to show it, as she would have said. "I guess you want to build there yourself." She insensibly got a little nearer to her husband. They liked to talk to each other in that blunt way; it is the New England way of expressing perfect confidence and tenderness.

"Well, I guess I do," said Lapham, not insisting upon the unselfish view of the matter. "I always did like the water side of Beacon. There aint a sightlier place in the world for a house. And some day there's bound to be a drive-way all along behind them houses, between them and the water, and then a lot there is going to be worth the gold that will cover it—coin. I've had offers for that lot, Pert, twice over what I give for it. Yes, I *have*. Don't you want to ride over there some afternoon with me and see it?"

"I'm satisfied where we be, Si," said Mrs. Lapham, recurring to the parlance of her youth in her pathos at her husband's kindness. She sighed anxiously, for she felt the trouble a woman knows in view of any great change. They had often talked of altering over the house in which they lived, but they had never come to it; and they had often talked of building, but it had always been a house in the country that they had thought of. "I wish you had sold that lot."

"I haint," said the Colonel, briefly.

"I don't know as I feel much like changing our way of living."

"Guess we could live there pretty much as we live here. There's all kinds of people on Beacon street; you mustn't think they're all big-bugs. I know one party that lives in a house he built to sell, and his wife don't keep any girl. You can have just as much style there as you want, or just as little. I guess we live as well as most of 'em now, and set as good a table. And if you come to style, I don't know as anybody has got more of a right to put it on than what we have."

"Well, I don't want to build on Beacon street, Si," said Mrs. Lapham, gently.

"Just as you please, Persis. I aint in any hurry to leave."

Mrs. Lapham stood flapping the check which she held in her right hand against the edge of her left.

The Colonel still sat looking up at her face, and watching the effect of the poison of ambition which he had artfully instilled into her mind.[6]

She sighed again—a yielding sigh. "What are you going to do this afternoon?"

"I'm going to take a turn on the Brighton road," said the Colonel.

"I don't believe but what I should like to go along," said his wife.

"All right. You hain't ever rode behind that mare yet, Pert, and I want you should see me let her out once. They say the snow's all packed down already, and the going is A 1."

At four o'clock in the afternoon, with a cold, red winter sunset before them, the Colonel and his wife were driving slowly down Beacon street in the light, high-seated cutter, where, as he said, they were a pretty tight fit. He was holding the mare in till the time came to speed her, and the mare was springily jolting over the snow, looking intelligently from side to side, and cocking this ear and that, while from her nostrils, her head tossing easily, she blew quick, irregular whiffs of steam.

"Gay, ain't she?" proudly suggested the Colonel.

"She *is* gay," assented his wife.

They met swiftly dashing sleighs, and let them pass on either hand, down the beautiful avenue narrowing with an admirably even skyline in the perspective. They were not in a hurry. The mare jounced easily along, and they talked of the different houses on either side of the way. They had a crude taste in architecture, and they admired the worst. There were women's faces at many of the handsome windows, and once in a while a young man on the pavement caught his hat suddenly from his head, and bowed in response to some salutation from within.

"I don't think our girls would look very bad behind one of those big panes," said the Colonel.

"No," said his wife, dreamily.

"Where's the young man? Did he come with them?"

"No; he was to spend the winter with a friend of his that has a ranch in Texas. I guess he's got to do something."

"Yes; gentlemaning as a profession has got to play out in a generation or two."

Neither of them spoke of the lot, though Lapham knew perfectly well what his wife had come with him for, and she was aware that he knew it. The time came when he brought the mare down to a walk, and then slowed up almost to a stop, while they both turned their heads to the right and looked at the vacant lot, through which showed the frozen stretch of the Back Bay, a section of the Long Bridge, and the roofs and smoke-stacks of Charlestown.

"Yes, it's sightly," said Mrs. Lapham, lifting her hand from the reins, on which she had unconsciously laid it.

Lapham said nothing, but he let the mare out a little.

The sleighs and cutters were thickening round them. On the Milldam* it became difficult to restrict the mare to the long, slow trot into which he let her break. The beautiful landscape widened to right and left of them, with the sunset redder and redder, over the low, irregular hills before them. They crossed the Milldam into Longwood, and here, from the crest of the first upland, stretched two endless lines, in which thousands of cutters went and came. Some of the drivers were already speeding their horses, and these shot to and fro on inner lines, between the slowly moving vehicles on either side of the road. Here and there a burly mounted police-man, bulging over the pommel† of his McClellan saddle, jolted by, silently gesturing and directing the course, and keeping it all under the eye of the law. It was what Bartley Hubbard called "a carnival of fashion and gayety on the Brighton road," in his account of it. But most of the people in those elegant sleighs and cutters had so little the air of the great world that one knowing it at all must have wondered where they and their money came from; and the gayety of the men, at least, was expressed, like that of Colonel Lapham, in a grim, almost fierce, alertness; the women wore an air of courageous apprehension. At a certain point the Colonel said, "I'm going to let her out, Pert," and he lifted and then dropped the reins lightly on the mare's back.

She understood the signal, and, as an admirer said, "she laid down to her work." Nothing in the immutable iron of Lapham's face betrayed his sense of triumph, as the mare left everything behind her on the road. Mrs. Lapham, if she felt fear, was too busy holding her flying wraps about her, and shielding her face from the scud of ice flung from the mare's heels, to betray it; except for the rush of her feet, the mare was as silent as the people behind her; the muscles

---

*Now called Beacon Street.
†Raised, rounded front part of a saddle.

of her back and thighs worked more and more swiftly, like some
mechanism responding to an alien force, and she shot to the end of
the course, grazing a hundred encountered and rival sledges in her
passage, but unmolested by the policemen, who probably saw that
the mare and the Colonel knew what they were about, and, at any
rate, were not the sort of men to interfere with trotting like that. At
the end of the heat Lapham drew her in, and turned off on a side
street into Brookline.

"Tell you what, Pert," he said, as if they had been quietly jogging
along, with time for uninterrupted thought since he last spoke, "I've
about made up my mind to build on that lot."

"All right, Silas," said Mrs. Lapham; "I suppose you know what
you're about. Don't build on it for me, that's all."

When she stood in the hall at home, taking off her things, she
said to the girls, who were helping her, "Some day your father will
get killed with that mare."

"Did he speed her?" asked Penelope, the elder. She was named
after her grandmother, who had in her turn inherited from another
ancestress the name of the Homeric matron whose peculiar merits
won her a place even among the Puritan Faiths, Hopes, Temper-
ances, and Prudences. Penelope was the girl whose odd, serious
face had struck Bartley Hubbard in the photograph of the family
group Lapham showed him on the day of the interview. Her large
eyes, like her hair, were brown; they had the peculiar look of near-
sighted eyes which is called mooning; her complexion was of a
dark pallor.

Her mother did not reply to a question which might be considered already answered. "He says he's going to build on that lot of his,"
she next remarked, unwinding the long veil which she had tied round
her neck to hold her bonnet on. She put her hat and cloak on the hall
table, to be carried upstairs later, and they all went in to tea: creamed
oysters, birds, hot biscuit, two kinds of cake, and dishes of stewed and
canned fruit and honey. The women dined alone at one, and the Colonel at the same hour down-town. But he liked a good hot meal when
he got home in the evening. The house flared with gas, and the Colonel, before he sat down, went about shutting the registers, through
which a welding heat came voluming up from the furnace.

"I'll be the death of that darkey yet," he said, "if he don't stop
making on such a fire. The only way to get any comfort out of your
furnace is to take care of it yourself."

"Well," answered his wife from behind the tea-pot, as he sat
down at table with this threat, "there's nothing to prevent you, Si.
And you can shovel the snow, too, if you want to—till you get over
to Beacon street, anyway."

"I guess I can keep my own sidewalk on Beacon street clean, if I
take the notion."

"I should like to see you at it," retorted his wife.

"Well, you keep a sharp lookout, and may be you will."

Their taunts were really expressions of affectionate pride in each
other. They liked to have it, give and take, that way, as they would
have said, right along.

"A man can be a man on Beacon street as well as anywhere, I
guess."

"Well, I'll do the wash, as I used to in Lumberville," said
Mrs. Lapham. "I presume you'll let me have set tubs, Si. You know I
aint so young, any more." She passed Irene a cup of Oolong tea,—
none of them had a sufficiently cultivated palate for Souchong,—and
the girl handed it to her father.

"Papa," she asked, "you don't really mean that you are going to
build over there?"

"Don't I? You wait and see," said the Colonel, stirring his tea.

"I don't believe you do," pursued the girl.

"Is that so? I presume you'd hate to have me. Your mother does."
He said *doos*, of course.

Penelope took the word. "I go in for it. I don't see any use in not
enjoying money, if you've got it to enjoy. That's what it's for, I suppose; though you mightn't always think so." She had a slow, quaint
way of talking, that seemed a pleasant personal modification of some
ancestral Yankee drawl, and her voice was low and cozy, and so far
from being nasal that it was a little hoarse.

"I guess the ayes has it, Pen," said her father. "How would it
do to let Irene and your mother stick in the old place here, and us
go into the new house?" At times the Colonel's grammar failed
him.

The matter dropped, and the Laphams lived on as before, with joking recurrences to the house on the water side of Beacon. The Colonel seemed less in earnest than any of them about it; but that was his way, his girls said; you never could tell when he really meant a thing.

III

Toward the end of the winter there came a newspaper addressed to Miss Irene Lapham; it proved to be a Texas newspaper, with a complimentary account of the ranch of the Hon. Loring G. Stanton, which the representative of the journal had visited.

"It must be his friend," said Mrs. Lapham, to whom her daughter brought the paper; "the one he's staying with."

The girl did not say anything, but she carried the paper to her room, where she scanned every line of it for another name. She did not find it, but she cut the notice out and stuck it into the side of her mirror, where she could read it every morning when she brushed her hair, and the last thing at night when she looked at herself in the glass just before turning off the gas. Her sister often read it aloud, standing behind her and rendering it with elocutionary effects.

"The first time I ever heard of a love-letter in the form of a puff to a cattle-ranch. But perhaps that's the style on the Hill."

Mrs. Lapham told her husband of the arrival of the paper, treating the fact with an importance that he refused to see in it.

"How do you know the fellow sent it, anyway?" he demanded.

"Oh, I know he did."

"I don't see why he couldn't write to 'Rene, if he really meant anything."

"Well, I guess that wouldn't be their way," said Mrs. Lapham; she did not at all know what their way would be.

When the spring opened Colonel Lapham showed that he had been in earnest about building on the New Land. His idea of a house was a brown-stone front, four stories high, and a French roof with an air-chamber above. Inside, there was to be a reception-room on the street and a dining-room back. The parlors were to be on the second floor, and finished in black walnut or parti-colored paint. The chambers were to be on the three floors above, front and rear, with side rooms over the front door. Black walnut was to be used everywhere except in the attic, which was to be painted and grained to look like black walnut. The whole was to be very high-studded, and there were to be handsome cornices and elaborate center-pieces throughout, except, again, in the attic.

These ideas he had formed from the inspection of many new buildings which he had seen going up, and which he had a passion for looking into. He was confirmed in his ideas by a master-builder who had put up a great many houses on the Back Bay as a speculation, and who told him that if he wanted to have a house in the style, that was the way to have it.

The beginnings of the process by which Lapham escaped from the master-builder and ended in the hands of an architect are so obscure that it would be almost impossible to trace them. But it all happened, and Lapham promptly developed his ideas of black-walnut finish, high-studding, and cornices. The architect was able to conceal the shudder which they must have sent through him. He was skillful, as nearly all architects are, in playing upon that simple instrument Man. He began to touch Colonel Lapham's stops.

"Oh, certainly, have the parlors high-studded. But you've seen some of those pretty, old-fashioned country-houses, haven't you, where the entrance-story is very low-studded?"

"Yes," Lapham assented.

"Well, don't you think something of that kind would have a very nice effect? Have the entrance-story low-studded, and your parlors on the next floor as high as you please. Put your little reception-room here beside the door, and get the whole width of your house frontage for a square hall, and an easy low-tread staircase running up three sides of it. I'm sure Mrs. Lapham would find it much pleasanter." The architect caught toward him a scrap of paper lying on the table at which they were sitting and sketched his idea. "Then have your dining-room behind the hall, looking on the water."

He glanced at Mrs. Lapham, who said, "Of course," and the architect went on:

"That gets you rid of one of those long, straight, ugly staircases,"—until that moment Lapham had thought a long, straight staircase the chief ornament of a house,—"and gives you an effect of amplitude and space."

"That's so!" said Mrs. Lapham. Her husband merely made a noise in his throat.

"Then, were you thinking of having your parlors together, connected by folding doors?" asked the architect deferentially.

"Yes, of course," said Lapham. "They're always so, ain't they?"

"Well, nearly," said the architect. "I was wondering how would it do to make one large square room at the front, taking the whole breadth of the house, and, with this hall-space between, have a music-room back for the young ladies?"

Lapham looked helplessly at his wife, whose quicker apprehension had followed the architect's pencil with instant sympathy. "First-rate!" she cried.

The Colonel gave way. "I guess that would do. It'll be kind of odd, wont it?"

"Well, I don't know," said the architect. "Not so odd, I hope, as the other thing will be a few years from now." He went on to plan the rest of the house, and he showed himself such a master in regard to all the practical details that Mrs. Lapham began to feel a motherly affection for the young man, and her husband could not deny in his heart that the fellow seemed to understand his business. He stopped walking about the room, as he had begun to do when the architect and Mrs. Lapham entered into the particulars of closets, drainage, kitchen arrangements, and all that, and came back to the table. "I presume," he said, "you'll have the drawing-room finished in black walnut?"

"Well, yes," replied the architect, "if you like. But some less expensive wood can be made just as effective with paint. Of course you can paint black walnut, too."

"Paint it?" gasped the Colonel.

"Yes," said the architect quietly. "White, or a little off white."

Lapham dropped the plan he had picked up from the table. His wife made a little move toward him of consolation or support.

"Of course," resumed the architect, "I know there has been a great craze for black walnut. But it's an ugly wood; and for a drawing-room there is really nothing like white paint. We should want to introduce a little gold here and there. Perhaps we might run a painted frieze round under the cornice—garlands of roses on a gold ground; it would tell wonderfully in a white room."

The Colonel returned less courageously to the charge. "I presume you'll want Eastlake* mantel-shelves and tiles?" He meant this for a sarcastic thrust at a prevailing foible of the profession.

"Well, no," gently answered the architect. "I was thinking perhaps a white marble chimney-piece, treated in the refined Empire style, would be the thing for that room."

"White marble!" exclaimed the Colonel. "I thought that had gone out long ago."

"Really beautiful things can't go out. They may disappear for a little while, but they must come back. It's only the ugly things that stay out after they've had their day."

Lapham could only venture very modestly, "Hard-wood floors?"

"In the music-room, of course," consented the architect.

"And in the drawing-room?"

"Carpet. Some sort of moquette,† I should say. But I should prefer to consult Mrs. Lapham's taste in that matter."

"And in the other rooms?"

"Oh, carpets, of course."

"And what about the stairs?"

"Carpet. And I should have the rail and banisters white— banisters turned or twisted."

The Colonel said under his breath, "Well, I'm dumned!" but he gave no utterance to his astonishment in the architect's presence. When he went at last,—the session did not end till eleven o'clock,— Lapham said, "Well, Pert, I guess that fellow's fifty years behind, or ten years ahead. I wonder what the Ongpeer style is?"

"I don't know. I hated to ask. But he seemed to understand what he was talking about. I declare, he knows what a woman wants in a house better than she does herself."

"And a man's simply nowhere in comparison," said Lapham. But he respected a fellow who could beat him at every point, and have a reason ready, as this architect had; and when he recovered from the daze into which the complete upheaval of all his preconceived notions had left him, he was in a fit state to swear by the architect. It

---

*English designer Charles Eastlake (1836–1906), whose work influenced post–Civil War interior home design.
†Thick, velvety, tufted fabric used in carpets or upholstery.

seemed to him that he had discovered the fellow (as he always called him) and owned him now, and the fellow did nothing to disturb this impression. He entered into that brief but intense intimacy with the Laphams which the sympathetic architect holds with his clients. He was privy to all their differences of opinion and all their disputes about the house. He knew just where to insist upon his own ideas, and where to yield. He was really building several other houses, but he gave the Laphams the impression that he was doing none but theirs.

The work was not begun till the frost was thoroughly out of the ground, which that year was not before the end of April. Even then it did not proceed very rapidly. Lapham said they might as well take their time to it; if they got the walls up and the thing closed in before the snow flew, they could be working at it all winter. It was found necessary to dig for the kitchen; at that point the original salt marsh lay near the surface, and before they began to put in the piles for the foundation they had to pump. The neighborhood smelt like the hold of a ship after a three years' voyage. People who had cast their fortunes with the New Land went by professing not to notice it; people who still "hung on to the Hill" put their handkerchiefs to their noses, and told each other the old terrible stories of the material used in filling up the Back Bay.

Nothing gave Lapham so much satisfaction in the whole construction of his house as the pile-driving. When this began, early in the summer, he took Mrs. Lapham every day in his buggy and drove round to look at it; stopping the mare in front of the lot, and watching the operation with even keener interest than the little loafing Irish boys who superintended it in force. It pleased him to hear the portable engine chuckle out a hundred thin whiffs of steam, in carrying the big iron weight to the top of the framework above the pile, then seem to hesitate, and cough once or twice in pressing the weight against the detaching apparatus. There was a moment in which the weight had the effect of poising before it fell; then it dropped with a mighty whack on the iron-bound head of the pile and drove it a foot into the earth.

"By gracious!" he would say, "there ain't anything like that in this world for business, Persis!"

Mrs. Lapham suffered him to enjoy the sight twenty or thirty times before she said, "Well, now drive on, Si."

By the time the foundation was in and the brick walls had begun to go up, there were so few people left in the neighborhood that she might indulge with impunity her husband's passion for having her clamber over the floor-timbers and the skeleton staircases with him. Many of the householders had boarded up their front doors before the buds had begun to swell and the assessor to appear in early May; others had followed soon; and Mrs. Lapham was as safe from remark as if she had been in the depth of the country. Ordinarily she and her girls left town early in July, going to one of the hotels at Nantasket, where it was convenient for the Colonel to get to and from his business by the boat. But this summer they were all lingering a few weeks later, under the novel fascination of the new house, as they called it, as if there were no other in the world.

Lapham drove there with his wife after he had set Bartley Hubbard down at the "Events" office, but on this day something happened that interfered with the solid pleasure they usually took in going over the house. As the Colonel turned from casting anchor at the mare's head with the hitching-weight, after helping his wife to alight, he encountered a man to whom he could not help speaking, though the man seemed to share his hesitation if not his reluctance at the necessity. He was a tallish, thin man, with a dust-colored face, and a dead, clerical air, which somehow suggested at once feebleness and tenacity.

Mrs. Lapham held out her hand to him.

"Why, Mr. Rogers!" she exclaimed, and then, turning toward her husband, seemed to refer the two men to each other. They shook hands, but Lapham did not speak. "I didn't know you were in Boston," pursued Mrs. Lapham. "Is Mrs. Rogers with you?"

"No," said Mr. Rogers, with a voice which had the flat, succinct sound of two pieces of wood clapped together. "Mrs. Rogers is still in Chicago."

A little silence followed, and then Mrs. Lapham said:

"I presume you are quite settled out there."

"No; we have left Chicago. Mrs. Rogers has merely remained to finish up a little packing."

"Oh, indeed! Are you coming back to Boston?"

"I cannot say as yet. We some think of so doing."

Lapham turned away and looked up at the building. His wife

pulled a little at her glove, as if embarrassed or even pained. She tried to make a diversion.

"We are building a house," she said, with a meaningless laugh.

"Oh, indeed," said Mr. Rogers, looking up at it.

Then no one spoke again, and she said, helplessly:

"If you come to Boston, I hope I shall see Mrs. Rogers."

"She will be happy to have you call," said Mr. Rogers.

He touched his hat-brim, and made a bow forward rather than in Mrs. Lapham's direction.

She mounted the planking that led into the shelter of the bare brick walls, and her husband slowly followed. When she turned her face toward him her cheeks were burning, and tears that looked hot stood in her eyes.

"You left it all to me!" she cried. "Why couldn't you speak a word?"

"I hadn't anything to say to him," replied Lapham sullenly.

They stood awhile, without looking at the work which they had come to enjoy, and without speaking to each other.

"I suppose we might as well go on," said Mrs. Lapham at last, as they returned to the buggy. The Colonel drove recklessly toward the Milldam. His wife kept her veil down and her face turned from him. After a time she put her handkerchief up under her veil and wiped her eyes, and he set his teeth and squared his jaw.

"I don't see how he always manages to appear just at the moment when he seems to have gone fairly out of our lives, and blight everything," she whimpered.

"I supposed he was dead," said Lapham.

"Oh, don't say such a thing! It sounds as if you wished it."

"Why do you mind it? What do you let him blight everything for?"

"I can't help it, and I don't believe I ever shall. I don't know as his being dead would help it any. I can't ever see him without feeling just as I did at first."

"I tell you," said Lapham, "it was a perfectly square thing. And I wish, once for all, you would quit bothering about it. My conscience is easy as far as he's concerned, and it always was."

"And I can't look at him without feeling as if you'd ruined him, Silas."

"Don't look at him, then," said her husband with a scowl.

"I want you should recollect in the first place, Persis, that I never wanted a partner."

"If he hadn't put his money in when he did, you'd 'a' broken down."

"Well, he got his money out again, and more too," said the Colonel with a sulky weariness.

"He didn't want to take it out."

"I gave him his choice: buy out or go out."

"You know he couldn't buy out then. It was no choice at all."

"It was a business chance."

"No; you had better face the truth, Silas. It was no chance at all. You crowded him out. A man that had saved you! No, you had got greedy, Silas. You had made your paint your god, and you couldn't bear to let anybody else share in its blessings."

"I tell you he was a drag and a brake on me from the word go. You say he saved me. Well, if I hadn't got him out he'd 'a' ruined me sooner or later. So it's an even thing, and far forth as that goes."

"No, it aint an even thing, and you kow it, Silas. Oh, if I could only get you once to acknowledge that you did wrong about it, then I should have some hope. I don't say you meant wrong exactly, but you took an advantage. Yes, you took an advantage! You had him where he couldn't help himself, and then you wouldn't show him any mercy."

"I'm sick of this," said Lapham. "If you'll 'tend to the house, I'll manage my business without your help."

"You were very glad of my help once."

"Well, I'm tired of it now. Don't meddle."

"I will meddle. When I see you hardening yourself in a wrong thing, it's time for me to meddle, as you call it, and I will. I can't ever get you to own up the least bit about Rogers, and I feel as if it was hurting you all the while."

"What do you want I should own up about a thing for when I don't feel wrong? I tell you Rogers hain't got anything to complain of, and that's what I told you from the start. It's a thing that's done every day. I was loaded up with a partner that didn't know anything, and couldn't do anything, and I unloaded; that's all."

"You unloaded just at the time when you knew that your paint was going to be worth about twice what it ever had been; and you wanted all the advantage for yourself."

"I had a right to it. I made the success."

"Yes, you made it with Rogers's money; and when you'd made it you took his share of it. I guess you thought of that when you saw him, and that's why you couldn't look him in the face."

At these words Lapham lost his temper.

"I guess you don't want to ride with me any more today," he said, turning the mare abruptly round.

"I'm as ready to go back as what you are," replied his wife. "And don't you ask me to go to that house with you any more. You can sell it, for all me. I sha'n't live in it. There's blood on it."

IV

The silken texture of the marriage tie bears a daily strain of wrong and insult to which no other human relation can be subjected without lesion; and sometimes the strength that knits society together might appear to the eye of faltering faith the curse of those immediately bound by it. Two people by no means reckless of each other's rights and feelings, but even tender of them for the most part, may tear at each other's heart-strings in this sacred bond with perfect impunity; though if they were any other two they would not speak or look at each other again after the outrages they exchange. It is certainly a curious spectacle, and doubtless it ought to convince an observer of the divinity of the institution. If the husband and wife are blunt, outspoken people like the Laphams, they do not weigh their words; if they are more refined, they weigh them very carefully, and know accurately just how far they will carry, and in what most sensitive spot they may be planted with most effect.

Lapham was proud of his wife, and when he married her it had been a rise in life for him. For a while he stood in awe of his good fortune, but this could not last, and he simply remained supremely satisfied with it. The girl who had taught school with a clear head and a strong hand was not afraid of work; she encouraged and helped him from the first, and bore her full share of the common burden. She had health, and she did not worry his life out with peevish complaints and vagaries; she had sense and principle, and in their simple lot she did what was wise and right. Their marriage was hallowed by an early sorrow: they lost their boy, and it was years before they could look each other in the face and speak of him. No one gave up more than they when they gave up each other, and Lapham went to the war. When he came back and began to work, her zeal and courage formed the spring of his enterprise. In that affair of the partnership she had tried to be his conscience, but perhaps she would have defended him if he had accused himself; it was one of those things in this life which seem destined to await justice, or at least judgment, in the next. As he said, Lapham had dealt fairly by his partner in money; he had let Rogers take more money out of the business than he put into it; he had, as he said, simply forced out of it

a timid and inefficient participant in advantages which he had created. But Lapham had not created them all. He had been dependent at
one time on his partner's capital. It was a moment of terrible trial.
Happy is the man forever after who can choose the ideal, the unselfish part in such an exigency! Lapham could not rise to it. He did
what he could maintain to be perfectly fair. The wrong, if any,
seemed to be condoned to him, except when from time to time his
wife brought it up. Then all the question stung and burned anew, and
had to be reasoned out and put away once more. It seemed to have
an inextinguishable vitality. It slept, but it did not die.

His course did not shake Mrs. Lapham's faith in him. It astonished
her at first, and it always grieved her that he could not see that he was
acting solely in his own interest. But she found excuses for him,
which at times she made reproaches. She vaguely perceived that his
paint was something more than business to him; it was a sentiment,
almost a passion. He could not share its management and its profit
with another without a measure of self-sacrifice far beyond that which
he must make with something less personal to him. It was the poetry
of that nature, otherwise so intensely prosaic; and she understood this,
and for the most part forbore. She knew him good and true and blame-
less in all his life, except for this wrong, if it were a wrong; and it
was only when her nerves tingled intolerably with some chance re-
newal of the pain she had suffered that she shared her anguish with
him in true wifely fashion.

With those two there was never anything like an explicit reconciliation. They simply ignored a quarrel; and Mrs. Lapham had only
to say a few days after at breakfast, "I guess the girls would like to go
round with you this afternoon, and look at the new house," in order
to make her husband grumble out as he looked down into his coffee-
cup, "I guess we better all go, hadn't we?"

"Well, I'll see," she said.

There was not really a great deal to look at when Lapham arrived
on the ground in his four-seated beach-wagon. But the walls were
up, and the studding had already given skeleton shape to the interior. The floors were roughly boarded over, and the stairways were
in place, with provisional treads rudely laid. They had not begun to
lath and plaster yet, but the clean, fresh smell of the mortar in the
walls mingling with the pungent fragrance of the pine shavings

neutralized the Venetian odor that drew in over the water. It was pleasantly shady there, though for the matter of that the heat of the morning had all been washed out of the atmosphere by a tide of east wind setting in at noon, and the thrilling, delicious cool of a Boston summer afternoon bathed every nerve.

The foreman went about with Mrs. Lapham, showing her where the doors were to be; but Lapham soon tired of this, and having found a pine stick of perfect grain, he abandoned himself to the pleasure of whittling it in what was to be the reception-room, where he sat looking out on the street from what was to be the bay-window. Here he was presently joined by his girls, who, after locating their own room on the water side above the music-room, had no more wish to enter into details than their father.

"Come and take a seat in the bay-window, ladies," he called out to them, as they looked in at him through the ribs of the wall. He jocosely made room for them on the trestle on which he sat.

They came gingerly and vaguely forward, as young ladies do when they wish not to seem to be going to do a thing they have made up their minds to do. When they had taken their places on their trestle, they could not help laughing with scorn, open and acceptable to their father; and Irene curled her chin up, in a little way she had, and said, "How ridiculous!" to her sister.

"Well, I can tell you what," said the Colonel, in fond enjoyment of their young-ladyishness, "your mother wasn't ashamed to sit with me on a trestle when I called her out to look at the first coat of my paint that I ever tried on a house."

"Yes; we've heard that story," said Penelope, with easy security of her father's liking what she said. "We were brought up on that story."

"Well, it's a good story," said her father.

At that moment a young man came suddenly in range, who began to look up at the signs of building as he approached. He dropped his eyes in coming abreast of the bay-window, where Lapham sat with his girls, and then his face lightened, and he took off his hat and bowed to Irene. She rose mechanically from the trestle, and her face lightened too. She was a very pretty figure of a girl, after our fashion of girls, round and slim and flexible, and her face was admirably regular. But her great beauty—and it was very great—was in her coloring. This was of an effect for which there is no word but delicious, as we use it of fruit or flowers. She had red hair, like her father in his earlier days, and the tints of her cheeks and temples were such as suggested May-flowers and apple-blossoms and peaches. Instead of the gray that often dulls this complexion, her eyes were of a blue at once intense and tender, and they seemed to burn on what they looked at with a soft, lambent flame. It was well understood by her sister and mother that her eyes always expressed a great deal more than Irene ever thought or felt; but this is not saying that she was not a very sensible girl and very honest.

The young man faltered perceptibly, and Irene came a little forward, and then there gushed from them both a smiling exchange of greeting, of which the sum was that he supposed she was out of town, and that she had not known that he had got back. A pause ensued, and flushing again in her uncertainty as to whether she ought or ought not to do it, she said, "My father, Mr. Corey; and my sister."

The young man took off his hat again, showing his shapely head, with a line of wholesome sunburn ceasing where the recently and closely clipped hair began. He was dressed in a fine summer check, with a blue white-dotted neckerchief, and he had a white hat, in which he looked very well when he put it back on his head. His whole dress seemed very fresh and new, and, in fact, he had cast aside his Texan habiliments only the day before.

"How do you do, sir?" said the Colonel, stepping to the window, and reaching out of it the hand which the young man advanced to take. "Wont you come in? We're at home here. House I'm building."

"Oh, indeed?" returned the young man; and he came promptly up the steps, and through its ribs into the reception-room.

"Have a trestle?" asked the Colonel, while the girls exchanged little shocks of terror and amusement at the eyes.

"Thank you," said the young man, simply, and sat down.

"Mrs. Lapham is upstairs interviewing the carpenter, but she'll be down in a minute."

"I hope she's quite well," said Corey. "I supposed—I was afraid she might be out of town."

"Well, we are off to Nantasket next week. The house kept us in town pretty late."

"It must be very exciting, building a house," said Corey to the elder sister.

"Yes, it is," she assented, loyally refusing in Irene's interest the opportunity of saying anything more.

Corey turned to the latter. "I suppose you've all helped to plan it?"

"Oh, no; the architect and mamma did that."

"But they allowed the rest of us to agree, when we were good," said Penelope.

Corey looked at her, and saw that she was shorter than her sister, and had a dark complexion.

"It's very exciting," said Irene.

"Come up," said the Colonel, rising, "and look round if you'd like to."

"I should like to, very much," said the young man.

He helped the young ladies over crevasses of carpentry and along narrow paths of planking, on which they had made their way unassisted before. The elder sister left the younger to profit solely by these offices as much as possible. She walked between them and her father, who went before, lecturing on each apartment and taking the credit of the whole affair more and more as he talked on.

"There!" he said, "we're going to throw out a bay-window here, so as get the water all the way up and down. This is my girls' room," he added, looking proudly at them both.

It seemed terribly intimate. Irene blushed deeply and turned her head away.

But the young man took it all, apparently, as simply as their father. "What a lovely lookout," he said. The Back Bay spread its glassy sheet before them, empty but for a few smaller boats and a large schooner, with her sails close-furled and dripping like snow from her spars, which a tug was rapidly towing toward Cambridge. The carpentry of that city, embanked and embowered in foliage, shared the picturesqueness of Charlestown in the distance.

"Yes," said Lapham, "I go in for using the best rooms in your house yourself. If people come to stay with you, they can put up with the second best. Though we don't intend to have any second best. There aint going to be an unpleasant room in the whole house, from top to bottom."

"Oh, I wish papa wouldn't brag so!" breathed Irene to her sister, where they stood a little apart looking away together.

The Colonel went on. "No, sir," he swelled out, "I have gone in for making a regular job of it. I've got the best architect in Boston, and I'm building a house to suit myself. And if money can do it, I guess I'm going to be suited."

"It seems very delightful," said Corey, "and very original."

"Yes, sir. That fellow hadn't talked five minutes before I saw that he knew what he was about every time."

"I wish mamma would come!" breathed Irene again. "I shall certainly go through the floor if papa says anything more."

"They are making a great many very pretty houses nowadays," said the young man. "It's very different from the old-fashioned building."

"Well," said the Colonel, with a large toleration of tone and a deep breath that expanded his ample chest, "we spend more on our houses nowadays. I started out to build a forty-thousand-dollar house. Well, sir! that fellow has got me in for more than sixty thousand already, and I doubt if I get out of it much under a hundred. You can't have a nice house for nothing. It's just like ordering a picture of a painter. You pay him enough, and he can afford to paint you a first-class picture; and if you don't, he can't. That's all there is of it. Why, they tell me that A.T. Stewart gave one of those French fellows sixty thousand dollars for a little seven-by-nine picture the other day. Yes, sir, give an architect money enough and he'll give you a nice house, every time."

"I've heard that they're sharp at getting money to realize their ideas," assented the young man, with a laugh.

"Well, I should say so!" exclaimed the Colonel. "They come to you with an improvement that you can't resist. It has good looks and common sense and everything in its favor, and it's like throwing money away to refuse. And they always manage to get you when your wife is around, and then you're helpless."

The Colonel himself set the example of laughing at this joke, and the young man joined him less obstreperously. The girls turned, and he said: "I don't think I ever saw this view to better advantage. It's surprising how well the Memorial Hall and the Cambridge spires work up, over there. And the sunsets must be magnificent."

Lapham did not wait for them to reply.

"Yes, sir, it's about the sightliest view I know of. I always did like the water side of Beacon. Long before I owned property here, or ever expected to, m'wife and I used to ride down this way, and stop the buggy to get this view over the water. When people talk to me about the Hill, I can understand 'em. It's snug, and it's old-fashioned, and it's where they've always lived. But when they talk about Commonwealth Avenue, I don't know what they mean. It don't hold a candle to the water side of Beacon. You've got just as much wind over there, and you've got just as much dust, and all the view you've got is the view across the street. No, sir! When you come to the Back Bay at all, give me the water side of Beacon."

"Oh, I think you're quite right," said the young man. "The view here is everything."

Irene looked "I wonder what papa is going to say next!" at her sister, when their mother's voice was heard overhead, approaching the opening in the floor where the stairs were to be; and she presently appeared, with one substantial foot a long way ahead. She was followed by the carpenter, with his rule sticking out of his overalls pocket, and she was still talking to him about some measurements they had been taking, when they reached the bottom, so that Irene had to say, "Mamma, Mr. Corey," before Mrs. Lapham was aware of him.

He came forward with as much grace and speed as the uncertain footing would allow, and Mrs. Lapham gave him a stout squeeze of her comfortable hand.

"Why, Mr. Corey! When did you get back?"

"Yesterday. It hardly seems as if I had got back. I didn't expect to find you in a new house."

"Well, you are our first caller. I presume you won't expect I should make excuses for the state you find it in. Has the Colonel been doing the honors?"

"Oh, yes. And I've seen more of your house than I ever shall again, I suppose."

"Well, I hope not," said Lapham. "There'll be several chances to see us in the old one yet, before we leave."

He probably thought this a neat, off-hand way of making the invitation, for he looked at his womankind as if he might expect their admiration.

"Oh, yes, indeed!" said his wife. "We shall be very glad to see Mr. Corey, any time."

"Thank you; I shall be glad to come."

He and the Colonel went before, and helped the ladies down the difficult descent. Irene seemed less sure-footed than the others; she clung to the young man's hand an imperceptible moment longer than need be, or else he detained her. He found opportunity of saying, "It's so pleasant seeing you again," adding, "All of you."

"Thank you," said the girl. "They must all be glad to have you at home again."

Corey laughed.

"Well, I suppose they would be, if they were at home to have me. But the fact is, there's nobody in the house but my father and myself, and I'm only on my way to Bar Harbor."

"Oh! Are they there?"

"Yes; it seems to be the only place where my mother can get just the combination of sea and mountain air that she wants."

"We go to Nantasket—it's convenient for papa; and I don't believe we shall go anywhere else this summer, mamma's so taken up with building. We do nothing but talk house; and Pen says we eat and sleep house. She says it would be a sort of relief to go and live in tents for a while."

"She seems to have a good deal of humor," the young man ventured, upon the slender evidence.

The others had gone to the back of the house a moment, to look at some suggested change. Irene and Corey were left standing in the doorway. A lovely light of happiness played over her face and etherealized its delicious beauty. She had some ado to keep herself from smiling outright, and the effort deepened the dimples in her cheeks; she trembled a little, and the pendants shook in the tips of her pretty ears.

The others came back directly, and they all descended the front steps together. The Colonel was about to renew his invitation, but he caught his wife's eye, and, without being able to interpret its warning exactly, was able to arrest himself, and went about gathering up the hitching-weight, while the young man handed the ladies into the beach-wagon. Then he lifted his hat, and the ladies all bowed, and the Laphams drove off, Irene's blue ribbons fluttering backward from her hat, as if they were her clinging thoughts.

"So that's young Corey, is it?" said the Colonel, letting the stately stepping, tall coupé horse make his way homeward at will with the beach-wagon. "Well, he aint a bad-looking fellow, and he's got a good, fair and square, honest eye. But I don't see how a fellow like that, that's had every advantage in this world, can hang round home and let his father support him. Seems to me, if I had his health and his education, I should want to strike out and do something for myself."

The girls on the back seat had hold of each other's hands, and they exchanged electrical pressures at the different points their father made.

"I presume," said Mrs. Lapham, "that he was down in Texas looking after something."

"He's come back without finding it, I guess."

"Well, if his father has the money to support him, and don't complain of the burden, I don't see why we should."

"Oh, I know it's none of my business; but I don't like the principle. I like to see a man *act* like a man. I don't like to see him taken care of like a young lady. Now, I suppose that fellow belongs to two or three clubs, and hangs around 'em all day, lookin' out the window,— I've seen 'em,—instead of tryin' to hunt up something to do for an honest livin'."

"If I was a young man," Penelope struck in, "I would belong to twenty clubs, if I could find them, and I would hang around them all, and look out the window till I dropped."

"Oh, you would, would you?" demanded her father, delighted with her defiance, and twisting his fat head around over his shoulder to look at her. "Well, you wouldn't do it on *my* money, if you were a son of *mine*, young lady."

"Oh, you wait and see," retorted the girl.

This made them all laugh. But the Colonel recurred seriously to the subject that night, as he was winding up his watch preparatory to putting it under his pillow.

"I could make a man of that fellow, if I had him in the business with me. There's stuff in him. But I spoke up the way I did because I didn't choose Irene should think I would stand any kind of a loafer 'round—I don't care who he is, or how well educated or brought up. And I guess, from the way Pen spoke up, that 'Rene saw what I was driving at."

The girl, apparently, was less anxious about her father's ideas and principles than about the impression which he had made upon the young man. She talked it over and over with her sister before they went to bed, and she asked in despair, as she stood looking at Penelope brushing out her hair before the glass,

"Do you suppose he'll think papa always talks in that bragging way?"

"He'll be right if he does," answered her sister. "It's the way father always does talk. You never noticed it so much, that's all. And I guess if he can't make allowance for father's bragging, he'll be a little too good. I enjoyed hearing the Colonel go on."

"I know you did," returned Irene in distress. Then she sighed. "Didn't you think he looked very nice?"

"Who? The Colonel?" Penelope had caught up the habit of calling her father so from her mother, and she used his title in all her jocose and perverse moods.

"You know very well I don't mean papa," pouted Irene.

"Oh! Mr. Corey! Why didn't you say Mr. Corey if you meant Mr. Corey? If I meant Mr. Corey, I should say Mr. Corey. It isn't swearing! Corey, Corey, Co——"

Her sister clapped her hand over her mouth. "Will you hush, you wretched thing?" she whimpered. "The whole house can hear you."

"Oh, yes, they can hear me all over the square. Well, I think he looked well enough for a plain youth, who hadn't taken his hair out of curl-papers for some time."

"It *was* clipped pretty close," Irene admitted; and they both laughed at the drab effect of Mr. Corey's skull, as they remembered it. "Did you like his nose?" asked Irene, timorously.

"Ah, now you're *coming* to something," said Penelope. "I don't know whether, if I had so much of a nose, I should want it all Roman."

"I don't see how you can expect to have a nose part one kind and part another," argued Irene.

"Oh, I do. Look at mine!" She turned aside her face, so as to get a three-quarters view of her nose in the glass, and crossing her hands, with the brush in one of them, before her, regarded it judicially. "Now, my nose started Grecian, but changed its mind before it got over the bridge, and concluded to be snub the rest of the way."

"You've got a very pretty nose, Pen," said Irene, joining in the contemplation of its reflex in the glass.

"Don't say that in hopes of getting me to compliment *his*, Mrs."—she stopped, and then added deliberately—"C.!"

Irene also had her hair-brush in her hand, and now she sprang at her sister and beat her very softly on the shoulder with the flat of it. "You mean thing!" she cried, between her shut teeth, blushing hotly.

"Well, D., then," said Penelope. "You've nothing to say against D.? Though I think C. is just as nice an initial."

"Oh!" cried the younger, for all expression of unspeakable things.

"I think he has very good eyes," admitted Penelope.

"Oh, he *has*! And didn't you like the way his sack-coat set? So close to him, and yet free—kind of peeling away at the lapels?"

"Yes, I should say he was a young man of great judgment. He knows how to choose his tailor."

Irene sat down on the edge of a chair. "It was so nice of you, Pen, to come in, that way, about clubs."

"Oh, I didn't mean anything by it except opposition," said Penelope. "I couldn't have father swelling on so, without saying something."

"How he *did* swell!" sighed Irene. "Wasn't it a relief to have mamma come down, even if she did seem to be all stocking at first?"

The girls broke into a wild giggle and hid their faces in each other's necks. "I thought I *should* die," said Irene.

" 'It's just like ordering a painting,' " said Penelope, recalling her father's talk, with an effect of dreamy absent-mindedness. " 'You give the painter money enough, and he can afford to paint you a first-class picture. Give an architect money enough, and he'll give you a first-class house, every time.' "

"Oh, wasn't it awful!" moaned her sister. "No one would ever have supposed that he had fought the very idea of an architect for weeks, before he gave in."

Penelope went on. " 'I always did like the water side of Beacon—long before I owned property there. When you come to the Back Bay at all, give me the water side of Beacon.' "

"Ow-w-w-w!" shrieked Irene. "*Do* stop!"

The door of their mother's chamber opened below, and the voice of the real Colonel called, "What are you doing up there, girls? Why don't you go to bed?"

This extorted nervous shrieks from both of them. The Colonel heard a sound of scurrying feet, whisking drapery, and slamming doors. Then he heard one of the doors opened again, and Penelope said, "I was only repeating something you said when you talked to Mr. Corey."

"Very well, now," answered the Colonel. "You postpone the rest of it till to-morrow at breakfast, and see that you're up in time to let me hear it."

V

At the same moment young Corey let himself in at his own door with his latch-key, and went to the library, where he found his father turning the last leaves of a story in the "Revue des Deux Mondes."* He was a white-mustached old gentleman, who had never been able to abandon his *pince-nez* for the superior comfort of spectacles, even in the privacy of his own library. He knocked the glasses off as his son came in, and looked up at him with lazy fondness, rubbing the two red marks that they always leave on the side of the nose.

"Tom," he said, "where did you get such good clothes?"

"I stopped over a day in New York," replied the son, finding himself a chair. "I'm glad you like them."

"Yes, I always do like your clothes, Tom," returned the father thoughtfully, swinging his glasses. "But I don't see how you can afford 'em. I can't."

"Well, sir," said the son, who dropped the sir into his speech with his father, now and then, in an old-fashioned way that was rather charming, "you see I have an indulgent parent."

"Smoke?" suggested the father, pushing toward his son a box of cigarettes, from which he had taken one.

"No, thank you," said the son. "I've dropped that."

"Ah, is that so?" The father began to feel about on the table for matches, in the purblind fashion of elderly men. His son rose, lighted one, and handed it to him. "Well,—oh, thank you, Tom!— I believe some statisticians prove that if you will give up smoking you can dress very well on the money your tobacco costs, even if you haven't got an indulgent parent. But I'm too old to try. Though, I confess, I should rather like the clothes. Whom did you find at the club?"

"There were a lot of fellows there," said young Corey, watching the accomplished fumigation of his father in an absent way.

"It's astonishing what a hardy breed the young club-men are," observed his father. "All summer through, in weather that sends

---

*Distinguished French intellectual journal.

the sturdiest female flying to the sea-shore, you find the clubs filled with young men, who don't seem to mind the heat in the least."

"Boston isn't a bad place, at the worst, in summer," said the son, declining to take up the matter in its ironical shape.

"I dare say it isn't, compared with Texas," returned the father, smoking tranquilly on. "But I don't suppose you find many of your friends in town outside of the club."

"No; you're requested to ring at the rear door, all the way down Beacon street and up Commonwealth Avenue. It's rather a blank reception for the returning prodigal."

"Ah, the prodigal must take his chance if he comes back out of season. But I'm glad to have you back, Tom, even as it is, and I hope you're not going to hurry away. You must give your energies a rest."

"I'm sure you never had to reproach me with abnormal activty," suggested the son, taking his father's jokes in good part.

"No, I don't know that I have," admitted the elder. "You've always shown a fair degree of moderation, after all. What do you think of taking up next? I mean after you have embraced your mother and sisters at Mount Desert. Real estate? It seems to me that it is about time for you to open out as a real-estate broker. Or did you ever think of matrimony?"

"Well, not just in that way, sir," said the young man. "I shouldn't quite like to regard it as a career, you know."

"No, no. I understand that. And I quite agree with you. But you know I've always contended that the affections could be made to combine pleasure and profit. I wouldn't have a man marry for money,—that would be rather bad,—but I don't see why, when it comes to falling in love, a man shouldn't fall in love with a rich girl as easily as a poor one. Some of the rich girls are very nice, and I should say that the chances of a quiet life with them were rather greater. They've always had everything, and they wouldn't be so ambitious and uneasy. Don't you think so?"

"It would depend," said the son, "upon whether a girl's people had been rich long enough to have given her position before she married. If they hadn't, I don't see how she would be any better than a poor girl in that respect."

"Yes, there's sense in that. But the suddenly rich are on a level with any of us nowadays. Money buys position at once. I don't say that it isn't all right. The world generally knows what it's about, and knows how to drive a bargain. I dare say it makes the new rich pay too much. But there's no doubt but money is to the fore now. It is the romance, the poetry of our age. It's the thing that chiefly strikes the imagination. The Englishmen who come here are more curious about the great new millionaires than about any one else, and they respect them more. It's all very well. I don't complain of it."

"And you would like a rich daughter-in-law, quite regardless, then?"

"Oh, not quite so bad as that, Tom," said his father. "A little youth, a little beauty, a little good sense and pretty behavior—one mustn't object to those things; and they go just as often with money as without it. And I suppose I should like her people to be rather grammatical."

"It seems to me that you're exacting, sir," said the son. "How can you expect people who have been strictly devoted to business to be grammatical? Isn't that rather too much?"

"Perhaps it is. Perhaps you're right. But I understood your mother to say that those benefactors of hers, whom you met last summer, were very passably grammatical."

"The father isn't."

The elder, who had been smoking with his profile toward his son, now turned his face full upon him. "I didn't know you had seen him?"

"I hadn't until today," said young Corey, with a little heightening of his color. "But I was walking down street this afternoon, and happened to look round at a new house someone was putting up, and I saw the whole family in the window. It appears that Mr. Lapham is building the house."

The elder Corey knocked the ash of his cigarette into the holder at his elbow. "I am more and more convinced, the longer I know you, Tom, that we are descended from Giles Corey. The gift of holding one's tongue seems to have skipped me, but you have it in full force. I can't say just how you would behave under

peine forte et dure,* but under ordinary pressure you are certainly able
to keep your own counsel. Why didn't you mention this encounter
at dinner? You weren't asked to plead to an accusation of witchcraft."

"No, not exactly," said the young man. "But I didn't quite see my
way to speaking of it. We had a good many other things before us."

"Yes, that's true. I suppose you wouldn't have mentioned it now
if I hadn't led up to it, would you?"

"I don't know, sir. It was rather on my mind to do so. Perhaps it
was I who led up to it."

His father laughed. "Perhaps you did, Tom; perhaps you did.
Your mother would have known you were leading up to something,
but I'll confess that I didn't. What is it?"

"Nothing very definite. But do you know that in spite of his syntax I rather liked him?"

The father looked keenly at the son; but unless the boy's full confidence was offered, Corey was not the man to ask it. "Well?" was all
that he said.

"I suppose that in a new country one gets to looking at people
a little out of our tradition; and I dare say that if I hadn't passed a
winter in Texas I might have found Colonel Lapham rather too
much."

"You mean that there are worse things in Texas?"

"Not that exactly. I mean that I saw it wouldn't be quite fair to
test him by our standards."

"This comes of the error which I have often deprecated," said
the elder Corey. "In fact I am always saying that the Bostonian ought
never to leave Boston. Then he knows—and then only—that there
can be no standard but ours. But we are constantly going away, and
coming back with our convictions shaken to their foundations. One
man goes to England, and returns with the conception of a grander
social life; another comes home from Germany with the notion of

---

*Legal term for death by torture (French). Giles Corey's wife, Martha, was accused
in the Salem witch trials of 1692. She was hanged, and according to a contemporary account, he was "pressed to death" with heavy weights for "standing mute," refusing to testify against her; the two appear as characters in Arthur Miller's 1953
play *The Crucible.*

a more searching intellectual activity; a fellow just back from Paris has the absurdest ideas of art and literature; and you revert to us from the cowboys of Texas, and tell us to our faces that we ought to try Papa Lapham by a jury of his peers. It ought to be stopped—it ought, really. The Bostonian who leaves Boston ought to be condemned to perpetual exile."

The son suffered the father to reach his climax with smiling patience. When he asked finally, "What are the characteristics of Papa Lapham that place him beyond our jurisdiction?" the younger Corey crossed his long legs, and leaned forward to take one of his knees between his hands.

"Well, sir, he bragged, rather."

"Oh, I don't know that bragging should exempt him from the ordinary processes. I've heard other people brag in Boston."

"Ah, not just in that personal way—not about money."

"No, that was certainly different."

"I don't mean," said the young fellow, with the scrupulosity which people could not help observing and liking in him, "that it was more than an indirect expression of satisfaction in the ability to spend."

"No. I should be glad to express something of the kind myself, if the facts would justify me."

The son smiled tolerantly again. "But if he was enjoying his money in that way, I didn't see why he shouldn't show his pleasure in it. It might have been vulgar, but it wasn't sordid. And I don't know that it was vulgar. Perhaps his successful strokes of business were the romance of his life——"

The father interrupted with a laugh. "The girl must be uncommonly pretty. What did she seem to think of her father's brag?"

"There were two of them," answered the son evasively.

"Oh, two! And is the sister pretty, too?"

"Not pretty, but rather interesting. She is like her mother."

"Then the pretty one isn't the father's pet?"

"I can't say, sir. I don't believe," added the young fellow, "that I can make you see Colonel Lapham just as I did. He struck me as very simple-hearted and rather wholesome. Of course he could be tiresome; we all can; and I suppose his range of ideas is limited. But he is a force, and not a bad one. If he hasn't got over being surprised at the effect of rubbing his lamp———"

"Oh, one could make out a case. I suppose you know what you are about, Tom. But remember that we are Essex County people, and that in savor we are just a little beyond the salt of the earth. I will tell you plainly that I don't like the notion of a man who has rivaled the hues of nature in her wildest haunts with the tints of his mineral paint; but I don't say there are not worse men. He isn't to my taste, though he might be ever so much to my conscience."

"I suppose," said the son, "that there is nothing really to be ashamed of in mineral paint. People go into all sorts of things."

His father took his cigarette from his mouth and once more looked his son full in the face. "Oh, is that it?"

"It has crossed my mind," admitted the son. "I must do something. I've wasted time and money enough. I've seen much younger men all through the West and Southwest taking care of themselves. I don't think I was particularly fit for anything out there, but I am ashamed to come back and live upon you, sir."

His father shook his head with an ironical sigh. "Ah, we shall never have a real aristocracy while this plebeian reluctance to live upon a parent or a wife continues the animating spirit of our youth. It strikes at the root of the whole feudal system. I really think you owe me an apology, Tom. I supposed you wished to marry the girl's money, and here you are, basely seeking to go into business with her father."

Young Corey laughed again like a son who perceives that his father is a little antiquated, but keeps a filial faith in his wit. "I don't know that it's quite so bad as that; but the thing had certainly crossed my mind. I don't know how it's to be approached, and I don't know that it's at all possible. But I confess that I 'took to' Colonel Lapham from the moment I saw him. He looked as if he 'meant business,' and I mean business too."

The father smoked thoughtfully. "Of course people do go into all sorts of things, as you say, and I don't know that one thing is more ignoble than another, if it's decent, and large enough. In my time you would have gone into the China trade or the India trade—though I didn't; and a little later cotton would have been your manifest destiny—though it wasn't mine; but now a man may do almost anything. The real-estate business is pretty full. Yes, if you have a deep inward vocation for it, I don't see why mineral paint shouldn't do. I fancy it's easy enough approaching the matter. We will invite Papa Lapham to dinner, and talk it over with him."

"Oh, I don't think that would be exactly the way, sir," said the son, smiling at his father's patrician unworldliness.

"No? Why not?"

"I'm afraid it would be a bad start. I don't think it would strike him as business-like."

"I don't see why he should be punctilious, if we're not."

"Ah, we might say that if he were making the advances."

"Well, perhaps you are right, Tom. What is your idea?"

"I haven't a very clear one. It seems to me I ought to get some business friend of ours, whose judgment he would respect, to speak a good word for me."

"Give you a character?"

"Yes. And of course I must go to Colonel Lapham. My notion would be to inquire pretty thoroughly about him, and then, if I liked the look of things, to go right down to Republic street and let him see what he could do with me, if anything."

"That sounds tremendously practical to me, Tom, though it may be just the wrong way. When are you going down to Mount Desert?"

"To-morrow, I think, sir," said the young man. "I shall turn it over in my mind while I'm off."

The father rose, showing something more than his son's height, with a very slight stoop, which the son's figure had not. "Well," he said, whimsically, "I admire your spirit, and I don't deny that it is justified by necessity. It's a consolation to think that while I've been spending and enjoying, I have been preparing the noblest future for you—a future of industry and self-reliance. You never could draw, but this scheme of going into the mineral-paint business shows that you have inherited something of my feeling for color."

The son laughed once more, and waiting till his father was well on his way upstairs, turned out the gas and then hurried after him and preceded him into his chamber. He glanced over it, to see that everything was there, to his father's hand. Then he said, "Good-night, sir," and the elder responded, "Good-night, my son," and the son went to his own room.

Over the mantel in the elder Corey's room hung a portrait which he had painted of his own father, and now he stood a moment and looked at this as if struck by something novel in it. The resemblance between his son and the old India merchant, who had followed the trade from Salem to Boston when the larger city drew it away from the smaller, must have been what struck him. Grandfather and grandson had both the Roman nose which appears to have flourished chiefly at the formative period of the republic, and which occurs more rarely in the descendants of the conscript fathers, though it still characterizes the profiles of a good many Boston ladies. Bromfield Corey had not inherited it, and he had made his straight nose his defense when the old merchant accused him of a want of energy. He said, "What could a man do whose unnatural father had left his own nose away from him?" This amused but did not satisfy the merchant. "You must do something," he said; "and it's for you to choose. If you don't like the India trade, go into something else. Or, take up law or medicine. No Corey yet ever proposed to do nothing." "Ah, then, it's quite time one of us made a beginning," urged the man who was then young, and who was now old, looking into the somewhat fierce eyes of his father's portrait. He had inherited as little of the fierceness as of the nose, and there was nothing predatory in his son either, though the aquiline beak had come down to him in such force. Bromfield Corey liked his son Tom for the gentleness which tempered his energy.

"Well, let us compromise," he seemed to be saying to his father's portrait. "I will travel." "Travel? How long?" the keen eyes demanded. "Oh, indefinitely. I wont be hard with you, father." He could see the eyes soften, and the smile of yielding come over his father's face; the merchant could not resist a son who was so much like his dead mother. There was some vague understanding between them that Bromfield Corey was to come back and go into business after a time, but he never did so. He traveled about over Europe, and traveled handsomely, frequenting good society everywhere, and getting himself presented at several courts, at a period when it was a distinction to do so. He had always sketched, and with his father's leave he fixed himself at Rome, where he remained studying art and rounding the being inherited from his Yankee progenitors, till there was very little left of the ancestral angularities. After ten years he came home and painted that portrait of his father. It was very good, if a little amateurish, and he might have made himself a name as a painter of portraits if he had not had so much money. But he had plenty of money, though by this time he was married and beginning to have a family. It was absurd for him to paint portraits for pay, and ridiculous to paint them for nothing; so he did not paint them at all. He continued a dilettante, never quite abandoning his art, but working at it fitfully, and talking more about it than working at it. He had his theory of Titian's method; and now and then a Bostonian insisted upon buying a picture of him. After a while he hung it more and more inconspicuously, and said apologetically, "Oh, yes! that's one of Bromfield Corey's things. It has nice qualities, but it's amateurish."

In process of time the money seemed less abundant. There were shrinkages of one kind and another, and living had grown much more expensive and luxurious. For many years he talked about going back to Rome, but he never went, and his children grew up in the usual way. Before he knew it his son had him out to his class-day spread at Harvard, and then he had his son on his hands. The son made various unsuccessful provisions for himself, and still continued upon his father's hands, to their common dissatisfaction, though it was chiefly the younger who repined. He had the Roman nose and the energy without the opportunity, and at one of the reversions his father said to him, "You ought not to have that nose, Tom; then you would do very well. You would go and travel, as I did."

Lapham and his wife continued talking after he had quelled the disturbance in his daughters' room overhead; and their talk was not altogether of the new house.

"I tell you," he said, "if I had that fellow in the business with me I would make a man of him."

"Well, Silas Lapham," returned his wife, "I do believe you've got mineral paint on the brain. Do you suppose a fellow like young Corey, brought up the way he's been, would touch mineral paint with a ten-foot pole?"

"Why not?" haughtily asked the Colonel.

"Well, if you don't know already, there's no use trying to tell you."

VI

The Coreys had always had a house at Nahant, but after letting it for a season or two they found they could get on without it, and sold it at the son's instance, who foresaw that if things went on as they were going, the family would be straitened to the point of changing their mode of life altogether. They began to be of the people of whom it was said that they staid in town very late; and when the ladies did go away, it was for a brief summering in this place and that. The father remained at home altogether; and the son joined them in the intervals of his enterprises, which occurred only too often.

At Bar Harbor, where he now went to find them, after his winter in Texas, he confessed to his mother that there seemed no very good opening there for him. He might do as well as Loring Stanton, but he doubted if Stanton was doing very well. Then he mentioned the new project which he had been thinking over. She did not deny that there was something in it, but she could not think of any young man who had gone into such a business as that, and it appeared to her that he might as well go into a patent medicine or a stove-polish.

"There was one of his hideous advertisements," she said, "painted on a reef that we saw as we came down."

Corey smiled. "Well, I suppose, if it was in a good state of preservation, that is proof positive of the efficacy of the paint on the hulls of vessels."

"It's very distasteful to me, Tom," said his mother; and if there was something else in her mind, she did not speak more plainly of it than to add: "It's not only the kind of business, but the kind of people you would be mixed up with."

"I thought you didn't find them so very bad," suggested Corey.

"I hadn't seen them in Nankeen Square then."

"You can see them on the water side of Beacon street when you go back."

Then he told of his encounter with the Lapham family in their new house. At the end his mother merely said, "It is getting very common down there," and she did not try to oppose anything further to his scheme.

The young man went to see Colonel Lapham shortly after his return to Boston. He paid his visit at Lapham's office, and if he had studied simplicity in his summer dress he could not have presented himself in a figure more to the mind of a practical man. His hands and neck still kept the brown of the Texan suns and winds, and he looked as business-like as Lapham himself.

He spoke up promptly and briskly in the outer office, and caused the pretty girl to look away from her copying at him. "Is Mr. Lapham in?" he asked; and after that moment for reflection which an array of book-keepers so addressed likes to give the inquirer, a head was lifted from a ledger and nodded toward the inner office.

Lapham had recognized the voice, and he was standing, in considerable perplexity of mind, to receive Corey, when the young man opened his painted glass door. It was a hot afternoon, and Lapham was in his shirt-sleeves. Scarcely a trace of the boastful hospitality with which he had welcomed Corey to his house a few days before lingered in his present address. He looked at the young man's face, as if he expected him to dispatch whatever unimaginable affair he had come upon.

"Won't you sit down? How are you? You'll excuse me," he added, in brief allusion to the shirt-sleeves. "I'm about roasted."

Corey laughed. "I wish you'd let me take off my coat."

"Why, take it off!" cried the Colonel, with instant pleasure. There is something in human nature which causes the man in his shirt-sleeves to wish all other men to appear in the same dishabille.

"I will, if you ask me after I've talked with you two minutes," said the young fellow, companionably pulling up the chair offered him toward the desk where Lapham had again seated himself. "But perhaps you haven't got two minutes to give me?"

"Oh, yes, I have," said the Colonel. "I was just going to knock off. I can give you twenty, and then I shall have fifteen minutes to catch the boat."

"All right," said Corey. "I want you to take me into the mineral paint business."

The Colonel sat dumb. He twisted his thick neck, and looked round at the door to see if it was shut. He would not have liked to have any of those fellows outside hear him, but there is no saying what sum of money he would not have given if his wife had been there to hear what Corey had just said.

"I suppose," continued the young man, "I could have got several people whose names you know to back my industry and sobriety, and say a word for my business capacity. But I thought I wouldn't trouble anybody for certificates till I found whether there was a chance, or the ghost of one, of your wanting me. So I came straight to you."

Lapham gathered himself together as well as he could. He had not yet forgiven Corey for Mrs. Lapham's insinuation that he would feel himself too good for the mineral paint business; and though he was dispersed by that astounding shot at first, he was not going to let any one even hypothetically despise his paint with impunity. "How do you think I am going to take you on?" They took on hands at the works; and Lapham put it as if Corey were a hand coming to him for employment. Whether he satisfied himself by this or not, he reddened a little after he had said it.

Corey answered, ignorant of the offense: "I haven't a very clear idea, I'm afraid; but I've been looking a little into the matter from the outside——"

"I hope you hain't been paying any attention to that fellow's stuff in the 'Events'?" Lapham interrupted. Since Bartley's interview had appeared, Lapham had regarded it with very mixed feelings. At first it gave him a glow of secret pleasure, blended with doubt as to how his wife would like the use Bartley had made of her in it. But she had not seemed to notice it much, and Lapham had experienced the gratitude of the man who escapes. Then his girls had begun to make fun of it; and though he did not mind Penelope's jokes much, he did not like to see that Irene's gentility was wounded. Business friends met him with the kind of knowing smile about it that implied their sense of the fraudulent character of its praise—the smile of men who had been there and who knew how it was themselves. Lapham had his misgivings as to how his clerks and underlings looked at it; he treated them with stately severity for a while after it came out, and he ended by feeling rather sore about it. He took it for granted that everybody had read it.

"I don't know what you mean," replied Corey. "I don't see the 'Events' regularly."

"Oh, it was nothing. They sent a fellow down here to interview me, and he got everything about as twisted as he could."

"I believe they always do," said Corey. "I hadn't seen it. Perhaps it came out before I got home."

"Perhaps it did."

"My notion of making myself useful to you was based on a hint I got from one of your own circulars."

Lapham was proud of those circulars; he thought they read very well. "What was that?"

"I could put a little capital into the business," said Corey, with the tentative accent of a man who chances a thing. "I've got a little money, but I didn't imagine you cared for anything of that kind."

"No, sir, I don't," returned the Colonel bluntly. "I've had one partner, and one's enough."

"Yes," assented the young man, who doubtless had his own ideas as to eventualities—or perhaps rather had the vague hopes of youth. "I didn't come to propose a partnership. But I see that you are introducing your paint into the foreign markets, and there I really thought I might be of use to you, and to myself, too."

"How?" asked the Colonel scantly.

"Well, I know two or three languages pretty well. I know French, and I know German, and I've got a pretty fair sprinkling of Spanish."

"You mean that you can talk them?" asked the Colonel, with the mingled awe and slight that such a man feels for such accomplishments.

"Yes; and I can write an intelligible letter in either of them."

Lapham rubbed his nose. "It's easy enough to get all the letters we want translated."

"Well," pursued Corey, not showing his discouragement if he felt any, "I know the countries where you want to introduce this paint of yours. I've been there. I've been in Germany and France, and I've been in South America and Mexico; I've been in Italy, of course. I believe I could go to any of those countries and place it to advantage."

Lapham had listened with a trace of persuasion in his face, but now he shook his head.

"It's placing itself as fast as there's any call for it. It wouldn't pay us to send anybody out to look after it. Your salary and expenses would eat up about all we should make on it."

"Yes," returned the young man intrepidly, "if you had to pay me any salary and expenses."

"You don't propose to work for nothing?"

"I propose to work for a commission." The Colonel was beginning to shake his head again, but Corey hurried on. "I haven't come to you without making some inquiries about the paint, and I know how it stands with those who know best. I believe in it."

Lapham lifted his head and looked at the young man, deeply moved.

"It's the best paint in God's universe," he said, with the solemnity of prayer.

"It's the best in the market," said Corey; and he repeated, "I believe in it."

"You believe in it," began the Colonel, and then he stopped. If there had really been any purchasing power in money, a year's income would have bought Mrs. Lapham's instant presence. He warmed and softened to the young man in every way, not only because he must do so to any one who believed in his paint, but because he had done this innocent person the wrong of listening to a defamation of his instinct and good sense, and had been willing to see him suffer for a purely supposititious offense.

Corey rose.

"You mustn't let me outstay my twenty minutes," he said, taking out his watch. "I don't expect you to give a decided answer on the spot. All that I ask is that you'll consider my proposition."

"Don't hurry," said Lapham. "Sit still! I want to tell you about this paint," he added, in a voice husky with the feeling that his hearer could not divine. "I want to tell you *all* about it."

"I could walk with you to the boat," suggested the young man.

"Never mind the boat! I can take the next one. Look here!" The Colonel pulled open a drawer, as Corey sat down again, and took out a photograph of the locality of the mine. "Here's where we get it. This photograph don't half do the place justice," he said, as if the imperfect art had slighted the features of a beloved face. "It's one of the sightliest places in the country, and here's the very spot"—he covered it with his huge forefinger—"where my father found that paint, more than forty—years—ago. Yes, sir!"

He went on, and told the story in unsparing detail, while his chance for the boat passed unheeded, and the clerks in the outer office hung up their linen office coats and put on their seersucker or flannel street coats. The young lady went, too, and nobody was left but the porter, who made from time to time a noisy demonstration of fastening a distant blind, or putting something in place. At last the Colonel roused himself from the autobiographical delight of the history of his paint. "Well, sir, that's the story."

"It's an interesting story," said Corey, with a long breath, as they rose together, and Lapham put on his coat.

"That's what it is," said the Colonel. "Well!" he added, "I don't see but what we've got to have another talk about this thing. It's a surprise to me, and I don't see exactly how you're going to make it pay."

"I'm willing to take the chances," answered Corey. "As I said, I believe in it. I should try South America first. I should try Chile."

"Look here!" said Lapham, with his watch in his hand, "I like to get things over. We've just got time for the six o'clock boat. Why don't you come down with me to Nantasket? I can give you a bed as well as not. And then we can finish up."

The impatience of youth in Corey responded to the impatience of temperament in his elder.

"Why, I don't see why I shouldn't," he allowed himself to say. "I confess I should like to have it finished up myself, if it could be finished up in the right way."

"Well, we'll see. Dennis!" Lapham called to the remote porter, and the man came. "Want to send any word home?" he asked Corey.

"No; my father and I go and come as we like, without keeping account of each other. If I don't come home, he knows that I'm not there. That's all."

"Well, that's convenient. You'll find you can't do that when you're married. Never mind, Dennis," said the Colonel.

He had time to buy two newspapers on the wharf before he jumped on board the steam-boat with Corey. "Just made it," he said; "and that's what I like to do. I can't stand it to be aboard much more than a minute before she shoves out." He gave one of the newspapers to Corey as he spoke, and set him the example of catching up a camp-stool on their way to that point on the boat which his experience had taught him was the best. He opened his paper at once and began to run over its news, while the young man watched the spectacular recession of the city, and was vaguely conscious of the people about him, and of the gay life of the water round the boat. The air freshened; the craft thinned in number; they met larger sail, lagging slowly inward in the afternoon light; the islands of the bay waxed and waned as the steamer approached and left them behind.

"I hate to see them stirring up those Southern fellows again," said the Colonel, speaking into the paper on his lap. "Seems to me it's time to let those old issues go."

"Yes," said the young man. "What are they doing now?"

"Oh, stirring up the Confederate brigadiers in Congress.* I don't like it. Seems to me, if our party haint got any other stock-in-trade, we better shut up shop altogether." Lapham went on, as he scanned his newspaper, to give his ideas of public questions, in a fragmentary way, while Corey listened patiently, and waited for him to come back to business. He folded up his paper at last, and stuffed it into his coat pocket. "There's one thing I always make it a rule to do," he said, "and that is to give my mind a complete rest from business while I'm going down on the boat. I like to get the fresh air all through me, soul and body. I believe a man can give his mind a rest, just the same as he can give his legs a rest, or his back. All he's got to do is to use his will-power. Why, I suppose, if I hadn't adopted some such rule, with the strain I've had on me for the last ten years, I should 'a' been a dead man long ago. That's the reason I like a horse. You've got to give your mind to the horse; you can't help it, unless you want to break your neck; but a boat's different, and there you got to use your will-power. You got to take your mind right up and put it where you want it. I make it a rule to read the paper on the boat—Hold on!" he interrupted himself to prevent Corey from paying his fare to the man who had come round for it. "I've got tickets. And when I get through the paper, I try to get somebody to talk to, or I watch the people. It's an astonishing thing to me where they all come from. I've been riding up and down on these boats for six or seven years, and I don't know but very few of the faces I see on board. Seems to be a perfectly fresh lot every time. Well, of course! Town's full of strangers in the summer season, anyway, and folks keep coming down from the country. They think it's a great thing to get down to the beach, and

---

*Former Confederate officers active in the Democratic Party.

they've all heard of the electric light on the water, and they want to see it. But you take faces now! The astonishing thing to me is not what a face tells, but what it don't tell. When you think of what a man is, or a woman is, and what most of 'em have been through before they get to be thirty, it seems as if their experience would burn right through. But it don't. I like to watch the couples, and try to make out which are engaged, or going to be, and which are married, or better be. But half the time I can't make any sort of guess. Of course, where they're young and kittenish, you can tell; but where they're anyways on, you can't. Heigh?"

"Yes, I think you're right," said Corey, not perfectly reconciled to philosophy in the place of business, but accepting it as he must.

"Well," said the Colonel, "I don't suppose it was meant we should know what was in each other's minds. It would take a man out of his own hands. As long as he's in his own hands, there's some hopes of his doing something with himself; but if a fellow has been found out—even if he hasn't been found out to be so very bad—it's pretty much all up with him. No, sir. I don't want to know people through and through."

The greater part of the crowd on board—and, of course, the boat was crowded—looked as if they might not only be easily but safely known. There was little style and no distinction among them; they were people who were going down to the beach for the fun or the relief of it, and were able to afford it. In face they were commonplace, with nothing but the American poetry of vivid purpose to light them up, where they did not wholly lack fire. But they were nearly all shrewd and friendly-looking, with an apparent readiness for the humorous intimacy native to us all. The women were dandified in dress, according to their means and taste, and the men differed from each other in degrees of indifference to it. To a straw-hatted population, such as ours is in summer, no sort of personal dignity is possible. We have not even the power over observers which comes from the fantasticality of an Englishman when he discards the conventional dress. In our straw hats and our serge or flannel sacks we are no more imposing than a crowd of boys.

"Some day," said Lapham, rising as the boat drew near the wharf of the final landing, "there's going to be an awful accident on these boats. Just look at that jam."

He meant the people thickly packed on the pier, and under strong restraint of locks and gates, to prevent them from rushing on board the boat and possessing her for the return trip before she had landed her Nantasket passengers.

"Overload 'em every time," he continued, with a sort of dry, impersonal concern at the impending calamity, as if it could not possibly include him. "They take about twice as many as they ought to carry, and about ten times as many as they could save if anything happened. Yes, sir, it's bound to come. Hello! There's my girl!" He took out his folded newspaper and waved it toward a group of phaetons and barouches* drawn up on the pier a little apart from the pack of people, and a lady in one of them answered with a flourish of her parasol.

When he had made his way with his guest through the crowd, she began to speak to her father before she noticed Corey. "Well, Colonel, you've improved your last chance. We've been coming to every boat since four o'clock,—or Jerry has,—and I told mother that I would come myself once, and see if I couldn't fetch you; and if I failed, you could walk next time. You're getting perfectly spoiled."

The Colonel enjoyed letting her scold him to the end before he said, with a twinkle of pride in his guest and satisfaction in her probably being able to hold her own against any discomfiture, "I've brought Mr. Corey down for the night with me, and I was showing him things all the way, and it took time."

The young fellow was at the side of the open beach-wagon, making a quick, gentlemanly bow, and Penelope Lapham was cozily drawling, "Oh, how do you do, Mr. Corey?" before the Colonel had finished his explanation.

"Get right in there, alongside of Miss Lapham, Mr. Corey," he said, pulling himself up into the place beside the driver. "No, no," he had added quickly, at some signs of polite protest in the young man, "I don't give up the best place to anybody. Jerry, suppose you let me have hold of the leathers a minute."

This was his way of taking the reins from the driver; and in half the time he specified, he had skillfully turned the vehicle on the pier,

*Two- and four-seat horse-drawn carriages.

among the crooked lines and groups of foot-passengers, and was spinning up the road toward the stretch of verandaed hotels and restaurants in the sand along the shore. "Pretty gay down here," he said, indicating all this with a turn of his whip, as he left it behind him. "But I've got about sick of hotels; and this summer I made up my mind that I'd take a cottage. Well, Pen, how are the folks?" He looked half-way round for her answer, and with the eye thus brought to bear upon her he was able to give her a wink of supreme content. The Colonel, with no sort of ulterior design, and nothing but his triumph over Mrs. Lapham definitely in his mind, was feeling, as he would have said, about right.

The girl smiled a daughter's amusement at her father's boyishness. "I don't think there's much change since morning. Did Irene have a headache when you left?"

"No," said the Colonel.

"Well, then, there's that to report."

"Pshaw!" said the Colonel, with vexation in his tone.

"I'm sorry Miss Irene isn't well," said Corey politely.

"I think she must have got it from walking too long on the beach. The air is so cool here that you forget how hot the sun is."

"Yes, that's true," assented Corey.

"A good night's rest will make it all right," suggested the Colonel, without looking round. "But you girls have got to look out."

"If you're fond of walking," said Corey, "I suppose you find the beach a temptation."

"Oh, it isn't so much that," returned the girl. "You keep walking on and on because it's so smooth and straight before you. We've been here so often that we know it all by heart—just how it looks at high tide, and how it looks at low tide, and how it looks after a storm. We're as well acquainted with the crabs and stranded jellyfish as we are with the children digging in the sand and the people sitting under umbrellas. I think they're always the same, all of them."

The Colonel left the talk to the young people. When he spoke next it was to say, "Well, here we are!" and he turned from the highway and drove up in front of a brown cottage with a vermilion roof, and a group of geraniums clutching the rock that cropped up in the loop formed by the road. It was treeless and bare all round, and the ocean, unnecessarily vast, weltered away a little more than a stone's cast from the cottage. A hospitable smell of supper filled the air, and Mrs. Lapham was on the veranda, with that demand in her eyes for her belated husband's excuses, which she was obliged to check on her tongue at sight of Corey.

VII

The exultant Colonel swung himself lightly down from his seat. "I've brought Mr. Corey with me," he nonchalantly explained.

Mrs. Lapham made their guest welcome, and the Colonel showed him to his room, briefly assuring himself that there was nothing wanting there. Then he went to wash his own hands, carelessly ignoring the eagerness with which his wife pursued him to their chamber.

"What gave Irene a headache?" he asked, making himself a fine lather for his hairy paws.

"Never you mind Irene," promptly retorted his wife. "How came he to come? Did you press him? If you did, I'll never forgive you, Silas!"

The Colonel laughed, and his wife shook him by the shoulder to make him laugh lower. " 'Sh!" she whispered. "Do you want him to hear *every* thing? Did you urge him?"

The Colonel laughed the more. He was going to get all the good out of this. "No, I didn't urge him. Seemed to want to come."

"I don't believe it. Where did you meet him?"

"At the office."

"What office?"

"Mine."

"Nonsense! What was he doing there?"

"Oh, nothing much."

"What did he come for?"

"Come for? Oh! He *said* he wanted to go into the mineral paint business."

Mrs. Lapham dropped into a chair, and watched his bulk shaken with smothered laughter. "Silas Lapham," she gasped, "if you try to get off any more of those things on me——"

The Colonel applied himself to the towel. "Had a notion he could work it in South America. I don't know what he's up to."

"Never mind!" cried his wife. "I'll get even with you *yet*."

"So I told him he had better come down and talk it over," continued the Colonel, in well-affected simplicity. "I knew he wouldn't touch it with a ten-foot pole."

"Go on!" threatened Mrs. Lapham.

"Right thing to do, wa'n't it?"

A tap was heard at the door, and Mrs. Lapham answered it. A maid announced supper. "Very well," she said, "come to tea now. But I'll make you pay for this, Silas."

Penelope had gone to her sister's room as soon as she entered the house.

"Is your head any better, 'Rene?" she asked.

"Yes, a little," came a voice from the pillows. "But I shall not come to tea. I don't want anything. If I keep still, I shall be all right by morning."

"Well, I'm sorry," said the elder sister. "He's come down with father."

"He hasn't! Who?" cried Irene, starting up in simultaneous denial and demand.

"Oh, well, if you say he hasn't, what's the use of my telling you who?"

"Oh, how can you treat me so!" moaned the sufferer. "What do you mean, Pen?"

"I guess I'd better not tell you," said Penelope, watching her like a cat playing with a mouse. "If you're not coming to tea, it would just excite you for nothing."

The mouse moaned and writhed upon the bed.

"Oh, I wouldn't treat *you* so!"

The cat seated herself across the room and asked quietly:

"Well, what could you do if it *was* Mr. Corey? You couldn't come to tea, you say. But *he'll* excuse you. I've told him you had a headache. Why, of course you can't come! It would be too barefaced. But you needn't be troubled, Irene; I'll do my best to make the time pass pleasantly for him." Here the cat gave a low titter, and the mouse girded itself up with a momentary courage and self-respect.

"I should think you would be ashamed to come here and tease me so."

"I don't see why you shouldn't believe me," argued Penelope. "Why shouldn't he come down with father, if father asked him? and he'd be sure to if he thought of it. I don't see any p'ints about that frog that's any better than any other frog."

The sense of her sister's helplessness was too much for the tease;

she broke down in a fit of smothered laughter, which convinced her victim that it was nothing but an ill-timed joke.

"Well, Pen, I wouldn't use you so," she whimpered.

Penelope threw herself on the bed beside her.

"Oh, poor Irene! He is here. It's a solemn fact." And she caressed and soothed her sister, while she choked with laughter. "You must get up and come out. I don't know what brought him here, but here he is."

"It's too late now," said Irene, desolately. Then she added, with a wilder despair: "What a fool I was to take that walk!"

"Well," coaxed her sister, "come out and get some tea. The tea will do you good."

"No, no; I can't come. But send me a cup here."

"Yes, and then perhaps you can see him later in the evening."

"I shall not see him at all."

An hour after Penelope came back to her sister's room and found her before her glass. "You might as well have kept still, and been well by morning, 'Rene," she said. "As soon as we were done father said, 'Well, Mr. Corey and I have got to talk over a a little matter of business, and we'll excuse you, ladies.' He looked at mother in a way that I guess was pretty hard to bear. 'Rene, you ought to have heard the Colonel swelling at supper. It would have made you feel that all he said the other day was nothing."

Mrs. Lapham suddenly opened the door.

"Now, see here, Pen," she said, as she closed it behind her, "I've had just as much as I can stand from your father, and if you don't tell me this instant what it all means——"

She left the consequences to imagination, and Penelope replied, with her mock soberness:

"Well, the Colonel does seem to be on his high horse, ma'am. But you mustn't ask me what his business with Mr. Corey is, for I don't know. All that I know is that I met them at the landing, and that they conversed all the way down—on literary topics."

"Nonsense! What do you think it is?"

"Well, if you want my candid opinion, I think this talk about business is nothing but a blind. It seems a pity Irene shouldn't have been up to receive him," she added.

Irene cast a mute look of imploring at her mother, who was too much preoccupied to afford her the protection it asked.

"Your father said he wanted to go into the business with him."

Irene's look changed to a stare of astonishment and mystification, but Penelope preserved her imperturbability.

"Well, it's a lucrative business, I believe."

"Well, I don't believe a word of it!" cried Mrs. Lapham. "And so I told your father."

"Did it seem to convince him?" inquired Penelope.

Her mother did not reply. "I know one thing," she said. "He's got to tell me every word, or there'll be no sleep for him this night."

"Well, ma'am," said Penelope, breaking down in one of her queer laughs, "I shouldn't be a bit surprised if you were right."

"Go on and dress, Irene," ordered her mother, "and then you and Pen come out into the parlor. They can have just two hours for business, and then we must all be there to receive him. You haven't got headache enough to hurt you."

"Oh, it's all gone now," said the girl.

At the end of the limit she had given the Colonel, Mrs. Lapham looked into the dining-room, which she found blue with his smoke.

"I think you gentlemen will find the parlor pleasanter now, and we can give it up to you."

"Oh, no, you needn't," said her husband. "We've got about through." Corey was already standing, and Lapham rose too. "I guess we can join the ladies now. We can leave that little point till to-morrow."

Both of the young ladies were in the parlor when Corey entered with their father, and both were frankly indifferent to the few books and the many newspapers scattered about on the table where the large lamp was placed. But after Corey had greeted Irene he glanced at the novel under his eye, and said, in the dearth that sometimes befalls people at such times: "I see you're reading 'Middlemarch.'* Do you like George Eliot?"

"Who?" asked the girl.

Penelope interposed. "I don't believe Irene's read it yet. I've just got it out of the library; I heard so much talk about it. I wish she would let you find out a little about the people for yourself," she added. But here her father struck in:

---

*Novel by George Eliot, published in 1872.

"I can't get the time for books. It's as much as I can do to keep up with the newspapers; and when night comes, I'm tired, and I'd rather go out to the theater, or a lecture, if they've got a good stere-opticon* to give you views of the places. But I guess we all like a play better than 'most anything else. I want something that'll make me laugh. I don't believe in tragedy. I think there's enough of that in real life without putting it on the stage. Seen 'Joshua Whitcomb'?"†

The whole family joined in the discussion, and it appeared that they all had their opinions of the plays and actors. Mrs. Lapham brought the talk back to literature. "I guess Penelope does most of our reading."

"Now, mother, you're not going to put it all on me!" said the girl, in comic protest.

Her mother laughed, and then added, with a sigh: "I used to like to get hold of a good book when I was a girl; but we weren't allowed to read many novels in those days. My mother called them all lies. And I guess she wasn't so very far wrong about some of them."

"They're certainly fictions," said Corey, smiling.

"Well, we do buy a good many books, first and last," said the Colonel, who probably had in mind the costly volumes which they presented to one another on birthdays and holidays. "But I get about all the reading I want in the newspapers. And when the girls want a novel, I tell 'em to get it out of the library. That's what the library's for. Phew!" he panted, blowing away the whole unprofitable subject. "How close you women-folks like to keep a room! You go down to the sea-side or up to the mountains for a change of air, and then you cork yourselves into a room so tight you don't have any air at all. Here! You girls get on your bonnets and go and show Mr. Corey the view of the hotels from the rocks."

Corey said that he should be delighted. The girls exchanged looks with each other, and then with their mother. Irene curved her pretty chin in comment upon her father's incorrigibility, and Penelope made a droll mouth, but the Colonel remained serenely content with his finesse. "I got 'em out of the way," he said, as soon as they

---

*Wide-angle slide projector that joined several images.
†Popular vaudeville sketch by Denman Thompson about rural New Englanders, dating from 1871; it evolved into the long-running stage comedy *The Old Homestead*.

were gone, and before his wife had time to fall upon him, "because I've got through my talk with him, and now I want to talk with you. It's just as I said, Persis; he wants to go into the business with me."

"It's lucky for you," said his wife, meaning that now he would not be made to suffer for attempting to hoax her. But she was too intensely interested to pursue that matter further. "What in the world do you suppose he means by it?"

"Well, I should judge by his talk that he had been trying a good many different things since he left college, and he haint found just the thing he likes—or the thing that likes him. It aint so easy. And now he's got an idea that he can take hold of the paint and push it in other countries—push it in Mexico and push it in South America. He's a splendid Spanish scholar,"—this was Lapham's version of Corey's modest claim to a smattering of the language,—"and he's been among the natives enough to know their ways. And he believes in the paint," added the Colonel.

"I guess he believes in something else besides the paint," said Mrs. Lapham.

"What do you mean?"

"Well, Silas Lapham, if you can't see now that he's after Irene, I don't know what ever can open your eyes. That's all."

The Colonel pretended to give the idea silent consideration, as if it had not occurred to him before. "Well, then, all I've got to say is, that he's going a good way round. I don't say you're wrong, but if it's Irene, I don't see why he should want to go off to South America to get her. And that's what he proposes to do. I guess there's some paint about it too, Persis. He says he believes in it,"—the Colonel devoutly lowered his voice,—"and he's willing to take the agency on his own account down there, and run it for a commission on what he can sell."

"Of course! He isn't going to take hold of it any way so as to feel beholden to you. He's got too much pride for that."

"He aint going to take hold of it at all, if he don't mean paint in the first place and Irene afterward. I don't object to him, as I know, either way, but the two things wont mix; and I don't propose he shall pull the wool over my eyes—or anybody else. But, as far as heard from, up to date, he means paint first, last, and all the time. At any rate, I'm going to take him on that basis. He's got some pretty good ideas about it, and he's been stirred up by this talk, just now, about getting our manufactures into the foreign markets. There's an overstock in everything, and we've got to get rid of it, or we've got to shut down till the home demand begins again. We've had two or three such flurries before now, and they didn't amount to much. They say we can't extend our commerce under the high tariff system we've got now, because there ain't any sort of reciprocity on our side,—we want to have the other fellows show all the reciprocity,—and the English have got the advantage of us every time. I don't know whether it's so or not; but I don't see why it should apply to my paint. Anyway, he wants to try it, and I've about made up my mind to let him. Of course I ain't going to let him take all the risk. I believe in the paint too, and I shall pay his expenses anyway."

"So you want another partner after all?" Mrs. Lapham could not forbear saying.

"Yes, if that's your idea of a partner. It isn't mine," returned her husband dryly.

"Well, if you've made up your mind, Si, I suppose you're ready for advice," said Mrs. Lapham.

The Colonel enjoyed this. "Yes, I *am*. What have you got to say against it?"

"I don't know as I've got anything. I'm satisfied if you are."

"Well?"

"When is he going to start for South America?"

"I shall take him into the office awhile. He'll get off some time in the winter. But he's got to know the business first."

"Oh, indeed! Are you going to take him to board in the family?"

"What are you after, Persis?"

"Oh, nothing! I presume he will feel free to visit in the family, even if he don't board with us."

"I presume he will."

"And if he don't use his privileges, do you think he'll be a fit person to manage your paint in South America?"

The Colonel reddened consciously. "I'm not taking him on that basis."

"Oh, yes, you are! You may pretend you aint to yourself, but you mustn't pretend so to me. Because I know you."

The Colonel laughed. "Pshaw!" he said.

Mrs. Lapham continued: "I don't see any harm in hoping that he'll take a fancy to her. But if you really think it wont do to mix the two things, I advise you not to take Mr. Corey into the business. It will do all very well if he *does* take a fancy to her; but if he don't, you know how you'll feel about it. And I know you well enough, Silas, to know that you can't do him justice if that happens. And I don't think it's right you should take this step unless you're pretty sure. I can see that you've set your heart on this thing———"

"I haven't set my heart on it at all," protested Lapham.

"And if you can't bring it about, you're going to feel unhappy over it," pursued his wife, regardless of his protest.

"Oh, very well," he said. "If you know more about what's in my mind than I do, there's no use arguing, as I can see."

He got up, to carry off his consciousness, and sauntered out of the door on to his piazza. He could see the young people down on the rocks, and his heart swelled in his breast. He had always said that he did not care what a man's family was, but the presence of young Corey as an applicant to him for employment, as his guest, as the possible suitor of his daughter, was one of the sweetest flavors that he had yet tasted in his success. He knew who the Coreys were very well, and, in his simple, brutal way, he had long hated their name as a symbol of splendor which, unless he should live to see at least three generations of his descendants gilded with mineral paint, he could not hope to realize in his own. He was acquainted in a business way with the tradition of old Phillips Corey, and he had heard a great many things about the Corey who had spent his youth abroad and his father's money everywhere, and done nothing but say smart things. Lapham could not see the smartness of some of them which had been repeated to him. Once he had encountered the fellow, and it seemed to Lapham that the tall, slim, white-mustached man, with the slight stoop, was everything that was offensively aristocratic. He had bristled up aggressively at the name when his wife told how she had made the acquaintance of the fellow's family the summer before, and he had treated the notion of young Corey's caring for Irene with the contempt which such a ridiculous superstition deserved. He had made up his mind about young Corey beforehand; yet when he met him he felt an instant liking for him, which he frankly acknowledged, and he had begun to assume the burden of his wife's superstition, of which she seemed now ready to accuse him of being the inventor.

Nothing had moved his thick imagination like this day's events since the girl who taught him spelling and grammar in the school at Lumberville had said she would have him for her husband.

The dark figures, stationary on the rocks, began to move, and he could see that they were coming toward the house. He went indoors so as not to appear to have been watching them.

VIII

A week after she had parted with her son at Bar Harbor, Mrs. Corey suddenly walked in upon her husband in their house in Boston. He was at breakfast, and he gave her the patronizing welcome with which the husband who has been staying in town all summer receives his wife when she drops down upon him from the mountains or the sea-side. For a little moment she feels herself strange in the house, and suffers herself to be treated like a guest, before envy of his comfort vexes her back into possession and authority. Mrs. Corey was a lady, and she did not let her envy take the form of open reproach.

"Well, Anna, you find me here in the luxury you left me to. How did you leave the girls?"

"The girls were well," said Mrs. Corey, looking absently at her husband's brown velvet coat, in which he was so handsome. No man had ever grown gray more beautifully. His hair, while not remaining dark enough to form a theatrical contrast with his mustache, was yet some shades darker, and, in becoming a little thinner, it had become a little more gracefully wavy. His skin had the pearly tint which that of elderly men sometimes assumes, and the lines which time had traced upon it were too delicate for the name of wrinkles. He had never had any personal vanity, and there was no consciousness in his good looks now.

"I am glad of that. The boy I have with me," he returned; "that is, when he is with me."

"Why, where is he?" demanded the mother.

"Probably carousing with the boon Lapham somewhere. He left me yesterday afternoon to go and offer his allegiance to the Mineral Paint King, and I haven't seen him since."

"Bromfield!" cried Mrs. Corey. "Why didn't you stop him?"

"Well, my dear, I'm not sure that it isn't a very good thing."

"A good thing? It's horrid!"

"No, I don't think so. It's decent. Tom had found out— without consulting the landscape, which I believe proclaims it everywhere——"

"Hideous!"

"That it's really a good thing; and he thinks that he has some ideas in regard to its dissemination in the parts beyond seas."

"Why shouldn't he go into something else?" lamented the mother.

"I believe he has gone into nearly everything else, and come out of it. So there is a chance of his coming out of this. But as I had nothing to suggest in place of it, I thought it best not to interfere. In fact, what good would my telling him that mineral paint was nasty have done? I dare say you told him it was nasty."

"Yes! I did."

"And you see with what effect, though he values your opinion three times as much as he values mine. Perhaps you came up to tell him again that it was nasty?"

"I feel very unhappy about it. He is throwing himself away. Yes, I should like to prevent it if I could!"

The father shook his head.

"If Lapham hasn't prevented it, I fancy it's too late. But there may be some hopes of Lapham. As for Tom's throwing himself away, I don't know. There's no question but he is one of the best fellows under the sun. He's tremendously energetic, and he has plenty of the kind of sense which we call horse; but he isn't brilliant. No, Tom is not brilliant. I don't think he would get on in a profession, and he's instinctively kept out of everything of the kind. But he has got to do something. What shall he do? He says mineral paint, and really I don't see why he shouldn't. If money is fairly and honestly earned, why should we pretend to care what it comes out of, when we don't really care? That superstition is exploded everywhere."

"Oh, it isn't the paint alone," said Mrs. Corey; and then she perceptibly arrested herself, and made a diversion in continuing: "I wish he had married someone."

"With money?" suggested her husband. "From time to time I have attempted Tom's corruption from that side, but I suspect Tom has a conscience against it, and I rather like him for it. I married for love myself," said Corey, looking across the table at his wife.

She returned his look tolerantly, though she felt it right to say, "What nonsense!"

"Besides," continued her husband, "if you come to money, there is the paint princess. She will have plenty."

"Ah, that's the worst of it," sighed the mother. "I suppose I could get on with the paint——"

"But not with the princess? I thought you said she was a very pretty, well-behaved girl?"

"She is very pretty, and she is well-behaved; but there is nothing of her. She is insipid; she is very insipid."

"But Tom seemed to like her flavor, such as it was?"

"How can I tell? We were under a terrible obligation to them, and I naturally wished him to be polite to them. In fact, I asked him to be so."

"And he was too polite?"

"I can't say that he was. But there is no doubt that the child is extremely pretty."

"Tom says there are two of them. Perhaps they will neutralize each other."

"Yes, there is another daughter," assented Mrs. Corey. "I don't see how you can joke about such things, Bromfield," she added.

"Well, I don't either, my dear, to tell you the truth. My hardihood surprises me. Here is a son of mine whom I see reduced to making his living by a shrinkage in values. It's very odd," interjected Corey, "that some values should have this peculiarity of shrinking. You never hear of values in a picture shrinking; but rents, stocks, real estate—all those values shrink abominably. Perhaps it might be argued that one should put all his values into pictures; I've got a good many of mine there."

"Tom needn't earn his living," said Mrs. Corey, refusing her husband's jest. "There's still enough for all of us."

"That is what I have sometimes urged upon Tom. I have proved to him that with economy, and strict attention to business, he need do nothing as long as he lives. Of course he would be somewhat restricted, and it would cramp the rest of us; but it is a world of sacrifices and compromises. He couldn't agree with me, and he was not in the least moved by the example of persons of quality in Europe, which I alleged in support of the life of idleness. It appears that he wishes to do something—to do something for himself. I am afraid that Tom is selfish."

Mrs. Corey smiled wanly. Thirty years before, she had married the rich young painter in Rome, who said so much better things than he painted—charming things, just the things to please the fancy of a girl who was disposed to take life a little too seriously and practically. She saw him in a different light when she got him home to Boston; but he had kept on saying the charming things, and he had not done much else. In fact, he had fulfilled the promise of his youth. It was a good trait in him that he was not actively but only passively extravagant. He was not adventurous with his money; his tastes were as simple as an Italian's; he had no expensive habits. In the process of time he had grown to lead a more and more secluded life. It was hard to get him out anywhere, even to dinner. His patience with their narrowing circumstances had a pathos which she felt the more she came into charge of their joint life. At times it seemed too bad that the children and their education and pleasures should cost so much. She knew, besides, that if it had not been for them she would have gone back to Rome with him, and lived princely there for less than it took to live respectably in Boston.

"Tom hasn't consulted me," continued his father, "but he has consulted other people. And he has arrived at the conclusion that mineral paint is a good thing to go into. He has found out all about it, and about its founder or inventor. It's quite impressive to hear him talk. And if he must do something for himself, I don't see why his egotism shouldn't as well take that form as another. Combined with the paint princess, it isn't so agreeable; but that's only a remote possibility, for which your principal ground is your motherly solicitude. But even if it were probable and imminent, what could you do? The chief consolation that we American parents have in these matters is that we can do nothing. If we were Europeans, even English, we should take some cognizance of our children's love affairs, and in some measure teach their young affections how to shoot. But it is our custom to ignore them until they have shot, and then they ignore us. We are altogether too delicate to arrange the marriages of our children; and when they have arranged them we don't like to say anything, for fear we should only make bad worse. The right way is for us to school ourselves to indifference. That is what the young people have to do elsewhere, and that is the only logical result of our position here. It is absurd for us to have any feeling about what we don't interfere with."

"Oh, people do interfere with their children's marriages very often," said Mrs. Corey.

"Yes, but only in a half-hearted way, so as not to make it disagreeable for themselves if the marriages go on in spite of them, as they're pretty apt to do. Now, my idea is that I ought to cut Tom off with a shilling. That would be very simple, and it would be economical. But you would never consent, and Tom wouldn't mind it."

"I think our whole conduct in regard to such things is wrong," said Mrs. Corey.

"Oh, very likely. But our whole civilization is based upon it. And who is going to make a beginning? To which father in our acquaintance shall I go and propose an alliance for Tom with his daughter? I should feel like an ass. And will you go to some mother, and ask her sons in marriage for our daughters? You would feel like a goose. No; the only motto for us is, Hands off altogether."

"I shall certainly speak to Tom when the time comes," said Mrs. Corey.

"And I shall ask leave to be absent from your discomfiture, my dear," answered her husband.

The son returned that afternoon, and confessed his surprise at finding his mother in Boston. He was so frank that she had not quite the courage to confess in turn why she had come, but trumped up an excuse.

"Well, mother," he said promptly, "I have made an engagement with Mr. Lapham."

"Have you, Tom?" she asked faintly.

"Yes. For the present I am going to have charge of his foreign correspondence, and if I see my way to the advantage I expect to find in it, I am going out to manage that side of his business in South America and Mexico. He's behaved very handsomely about it. He says that if it appears for our common interest, he shall pay me a salary as well as a commission. I've talked with Uncle Jim, and he thinks it's a good opening."

"Your Uncle Jim does?" queried Mrs. Corey in amaze.

"Yes; I consulted him the whole way through, and I've acted on his advice."

This seemed an incomprehensible treachery on her brother's part.

"Yes; I thought you would like to have me. And besides, I couldn't possibly have gone to any one so well fitted to advise me."

His mother said nothing. In fact, the mineral paint business, however painful its interest, was, for the moment, superseded by a more poignant anxiety. She began to feel her way cautiously toward this.

"Have you been talking about your business with Mr. Lapham all night?"

"Well, pretty much," said her son, with a guiltless laugh. "I went to see him yesterday afternoon, after I had gone over the whole ground with Uncle Jim, and Mr. Lapham asked me to go down with him and finish up."

"Down?" repeated Mrs. Corey.

"Yes, to Nantasket. He has a cottage down there."

"At Nantasket?" Mrs. Corey knitted her brows a little. "What in the world can a cottage at Nantasket be like?"

"Oh, very much like a 'cottage' anywhere. It has the usual allowance of red roof and veranda. There are the regulation rocks by the sea; and the big hotels on the beach about a mile off, flaring away with electric lights and roman-candles at night. We didn't have them at Nahant."

"No," said his mother. "Is Mrs. Lapham well? And her daughter?"

"Yes, I think so," said the young man. "The young ladies walked me down to the rocks in the usual way after dinner, and then I came back and talked paint with Mr. Lapham till midnight. We didn't settle anything till this morning coming up on the boat."

"What sort of people do they seem to be at home?"

"What sort? Well, I don't know that I noticed." Mrs. Corey permitted herself the first part of a sigh of relief; and her son laughed, but apparently not at her. "They're just reading 'Middlemarch.' They say there's so much talk about it. Oh, I suppose they're very good people. They seemed to be on very good terms with each other."

"I suppose it's the plain sister who's reading 'Middlemarch.' "

"Plain? Is she plain?" asked the young man, as if searching his consciousness. "Yes, it's the older one who does the reading, apparently. But I don't believe that even she overdoes it. They like to talk better. They reminded me of Southern people in that." The young man smiled, as if amused by some of his impressions of the Lapham family. "The living, as the country people call it, is tremendously good. The Colonel—he's a colonel—talked of the coffee as his wife's coffee, as if she had personally made it in the kitchen, though I believe it was merely inspired by her. And there was everything in the house that money could buy. But money has its limitations."

This was a fact which Mrs. Corey was beginning to realize more and more unpleasantly in her own life; but it seemed to bring her a certain comfort in its application to the Laphams. "Yes, there is a point where taste has to begin," she said.

"They seemed to want to apologize to me for not having more books," said Corey. "I don't know why they should. The Colonel said they bought a good many books, first and last; but apparently they don't take them to the sea-side."

"I dare say they *never* buy a *new* book. I've met some of these moneyed people lately, and they lavish on every conceivable luxury, and then borrow books, and get them in the cheap paper editions."

"I fancy that's the way with the Lapham family," said the young man, smilingly. "But they are very good people. The other daughter is humorous."

"Humorous?" Mrs. Corey knitted her brows in some perplexity. "Do you mean like Mrs. Sayre?" she asked, naming the lady whose name must come into every Boston mind when humor is mentioned.

"Oh, no; nothing like that. She never says anything that you can remember; nothing in flashes or ripples; nothing the least literary. But it's a sort of droll way of looking at things; or a droll medium through which things present themselves. I don't know. She tells what she's seen, and mimics a little."

"Oh," said Mrs. Corey, coldly. After a moment she asked: "And is Miss Irene as pretty as ever?"

"She's a wonderful complexion," said the son, unsatisfactorily. "I shall want to be by when father and Colonel Lapham meet," he added, with a smile.

"Ah, yes, your father!" said the mother, in that way in which a wife at once compassionates and censures her husband to their children.

"Do you think it's really going to be a trial to him?" asked the young man, quickly.

"No, no, I can't say it is. But I confess I wish it was some other business, Tom."

"Well, mother, I don't see why. The principal thing looked at now is the amount of money; and while I would rather starve than touch a dollar that was dirty with any sort of dishonesty——"

"Of course you would, my son!" interposed his mother, proudly.

"I shouldn't at all mind its having a little mineral paint on it. I'll use my influence with Colonel Lapham—if I ever have any—to have his paint scraped off the landscape."

"I suppose you wont begin till the autumn."

"Oh, yes, I shall," said the son, laughing at his mother's simple ignorance of business. "I shall begin to-morrow morning."

"To-morrow morning!"

"Yes. I've had my desk appointed already, and I shall be down there at nine in the morning to take possession."

"Tom!" cried his mother, "why do you think Mr. Lapham has taken you into business so readily? I've always heard that it was so hard for young men to get in."

"And do you think I found it easy with him? We had about twelve hours' solid talk."

"And you don't suppose it was any sort of—personal consideration?"

"Why, I don't know exactly what you mean, mother. I suppose he likes me."

Mrs. Corey could not say just what she meant. She answered, ineffectually enough:

"Yes. You wouldn't like it to be a favor, would you?"

"I think he's a man who may be trusted to look after his own interest. But I don't mind his beginning by liking me. It'll be my own fault if I don't make myself essential to him."

"Yes," said Mrs. Corey.

"Well," demanded her husband, at their first meeting after her interview with their son, "what did you say to Tom?"

"Very little, if anything. I found him with his mind made up, and it would only have distressed him if I had tried to change it."

"That is precisely what I said, my dear."

"Besides, he had talked the matter over fully with James, and seems to have been advised by him. I can't understand James."

"Oh! it's in regard to the paint, and not the princess, that he's made up his mind. Well, I think you were wise to let him alone, Anna. We represent a faded tradition. We don't really care what business a man is in, so it is large enough, and he doesn't advertise offensively; but we think it fine to affect reluctance."

"Do you really feel so, Bromfield?" asked his wife, seriously.

"Certainly I do. There was a long time in my misguided youth when I supposed myself some sort of porcelain; but it's a relief to be of the common clay, after all, and to know it. If I get broken, I can be easily replaced."

"If Tom must go into such a business," said Mrs. Corey, "I'm glad James approves of it."

"I'm afraid it wouldn't matter to Tom if he didn't; and I don't know that I should care," said Corey, betraying the fact that he had perhaps had a good deal of his brother-in-law's judgment in the course of his life. "You had better consult him in regard to Tom's marrying the princess."

"There is no necessity at present for that," said Mrs. Corey, with dignity. After a moment, she asked, "Should you feel quite so easy if it were a question of that, Bromfield?"

"It would be a little more personal."

"You feel about it as I do. Of course, we have both lived too long, and seen too much of the world, to suppose we can control such things. The child is good, I haven't the least doubt, and all those things can be managed so that they wouldn't disgrace us. But she has had a certain sort of bringing up. I should prefer Tom to marry a girl with another sort, and this business venture of his increases the chances that he wont. That's all."

"'Tis not so deep as a well, nor so wide as a church door, but 'twill serve.'"*

"I shouldn't like it."

"Well, it hasn't happened yet."

"Ah, you never can realize anything beforehand."

"Perhaps that has saved me some suffering. But you have at least the consolation of two anxieties at once. I always find that a great advantage. You can play one off against the other."

---

*Lines spoken by Mercutio in Shakespeare's *Romeo and Juliet* (act 3, scene 1), making light of his fatal wound.

Mrs. Corey drew a long breath as if she did not experience the suggested consolation; and she arranged to quit, the following afternoon, the scene of her defeat, which she had not had the courage to make a battle-field. Her son went down to see her off on the boat, after spending his first day at his desk in Lapham's office. He was in a gay humor, and she departed in a reflected gleam of his good spirits. He told her all about it, as he sat talking with her at the stern of the boat, lingering till the last moment, and then stepping ashore, with as little waste of time as Lapham himself, on the gang-plank which the deck-hands had laid hold of. He touched his hat to her from the wharf to reassure her of his escape from being carried away with her, and the next moment his smiling face hid itself in the crowd.

He walked on smiling up the long wharf, encumbered with trucks and hacks and piles of freight, and, taking his way through the deserted business streets beyond this bustle, made a point of passing the door of Lapham's warehouse, on the jambs of which his name and paint were lettered in black on a square ground of white. The door was still open, and Corey loitered a moment before it, tempted to go upstairs and fetch away some foreign letters which he had left on his desk, and which he thought he might finish up at home. He was in love with his work, and he felt the enthusiasm for it which nothing but the work we can do well inspires in us. He believed that he had found his place in the world, after a good deal of looking, and he had the relief, the repose, of fitting into it. Every little incident of the momentous, uneventful day was a pleasure in his mind, from his sitting down at his desk, to which Lapham's boy brought him the foreign letters, till his rising from it an hour ago. Lapham had been in view within his own office, but he had given Corey no formal reception, and had, in fact, not spoken to him till toward the end of the forenoon, when he suddenly came out of his den with some more letters in his hand, and after a brief "How d'ye do?" had spoken a few words about them, and left them with him. He was in his shirt-sleeves again, and his sanguine person seemed to radiate the heat with which he suffered. He did not go out to lunch, but had it brought to him in his office, where Corey saw him eating it before he left his own desk to go out and perch on a swinging seat before the long counter of a down-town restaurant. He observed that all the others lunched at twelve, and he resolved to anticipate his usual hour. When he returned, the pretty girl who had been clicking away at a type-writer all the morning was neatly putting out of sight the evidences of pie from the table where her machine stood, and was preparing to go on with her copying. In his office Lapham lay asleep in his arm-chair, with a newspaper over his face.

Now, while Corey lingered at the entrance to the stairway, these two came down the stairs together, and he heard Lapham saying, "Well, then, you better get a divorce."

He looked red and excited, and the girl's face, which she veiled at sight of Corey, showed traces of tears. She slipped round him into the street.

But Lapham stopped, and said, with the show of no feeling but surprise: "Hello, Corey! Did you want to go up?"

"Yes; there were some letters I hadn't quite got through with."

"You'll find Dennis up there. But I guess you better let them go till to-morrow. I always make it a rule to stop work when I'm done."

"Perhaps you're right," said Corey, yielding.

"Come along down as far as the boat with me. There's a little matter I want to talk over with you."

It was a business matter, and related to Corey's proposed connection with the house.

The next day the head book-keeper, who lunched at the long counter of the same restaurant with Corey, began to talk with him about Lapham. Walker had not apparently got his place by seniority; though, with his bald head, and round, smooth face, one might have taken him for a plump elder, if he had not looked equally like a robust infant. The thick, drabbish-yellow mustache was what arrested decision in either direction, and the prompt vigor of all his movements was that of a young man of thirty, which was really Walker's age. He knew, of course, who Corey was, and he had waited for a man who might look down on him socially to make the overtures toward something more than business acquaintance; but, these made, he was readily responsive, and drew freely on his philosophy of Lapham and his affairs.

"I think about the only difference between people in this world is that some know what they want, and some don't. Well, now," said Walker, beating the bottom of his salt-box to make the salt come out, "the old man knows what he wants every time. And generally he gets it. Yes, sir, he generally gets it. He knows what he's about, but I'll be blessed if the rest of us do half the time. Anyway, we don't till he's ready to let us. You take my position in most business houses. It's confidential. The head book-keeper knows right along pretty much everything the house has got in hand. I'll give you my word I don't. He may open up to you a little more in your department, but, as far as the rest of us go, he don't open up any more than an oyster on a hot brick. They say he had a partner once; I guess he's dead. I wouldn't like to be the old man's partner. Well, you see, this paint of his is like his heart's blood. Better not try to joke him about it. I've seen people come in occasionally and try it. They didn't get much fun out of it."

While he talked, Walker was plucking up morsels from his plate, tearing off pieces of French bread from the long loaf, and feeding them into his mouth in an impersonal way, as if he were firing up an engine.

"I suppose he thinks," suggested Corey, "that if he doesn't tell, nobody else will."

Walker took a draught of beer from his glass, and wiped the foam from his mustache.

"Oh, but he carries it too far! It's a weakness with him. He's just so about everything. Look at the way he keeps it up about that type-writer girl of his. You'd think she was some princess traveling incognito. There isn't one of us knows who she is, or where she came from, or who she belongs to. He brought her and her machine into the office one morning, and set 'em down at a table, and that's all there is about it, as far as we're concerned. It's pretty hard on the girl, for I guess she'd like to talk; and to any one that didn't know the old man—" Walker broke off and drained his glass of what was left in it.

Corey thought of the words he had overheard from Lapham to the girl. But he said, "She seems to be kept pretty busy."

"Oh, yes," said Walker; "there aint much loafing round the place, in any of the departments, from the old man's down. That's just what I say. He's got to work just twice as hard, if he wants to keep everything in his own mind. But he aint afraid of work. That's one good thing about him. And Miss Dewey has to keep step with the rest of us. But she don't look like one that would take to it naturally. Such a pretty girl as that generally thinks she does enough when she looks her prettiest."

"She's a pretty girl," said Corey, non-committally. "But I suppose a great many pretty girls have to earn their living."

"Don't any of 'em like to do it," returned the book-keeper. "They think it's a hardship, and I don't blame 'em. They have got a right to get married, and they ought to have the chance. And Miss Dewey's smart, too. She's as bright as a biscuit. I guess she's had trouble. I shouldn't be much more than half surprised if Miss Dewey wasn't Miss Dewey, or hadn't always been. Yes, sir," continued the book-keeper, who prolonged the talk as they walked back to Lapham's warehouse together, "I don't know exactly what it is,—it isn't any one thing in particular,—but I should say that girl had been married. I wouldn't speak so freely to any of the rest, Mr. Corey,—I want you to understand that,—and it isn't any of my business, anyway; but that's my opinion."

Corey made no reply, as he walked beside the book-keeper, who continued:

"It's curious what a difference marriage makes in people. Now, I know that I don't look any more like a bachelor of my age than I do like the man in the moon, and yet I couldn't say where the difference came in, to save me. And it's just so with a woman. The minute you catch sight of her face, there's something in it that tells you whether she's married or not. What do you suppose it is?"

"I'm sure I don't know," said Corey, willing to laugh away the topic. "And from what I read occasionally of some people who go about repeating their happiness, I shouldn't say that the intangible evidences were always unmistakable."

"Oh, of course," admitted Walker, easily surrendering his position. "All signs fail in dry weather. Hello! What's that?" He caught Corey by the arm, and they both stopped.

At a corner, half a block ahead of them, the summer noon solitude of the place was broken by a bit of drama. A man and woman issued from the intersecting street, and at the moment of coming into sight the man, who looked like a sailor, caught the woman by the arm, as if to detain her. A brief struggle ensued, the woman trying to free herself, and the man half coaxing, half scolding. The spectators could now see that he was drunk; but before they could decide whether it was a case for their interference or not, the woman suddenly set both hands against the man's breast and gave him a quick push. He lost his footing and tumbled into a heap in the gutter. The woman faltered an instant, as if to see whether he was seriously hurt, and then turned and ran.

When Corey and the book-keeper reëntered the office, Miss Dewey had finished her lunch, and was putting a sheet of paper into her type-writer. She looked up at them with her eyes of turquoise blue, under her low white forehead, with the hair neatly rippled over it, and then began to beat the keys of her machine.

IX

Lapham had the pride which comes of self-making, and he would not openly lower his crest to the young fellow he had taken into his business. He was going to be obviously master in his own place to every one; and during the hours of business he did nothing to distinguish Corey from the half-dozen other clerks and book-keepers in the outer office, but he was not silent about the fact that Bromfield Corey's son had taken a fancy to come to him. "Did you notice that fellow at the desk facing my type-writer girl? Well, sir, that's the son of Bromfield Corey—old Phillips Corey's grandson. And I'll say this for him, that there isn't a man in the office that looks after his work better. There isn't anything he's too good for. He's right here at nine every morning, before the clock gets in the word. I guess it's his grandfather coming out in him. He's got charge of the foreign correspondence. We're pushing the paint everywhere." He flattered himself that he did not lug the matter in. He had been warned against that by his wife, but he had the right to do Corey justice, and his brag took the form of illustration. "Talk about training for business—I tell you it's all in the man himself! I used to believe in what old Horace Greeley* said about college graduates being the poorest kind of horned cattle; but I've changed my mind a little. You take that fellow Corey. He's been through Harvard, and he's had about every advantage that a fellow could have. Been everywhere, and talks half a dozen languages like English. I suppose he's got money enough to live without lifting a hand, any more than his father does; son of Bromfield Corey, you know. But the thing was in him. He's a natural-born business man; and I've had many a fellow with me that had come up out of the street, and worked hard all his life, without ever losing his original opposition to the thing. But Corey likes it. I believe the fellow would like to stick at that desk of his night and day. I don't know where he got it. I guess it must be his grandfather, old Phillips Corey; it often skips a generation, you know. But what I say is, a thing has got to be born in a man; and if it ain't born in him,

*Founder and editor of the New York Tribune, whose best-known advice was "Go West, young man."

all the privations in the world won't put it there, and if it is, all the college training won't take it out."

Sometimes Lapham advanced these ideas at his own table, to a guest whom he had brought to Nantasket for the night. Then he suffered exposure and ridicule at the hands of his wife, when opportunity offered. She would not let him bring Corey down to Nantasket at all.

"No, indeed!" she said. "I am not going to have them think we're running after him. If he wants to see Irene, he can find out ways of doing it for himself."

"Who wants him to see Irene?" retorted the Colonel angrily.

"I do," said Mrs. Lapham. "And I want him to see her without any of your connivance, Silas. I'm not going to have it said that I put my girls at anybody. Why don't you invite some of your other clerks?"

"He ain't just like the other clerks. He's going to take charge of a part of the business. It's quite another thing."

"Oh, indeed!" said Mrs. Lapham vexatiously. "Then you *are* going to take a partner."

"I shall ask him down if I choose!" returned the Colonel, disdaining her insinuation.

His wife laughed with the fearlessness of a woman who knows her husband.

"But you won't choose when you've thought it over, Si." Then she applied an emollient to his chafed surface. "Don't you suppose I feel as you do about it? I know just how proud you are, and I'm not going to have you do anything that will make you feel meeching* afterward. You just let things take their course. If he wants Irene, he's going to find out some way of seeing her; and if he don't, all the plotting and planning in the world isn't going to make him."

"Who's plotting?" again retorted the Colonel, shuddering at the utterance of hopes and ambitions which a man hides with shame, but a woman talks over as freely and coolly as if they were items of a milliner's bill.

"Oh, not *you*!" exulted his wife. "I understand what *you* want. You

---

*Skulking, cowardly.

want to get this fellow, who is neither partner nor clerk, down here to talk business with him. Well, now, you just talk business with him at the office."

The only social attention which Lapham succeeded in offering Corey was to take him in his buggy, now and then, for a spin out over the Milldam. He kept the mare in town, and on a pleasant afternoon he liked to knock off early, as he phrased it, and let the mare out a little. Corey understood something about horses, though in a passionless way, and he would have preferred to talk business when obliged to talk horse. But he deferred to his business superior with the sense of discipline which is innate in the apparently insubordinate American nature. If Corey could hardly have helped feeling the social difference between Lapham and himself, in his presence he silenced his traditions, and showed him all the respect that he could have exacted from any of his clerks. He talked horse with him, and when the Colonel wished he talked house. Besides himself and his paint Lapham had not many other topics; and if he had a choice between the mare and the edifice on the water side of Beacon street, it was just now the latter. Sometimes, in driving in or out, he stopped at the house, and made Corey his guest there, if he might not at Nantasket; and one day it happened that the young man met Irene there again. She had come up with her mother alone, and they were in the house, interviewing the carpenter as before, when the Colonel jumped out of his buggy and cast anchor at the pavement. More exactly, Mrs. Lapham was interviewing the carpenter, and Irene was sitting in the bow-window on a trestle, and looking out at the driving. She saw him come up with her father, and bowed and blushed. Her father went on upstairs to find her mother, and Corey pulled up another trestle which he found in the back part of the room. The first floorings had been laid throughout the house, and the partitions had been lathed so that one could realize the shape of the interior.

"I suppose you will sit at this window a good deal," said the young man.

"Yes, I think it will be very nice. There's so much more going on than there is in the Square."

"It must be very interesting to you to see the house grow."

"It is. Only it doesn't seem to grow so fast as I expected."

"Why, I'm amazed at the progress your carpenter has made every time I come."

The girl looked down, and then lifting her eyes she said, with a sort of timorous appeal:

"I've been reading that book since you were down at Nantasket."

"Book?" repeated Corey, while she reddened with disappointment. "Oh, yes. 'Middlemarch.' Did you like it?"

"I haven't got through with it yet. Pen has finished it."

"What does she think of it?"

"Oh, I think she likes it very well. I haven't heard her talk about it much. Do you like it?"

"Yes; I liked it immensely. But it's several years since I read it."

"I didn't know it was so old. It's just got into the Seaside Library," she urged, with a little sense of injury in her tone.

"Oh, it hasn't been out such a very great while," said Corey, politely. "It came a little before 'Daniel Deronda.' "*

The girl was again silent. She followed the curl of a shaving on the floor with the point of her parasol.

"Do you like that Rosamond Vincy?"† she asked, without looking up.

Corey smiled in his kind way.

"I didn't suppose she was expected to have any friends. I can't say I liked her. But I don't think I disliked her so much as the author does. She's pretty hard on her good-looking"—he was going to say girls, but as if that might have been rather personal, he said—"people."

"Yes, that's what Pen says. She says she doesn't give her any chance to be good. She says she should have been just as bad as Rosamond if she had been in her place."

The young man laughed. "Your sister is very satirical, isn't she?"

"I don't know," said Irene, still intent upon the convolutions of the shaving. "She keeps us laughing. Papa thinks there's nobody that can talk like her." She gave the shaving a little toss from her, and took

---

*George Eliot's last novel, published in installments in 1876.

†Character in George Eliot's *Middlemarch*, a vain, restless, beautiful woman for whom her husband, a gifted physician, sacrifices his career.

the parasol up across her lap. The unworldliness of the Lapham girls did not extend to their dress; Irene's costume was very stylish, and she governed her head and shoulders stylishly. "We are going to have the back room upstairs for a music-room and library," she said abruptly.

"Yes?" returned Corey. "I should think that would be charming."

"We expected to have book-cases, but the architect wants to build the shelves in."

The fact seemed to be referred to Corey for his comment.

"It seems to me that would be the best way. They'll look like part of the room then. You can make them low, and hang your pictures above them."

"Yes, that's what he said." The girl looked out of the window in adding, "I presume with nice bindings it will look very well."

"Oh, nothing furnishes a room like books."

"No. There will have to be a good many of them."

"That depends upon the size of your room and the number of your shelves."

"Oh, of course! I presume," said Irene, thoughtfully, "we shall have to have Gibbon."*

"If you want to read him," said Corey, with a laugh of sympathy for an imaginable joke.

"We had a great deal about him at school. I believe we had one of his books. Mine's lost, but Pen will remember."

The young man looked at her, and then said, seriously, "You'll want Greene, of course, and Motley, and Parkman."†

"Yes. What kind of writers are they?"

"They're historians, too."

"Oh, yes; I remember now. That's what Gibbon was. Is it Gibbon or Gibbons?"

The young man decided the point with apparently superfluous delicacy. "Gibbon, I think."

---

*Edward Gibbon (1737–1794), the most celebrated British historian, author of The Decline and Fall of the Roman Empire.
†George Washington Greene (1811–1883), John Lothrop Motley (1814–1877), and Francis Parkman (1823–1893) were leading American historians.

"There used to be so many of them," said Irene, gayly. "I used to get them mixed up with each other, and I couldn't tell them from the poets. Should you want to have poetry?"

"Yes; I suppose some edition of the English poets."

"We don't any of us like poetry. Do you like it?"

"I'm afraid I don't very much," Corey owned. "But, of course, there was a time when Tennyson was a great deal more to me than he is now."

"We had something about him at school, too. I think I remember the name. I think we ought to have *all* the American poets."

"Well, not all. Five or six of the best: you want Longfellow and Bryant and Whittier and Holmes and Emerson and Lowell."*

The girl listened attentively, as if making mental note of the names.

"And Shakspere," she added. "Don't you like Shakspere's plays?"

"Oh, yes, very much."

"I used to be perfectly crazy about his plays. Don't you think 'Hamlet' is splendid? We had ever so much about Shakspere. Weren't you perfectly astonished when you found out how many other plays of his there were? I always thought there was nothing but 'Hamlet' and 'Romeo and Juliet' and 'Macbeth' and 'Richard III' and 'King Lear,' and that one that Robeson and Crane have—oh, yes! 'Comedy of Errors.' "

"Those are the ones they usually play," said Corey.

"I presume we shall have to have Scott's works,"† said Irene, returning to the question of books.

"Oh, yes."

"One of the girls used to think he was *great*. She was always talking about Scott." Irene made a pretty little, amiably contemptuous mouth. "He isn't American, though?" she suggested.

"No," said Corey; "he's Scotch, I believe."

Irene passed her glove over her forehead. "I always get him mixed

*Henry Wadsworth Longfellow (1807–1882), William Cullen Bryant (1794–1878), John Greenleaf Whittier (1807–1892), Oliver Wendell Holmes (1809–1894), Ralph Waldo Emerson (1803–1882), and James Russell Lowell (1819–1891), the best-known American poets of the day, were also friends and patrons of Howells.
†Sir Walter Scott (1771–1832), Scottish poet and author of a celebrated series of historical novels, including *Ivanhoe*.

up with Cooper.* Well, papa has got to get them. If we have a library, we have got to have books in it. Pen says it's perfectly ridiculous having one. But papa thinks whatever the architect says is right. He fought him hard enough at first. I don't see how any one can keep the poets and the historians and novelists separate in their mind. Of course papa will buy them if we say so. But I don't see how I'm ever going to tell him which ones." The joyous light faded out of her face and left it pensive.

"Why, if you like," said the young man, taking out his pencil, "I'll put down the names we've been talking about."

He clapped himself on his breast pockets to detect some lurking scrap of paper.

"Will you?" she cried delightedly. "Here! take one of my cards," and she pulled out her card-case. "The carpenter writes on a three-cornered block and puts it into his pocket, and it's so uncomfortable he can't help remembering it. Pen says she's going to adopt the three-cornered-block plan with papa."

"Thank you," said Corey. "I believe I'll use your card." He crossed over to her, and after a moment sat down on the trestle beside her. She looked over the card as he wrote. "Those are the ones we mentioned, but perhaps I'd better add a few others."

"Oh, thank you," she said, when he had written the card full on both sides. "He has got to get them in the nicest binding, too. I shall tell him about their helping to furnish the room, and then he can't object." She remained with the card, looking at it rather wistfully.

Perhaps Corey divined her trouble of mind.

"If he will take that to any book-seller, and tell him what bindings he wants, he will fill the order for him."

"Oh, thank you very much," she said, and put the card back into her card-case with great apparent relief. Then she turned her lovely face toward the young man, beaming with the triumph a woman feels in any bit of successful manœuvring, and began to talk with recovered gayety of other things, as if, having got rid of a matter

---

*James Fenimore Cooper (1789–1851), novelist who wrote stories of adventure and the American frontier, best known for his Leatherstocking Tales, including *The Last of the Mohicans*.

annoying out of all proportion to its importance, she was now going to indemnify herself.

Corey did not return to his own trestle. She found another shaving within reach of her parasol, and began poking that with it, and trying to follow it through its folds. Corey watched her awhile.

"You seem to have a great passion for playing with shavings," he said. "Is it a new one?"

"New what?"

"Passion."

"I don't know," she said, dropping her eyelids, and keeping on with her effort. She looked shyly aslant at him. "Perhaps you don't approve of playing with shavings?"

"Oh, yes, I do. I admire it very much. But it seems rather difficult. I've a great ambition to put my foot on the shaving's tail and hold it for you."

"Well," said the girl.

"Thank you," said the young man. He did so, and now she ran her parasol point easily through it. They looked at each other and laughed. "That was wonderful. Would you like to try another?" he asked.

"No, I thank you," she replied. "I think one will do."

They both laughed again, for whatever reason or no reason, and then the young girl became sober. To a girl everything a young man does is of significance; and if he holds a shaving down with his foot while she pokes through it with her parasol, she must ask herself what he means by it.

"They seem to be having rather a long interview with the carpenter today," said Irene, looking vaguely toward the ceiling. She turned with polite ceremony to Corey. "I'm afraid you're letting them keep you. You mustn't."

"Oh, no. You're letting me stay," he returned.

She bridled, and bit her lip for pleasure. "I presume they will be down before a great while. Don't you like the smell of the wood and the mortar? It's so fresh."

"Yes, it's delicious." He bent forward and picked up from the floor the shaving with which they had been playing, and put it to his nose. "It's like a flower. May I offer it to you?" he asked, as if it had been one.

"Oh, thank you, thank you!" She took it from him and put it into her belt, and then they both laughed once more.

Steps were heard descending. When the elder people reached the floor where they were sitting, Corey rose and presently took his leave.

"What makes you so solemn, 'Rene?" asked Mrs. Lapham.

"Solemn?" echoed the girl. "I'm not a bit solemn. What *can* you mean?"

Corey dined at home that evening, and as he sat looking across the table at his father, he said, "I wonder what the average literature of non-cultivated people is."

"Ah," said the elder, "I suspect the average is pretty low even with cultivated people. You don't read a great many books yourself, Tom."

"No, I don't," the young man confessed. "I read more books when I was with Stanton, last winter, than I had since I was a boy. But I read them because I must—there was nothing else to do. It wasn't because I was fond of reading. Still, I think I read with some sense of literature and the difference between authors. I don't suppose that people generally do that; I have met people who had read books without troubling themselves to find out even the author's name, much less trying to decide upon his quality. I suppose that's the way the vast majority of people read."

"Yes. If authors were not almost necessarily recluses, and ignorant of the ignorance about them, I don't see how they could endure it. Of course they are fated to be overwhelmed by oblivion at last, poor fellows; but to see it weltering all round them while they are in the very act of achieving immortality must be tremendously discouraging. I don't suppose that we who have the habit of reading, and at least a nodding acquaintance with literature, can imagine the bestial darkness of the great mass of people—even people whose houses are rich, and whose linen is purple and fine. But occasionally we get glimpses of it. I suppose you found the latest publications lying all about in Lapham cottage when you were down there?"

Young Corey laughed. "It wasn't exactly cumbered with them."

"No?"

"To tell the truth, I don't suppose they ever buy books. The young ladies get novels that they hear talked of out of the circulating library."

"Had they knowledge enough to be ashamed of their ignorance?"

"Yes, in certain ways—to a certain degree."

"It's a curious thing, this thing we call civilization," said the elder, musingly. "We think it is an affair of epochs and of nations. It's really an affair of individuals. One brother will be civilized and the other a barbarian. I've occasionally met young girls who were so brutally, insolently, willfully indifferent to the arts which make civilization that they ought to have been clothed in the skins of wild beasts and gone about barefoot with clubs over their shoulders. Yet they were of polite origin, and their parents were at least respectful of the things that these young animals despised."

"I don't think that is exactly the case with the Lapham family," said the son, smiling. "The father and mother rather apologized about not getting time to read, and the young ladies by no means scorned it."

"They are quite advanced!"

"They are going to have a library in their Beacon street house."

"Oh, poor things! How are they ever going to get the books together?"

"Well, sir," said the son, coloring a little, "I have been indirectly applied to for help."

"You, Tom!" His father dropped back in his chair and laughed.

"I recommended the standard authors," said the son.

"Oh, I never supposed your prudence would be at fault, Tom!"

"But seriously," said the young man, generously smiling in sympathy with his father's enjoyment, "they're not unintelligent people. They are very quick, and they are shrewd and sensible."

"I have no doubt that some of the Sioux are so. But that is not saying that they are civilized. All civilization comes through literature now, especially in our country. A Greek got his civilization by talking and looking, and in some measure a Parisian may still do it. But we, who live remote from history and monuments, we must read or we must barbarize. Once we were softened, if not polished, by religion; but I suspect that the pulpit counts for much less now in civilizing."

"They're enormous devourers of newspapers, and theatergoers;

and they go a great deal to lectures. The Colonel prefers them with the stereopticon."

"They might get a something in that way," said the elder, thoughtfully. "Yes, I suppose one must take those things into account—especially the newspapers and the lectures. I doubt if the theater is a factor in civilization among us. I dare say it doesn't deprave a great deal, but from what I've seen of it I should say that it was intellectually degrading. Perhaps they might get some sort of lift from it; I don't know. Tom!" he added, after a moment's reflection. "I really think I ought to see this patron of yours. Don't you think it would be rather decent in me to make his acquaintance?"

"Well, if you have the fancy, sir," said the young man. "But there's no sort of obligation. Colonel Lapham would be the last man in the world to want to give our relation any sort of social character. The meeting will come about in the natural course of things."

"Ah, I didn't intend to propose anything immediate," said the father. "One can't do anything in the summer, and I should prefer your mother's superintendence. Still, I can't rid myself of the idea of a dinner. It appears to me that there ought to be a dinner."

"Oh, pray don't feel that there's any necessity."

"Well," said the elder, with easy resignation, "there's at least no hurry."

"There is one thing I don't like," said Lapham, in the course of one of those talks which came up between his wife and himself concerning Corey, "or at least I don't understand it; and that's the way his father behaves. I don't want to force myself on any man; but it seems to me pretty queer the way he holds off. I should think he would take enough interest in his son to want to know something about his business. What is he afraid of?" demanded Lapham angrily. "Does he think I'm going to jump at a chance to get in with him, if he gives me one? He's mightily mistaken if he does. I don't want to know him."

"Silas," said his wife, making a wife's free version of her husband's words, and replying to their spirit rather than their letter, "I hope you never said a word to Mr. Corey to let him know the way you feel."

"I never mentioned his father to him!" roared the Colonel. "That's the way I feel about it!"

"Because it would spoil everything. I wouldn't have them think we cared the least thing in the world for their acquaintance. We shouldn't be a bit better off. We don't know the same people they do, and we don't care for the same kind of things."

Lapham was breathless with resentment of his wife's implication. "Don't I tell you," he gasped, "that I don't want to know them? Who began it? They're friends of yours if they're anybody's."

"They're distant acquaintances of mine," returned Mrs. Lapham quietly; "and this young Corey is a clerk of yours. And I want we should hold ourselves so that when they get ready to make the advances we can meet them half-way or not, just as we choose."

"That's what grinds me," cried her husband. "Why should we wait for them to make the advances? Why shouldn't we make 'em? Are they any better than we are? My note of hand would be worth ten times what Bromfield Corey's is on the street to-day. And I made my money. I haven't loafed my life away."

"Oh, it isn't what you've got, and it isn't what you've done exactly. It's what you are."

"Well, then, what's the difference?"

"None that really amounts to anything, or that need give you any trouble, if you don't think of it. But he's been all his life in society, and he knows just what to say and what to do, and he can talk about the things that society people like to talk about, and you—can't."

Lapham gave a furious snort. "And does that make him any better?"

"No. But it puts him where he can make the advances without demeaning himself, and it puts you where you can't. Now, look here, Silas Lapham! You understand this thing as well as I do. You know that I appreciate you, and that I'd sooner die than have you humble yourself to a living soul. But I'm not going to have you coming to me, and pretending that you can meet Bromfield Corey as an equal on his own ground. You can't. He's got a better education than you, and if he hasn't got more brains than you, he's got different. And he and his wife, and their fathers and grandfathers before 'em, have always had a high position, and you can't help it. If you want to know them, you've got to let them make the advances. If you don't, all well and good."

"I guess," said the chafed and vanquished Colonel, after a moment for swallowing the pill, "that they'd have been in a pretty fix if you'd waited to let them make the advances last summer."

"That was a different thing altogether. I didn't know who they were, or may be I should have waited. But all I say now is that if you've got young Corey into business with you, in hopes of our getting into society with his father, you better ship him at once. For I ain't going to have it on that basis."

"Who wants to have it on that basis?" retorted her husband.

"Nobody, if you don't," said Mrs. Lapham tranquilly.

Irene had come home with the shaving in her belt, unnoticed by her father, and unquestioned by her mother. But her sister saw it at once, and asked her what she was doing with it.

"Oh, nothing," said Irene, with a joyful smile of self-betrayal, taking the shaving carefully out, and laying it among the laces and ribbons in her drawer.

"Hadn't you better put it in water, 'Rene? It'll be all wilted by morning," said Pen.

"You mean thing!" cried the happy girl. "It isn't a flower!"

"Oh, I thought it was a whole bouquet. Who gave it to you?"

"I sha'n't tell you," said Irene saucily.

"Oh, well, never mind. Did you know Mr. Corey had been down here this afternoon, walking on the beach with me?"

"He wasn't—he wasn't at all! He was at the house with me. There! I've caught you fairly."

"Is that so?" drawled Penelope. "Then I never could guess who gave you that precious shaving."

"No, you couldn't!" said Irene, flushing beautifully. "And you may guess, and you may guess, and you may guess!" With her lovely eyes she coaxed her sister to keep on teasing her, and Penelope continued the comedy with the patience that women have for such things.

"Well, I'm not going to try, if it's no use. But I didn't know it had got to be the fashion to give shavings instead of flowers. But there's some sense in it. They can be used for kindlings when they get old, and you can't do anything with old flowers. Perhaps he'll get to sending 'em by the barrel."

Irene laughed for pleasure in this tormenting. "Oh, Pen, I want to tell you how it all happened."

"Oh, he did give it to you, then? Well, I guess I don't care to hear."

"You shall, and you've got to!" Irene ran and caught her sister, who feigned to be going out of the room, and pushed her into a chair. "There, now!" She pulled up another chair, and hemmed her in with it. "He came over, and sat down on the trestle alongside of me——"

"What? As close as you are to me now?"

"You wretch! I will give it to you! No, at a proper distance. And here was this shaving on the floor, that I'd been poking with my parasol——"

"To hide your embarrassment."

"Pshaw! I wasn't a bit embarrassed. I was just as much at my ease! And then he asked me to let him hold the shaving down with his foot, while I went on with my poking. And I said yes he might——"

"What a bold girl! You said he might hold a shaving down for you?"

"And then—and then—" continued Irene, lifting her eyes absently, and losing herself in the beatific recollection, "and then—Oh, yes! Then I asked him if he didn't like the smell of pine shavings. And then he picked it up, and said it smelt like a flower. And then he asked if he might offer it to me—just for a joke, you know. And I took it, and stuck it in my belt. And we had such a laugh! We got into a regular gale. And oh, Pen, what do you suppose he meant by it?" She suddenly caught herself to her sister's breast, and hid her burning face on her shoulder.

"Well, there used to be a book about the language of flowers. But I never knew much about the language of shavings, and I can't say exactly——"

"Oh, don't—don't, Pen!" and here Irene gave over laughing, and began to sob in her sister's arms.

"Why, 'Rene!" cried the elder girl.

"You know he didn't mean anything. He doesn't care a bit about me. He hates me! He despises me! Oh, what shall I do?"

A trouble passed over the face of the sister as she silently comforted the child in her arms; then the drolling light came back into her eyes. "Well, 'Rene, you haven't got to do anything. That's one advantage girls have got—if it is an advantage. I'm not always sure."

Irene's tears turned to laughing again. When she lifted her head it was to look into the mirror confronting them, where her beauty showed all the more brilliant for the shower that had passed over it. She seemed to gather courage from the sight.

"It must be awful to have to *do*," she said, smiling into her own face. "I don't see how they ever can."

"Some of 'em can't—especially when there's such a tearing beauty around."

"Oh, pshaw, Pen! You know that isn't so. You've got a real pretty mouth, Pen," she added thoughtfully, surveying the feature in the glass, and then pouting her own lips for the sake of that effect on them.

"It's a useful mouth," Penelope admitted; "I don't believe I could get along without it now, I've had it so long."

"It's got such a funny expression—just the mate of the look in your eyes; as if you were just going to say something ridiculous. He said, the very first time he saw you, that he knew you were humorous."

"Is it possible? It must be so, if the Grand Mogul said it. Why didn't you tell me so before, and not let me keep on going round just like a common person?"

Irene laughed as if she liked to have her sister take his praises in that way rather than another. "I've got such a stiff, prim kind of mouth," she said, drawing it down, and then looking anxiously at it.

"I hope you didn't put on that expression when he offered you the shaving. If you did, I don't believe he'll ever give you another splinter."

The severe mouth broke into a lovely laugh, and then pressed itself in a kiss against Penelope's cheek.

"There! Be done, you silly thing! I'm not going to have you accepting *me* before I've offered myself, *anyway*." She freed herself from her sister's embrace, and ran from her round the room.

Irene pursued her, in the need of hiding her face against her shoulder again. "Oh, Pen! Oh, Pen!" she cried.

The next day, at the first moment of finding herself alone with her eldest daughter, Mrs. Lapham asked, as if knowing that Penelope must have already made it subject of inquiry: "What was Irene doing with that shaving in her belt yesterday?"

"Oh, just some nonsense of hers with Mr. Corey. He gave it to her at the new house." Penelope did not choose to look up and meet her mother's grave glance.

"What do you think he meant by it?"

Penelope repeated Irene's account of the affair, and her mother listened without seeming to derive much encouragement from it.

"He doesn't seem like one to flirt with her," she said at last. Then, after a thoughtful pause: "Irene is as good a girl as ever breathed, and she's a perfect beauty. But I should hate the day when a daughter of mine was married for her beauty."

"You're safe as far as I'm concerned, mother."

Mrs. Lapham smiled ruefully. "She isn't really equal to him, Pen. I misdoubted that from the first, and it's been borne in upon me more and more ever since. She hasn't mind enough."

"I didn't know that a man fell in love with a girl's intellect," said Penelope quietly.

"Oh, no. He hasn't fallen in love with Irene at all. If he had, it wouldn't matter about the intellect."

Penelope let the self-contradiction pass.

"Perhaps he has, after all."

"No," said Mrs. Lapham. "She pleases him when he sees her. But he doesn't try to see her."

"He has no chance. You won't let father bring him here."

"He would find excuses to come without being brought, if he wished to come," said the mother. "But she isn't in his mind enough to make him. He goes away and doesn't think anything more about her. She's a child. She's a good child, and I shall always say it; but she's nothing but a child. No, she's got to forget him."

"Perhaps that won't be so easy."

"No, I presume not. And now your father has got the notion in his head, and he will move heaven and earth to bring it to pass. I can see that he's always thinking about it."

"The Colonel has a will of his own," observed the girl, rocking to and fro where she sat looking at her mother.

"I wish we had never met them!" cried Mrs. Lapham. "I wish we had never thought of building! I wish he had kept away from your father's business!"

"Well, it's too late now, mother," said the girl. "Perhaps it isn't so bad as you think."

"Well, we must stand it, anyway," said Mrs. Lapham, with the grim antique Yankee submission.

"Oh, yes, we've got to stand it," said Penelope, with the quaint modern American fatalism.

X

It was late June, almost July, when Corey took up his life in Boston again, where the summer slips away so easily. If you go out of town early, it seems a very long summer when you come back in October; but if you stay, it passes swiftly, and, seen foreshortened in its flight, seems scarcely a month's length. It has its days of heat, when it is very hot, but for the most part it is cool, with baths of the east wind that seem to saturate the soul with delicious freshness. Then there are stretches of gray, westerly weather, when the air is full of the sentiment of early autumn, and the frying of the grasshopper in the blossomed weed of the vacant lots on the Back Bay is intershot with the carol of crickets; and the yellowing leaf on the long slope of Mt. Vernon street smites the sauntering observer with tender melancholy. The caterpillar, gorged with the spoil of the lindens on Chestnut, and weaving his own shroud about him in his lodgment on the brickwork, records the passing of summer by mid-July; and if after that comes August, its breath is thick and short, and September is upon the sojourner before he has fairly had time to philosophize the character of the town out of season.

But it must have appeared that its most characteristic feature was the absence of everybody he knew. This was one of the things that commended Boston to Bromfield Corey during the summer; and if his son had any qualms about the life he had entered upon with such vigor, it must have been a relief to him that there was scarcely a soul left to wonder or pity. By the time people got back to town the fact of his connection with the mineral paint man would be an old story, heard afar off with different degrees of surprise, and considered with different degrees of indifference. A man has not reached the age of twenty-six in any community where he was born and reared without having had his capacity pretty well ascertained; and in Boston the analysis is conducted with an unsparing thoroughness which may fitly impress the un-Bostonian mind, darkened by the popular superstition that the Bostonians blindly admire one another. A man's qualities are sifted as closely in Boston as they doubtless were in Florence or Athens; and, if final mercy was shown in those cities because a man was, with all his limitations, an Athenian or Florentine, some abatement might as justly be made in Boston for like reason. Corey's powers had been gauged in college, and he had not given his world reason to think very differently of him since he came out of college. He was rated as an energetic fellow, a little indefinite in aim, with the smallest amount of inspiration that can save a man from being commonplace. If he was not commonplace, it was through nothing remarkable in his mind, which was simply clear and practical, but through some combination of qualities of the heart that made men trust him, and women call him sweet—a word of theirs which conveys otherwise indefinable excellences. Some of the more nervous and excitable said that Tom Corey was as sweet as he could live; but this perhaps meant no more than the word alone. No man ever had a son less like him than Bromfield Corey. If Tom Corey had ever said a witty thing, no one could remember it; and yet the father had never said a witty thing to a more sympathetic listener than his own son. The clear mind which produced nothing but practical results reflected everything with charming lucidity; and it must have been this which endeared Tom Corey to every one who spoke ten words with him. In a city where people have good reason for liking to shine, a man who did not care to shine must be little short of universally acceptable without any other effort for popularity; and those who admired and enjoyed Bromfield Corey loved his son. Yet, when it came to accounting for Tom Corey, as it often did in a community where every one's generation is known to the remotest degrees of cousinship, they could not trace his sweetness to his mother, for neither Anna Bellingham nor any of her family, though they were so many blocks of Wenham ice for purity and rectangularity, had ever had any such savor; and, in fact, it was to his father, whose habit of talk wronged it in himself, that they had to turn for this quality of the son's. They traced to the mother the traits of practicality and common sense in which he bordered upon the commonplace, and which, when they had dwelt upon them, made him seem hardly worth the close inquiry they had given him.

While the summer wore away he came and went methodically about his business, as if it had been the business of his life, sharing his father's bachelor liberty and solitude, and expecting with equal patience the return of his mother and sisters in the autumn. Once or twice he found time to run down to Mt. Desert and see them; and then he heard how the Philadelphia and New York people were getting in everywhere, and was given reason to regret the house at Nahant which he had urged to be sold. He came back and applied himself to his desk with a devotion that was exemplary rather than necessary; for Lapham made no difficulty about the brief absences which he asked, and set no term to the apprenticeship that Corey was serving in the office before setting off upon that mission to South America in the early winter, for which no date had yet been fixed.

The summer was a dull season for the paint as well as for everything else. Till things should brisk up, as Lapham said, in the fall, he was letting the new house take a great deal of his time. Æsthetic ideas had never been intelligibly presented to him before, and he found a delight in apprehending them that was very grateful to his imaginative architect. At the beginning, the architect had foreboded a series of mortifying defeats and disastrous victories in his encounters with his client; but he had never had a client who could be more reasonably led on from one outlay to another. It appeared that Lapham required but to understand or feel the beautiful effect intended, and he was ready to pay for it. His bull-headed pride was concerned in a thing which the architect made him see, and then he believed that he had seen it himself, perhaps conceived it. In some measure the architect seemed to share his delusion, and freely said that Lapham was very suggestive. Together they blocked out windows here, and bricked them up there; they changed doors and passages; pulled down cornices and replaced them with others of different design; experimented with costly devices of decoration, and went to extravagant lengths in novelties of finish. Mrs. Lapham, beginning with a woman's adventurousness in the unknown region, took fright at the reckless outlay at last, and refused to let her husband pass a certain limit. He tried to make her believe that a far-seeing economy dictated the expense; and that if he put the money into the house, he could get it out any time by selling it. She would not be persuaded.

"I don't want you should sell it. And you've put more money into it now than you'll ever get out again, unless you can find as big a goose to buy it, and that isn't likely. No, sir! You just stop at a hundred thousand, and don't you let him get you a cent beyond. Why, you're perfectly bewitched with that fellow! You've lost your head, Silas Lapham, and if you don't look out you'll lose your money too."

The Colonel laughed; he liked her to talk that way, and promised he would hold up awhile.

"But there's no call to feel anxious, Pert. It's only a question what to do with the money. I can reinvest it; but I never had so much of it to spend before."

"Spend it, then," said his wife; "don't throw it away! And how came you to have so much more money than you know what to do with, Silas Lapham?" she added.

"Oh, I've made a very good thing in stocks lately."

"In stocks? When did you take up gambling for a living?"

"Gambling? Stuff! What gambling? Who said it was gambling?"

"You have; many a time."

"Oh, yes, buying and selling on a margin. But this was a *bona fide* transaction. I bought at forty-three for an investment, and I sold at a hundred and seven; and the money passed both times."

"Well, you better let stocks alone," said his wife, with the conservatism of her sex. "Next time you'll buy at a hundred and seven and sell at forty-three. Then where'll you be?"

"Left," admitted the Colonel.

"You better stick to paint awhile yet."

The Colonel enjoyed this, too, and laughed again with the ease of a man who knows what he is about. A few days after that he came down to Nantasket with the radiant air which he wore when he had done a good thing in business and wanted his wife's sympathy. He did not say anything of what had happened till he was alone with her in their own room; but he was very gay the whole evening, and made several jokes which Penelope said nothing but very great prosperity could excuse: they all understood these moods of his.

"Well, what is it, Silas?" asked his wife when the time came. "Any more big-bugs wanting to go into the mineral paint business with you?"

"Something better than that."

"I could think of a good many better things," said his wife, with a sigh of latent bitterness. "What's this one?"

"I've had a visitor."

"Who?"

"Can't you guess?"

"I don't want to try. Who was it?"

"Rogers."

Mrs. Lapham sat down with her hands in her lap, and stared at the smile on her husband's face, where he sat facing her.

"I guess you wouldn't want to joke on that subject, Si," she said, a little hoarsely, "and you wouldn't grin about it unless you had some good news. I don't know what the miracle is, but if you could tell quick——"

She stopped like one who can say no more.

"I will, Persis," said her husband, and with that awed tone in which he rarely spoke of anything but the virtues of his paint. "He came to borrow money of me, and I lent him it. That's the short of it. The long——"

"Go on," said his wife, with gentle patience.

"Well, Pert, I was never so much astonished in my life as I was to see that man come into my office. You might have knocked me down with—I don't know what."

"I don't wonder. Go on!"

"And he was as much embarrassed as I was. There we stood, gaping at each other, and I hadn't hardly sense enough to ask him to take a chair. I don't know just how we got at it. And I don't remember just how it was that he said he came to come to me. But he had got hold of a patent right that he wanted to go into on a large scale, and there he was wanting me to supply him the funds."

"Go on!" said Mrs. Lapham, with her voice further in her throat.

"I never felt the way you did about Rogers, but I know how you always did feel, and I guess I surprised him with my answer. He had brought along a lot of stock as security——"

"You didn't take it, Silas!" his wife flashed out.

"Yes, I did, though," said Lapham. "You wait. We settled our business, and then we went into the old thing, from the very start. And we talked it all over. And when we got through we shook hands. Well, I don't know when it's done me so much good to shake hands with anybody."

"And you told him—you owned up to him that you were in the wrong, Silas?"

"No, I didn't," returned the Colonel, promptly; "for I wasn't. And before we got through, I guess he saw it the same as I did."

"Oh, no matter! so you had the chance to show how you felt."

"But I never felt that way," persisted the Colonel. "I've lent him the money, and I've kept his stocks. And he got what he wanted out of me."

"Give him back his stocks!"

"No, I sha'n't. Rogers came to borrow. He didn't come to beg. You needn't be troubled about his stocks. They're going to come up in time; but just now they're so low down that no bank would take them as security, and I've got to hold them till they do rise. I hope you're satisfied now, Persis," said her husband; and he looked at her with the willingness to receive the reward of a good action which we all feel when we have performed one. "I lent him the money you kept me from spending on the house."

"Truly, Si? Well, I'm satisfied," said Mrs. Lapham, with a deep, tremulous breath. "The Lord has been good to you, Silas," she continued, solemnly. "You may laugh if you choose, and I don't know as I believe in his interfering a great deal; but I believe he's interfered this time; and I tell you, Silas, it ain't always he gives people a chance to make it up to others in this life. I've been afraid you'd die, Silas, before you got the chance; but he's let you live to make it up to Rogers."

"I'm glad to be let live," said Lapham, stubbornly; "but I hadn't anything to make up to Milton K. Rogers. And if God has let me live for that——"

"Oh, say what you please, Si! Say what you please, now you've done it! I sha'n't stop you. You've taken the one spot—the one *speck*— off you that was ever there, and I'm satisfied."

"There wa'n't ever any speck there," Lapham held out, lapsing more and more into his vernacular; "and what I done, I done for you, Persis."

"And I thank you for your own soul's sake, Silas."

"I guess my soul's all right," said Lapham.

"And I want you should promise me one thing more."

"Thought you said you were satisfied?"

"I am. But I want you should promise me this: that you won't let anything tempt you—anything!—to ever trouble Rogers for that money you lent him. No matter what happens—no matter if you lose it all. Do you promise?"

"Why, I don't ever *expect* to press him for it. That's what I said to myself when I lent it. And of course I'm glad to have that old trouble healed up. I don't think I ever did Rogers any wrong, and I never did think so; but if I did do it—if I did—I'm willing to call it square, if I never see a cent of my money back again."

"Well, that's all," said his wife.

They did not celebrate his reconciliation with his old enemy—for such they had always felt him to be since he ceased to be an ally—by any show of joy or affection. It was not in their tradition, as stoical for the woman as for the man, that they should kiss or embrace each other at such a moment. She was content to have told him that he had done his duty, and he was content with her saying that. But before she slept she found words to add that she always feared the selfish part he had acted toward Rogers had weakened him, and left him less able to overcome any temptation that might beset him; and that was one reason why she could never be easy about it. Now she should never fear for him again.

This time he did not explicitly deny her forgiving impeachment.

"Well, it's all past and gone now, anyway; and I don't want you should think anything more about it."

He was man enough to take advantage of the high favor in which he stood when he went up to town, and to abuse it by bringing Corey down to supper. His wife could not help condoning the sin of disobedience in him at such a time. Penelope said that between the admiration she felt for the Colonel's boldness and her mother's forbearance, she was hardly in a state to entertain company that evening; but she did what she could.

Irene liked being talked to better than talking, and when her sister was by she was always, tacitly or explicitly, referring to her for confirmation of what she said. She was content to sit and look pretty as she looked at the young man and listened to her sister's drolling. She laughed, and kept glancing at Corey to make sure that he was understanding her. When they went out on the veranda to see the moon on the water, Penelope led the way and Irene followed.

They did not look at the moonlight long. The young man perched on the rail of the veranda, and Irene took one of the red-painted rocking-chairs where she could conveniently look at him and at her sister, who sat leaning forward lazily and running on, as the phrase is. That low, crooning note of hers was delicious; her face, glimpsed now and then in the moonlight as she turned it or lifted it a little, had a fascination which kept his eye. Her talk was very unliterary, and its effect seemed hardly conscious. She was far from epigram in her funning. She told of this trifle and that; she sketched the characters and looks of people who had interested her, and nothing seemed to have escaped her notice; she mimicked a little, but not much; she suggested, and then the affair represented itself as if without her agency. She did not laugh; when Corey stopped, she made a soft cluck in her throat, as if she liked his being amused, and went on again.

The Colonel, left alone with his wife for the first time since he had come from town, made haste to take the word. "Well, Pert, I've arranged the whole thing with Rogers, and I hope you'll be satisfied to know that he owes me twenty thousand dollars, and that I've got security from him to the amount of a fourth of that, if I was to force his stocks to a sale."

"How came he to come down with you?" asked Mrs. Lapham.

"Who? Rogers?"

"Mr. Corey."

"Corey? Oh!" said Lapham, affecting not to have thought she could mean Corey. "He proposed it."

"Likely!" jeered his wife, but with perfect amiability.

"It's so," protested the Colonel. "We got talking about a matter just before I left, and he walked down to the boat with me; and then he said if I didn't mind he guessed he'd come along down and go back on the return boat. Of course I couldn't let him do that."

"It's well for you you couldn't."

"And I couldn't do less than bring him here to tea."

"Oh, certainly not."

"But he ain't going to stay the night—unless," faltered Lapham, "you want him to."

"Oh, of course, I want him to! I guess he'll stay, probably."

"Well, you know how crowded that last boat always is, and he can't get any other now."

Mrs. Lapham laughed at the simple wile. "I hope you'll be just as well satisfied, Si, if it turns out he doesn't want Irene after all."

"Pshaw, Persis! What are you always bringing that up for?" pleaded the Colonel. Then he fell silent, and presently his rude, strong face was clouded with an unconscious frown.

"There!" cried his wife, startling him from his abstraction. "I see how you'd feel; and I hope that you'll remember who you've got to blame."

"I'll risk it," said Lapham, with the confidence of a man used to success.

From the veranda the sound of Penelope's lazy tone came through the closed windows, with joyous laughter from Irene and peals from Corey.

"Listen to that!" said her father within, swelling up with inexpressible satisfaction. "That girl can talk for twenty, right straight along. She's better than a circus any day. I wonder what she's up to now."

"Oh, she's probably getting off some of those yarns of hers, or telling about some people. She can't step out of the house without coming back with more things to talk about than most folks would bring back from Japan. There ain't a ridiculous person she's ever seen but what she's got something from them to make you laugh at; and I don't believe we've ever had anybody in the house since the girl could talk that she hain't got some saying from, or some trick that'll pint 'em out so't you can see 'em and hear 'em. Sometimes I want to stop her; but when she gets into one of her gales there ain't any standing up against her. I guess it's lucky for Irene that she's got Pen there to help entertain her company. I can't ever feel down where Pen is."

"That's so," said the Colonel. "And I guess she's got about as much culture as any of them. Don't you?"

"She reads a great deal," admitted her mother. "She seems to be at it the whole while. I don't want she should injure her health, and sometimes I feel like snatchin' the books away from her. I don't know as it's good for a girl to read so much, anyway, especially novels. I don't want she should get notions."

"Oh, I guess Pen'll know how to take care of herself," said Lapham.

"She's got sense enough. But she ain't so practical as Irene. She's more up in the clouds—more of what you may call a dreamer. Irene's wide-awake every minute; and I declare, any one to see these two together when there's anything to be done, or any lead to be taken, would say Irene was the oldest, nine times out of ten. It's only when they get to talking that you can see Pen's got twice as much brains."

"Well," said Lapham, tacitly granting this point, and leaning back in his chair in supreme content. "Did you ever see much nicer girls anywhere?"

His wife laughed at his pride. "I presume they're as much swans as anybody's geese."

"No; but honestly, now!"

"Oh, they'll do; but don't you be silly, if you can help it, Si."

The young people came in, and Corey said it was time for his boat. Mrs. Lapham pressed him to stay, but he persisted, and he would not let the Colonel send him to the boat; he said he would rather walk. Outside, he pushed along toward the boat, which presently he could see lying at her landing in the bay, across the sandy tract to the left of the hotels. From time to time he almost stopped in his rapid walk, as a man does whose mind is in a pleasant tumult; and then he went forward at a swifter pace.

"She's charming!" he said, and he thought he had spoken aloud. He found himself floundering about in the deep sand, wide of the path; he got back to it, and reached the boat just before she started. The clerk came to take his fare, and Corey looked radiantly up at him in his lantern-light, with a smile that he must have been wearing a long time; his cheek was stiff with it. Once some people who stood near him edged suddenly and fearfully away, and then he suspected himself of having laughed outright.

XI

Corey put off his set smile with the help of a frown, of which he first became aware after reaching home, when his father asked:

"Anything gone wrong with your department of the fine arts today, Tom?"

"Oh, no—no, sir," said the son, instantly relieving his brows from the strain upon them, and beaming again. "But I was thinking whether you were not perhaps right in your impression that it might be well for you to make Colonel Lapham's acquaintance before a great while."

"Has he been suggesting it in any way?" asked Bromfield Corey, laying aside his book and taking his lean knee between his clasped hands.

"Oh, not at all!" the young man hastened to reply. "I was merely thinking whether it might not begin to seem intentional, your not doing it."

"Well, Tom, you know I have been leaving it altogether to you——"

"Oh, I understand, of course, and I didn't mean to urge anything of the kind——"

"You are so very much more of a Bostonian than I am, you know, that I've been waiting your motion in entire confidence that you would know just what to do, and when to do it. If I had been left quite to my own lawless impulses, I think I should have called upon your *padrone* at once. It seems to me that my father would have found some way of showing that he expected as much as that from people placed in the relation to him that we hold to Colonel Lapham."

"Do you think so?" asked the young man.

"Yes. But you know I don't pretend to be an authority in such matters. As far as they go, I am always in the hands of your mother and you children."

"I'm very sorry, sir. I had no idea I was overruling your judgment. I only wanted to spare you a formality that didn't seem quite a necessity yet. I'm very sorry," he said again, and this time with more comprehensive regret. "I shouldn't like to have seemed remiss with a man who has been so considerate of me. They are all very good-natured."

"I dare say," said Bromfield Corey, with the satisfaction which no elder can help feeling in disabling the judgment of a younger man, "that it won't be too late if I go down to your office with you to-morrow."

"No, no. I didn't imagine your doing it at once, sir."

"Ah, but nothing can prevent me from doing a thing when once I take the bit in my teeth," said the father, with the pleasure which men of weak will sometimes take in recognizing their weakness. "How does their new house get on?"

"I believe they expect to be in it before New Year's."

"Will they be a great addition to society?" asked Bromfield Corey, with unimpeachable seriousness.

"I don't quite know what you mean," returned the son, a little uneasily.

"Ah, I see that you do, Tom."

"No one can help feeling that they are all people of good sense and—right ideas."

"Oh, that won't do. If society took in all the people of right ideas and good sense, it would expand beyond the calling capacity of its most active members. Even your mother's social conscientiousness could not compass it. Society is a very different sort of thing from good sense and right ideas. It is based upon them, of course, but the airy, graceful, winning superstructure which we all know demands different qualities. Have your friends got these qualities,—which may be felt, but not defined?"

The son laughed. "To tell you the truth, sir, I don't think they have the most elemental ideas of society, as we understand it. I don't believe Mrs. Lapham ever gave a dinner."

"And with all that money!" sighed the father.

"I don't believe they have the habit of wine at table. I suspect that when they don't drink tea and coffee with their dinner, they drink ice-water."

"Horrible!" said Bromfield Corey.

"It appears to me that this defines them."

"Oh, yes. There are people who give dinners, and who are not cognoscible.* But people who have never yet given a dinner, how is society to assimilate them?"

"It digests a great many people," suggested the young man.

"Yes; but they have always brought some sort of sauce piquante with them. Now, as I understand you, these friends of yours have no such sauce."

"Oh, I don't know about that!" cried the son.

"Oh, rude, native flavors, I dare say. But that isn't what I mean. Well, then, they must spend. There is no other way for them to win their way to general regard. We must have the Colonel elected to the Ten O'clock Club, and he must put himself down in the list of those willing to entertain. Any one can manage a large supper. Yes, I see a gleam of hope for him in that direction."

In the morning Bromfield Corey asked his son whether he should find Lapham at his place as early as eleven.

"I think you might find him even earlier. I've never been there before him. I doubt if the porter is there much sooner."

"Well, suppose I go with you, then?"

"Why, if you like, sir," said the son, with some deprecation.

"Oh, the question is, will *he* like?"

"I think he will, sir"; and the father could see that his son was very much pleased.

Lapham was rending an impatient course through the morning's news when they appeared at the door of his inner room. He looked up from the newspaper spread on the desk before him, and then he stood up, making an indifferent feint of not knowing that he knew Bromfield Corey by sight.

"Good-morning, Colonel Lapham," said the son, and Lapham waited for him to say further, "I wish to introduce my father."

Then he answered "Good-morning," and added rather sternly for the elder Corey, "How do you do, sir? Will you take a chair?" and he pushed him one.

They shook hands and sat down, and Lapham said to his subordinate, "Have a seat"; but young Corey remained standing, watching them in their observance of each other with an amusement which

---

*Knowable; suitable for social acquaintance.

was a little uneasy. Lapham made his visitor speak first by waiting for him to do so.

"I'm glad to make your acquaintance, Colonel Lapham, and I ought to have come sooner to do so. My father in your place would have expected it of a man in my place at once, I believe. But I can't feel myself altogether a stranger as it is. I hope Mrs. Lapham is well? And your daughter?"

"Thank you," said Lapham, "they're quite well."

"They were very kind to my wife——"

"Oh, that was nothing!" cried Lapham. "There's nothing Mrs. Lapham likes better than a chance of that sort. Mrs. Corey and the young ladies well?"

"Very well, when I heard from them. They're out of town."

"Yes, so I understood," said Lapham, with a nod toward the son. "I believe Mr. Corey, here, told Mrs. Lapham." He leaned back in his chair, stiffly resolute to show that he was not incommoded by the exchange of these civilities.

"Yes," said Bromfield Corey. "Tom has had the pleasure which I hope for of seeing you all. I hope you're able to make him useful to you here?" Corey looked round Lapham's room vaguely, and then out at the clerks in their railed inclosure, where his eye finally rested on an extremely pretty girl, who was operating a typewriter.

"Well, sir," replied Lapham, softening for the first time with this approach to business, "I guess it will be our own fault if we don't. By the way, Corey," he added, to the younger man, as he gathered up some letters from his desk, "here's something in your line. Spanish or French, I guess."

"I'll run them over," said Corey, taking them to his desk.

His father made an offer to rise.

"Don't go," said Lapham, gesturing him down again. "I just wanted to get him away a minute. I don't care to say it to his face,—I don't like the principle,—but since you ask me about it, I'd just as lief say that I've never had any young man take hold here equal to your son. I don't know as you care——"

"You make me very happy," said Bromfield Corey. "Very happy indeed. I've always had the idea that there was something in my son, if he could only find the way to work it out. And he seems to have gone into your business for the love of it."

"He went to work in the right way, sir! He told me about it. He looked into it. And that paint is a thing that will bear looking into."

"Oh, yes. You might think he had invented it, if you heard him celebrating it."

"Is that so?" demanded Lapham, pleased through and through. "Well, there ain't any other way. You've got to believe in a thing before you can put any heart in it. Why, I had a partner in this thing once, along back just after the war, and he used to be always wanting to tinker with something else. 'Why,' says I, 'you've got the best thing in God's universe now. Why ain't you satisfied?' I had to get rid of him at last. I stuck to my paint, and that fellow's drifted round pretty much all over the whole country, whittling his capital down all the while, till here the other day I had to lend him some money to start him new. No, sir, you've got to believe in a thing. And I believe in your son. And I don't mind telling you that, so far as he's gone, he's a success."

"That's very kind of you."

"No kindness about it. As I was saying the other day to a friend of mine, I've had many a fellow right out of the street that had to work hard all his life, and didn't begin to take hold like this son of yours."

Lapham expanded with profound self-satisfaction. As he probably conceived it, he had succeeded in praising, in a perfectly casual way, the supreme excellence of his paint, and his own sagacity and benevolence; and here he was sitting face to face with Bromfield Corey, praising his son to him, and receiving his grateful acknowledgments as if he were the father of some office-boy whom Lapham had given a place half out of charity.

"Yes, sir, when your son proposed to take hold here, I didn't have much faith in his ideas, that's the truth. But I had faith in him, and I saw that he meant business from the start. I could see it was born in him. Any one could."

"I'm afraid he didn't inherit it directly from me," said Bromfield Corey; "but it's in the blood, on both sides."

"Well, sir, we can't help those things," said Lapham, compassionately. "Some of us have got it, and some of us haven't. The idea is to make the most of what we *have* got."

"Oh, yes; that is the idea. By all means."

"And you can't ever tell what's in you till you try. Why, when I started this thing, I didn't more than half understand my own strength. I wouldn't have said, looking back, that I could have stood the wear and tear of what I've been through. But I developed as I went along. It's just like exercising your muscles in a gymnasium. You can lift twice or three times as much after you've been in training a month as you could before. And I can see that it's going to be just so with your son. His going through college won't hurt him,—he'll soon slough all that off,—and his bringing up won't; don't be anxious about it. I noticed in the army that some of the fellows that had the most go-ahead were fellows that hadn't ever had much more to do than girls before the war broke out. Your son will get along."

"Thank you," said Bromfield Corey, and smiled—whether because his spirit was safe in the humility he sometimes boasted, or because it was triply armed in pride against anything the Colonel's kindness could do.

"He'll get along. He's a good business man and he's a fine fellow. Must you go?" asked Lapham, as Bromfield Corey now rose more resolutely. "Well, glad to see you. It was natural you should want to come and see what he was about, and I'm glad you did. I should have felt just so about it. Here is some of our stuff," he said, pointing out the various packages in his office, including the Persis Brand.

"Ah, that's very nice, very nice indeed," said his visitor. "That color through the jar—very rich—delicious. Is Persis Brand a name?"

Lapham blushed.

"Well, Persis is. I don't know as you saw an interview that fellow published in the 'Events' awhile back?"

"What is the 'Events'?"

"Well, it's that new paper Witherby's started."

"No," said Bromfield Corey, "I haven't seen it. I read 'The Daily,'" he explained; by which he meant "The Daily Advertiser," the only daily there is in the old-fashioned Bostonian sense.

"He put a lot of stuff in my mouth that I never said," resumed Lapham; "but that's neither here nor there, so long as you haven't seen it. Here's the department your son's in," and he showed him the foreign labels. Then he took him out into the warehouse to see the large packages. At the head of the stairs, where his guest stopped to

nod to his son and say "Good-bye, Tom," Lapham insisted upon
going down to the lower door with him. "Well, call again," he said
in hospitable dismissal. "I shall always be glad to see you. There ain't
a great deal doing at this season." Bromfield Corey thanked him, and
let his hand remain perforce in Lapham's lingering grasp. "If you
ever like to ride after a good horse——" the Colonel began.

"Oh, no, no, no; thank you! The better the horse, the more I
should be scared. Tom has told me of your driving!"

"Ha, ha, ha!" laughed the Colonel. "Well! every one to his taste.
Well, good-morning, sir!" and he suffered him to go.

"Who is the old man blowing to this morning?" asked Walker,
the book-keeper, making an errand to Corey's desk.

"My father."

"Oh! That your father? I thought he must be one of your Italian
correspondents that you'd been showing round, or Spanish."

In fact, as Bromfield Corey found his way at his leisurely pace up
through the streets on which the prosperity of his native city was
founded, hardly any figure could have looked more alien to its life.
He glanced up and down the façades and through the crooked vistas
like a stranger, and the swarthy fruiterer of whom he bought an apple,
apparently for the pleasure of holding it in his hand, was not surprised that the purchase should be transacted in his own tongue.

Lapham walked back through the outer office to his own room
without looking at Corey, and during the day he spoke to him only
of business matters. That must have been his way of letting Corey see
that he was not overcome by the honor of his father's visit. But he
presented himself at Nantasket with the event so perceptibly on his
mind that his wife asked: "Well, Silas, has Rogers been borrowing
any more money of you? I don't want you should let that thing go
too far. You've done enough."

"You needn't be afraid. I've seen the last of Rogers for one
while." He hesitated, to give the fact an effect of no importance.
"Corey's father called this morning."

"Did he?" said Mrs. Lapham, willing to humor his feint of indifference. "Did *he* want to borrow some money too?"

"Not as I understood." Lapham was smoking at great ease, and
his wife had some crocheting on the other side of the lamp from
him.

The girls were on the piazza looking at the moon on the water again. "There's no man in it to-night," Penelope said, and Irene laughed forlornly.

"What did he want, then?" asked Mrs. Lapham.

"Oh, I don't know. Seemed to be just a friendly call. Said he ought to have come before."

Mrs. Lapham was silent awhile. Then she said: "Well, I hope you're satisfied now."

Lapham rejected the sympathy too openly offered. "I don't know about being satisfied. I wa'n't in any hurry to see him."

His wife permitted him this pretense also. "What sort of a person is he, anyway?"

"Well, not much like his son. There's no sort of business about him. I don't know just how you'd describe him. He's tall; and he's got white hair and a mustache; and his fingers are very long and limber. I couldn't help noticing them as he sat there with his hands on the top of his cane. Didn't seem to be dressed very much, and acted just like anybody. Didn't talk much. Guess I did most of the talking. Said he was glad I seemed to be getting along so well with his son. He asked after you and Irene; and he said he couldn't feel just like a stranger. Said you had been very kind to his wife. Of course I turned it off. Yes," said Lapham thoughtfully, with his hands resting on his knees, and his cigar between the fingers of his left hand, "I guess he meant to do the right thing, every way. Don't know as I ever saw a much pleasanter man. Dunno but what he's about the pleasantest man I ever did see." He was not letting his wife see in his averted face the struggle that revealed itself there—the struggle of stalwart achievement not to feel flattered at the notice of sterile elegance, not to be sneakingly glad of its amiability, but to stand up and look at it with eyes on the same level. God, who made us so much like himself, but out of the dust, alone knows when that struggle will end. The time had been when Lapham could not have imagined any worldly splendor which his dollars could not buy if he chose to spend them for it; but his wife's half discoveries, taking form again in his ignorance of the world, filled him with helpless misgiving. A cloudy vision of something unpurchasable, where he had supposed there was nothing, had cowed him in spite of the burly resistance of his pride.

"I don't see why he shouldn't be pleasant," said Mrs. Lapham. "He's never done anything else."

Lapham looked up consciously, with an uneasy laugh. "Pshaw, Persis! you never forget anything!"

"Oh, I've got more than that to remember. I suppose you asked him to ride after the mare?"

"Well," said Lapham, reddening guiltily, "he said he was afraid of a good horse."

"Then, of course, you hadn't asked him." Mrs. Lapham crocheted in silence, and her husband leaned back in his chair and smoked.

At last he said, "I'm going to push that house forward. They're loafing on it. There's no reason why we shouldn't be in it by Thanksgiving. I don't believe in moving in the dead of winter."

"We can wait till spring. We're very comfortable in the old place," answered his wife. Then she broke out on him: "What are you in such a hurry to get into that house for? Do you want to invite the Coreys to a house-warming?"

Lapham looked at her without speaking.

"Don't you suppose I can see through you? I declare, Silas Lapham, if I didn't know different, I should say you *were* about the biggest fool! Don't you know *anything?* Don't you know that it wouldn't do to ask those people to our house before they've asked us to theirs? They'd laugh in our faces!"

"I don't believe they'd laugh in our faces. What's the difference between our asking them and their asking us?" demanded the Colonel, sulkily.

"Oh, well! If you don't see!"

"Well, I *don't* see. But I don't want to ask them to the house. I suppose, if I want to, I can invite him down to a fish dinner at Taft's."

Mrs. Lapham fell back in her chair, and let her work drop in her lap with that "Tckk!" in which her sex knows how to express utter contempt and despair.

"What's the matter?"

"Well, if you *do* such a thing, Silas, I'll never speak to you again! It's no *use!* It's *no* use! I did think, after you'd behaved so well about Rogers, I might trust you a little. But I see I can't. I presume as long as you live you'll have to be nosed about like a perfect—I don't know what!"

"What are you making such a fuss about?" demanded Lapham, terribly crest-fallen, but trying to pluck up a spirit. "I haven't done anything yet. I can't ask your advice about anything any more without having you fly out. Confound it! I shall do as I please after this."

But as if he could not endure that contemptuous atmosphere, he got up, and his wife heard him in the dining-room pouring himself out a glass of ice-water, and then heard him mount the stairs to their room, and slam its door after him.

"Do you know what your father's wanting to do now?" Mrs. Lapham asked her eldest daughter, who lounged into the parlor a moment with her wrap stringing from her arm, while the younger went straight to bed. "He wants to invite Mr. Corey's father to a fish dinner at Taft's!"

Penelope was yawning with her hand on her mouth; she stopped, and, with a laugh of amused expectance, sank into a chair, her shoulders shrugged forward.

"Why! what in the world has put the Colonel up to that?"

"Put him up to it! There's that fellow, who ought have come to see him long ago, drops into his office this morning, and talks five minutes with him, and your father is flattered out of his five senses. He's crazy to get in with those people, and I shall have a perfect battle to keep him within bounds."

"Well, Persis, ma'am, you can't say but what you began it," said Penelope.

"Oh, yes, I began it," confessed Mrs. Lapham. "Pen," she broke out, "what do you suppose he means by it?"

"Who? Mr. Corey's father? What does the Colonel think?"

"Oh, the Colonel!" cried Mrs. Lapham. She added tremulously: "Perhaps he is right. He did seem to take a fancy to her last summer, and now if he's called in that way—" She left her daughter to distribute the pronouns aright, and resumed: "Of course, I should have said once that there wasn't any question about it. I should have said so last year; and I don't know what it is keeps me from saying so now. I suppose I know a little more about things than I did; and your father's being so bent on it sets me all in a twitter. He thinks his money can do everything. Well, I don't say but what it can, a good many. And 'Rene is as good a child as ever there was; and I don't see but what she's pretty-appearing enough to suit any one. She's pretty-behaved, too; and she is the most capable girl. I presume young men don't care very much for such things nowadays; but there ain't a great many girls can go right into the kitchen, and make such a custard as she did yesterday. And look at the way she does, through the whole house! She can't seem to go into a room without the things fly right into their places. And if she had to do it to-morrow, she could make all her own dresses a great deal better than them we pay to do it. I don't say but what he's about as nice a fellow as ever stepped. But there! I'm ashamed of going on so."

"Well, mother," said the girl after a pause, in which she looked as if a little weary of the subject, "why do you worry about it? If it's to be it'll be, and if it isn't——"

"Yes, that's what I tell your father. But when it comes to myself, I see how hard it is for him to rest quiet. I'm afraid we shall all do something we'll repent of afterwards."

"Well, ma'am," said Penelope, "I don't intend to do anything wrong; but if I do, I promise not to be sorry for it. I'll go that far. And I think I wouldn't be sorry for it beforehand, if I were in your place, mother. Let the Colonel go on! He likes to manœuvre, and he isn't going to hurt any one. The Corey family can take care of themselves, I guess."

She laughed in her throat, drawing down the corners of her mouth, and enjoying the resolution with which her mother tried to fling off the burden of her anxieties. "Pen! I believe you're right. You always do see things in such a light! There! I don't care if he brings him down every day."

"Well, ma'am," said Pen, "I don't believe 'Rene would, either. She's just so indifferent!"

The Colonel slept badly that night, and in the morning Mrs. Lapham came to breakfast without him.

"Your father ain't well," she reported. "He's had one of his turns."

"I should have thought he had two or three of them," said Penelope, "by the stamping round I heard. Isn't he coming to breakfast?"

"Not just yet," said her mother. "He's asleep, and he'll be all right if he gets his nap out. I don't want you girls should make any great noise."

"Oh, we'll be quiet enough," returned Penelope. "Well, I'm glad the Colonel isn't sojering. At first I thought he might be sojering." She broke into a laugh, and, struggling indolently with it, looked at her sister. "You don't think it'll be necessary for anybody to come down from the office and take orders from him while he's laid up, do you, mother?" she inquired.

"Pen!" cried Irene.

"He'll be well enough to go up on the ten o'clock boat," said the mother, sharply.

"I think papa works too hard all through the summer. Why don't you make him take a rest, mamma?" asked Irene.

"Oh, take a rest! The man slaves harder every year. It used to be so that he'd take a little time off now and then; but I declare, he hardly ever seems to breathe now away from his office. And this year he says he doesn't intend to go down to Lapham, except to see after the works for a few days. I don't know what to do with the man any more! Seems as if the more money he got, the more he wanted to get. It scares me to think what would happen to him if he lost it. I know one thing," concluded Mrs. Lapham. "He shall not go back to the office to-day."

"Then he won't go up on the ten o'clock boat," Pen reminded her.

"No, he won't. You can just drive over to the hotel as soon as you're through, girls, and telegraph that he's not well, and won't be at the office till to-morrow. I'm not going to have them send any-body down here to bother him."

"That's a blow," said Pen. "I didn't know but they might send——" she looked demurely at her sister—"Dennis!"

"Mamma!" cried Irene.

"Well, I declare, there's no living with this family any more," said Penelope.

"There, Pen, be done!" commanded her mother. But perhaps she did not intend to forbid her teasing. It gave a pleasant sort of reality to the affair that was in her mind, and made what she wished appear not only possible but probable.

Lapham got up and lounged about, fretting and rebelling as each boat departed without him, through the day; before night he became very cross, in spite of the efforts of the family to soothe him, and grumbled that he had been kept from going up to town. "I might as well have gone as not," he repeated, till his wife lost her patience.

"Well, you shall go to-morrow, Silas, if you have to be carried to the boat."

"I declare," said Penelope, "the Colonel don't pet worth a cent."

The six o'clock boat brought Corey. The girls were sitting on the piazza, and Irene saw him first.

"Oh, Pen!" she whispered, with her heart in her face; and Penelope had no time for mockery before he was at the steps.

"I hope Colonel Lapham isn't ill," he said, and they could hear their mother engaged in a moral contest with their father indoors.

"Go and put on your coat! I say you shall! It don't matter how he sees you at the office, shirt-sleeves or not. You're in a gentleman's house now—or you ought to be—and you sha'n't see company in your dressing-gown."

Penelope hurried in to subdue her mother's anger.

"Oh, he's very much better, thank you!" said Irene, speaking up loudly to drown the noise of the controversy.

"I'm glad of that," said Corey, and when she led him indoors the vanquished Colonel met his visitor in a double-breasted frock-coat, which he was still buttoning up. He could not persuade himself at once that Corey had not come upon some urgent business matter, and when he was clear that he had come out of civility, surprise mingled with his gratification that he should be the object of solicitude to the young man. In Lapham's circle of acquaintance they complained when they were sick, but they made no womanish inquiries after one another's health, and certainly paid no visits of sympathy till matters were serious. He would have enlarged upon the particulars of his indisposition if he had been allowed to do so; and after tea, which Corey took with them, he would have remained to entertain him if his wife had not sent him to bed. She followed him to see that he took some medicine she had prescribed for him, but she went first to Penelope's room, where she found the girl with a book in her hand, which she was not reading.

"You better go down," said the mother. "I've got to go to your father, and Irene is all alone with Mr. Corey; and I know she'll be on pins and needles without you're there to help make it go off."

"She'd better try to get along without me, mother," said Penelope soberly. "I can't always be with them."

"Well," replied Mrs. Lapham, "then I must. There'll be a perfect Quaker meeting down there."

"Oh, I guess 'Rene will find something to say if you leave her to herself. Or if she don't, he must. It'll be all right for you to go down when you get ready; but I sha'n't go till toward the last. If he's coming here to see Irene—and I don't believe he's come on father's account—he wants to see her and not me. If she can't interest him alone, perhaps he'd as well find it out now as any time. At any rate, I guess you'd better make the experiment. You'll know whether it's a success if he comes again."

"Well," said the mother, "may be you're right. I'll go down directly. It does seem as if he did mean something, after all."

Mrs. Lapham did not hasten to return to her guest. In her own girlhood it was supposed that if a young man seemed to be coming to see a girl, it was only common sense to suppose that he wished to see her alone; and her life in town had left Mrs. Lapham's simple traditions in this respect unchanged. She did with her daughter as her mother would have done with her.

Where Penelope sat with her book, she heard the continuous murmur of voices below, and after a long interval she heard her mother descend. She did not read the open book that lay in her lap, though she kept her eyes fast on the print. Once she rose and almost shut the door, so that she could scarcely hear; then she opened it wide again with a self-disdainful air, and resolutely went back to her book, which again she did not read. But she remained in her room till it was nearly time for Corey to return to his boat.

When they were alone again, Irene made a feint of scolding her for leaving her to entertain Mr. Corey.

"Why! didn't you have a pleasant call?" asked Penelope.

Irene threw her arms round her. "Oh, it was a *splendid* call! I didn't suppose I could make it go off so well. We talked nearly the whole time about you!"

"I don't think *that* was a very interesting subject."

"He kept asking about you. He asked everything. You don't know how much he thinks of you, Pen. Oh, Pen! what do you think made him come? Do you think he really did come to see how papa was?" Irene buried her face in her sister's neck.

Penelope stood with her arms at her side, submitting. "Well," she said, "I don't think he did, altogether."

Irene, all glowing, released her. "Don't you—don't you *really*? Oh! Pen, don't you think he *is* nice? Don't you think he's handsome? Don't you think I behaved horridly when we first met him this evening, not thanking him for coming? I know he thinks I've no manners. But it seemed as if it would be thanking him for coming to see me. Ought I to have asked him to come again, when he said good-night? I didn't; I couldn't. Do you believe he'll think I don't want him to? You don't believe he would keep coming if he didn't—want to——"

"He hasn't kept coming a great deal, yet," suggested Penelope.

"No; I know he hasn't. But if he—if he should?"

"Then I should think he wanted to."

"Oh, would you—*would* you? Oh, how good you always are, Pen! And you always say what you think. I wish there was someone coming to see you too. That's all that I don't like about it. Perhaps——He was telling about his friend there in Texas——"

"Well," said Penelope, "his friend couldn't call often from Texas. You needn't ask Mr. Corey to trouble about me, 'Rene. I think I can manage to worry along, if you're satisfied."

"Oh, I *am*, Pen. When do you suppose he'll come again?" Irene pushed some of Penelope's things aside on the dressing-case, to rest her elbow and talk at ease. Penelope came up and put them back.

"Well, not to-night," she said; "and if that's what you're sitting up for——"

Irene caught her round the neck again, and ran out of the room.

The Colonel was packed off on the eight o'clock boat the next morning; but his recovery did not prevent Corey from repeating his visit in a week. This time Irene came radiantly up to Penelope's room, where she had again withdrawn herself. "You must come down, Pen," she said. "He's asked if you're not well, and mamma says you've got to come."

After that Penelope helped Irene through with her calls, and talked them over with her far into the night after Corey was gone. But when the impatient curiosity of her mother pressed her for some opinion of the affair, she said, "You know as much as I do, mother."

"Don't he ever say anything to you about her—praise her up, any?"

"He's never mentioned Irene to me."

"He hasn't to me, either," said Mrs. Lapham, with a sigh of trouble. "Then what makes him keep coming?"

"I can't tell you. One thing, he says there isn't a house open in Boston where he's acquainted. Wait till some of his friends get back, and then if he keeps coming, it'll be time to inquire."

"Well!" said the mother; but as the weeks passed she was less and less able to attribute Corey's visits to his loneliness in town, and turned to her husband for comfort.

"Silas, I don't know as we ought to let young Corey keep coming so. I don't quite like it, with all his family away."

"He's of age," said the Colonel. "He can go where he pleases. It don't matter whether his family's here or not."

"Yes, but if they don't want he should come? Should you feel just right about letting him?"

"How're you going to stop him? I swear, Persis, I don't know what's got over you! What is it? You didn't use to be so. But to hear you talk, you'd think those Coreys were too good for this world, and we wa'n't fit for 'em to walk on."

"I'm not going to have 'em say we took an advantage of their being away and tolled him on."*

"I should like to hear 'em say it!" cried Lapham. "Or anybody!"

"Well," said his wife, relinquishing this point of anxiety, "I can't make out whether he cares anything for her or not. And Pen can't tell either; or else she won't."

"Oh, I guess he cares for her, fast enough," said the Colonel.

"I can't make out that he's said or done the first thing to show it."

"Well, I was better than a year getting my courage up."

"Oh, that was different," said Mrs. Lapham, in contemptuous dismissal of the comparison, and yet with a certain fondness. "I guess, if he cared for her, a fellow in his position wouldn't be long getting up his courage to speak to Irene."

Lapham brought his fist down on the table between them.

"Look here, Persis! Once for all, now, don't you ever let me hear you say anything like that again! I'm worth nigh on to a million, and

---

*Enticed him, drew him in (old-style usage).

I've made it every cent myself; and my girls are the equals of any-body, I don't care who it is. He ain't the fellow to take on any airs; but if he ever tries it with me, I'll send him to the right about mighty quick. I'll have a talk with him, if——"

"No, no; don't do that!" implored his wife. "I didn't mean any-thing. I don't know as I meant *anything*. He's just as unassuming as he can be, and I think Irene's a match for anybody. You just let things go on. It'll be all right. You never can tell how it is with young people. Perhaps *she's* offish. Now you ain't—you ain't going to say anything?"

Lapham suffered himself to be persuaded, the more easily, no doubt, because after his explosion he must have perceived that his pride itself stood in the way of what his pride had threatened. He contented himself with his wife's promise that she would never again present that offensive view of the case, and she did not remain with-out a certain support in his sturdy self-assertion.

XII

Mrs. Corey returned with her daughters in the early days of October, having passed three or four weeks at Intervale* after leaving Bar Harbor. They were somewhat browner than they were when they left town in June, but they were not otherwise changed. Lily, the elder of the girls, had brought back a number of studies of kelp and toadstools, with accessory rocks and rotten logs, which she would never finish up and never show any one, knowing the slightness of their merit. Nanny, the younger, had read a great many novels with a keen sense of their inaccuracy as representations of life, and had seen a great deal of life with a sad regret for its difference from fiction. They were both nice girls, accomplished, well dressed of course, and well-enough looking; but they had met no one at the seaside or the mountains whom their taste would allow to influence their fate, and they had come home to the occupations they had left, with no hopes and no fears to distract them.

In the absence of these they were fitted to take the more vivid interest in their brother's affairs, which they could see weighed upon their mother's mind after the first hours of greeting.

"Oh, it seems to have been going on, and your father has never written a word about it," she said, shaking her head.

"What good would it have done?" asked Nanny, who was little and fair, with rings of light hair that filled a bonnet-front very prettily; she looked best in a bonnet. "It would only have worried you. He could not have stopped Tom; you couldn't, when you came home to do it."

"I dare say papa didn't know much about it," suggested Lily. She was a tall, lean, dark girl, who looked as if she were not quite warm enough, and whom you always associated with wraps of different æsthetic effect after you had once seen her.

It is a serious matter always to the women of his family when a young man gives them cause to suspect that he is interested in some other woman. A son-in-law or brother-in-law does not enter the

---

*New Hampshire summer resort.

family; he need not be caressed or made anything of; but the son's or brother's wife has a claim upon his mother and sisters which they cannot deny. Some convention of their sex obliges them to show her affection, to like or to seem to like her, to take her to their intimacy, however odious she may be to them. With the Coreys it was something more than an affair of sentiment. They were by no means poor, and they were not dependent money-wise upon Tom Corey; but the mother had come, without knowing it, to rely upon his sense, his advice in everything, and the sisters, seeing him hitherto so indifferent to girls, had insensibly grown to regard him as altogether their own till he should be released, not by his marriage, but by theirs, an event which had not approached with the lapse of time. Some kinds of girls—they believed that they could readily have chosen a kind—might have taken him without taking him from them; but this generosity could not be hoped for in such a girl as Miss Lapham.

"Perhaps," urged their mother, "it would not be so bad. She seemed an affectionate little thing with her mother, without a great deal of character, though she was so capable about some things."

"Oh, she'll be an affectionate little thing with Tom too, you may be sure," said Nanny. "And that characterless capability becomes the most intense narrow-mindedness. She'll think we were against her from the beginning."

"She has no cause for that," Lily interposed, "and we shall not give her any."

"Yes, we shall," retorted Nanny. "We can't help it; and if we can't, her own ignorance would be cause enough."

"I can't feel that she's altogether ignorant," said Mrs. Corey, justly.

"Of course she can read and write," admitted Nanny.

"I can't imagine what he finds to talk about with her," said Lily.

"Oh, that's very simple," returned her sister. "They talk about themselves, with occasional references to each other. I have heard people 'going on' on the hotel piazzas. She's embroidering, or knitting, or tatting, or something of that kind; and he says she seems quite devoted to needle-work; and she says, yes, she has a perfect passion for it, and everybody laughs at her for it; but she can't help it, she always was so from a child, and supposes she always shall be,—with remote and minute particulars. And she ends by saying that perhaps he does not like people to tat, or knit, or embroider, or whatever. And he says, oh, yes, he does; what could make her think such a thing? but for his part he likes boating rather better, or if you're in the woods camping. Then she lets him take up one corner of her work, and perhaps touch her fingers; and that encourages him to say that he supposes nothing could induce her to drop her work long enough to go down on the rocks, or out among the huckleberry bushes; and she puts her head on one side, and says she doesn't know really. And then they go, and he lies at her feet on the rocks, or picks huckleberries and drops them in her lap, and they go on talking about themselves, and comparing notes to see how they differ from each other. And——"

"That will do, Nanny," said her mother.

Lily smiled autumnally. "Oh, disgusting!"

"Disgusting? Not at all!" protested her sister. "It's very amusing when you see it, and when you do it——"

"It's always a mystery what people see in each other," observed Mrs. Corey, severely.

"Yes," Nanny admitted, "but I don't know that there is much comfort for us in the application."

"No, there isn't," said her mother.

"The most that we can do is to hope for the best till we know the worst. Of course we shall make the best of the worst when it comes."

"Yes, and perhaps it would not be so very bad. I was saying to your father when I was here in July that those things can always be managed. You must face them as if they were nothing out of the way, and try not to give any cause for bitterness among ourselves."

"That's true. But I don't believe in too much resignation beforehand. It amounts to concession," said Nanny.

"Of course we should oppose it in all proper ways," returned her mother.

Lily had ceased to discuss the matter. In virtue of her artistic temperament, she was expected not to be very practical. It was her mother and her sister who managed, submitting to the advice and consent of Corey what they intended to do.

"Your father wrote me that he had called on Colonel Lapham at his place of business," said Mrs. Corey, seizing her first chance of approaching the subject with her son.

"Yes," said Corey. "A dinner was father's idea, but he came down to a call, at my suggestion."

"Oh," said Mrs. Corey, in a tone of relief, as if the statement threw a new light on the fact that Corey had suggested the visit. "He said so little about it in his letter that I didn't know just how it came about."

"I thought it was right they should meet," explained the son, "and so did father. I was glad that I suggested it, afterward; it was extremely gratifying to Colonel Lapham."

"Oh, it was quite right in every way. I suppose you have seen something of the family during the summer."

"Yes, a good deal. I've been down at Nantasket rather often."

Mrs. Corey let her eyes droop. Then she asked: "Are they well?"

"Yes, except Lapham himself, now and then. I went down once or twice to see him. He hasn't given himself any vacation this summer; he has such a passion for his business that I fancy he finds it hard being away from it at any time, and he's made his new house an excuse for staying———"

"Oh, yes, his house! Is it to be something fine?"

"Yes; it's a beautiful house. Seymour is doing it."

"Then, of course, it will be very handsome. I suppose the young ladies are very much taken up with it; and Mrs. Lapham."

"Mrs. Lapham, yes. I don't think the young ladies care so much about it."

"It must be for them. Aren't they ambitious?" asked Mrs. Corey, delicately feeling her way.

Her son thought awhile. Then he answered with a smile:

"No, I don't really think they are. They are unambitious, I should say." Mrs. Corey permitted herself a long breath. But her son added, "It's the parents who are ambitious for them," and her respiration became shorter again.

"Yes," she said.

"They're very simple, nice girls," pursued Corey. "I think you'll like the elder, when you come to know her."

When you come to know her. The words implied an expectation that the two families were to be better acquainted.

"Then she is more intellectual than her sister?" Mrs. Corey ventured.

"Intellectual?" repeated her son. "No; that isn't the word, quite. Though she certainly has more mind."

"The younger seemed very sensible."

"Oh, sensible, yes. And as practical as she's pretty. She can do all sorts of things, and likes to be doing them. Don't you think she's an extraordinary beauty?"

"Yes—yes, she is," said Mrs. Corey, at some cost.

"She's good, too," said Corey, "and perfectly innocent and transparent. I think you will like her the better the more you know her."

"I thought her very nice from the beginning," said the mother, heroically; and then nature asserted itself in her. "But I should be afraid that she might perhaps be a little bit tiresome at last; her range of ideas seemed so extremely limited."

"Yes, that's what I was afraid of. But, as a matter of fact, she isn't. She interests you by her very limitations. You can see the working of her mind, like that of a child. She isn't at all conscious even of her beauty."

"I don't believe young men can tell whether girls are conscious or not," said Mrs. Corey. "But I am not saying the Miss Laphams are not—" Her son sat musing, with an inattentive smile on his face. "What is it?"

"Oh, nothing. I was thinking of Miss Lapham and something she was saying. She's very droll, you know."

"The elder sister? Yes, you told me that. Can you see the workings of her mind too?"

"No; she's everything that's unexpected." Corey fell into another revery, and smiled again; but he did not offer to explain what amused him, and his mother would not ask.

"I don't know what to make of his admiring the girl so frankly," she said afterward to her husband. "That couldn't come naturally till after he had spoken to her, and I feel sure that he hasn't yet."

"You women haven't risen yet—it's an evidence of the backwardness of your sex—to a conception of the Bismarck* idea in diplomacy. If a man praises one woman, you still think he's in love

---

*Otto von Bismarck (1815–1898), German chancellor, skilled diplomat, architect of the unified German state.

with another. Do you mean that because Tom didn't praise the elder sister so much, he *has* spoken to *her?*"

Mrs. Corey refused the consequence, saying that it did not follow. "Besides, he did praise her."

"You ought to be glad that matters are in such good shape, then. At any rate, you can do absolutely nothing."

"Oh! I know it," sighed Mrs. Corey. "I wish Tom would be a little opener with me."

"He's as open as it's in the nature of an American-born son to be with his parents. I dare say if you'd ask him plumply what he meant in regard to the young lady, he would have told you—if he knew."

"Why, don't you think he does know, Bromfield?"

"I'm not at all sure he does. You women think that because a young man dangles after a girl, or girls, he's attached to them. It doesn't at all follow. He dangles because he must, and doesn't know what to do with his time, and because they seem to like it. I dare say that Tom has dangled a good deal in this instance because there was nobody else in town."

"Do you really think so?"

"I throw out the suggestion. And it strikes me that a young lady couldn't do better than stay in or near Boston during the summer. Most of the young men are here, kept by business through the week, with evenings available only on the spot, or a few miles off. What was the proportion of the sexes at the seashore and the mountains?"

"Oh, twenty girls at least for even an excuse of a man. It's shameful."

"You see, I am right in one part of my theory. Why shouldn't I be right in the rest?"

"I wish you were. And yet I can't say that I do. Those things are very serious with girls. I shouldn't like Tom to have been going to see those people if he meant nothing by it."

"And you wouldn't like it if he did. You are difficult, my dear." Her husband pulled an open newspaper toward him from the table.

"I feel that it wouldn't be at all like him to do so," said Mrs. Corey, going on to entangle herself in her words, as women often do when their ideas are perfectly clear. "Don't go to reading, please, Bromfield! I am really worried about this matter. I must know how much it means. I can't let it go on so. I don't see how you can rest easy without knowing."

"I don't in the least know what's going to become of me when I die; and yet I sleep well," replied Bromfield Corey, putting his newspaper aside.

"Ah, but this is a very different thing."

"So much more serious? Well, what can you do? We had this out when you were here in the summer, and you agreed with me then that we could do nothing. The situation hasn't changed at all."

"Yes, it has; it has continued the same," said Mrs. Corey, again expressing the fact by a contradiction in terms. "I think I must ask Tom outright."

"You know you can't do that, my dear."

"Then why doesn't he tell us?"

"Ah, that's what *he* can't do, if he's making love to Miss Irene—that's her name, I believe—on the American plan. He will tell us after he has told *her*. That was the way I did. Don't ignore our own youth, Anna. It was a long while ago, I'll admit."

"It was very different," said Mrs. Corey, a little shaken.

"I don't see how. I dare say Mamma Lapham knows whether Tom is in love with her daughter or not; and no doubt Papa Lapham knows it at second hand. But we shall not know it until the girl herself does. Depend upon that. Your mother knew, and she told your father; but my poor father knew nothing about it till we were engaged; and I had been hanging about—dangling, as you call it——"

"No, no; *you* called it that."

"Was it I?—for a year or more."

The wife could not refuse to be a little consoled by the image of her young love which the words conjured up, however little she liked its relation to her son's interest in Irene Lapham. She smiled pensively. "Then you think it hasn't come to an understanding with them yet?"

"An understanding? Oh, probably."

"An explanation, then?"

"The only logical inference from what we've been saying is that it hasn't. But I don't ask you to accept it on that account. May I read now, my dear?"

"Yes, you may read now," said Mrs. Corey, with one of those sighs which perhaps express a feminine sense of the unsatisfactoriness of husbands in general, rather than a personal discontent with her own.

"Thank you, my dear; then I think I'll smoke too," said Bromfield Corey, lighting a cigar.

She left him in peace, and she made no further attempt upon her son's confidence. But she was not inactive for that reason. She did not, of course, admit to herself, and far less to others, the motive with which she went to pay an early visit to the Laphams, who had now come up from Nantasket to Nankeen Square. She said to her daughters that she had always been a little ashamed of using her acquaintance with them to get money for her charity, and then seeming to drop it. Besides, it seemed to her that she ought somehow to recognize the business relation that Tom had formed with the father; they must not think that his family disapproved of what he had done.

"Yes, business is business," said Nanny, with a laugh. "Do you wish us to go with you again?"

"No; I will go alone this time," replied the mother with dignity.

Her coupé now found its way to Nankeen Square without difficulty, and she sent up a card, which Mrs. Lapham received in the presence of her daughter Penelope.

"I presume I've got to see her," she gasped.

"Well, don't look so guilty, mother," joked the girl; "you haven't been doing anything so *very* wrong."

"It seems as if I *had*. I don't know what's come over me. I wasn't afraid of the woman before, but now I don't seem to feel as if I could look her in the face. He's been coming here of his own accord, and I fought against his coming long enough, goodness knows. I didn't want him to come. And as far forth as that goes, we're as respectable as they are; and your father's got twice their money, any day. We've no need to go begging for their favor. I guess they were glad enough to get him in with your father."

"Yes, those are all good points, mother," said the girl; "and if you keep saying them over, and count a hundred every time before you speak, I guess you'll worry through."

Mrs. Lapham had been fussing distractedly with her hair and ribbons, in preparation for her encounter with Mrs. Corey. She now drew in a long quivering breath, stared at her daughter without seeing her, and hurried downstairs. It was true that when she met

Mrs. Corey before she had not been awed by her; but since then she had learned at least her own ignorance of the world, and she had talked over the things she had misconceived and the things she had shrewdly guessed so much that she could not meet her on the former footing of equality. In spite of as brave a spirit and as good a conscience as woman need have, Mrs. Lapham cringed inwardly, and tremulously wondered what her visitor had come for. She turned from pale to red, and was hardly coherent in her greetings; she did not know how they got to where Mrs. Corey was saying exactly the right things about her son's interest and satisfaction in his new business, and keeping her eyes fixed on Mrs. Lapham's, reading her uneasiness there, and making her feel, in spite of her indignant innocence, that she had taken a base advantage of her in her absence to get her son away from her and marry him to Irene. Then, presently, while this was painfully revolving itself in Mrs. Lapham's mind, she was aware of Mrs. Corey's asking if she was not to have the pleasure of seeing Miss Irene.

"No; she's out, just now," said Mrs. Lapham. "I don't know just when she'll be in. She went to get a book." And here she turned red again, knowing that Irene had gone to get the book because it was one that Corey had spoken of.

"Oh! I'm sorry," said Mrs. Corey. "I had hoped to see her. And your other daughter, whom I never met?"

"Penelope?" asked Mrs. Lapham, eased a little. "She is at home. I will go and call her." The Laphams had not yet thought of spending their superfluity on servants who could be rung for; they kept two girls and a man to look after the furnace, as they had for the last ten years. If Mrs. Lapham had rung in the parlor, her second girl would have gone to the street door to see who was there. She went upstairs for Penelope herself, and the girl, after some rebellious derision, returned with her.

Mrs. Corey took account of her, as Penelope withdrew to the other side of the room after their introduction, and sat down, indolently submissive on the surface to the tests to be applied, and following Mrs. Corey's lead of the conversation in her odd drawl.

"You young ladies will be glad to be getting into your new house," she said, politely.

"I don't know," said Penelope. "We're so used to this one."

Mrs. Corey looked a little baffled, but she said sympathetically, "Of course, you will be sorry to leave your old home."

Mrs. Lapham could not help putting in on behalf of her daughters: "I guess if it was left to the girls to say, we shouldn't leave it at all."

"Oh, indeed!" said Mrs. Corey; "are they so much attached? But I can quite understand it. My children would be heartbroken too if we were to leave the old place." She turned to Penelope. "But you must think of the lovely new house, and the beautiful position."

"Yes, I suppose we shall get used to them too," said Penelope, in response to this didactic consolation.

"Oh, I could even imagine your getting very fond of them," pursued Mrs. Corey, patronizingly. "My son has told me of the lovely outlook you're to have over the water. He thinks you have such a beautiful house. I believe he had the pleasure of meeting you all there when he first came home."

"Yes, I think he was our first visitor."

"He is a great admirer of your house," said Mrs. Corey, keeping her eyes very sharply, however politely, on Penelope's face, as if to surprise there the secret of any other great admiration of her son's that might helplessly show itself.

"Yes," said the girl, "he's been there several times with father; and he wouldn't be allowed to overlook any of its good points."

Her mother took a little more courage from her daughter's tranquillity.

"The girls make such fun of their father's excitement about his building, and the way he talks it into everybody."

"Oh, indeed!" said Mrs. Corey, with civil misunderstanding and inquiry.

Penelope flushed, and her mother went on: "I tell him he's more of a child about it than any of them."

"Young people are very philosophical nowadays," remarked Mrs. Corey.

"Yes, indeed," said Mrs. Lapham. "I tell them they've always had everything, so that nothing's a surprise to them. It was different with us in our young days."

"Yes," said Mrs. Corey, without assenting.

"I mean the Colonel and myself," explained Mrs. Lapham.

"Oh, yes—*yes!*" said Mrs. Corey.

"I'm sure," the former went on, rather helplessly, "*we* had to work hard enough for everything we got. And so we appreciated it."

"So many things were not done for young people then," said Mrs. Corey, not recognizing the early-hardships stand-point of Mrs. Lapham. "But I don't know that they are always the better for it now," she added, vaguely, but with the satisfaction we all feel in uttering a just commonplace.

"It's rather hard living up to blessings that you've always had," said Penelope.

"Yes," replied Mrs. Corey, distractedly, and coming back to her slowly from the virtuous distance to which she had absented herself. She looked at the girl searchingly again, as if to determine whether this were a touch of the drolling her son had spoken of. But she only added: "You will enjoy the sunsets on the Back Bay so much."

"Well, not unless they're new ones," said Penelope. "I don't believe I could promise to enjoy any sunsets that I was used to, a great deal."

Mrs. Corey looked at her with misgiving, hardening into dislike. "No," she breathed, vaguely. "My son spoke of the fine effect of the lights about the hotel from your cottage at Nantasket," she said to Mrs. Lapham.

"Yes, they're splendid!" exclaimed that lady. "I guess the girls went down every night with him to see them from the rocks."

"Yes," said Mrs. Corey, a little dryly; and she permitted herself to add: "He spoke of those rocks. I suppose both you young ladies spend a great deal of your time on them when you're there. At Nahant my children were constantly on them."

"Irene likes the rocks," said Penelope. "I don't care much about them,—especially at night."

"Oh, indeed! I suppose you find it quite as well looking at the lights comfortably from the veranda."

"No; you can't see them from the house."

"Oh," said Mrs. Corey. After a perceptible pause, she turned to Mrs. Lapham. "I don't know what my son would have done for a breath of sea air this summer, if you had not allowed him to come to Nantasket. He wasn't willing to leave his business long enough to go anywhere else."

"Yes, he's a born business man," responded Mrs. Lapham enthu-
siastically. "If it's born in you, it's bound to come out. That's what the
Colonel is always saying about Mr. Corey. He says it's born in him to
be a business man, and he can't help it." She recurred to Corey gladly
because she felt that she had not said enough of him when his
mother first spoke of his connection with the business. "I don't believe," she went on excitedly, "that Colonel Lapham has ever had
anybody with him that he thought more of."

"You have all been very kind to my son," said Mrs. Corey in acknowledgment, and stiffly bowing a little, "and we feel greatly indebted to you. Very much so."

At these grateful expressions Mrs. Lapham reddened once more,
and murmured that it had been very pleasant to them, she was sure.
She glanced at her daughter for support, but Penelope was looking at
Mrs. Corey, who doubtless saw her from the corner of her eyes,
though she went on speaking to her mother.

"I was sorry to hear from him that Mr.—Colonel?—Lapham had
not been quite well this summer. I hope he's better now?"

"Oh, yes, indeed," replied Mrs. Lapham; "he's all right now. He's
hardly ever been sick, and he don't know how to take care of himself. That's all. We don't any of us; we're all so well."

"Health is a great blessing," sighed Mrs. Corey.

"Yes, so it is. How is your oldest daughter?" inquired Mrs.
Lapham. "Is she as delicate as ever?"

"She seems to be rather better since we returned." And now Mrs.
Corey, as if forced to the point, said bunglingly that the young ladies
had wished to come with her, but had been detained. She based her
statement upon Nanny's sarcastic demand; and, perhaps seeing it
topple a little, she rose hastily, to get away from its fall. "But we shall
hope for some—some other occasion," she said vaguely, and she put
on a parting smile, and shook hands with Mrs. Lapham and Penelope, and then, after some lingering commonplaces, got herself out
of the house.

Penelope and her mother were still looking at each other, and
trying to grapple with the effect or purport of the visit, when Irene
burst in upon them from the outside.

"Oh, mamma! wasn't that Mrs. Corey's carriage just drove
away?"

Penelope answered with her laugh. "Yes! You've just missed the most delightful call, 'Rene. So easy and pleasant every way. Not a bit stiff! Mrs. Corey was so friendly! She didn't make me feel at all as if she'd bought me, and thought she'd given too much; and mother held up her head as if she were all wool and a yard wide, and she would just like to have anybody deny it."

In a few touches of mimicry she dashed off a sketch of the scene: her mother's trepidation, and Mrs. Corey's well-bred repose and polite scrutiny of them both. She ended by showing how she herself had sat huddled up in a dark corner, mute with fear.

"If she came to make us say and do the wrong thing, she must have gone away happy; and it's a pity you weren't here to help, Irene. I don't know that I aimed to make a bad impression, but I guess I succeeded—even beyond my deserts." She laughed; then suddenly she flashed out in fierce earnest. "If I missed doing anything that could make me as hateful to her as she made herself to me——" She checked herself, and began to laugh. Her laugh broke, and the tears started into her eyes; she ran out of the room, and up the stairs.

"What—what does it mean?" asked Irene, in a daze.

Mrs. Lapham was still in the chilly torpor to which Mrs. Corey's call had reduced her. Penelope's vehemence did not rouse her. She only shook her head absently, and said, "I don't know."

"Why should Pen care what impression she made? I didn't suppose it would make any difference to her whether Mrs. Corey liked her or not."

"I didn't, either. But I could see that she was just as nervous as she could be, every minute of the time. I guess she didn't like Mrs. Corey any too well from the start, and she couldn't seem to act like herself."

"Tell me about it, mamma," said Irene, dropping into a chair.

Mrs. Corey described the interview to her husband on her return home. "Well, and what are your inferences?" he asked.

"They were extremely embarrassed and excited—that is, the mother. I don't wish to do her injustice, but she certainly behaved consciously."

"You made her feel so, I dare say, Anna. I can imagine how terrible you must have been, in the character of an accusing spirit, too lady-like to say anything. What did you hint?"

"I hinted nothing," said Mrs. Corey, descending to the weakness of defending herself. "But I saw quite enough to convince me that the girl is in love with Tom, and the mother knows it."

"That was very unsatisfactory. I supposed you went to find out whether Tom was in love with the girl. Was she as pretty as ever?"

"I didn't see her; she was not at home; I saw her sister."

"I don't know that I follow you quite, Anna. But no matter. What was the sister like?"

"A thoroughly disagreeable young woman."

"What did she do?"

"Nothing. She's far too sly for that. But that was the impression."

"Then you didn't find her so amusing as Tom does?"

"I found her pert. There's no other word for it. She says things to puzzle you and put you out."

"Ah, that was worse than pert, Anna; that was criminal. Well, let us thank heaven the younger one is so pretty."

Mrs. Corey did not reply directly. "Bromfield," she said, after a moment of troubled silence, "I have been thinking over your plan, and I don't see why it isn't the right thing."

"What is my plan?" inquired Bromfield Corey.

"A dinner."

Her husband began to laugh. "Ah, you overdid the accusing-spirit business, and this is reparation." But Mrs. Corey hurried on, with combined dignity and anxiety:

"We can't ignore Tom's intimacy with them—it amounts to that; it will probably continue even if it's merely a fancy, and we must seem to know it; whatever comes of it, we can't disown it. They are very simple, unfashionable people, and unworldly; but I can't say that they are offensive, unless—unless," she added, in propitiation of her husband's smile, "unless the father—how *did* you find the father?" she implored.

"He will be very entertaining," said Corey, "if you start him on his paint. What was the disagreeable daughter like? Shall you have her?"

"She's little and dark. We must have them all," Mrs. Corey sighed. "Then you don't think a dinner would do?"

"Oh, yes, I do. As you say, we can't disown Tom's relation to them, whatever it is. We had much better recognize it, and make the best of the inevitable. I think a Lapham dinner would be delightful." He looked at her with delicate irony in his voice and smile, and she fetched another sigh, so deep and sore now that he laughed outright. "Perhaps," he suggested, "it would be the best way of curing Tom of his fancy, if he has one. He has been seeing her with the dangerous advantages which a mother knows how to give her daughter in the family circle, and with no means of comparing her with other girls. You must invite several other very pretty girls."

"Do you really think so, Bromfield?" asked Mrs. Corey, taking courage a little. "That might do." But her spirits visibly sank again. "I don't know any other girl half so pretty."

"Well, then, better bred."

"She is very lady-like, very modest, and pleasing."

"Well, more cultivated."

"Tom doesn't get on with such people."

"Oh, you wish him to marry her, I see."

"No, no——"

"Then you'd better give the dinner to bring them together, to promote the affair."

"You know I don't want to do that, Bromfield. But I feel that we must do something. If we don't, it has a clandestine appearance. It isn't just to them. A dinner won't leave us in any worse position, and may leave us in a better. Yes," said Mrs. Corey, after another thoughtful interval, "we must have them—have them all. It could be very simple."

"Ah, you can't give a dinner under a bushel, if I take your meaning, my dear. If we do this at all, we mustn't do it as if we were ashamed of it. We must ask people to meet them."

"Yes," sighed Mrs. Corey. "There are not many people in town yet," she added, with relief that caused her husband another smile. "There really seems a sort of fatality about it," she concluded, religiously.

"Then you had better not struggle against it. Go and reconcile Lily and Nanny to it as soon as possible."

Mrs. Corey blanched a little. "But don't you think it will be the best thing, Bromfield?"

"I do indeed, my dear. The only thing that shakes my faith in the scheme is the fact that I first suggested it. But if you have adopted it, it must be all right, Anna. I can't say that I expected it."

"No," said his wife, "it wouldn't do."

XIII

Having distinctly given up the project of asking the Laphams to dinner, Mrs. Corey was able to carry it out with the courage of sinners who have sacrificed to virtue by frankly acknowledging its superiority to their intended transgression. She did not question but the Laphams would come; and she only doubted as to the people whom she should invite to meet them. She opened the matter with some trepidation to her daughters, but neither of them opposed her; they rather looked at the scheme from her own point of view, and agreed with her that nothing had really yet been done to wipe out the obligation to the Laphams helplessly contracted the summer before, and strengthened by that ill-advised application to Mrs. Lapham for charity. Not only the principal of their debt of gratitude remained, but the accruing interest. They said, What harm could giving the dinner possibly do them? They might ask any or all of their acquaintance without disadvantage to themselves; but it would be perfectly easy to give the dinner just the character they chose, and still flatter the ignorance of the Laphams. The trouble would be with Tom, if he were really interested in the girl; but he could not say anything if they made it a family dinner; he could not feel anything. They had each turned in her own mind, as it appeared from a comparison of ideas, to one of the most comprehensive of those cousinships which form the admiration and terror of the adventurer in Boston society. He finds himself hemmed in and left out at every turn by ramifications that forbid him all hope of safe personality in his comments on people; he is never less secure than when he hears some given Bostonian denouncing or ridiculing another. If he will be advised, he will guard himself from concurring in these criticisms, however just they appear, for the probability is that their object is a cousin of not more than one remove from the censor. When the alien hears a group of Boston ladies calling one another, and speaking of all their gentlemen friends, by the familiar abbreviations of their Christian names, he must feel keenly the exile to which he was born; but he is then, at least, in comparatively little danger; while these latent and tacit cousinships open pitfalls at every step around him, in a society where Middlesexes have

161

married Essexes and produced Suffolks for two hundred and fifty years.

These conditions, however, so perilous to the foreigner, are a source of strength and security to those native to them. An uncertain acquaintance may be so effectually involved in the meshes of such a cousinship, as never to be heard of outside of it; and tremendous stories are told of people who have spent a whole winter in Boston, in a whirl of gayety, and who, the original guests of the Suffolks, discover upon reflection that they have met no one but Essexes and Middlesexes.

Mrs. Corey's brother James came first into her mind, and she thought with uncommon toleration of the easy-going, uncritical good-nature of his wife. James Bellingham had been the adviser of her son throughout, and might be said to have actively promoted his connection with Lapham. She thought next of the widow of her cousin, Henry Bellingham, who had let her daughter marry that Western steamboat man, and was fond of her son-in-law; she might be expected at least to endure the paint-king and his family. The daughters insisted so strongly upon Mrs. Bellingham's son, Charles, that Mrs. Corey put him down—if he were in town; he might be in Central America; he got on with all sorts of people. It seemed to her that she might stop at this: four Laphams, five Coreys, and four Bellinghams were enough.

"That makes thirteen," said Nanny. "You can have Mr. and Mrs. Sewell."

"Yes, that is a good idea," assented Mrs. Corey. "He is our minister, and it is very proper."

"I don't see why you don't have Robert Chase. It is a pity he shouldn't see her—for the color."

"I don't quite like the idea of that," said Mrs. Corey; "but we can have him too, if it won't make too many." The painter had married into a poorer branch of the Coreys, and his wife was dead. "Is there any one else?"

"There is Miss Kingsbury."

"We have had her so much. She will begin to think we are using her."

"She won't mind; she's so good-natured."

"Well, then," the mother summed up, "there are four Laphams,

five Coreys, four Bellinghams, one Chase, and one Kingsbury—
fifteen. Oh! and two Sewells. Seventeen. Ten ladies and seven gentlemen. It doesn't balance very well, and it's too large."

"Perhaps some of the ladies won't come," suggested Lily.

"Oh, the ladies always come," said Nanny.

Their mother reflected. "Well, I will ask them. The ladies will refuse in time to let us pick up some gentlemen somewhere; some
more artists. Why! we must have Mr. Seymour, the architect; he's a
bachelor, and he's building their house, Tom says."

Her voice fell a little when she mentioned her son's name, and
she told him of her plan, when he came home in the evening, with
evident misgiving.

"What are you doing it for, mother?" he asked, looking at her
with his honest eyes.

She dropped her own in a little confusion. "I won't do it at all,
my dear," she said, "if you don't approve. But I thought——You
know we have never made any proper acknowledgment of their
kindness to us at Baie St. Joan. Then in the winter, I'm ashamed to
say, I got money from her for a charity I was interested in; and I hate
the idea of merely using people in that way. And now your having
been at their house this summer—we can't seem to disapprove of
that; and your business relations to him——"

"Yes, I see," said Corey. "Do you think it amounts to a dinner?"

"Why, I don't know," returned his mother. "We shall have hardly
any one out of our family connection."

"Well," Corey assented, "it might do. I suppose what you wish
is to give them a pleasure."

"Why, certainly. Don't you think they'd like to come?"

"Oh, they'd like to come; but whether it would be a pleasure
after they were here is another thing. I should have said that if you
wanted to have them, they would enjoy better being simply asked to
meet our own immediate family."

"That's what I thought of in the first place, but your father
seemed to think it implied a social distrust of them; and we couldn't
afford to have that appearance, even to ourselves."

"Perhaps he was right."

"And besides, it might seem a little significant."

Corey seemed inattentive to this consideration. "Whom did you think of asking?" His mother repeated the names. "Yes, that would do," he said, with a vague dissatisfaction.

"I won't have it at all, if you don't wish, Tom."

"Oh, yes, have it; perhaps you ought. Yes, I dare say it's right. What did you mean by a family dinner seeming significant?"

His mother hesitated. When it came to that, she did not like to recognize in his presence the anxieties that had troubled her. But "I don't know," she said, since she must. "I shouldn't want to give that young girl, or her mother, the idea that we wished to make more of the acquaintance than—than you did, Tom."

He looked at her absent-mindedly, as if he did not take her meaning. But he said, "Oh, yes, of course," and Mrs. Corey, in the uncertainty in which she seemed destined to remain concerning this affair, went off and wrote her invitation to Mrs. Lapham. Later in the evening, when they again found themselves alone, her son said, "I don't think I understood you, mother, in regard to the Laphams. I think I do now. I certainly don't wish you to make more of the acquaintance than I have done. It wouldn't be right; it might be very unfortunate. Don't give the dinner!"

"It's too late now, my son," said Mrs. Corey. "I sent my note to Mrs. Lapham an hour ago." Her courage rose at the trouble which showed in Corey's face. "But don't be annoyed by it, Tom. It isn't a family dinner, you know, and everything can be managed without embarrassment. If we take up the affair at this point, you will seem to have been merely acting for us; and they can't possibly understand anything more."

"Well, well! Let it go! I dare say it's all right. At any rate, it can't be helped now."

"I don't wish to help it, Tom," said Mrs. Corey, with a cheerfulness which the thought of the Laphams had never brought her before. "I am sure it is quite fit and proper, and we can make them have a very pleasant time. They are good, inoffensive people, and we owe it to ourselves not to be afraid to show that we have felt their kindness to us, and his appreciation of you."

"Well," consented Corey. The trouble that his mother had suddenly cast off was in his tone; but she was not sorry. It was quite time that he should think seriously of his attitude toward these people if he had not thought of it before, but, according to his father's theory, had been merely dangling.

It was a view of her son's character that could hardly have pleased her in different circumstances; yet it was now unquestionably a consolation if not wholly a pleasure. If she considered the Laphams at all, it was with the resignation which we feel at the evils of others, even when they have not brought them on themselves.

Mrs. Lapham, for her part, had spent the hours between Mrs. Corey's visit and her husband's coming home from business in reaching the same conclusion with regard to Corey; and her spirits were at the lowest when they sat down to supper. Irene was downcast with her; Penelope was purposely gay; and the Colonel was beginning, after his first plate of the boiled ham,—which, bristling with cloves, rounded its bulk on a wide platter before him,—to take note of the surrounding mood, when the door-bell jingled peremptorily, and the girl left waiting on the table to go and answer it. She returned at once with a note for Mrs. Lapham, which she read, and then, after a helpless survey of her family, read again.

"Why, what is it, mamma?" asked Irene; while the Colonel, who had taken up his carving-knife for another attack on the ham, held it drawn half across it.

"Why, I don't know what it does mean," answered Mrs. Lapham tremulously, and she let the girl take the note from her.

Irene ran it over, and then turned to the name at the end with a joyful cry and a flush that burned to the top of her forehead. Then she began to read it once more.

The Colonel dropped his knife and frowned impatiently, and Mrs. Lapham said, "You read it out loud, if you know what to make of it, Irene." But Irene, with a nervous scream of protest, handed it to her father, who performed the office.

"DEAR MRS. LAPHAM:

"Will you and General Lapham——"

"I didn't know I was a general," grumbled Lapham. "I guess I shall have to be looking up my back pay. Who is it writes this, anyway?" he asked, turning the letter over for the signature.

"Oh, never mind. Read it through!" cried his wife, with a kindling glance of triumph at Penelope, and he resumed:

"*—and your daughters give us the pleasure of your company at dinner on Thursday, the 28th, at half-past six.*

"*Yours sincerely,*
"*ANNA B. COREY.*"

The brief invitation had been spread over two pages, and the Colonel had difficulties with the signature which he did not instantly surmount. When he had made out the name and pronounced it, he looked across at his wife for an explanation.

"I don't know what it all means," she said, shaking her head and speaking with a pleased flutter. "She was here this afternoon, and I should have said she had come to see how bad she *could* make us feel. I declare, I never felt so put down in my life by anybody."

"Why, what did she do? What did she say?" Lapham was ready, in his dense pride, to resent any affront to his blood, but doubtful, with the evidence of this invitation to the contrary, if any affront had been offered. Mrs. Lapham tried to tell him, but there was really nothing tangible; and when she came to put it into words, she could not make out a case. Her husband listened to her excited attempt, and then he said, with judicial superiority, "I guess nobody's been trying to make you feel bad, Persis. What would she go right home and invite you to dinner for, if she'd acted the way you say?"

In this view it did seem improbable, and Mrs. Lapham was shaken. She could only say, "Penelope felt just the way I did about it."

Lapham looked at the girl, who said, "Oh, I can't prove it! I begin to think it never happened. I guess it didn't."

"Humph!" said her father, and he sat frowning thoughtfully awhile—ignoring her mocking irony, or choosing to take her seriously. "You can't really put your finger on anything," he said to his wife, "and it ain't likely there *is* anything. Anyway, she's done the proper thing by you now."

Mrs. Lapham faltered between her lingering resentment and the appeals of her flattered vanity. She looked from Penelope's impassive face to the eager eyes of Irene. "Well—just as you *say*, Silas. I don't know as she *was* so very bad. I guess may be she was embarrassed some——"

"That's what I told you, mamma, from the start," interrupted Irene. "Didn't I tell you she didn't mean anything by it? It's just the way she acted at Baie St. Joan, when she got well enough to realize what you'd done for her!"

Penelope broke into a laugh. "Is that her way of showing her gratitude? I'm sorry I didn't understand that before."

Irene made no effort to reply. She merely looked from her mother to her father with a grieved face for their protection, and Lapham said, "When we've done supper, you answer her, Persis. Say we'll come."

"With one exception," said Penelope.

"What do you mean?" demanded her father, with a mouth full of ham.

"Oh, nothing of importance. Merely that I'm not going."

Lapham gave himself time to swallow his morsel, and his rising wrath went down with it. "I guess you'll change your mind when the time comes," he said. "Anyway, Persis, you say we'll all come, and then, if Penelope don't want to go, you can excuse her after we get there. That's the best way."

None of them, apparently, saw any reason why the affair should not be left in this way, or had a sense of the awful and binding nature of a dinner-engagement. If she believed that Penelope would not finally change her mind and go, no doubt Mrs. Lapham thought that Mrs. Corey would easily excuse her absence. She did not find it so simple a matter to accept the invitation. Mrs. Corey had said "Dear Mrs. Lapham," but Mrs. Lapham had her doubts whether it would not be a servile imitation to say "Dear Mrs. Corey" in return; and she was tormented as to the proper phrasing throughout and the precise temperature which she should impart to her politeness. She wrote an unpracticed, uncharacteristic round hand, the same in which she used to set the children's copies at school, and she subscribed herself, after some hesitation between her husband's given name and her own, "Yours truly, Mrs. S. Lapham."

Penelope had gone to her room, without waiting to be asked to advise or criticise; but Irene had decided upon the paper, and, on the whole, Mrs. Lapham's note made a very decent appearance on the page.

When the furnace-man came, the Colonel sent him out to post it in the box at the corner of the square. He had determined not to

say anything more about the matter before the girls, not choosing to
let them see that he was elated; he tried to give the effect of its being
an every-day sort of thing, abruptly closing the discussion with his
order to Mrs. Lapham to accept; but he had remained swelling behind his newspaper during her prolonged struggle with her note,
and he could no longer hide his elation when Irene followed her sister upstairs.

"Well, Pers," he demanded, "what do you say now?"

Mrs. Lapham had been sobered into something of her former
misgiving by her difficulties with her note. "Well, I don't know what
to say. I declare, I'm all mixed up about it, and I don't know as we've
begun as we can carry out in promising to go. I presume," she sighed,
"that we can all send some excuse at the last moment, if we don't
want to go."

"I guess we can carry out, and I guess we sha'n't want to send
any excuse," bragged the Colonel. "If we're ever going to be anybody
at all, we've got to go and see how it's done. I presume we've got to
give some sort of party when we get into the new house, and this
gives the chance to ask 'em back again. You can't complain now but
what they've made the advances, Persis?"

"No," said Mrs. Lapham, lifelessly; "I wonder why they wanted
to do it. Oh, I suppose it's all right," she added in deprecation of
the anger with her humility which she saw rising in her husband's
face; "but if it's all going to be as much trouble as that letter, I'd
rather be whipped. I don't know what I'm going to wear; or the
girls, either. I do wonder—I've heard that people go to dinner in
low-necks. Do you suppose it's the custom?"

"How should I know?" demanded the Colonel. "I guess you've
got clothes enough. Any rate, you needn't fret about it. You just go
round to White's, or Jordan & Marsh's,* and ask for a dinner dress. I
guess that'll settle it; they'll know. Get some of them imported
dresses. I see 'em in the window every time I pass; lots of 'em."

"Oh, it ain't the dress!" said Mrs. Lapham. "I don't suppose but
what we could get along with that; and I want to do the best we can
for the children; but I don't know what we're going to talk about to
those people when we get there. We haven't got anything in common

---

*Boston department stores.

with them. Oh, I don't say they're any better," she again made haste
to say in arrest of her husband's resentment. "I don't believe they are;
and I don't see why they should be. And there ain't anybody has got
a better right to hold up their head than you have, Silas. You've got
plenty of money, and you've made every cent of it."

"I guess I shouldn't amounted to much without you, Persis," interposed Lapham, moved to this justice by her praise.

"Oh, don't talk about *me!*" protested the wife. "Now that you've
made it all right about Rogers, there ain't a thing in this world
against you. But still, for all that, I can see—and I can feel it when I
can't see it—that we're different from those people. They're well-
meaning enough, and they'd excuse it, I presume, but we're too old
to learn to be like them."

"The children ain't," said Lapham, shrewdly.

"No, the children ain't," admitted his wife, "and that's the only
thing that reconciles me to it."

"You see how pleased Irene looked when I read it?"

"Yes, she was pleased."

"And I guess Penelope'll think better of it before the time
comes."

"Oh, yes, we do it for them. But whether we're doing the best
thing for 'em, goodness knows. I'm not saying anything against him.
Irene'll be a lucky girl to get him, if she wants him. But there! I'd ten
times rather she was going to marry such a fellow as you were, Si, that
had to make every inch of his own way, and she had to help him. It's
in her!"

Lapham laughed aloud for pleasure in his wife's fondness; but
neither of them wished that he should respond directly to it. "I
guess, if it wa'n't for me, he wouldn't have a much easier time. But
don't you fret! It's all coming out right. That dinner ain't a thing for
you to be uneasy about. It'll pass off perfectly easy and natural."

Lapham did not keep his courageous mind quite to the end of
the week that followed. It was his theory not to let Corey see that he
was set up about the invitation, and when the young man said politely that his mother was glad they were able to come, Lapham was
very short with him. He said yes, he believed that Mrs. Lapham and
the girls were going. Afterward he was afraid Corey might not understand that he was coming too; but he did not know how to approach

the subject again, and Corey did not, so he let it pass. It worried him
to see all the preparation that his wife and Irene were making, and
he tried to laugh at them for it; and it worried him to find that Penelope was making no preparation at all for herself, but only helping
the others. He asked her what should she do if she changed her mind
at the last moment and concluded to go, and she said she guessed she
should not change her mind, but if she did, she would go to White's
with him and get him to choose her an imported dress, he seemed
to like them so much. He was too proud to mention the subject again
to her.

Finally, all that dress-making in the house began to scare him
with vague apprehensions in regard to his own dress. As soon as he
had determined to go, an ideal of the figure in which he should go
presented itself to his mind. He should not wear any dress-coat, because, for one thing, he considered that a man looked like a fool in
a dress-coat, and, for another thing, he had none—had none on
principle. He would go in a frock-coat and black pantaloons, and
perhaps a white waistcoat, but a black cravat, anyway. But as soon as
he developed this ideal to his family, which he did in pompous dis-
dain of their anxieties about their own dress, they said he should not
go so. Irene reminded him that he was the only person without a
dress-coat at a corps-reunion dinner which he had taken her to some
years before, and she remembered feeling awfully about it at the
time. Mrs. Lapham, who would perhaps have agreed of herself, shook
her head with misgiving. "I don't see but what you'll have to get you
one, Si," she said. "I don't believe they *ever* go without 'em to a private house."

He held out openly, but on his way home the next day, in a sudden panic, he cast anchor before his tailor's door and got measured
for a dress-coat. After that he began to be afflicted about his waistcoat, concerning which he had hitherto been airily indifferent. He
tried to get opinion out of his family, but they were not so clear
about it as they were about the frock. It ended in their buying a book
of etiquette, which settled the question adversely to a white waistcoat. The author, however, after being very explicit in telling them
not to eat with their knives, and above all not to pick their teeth with
their forks,—a thing which he said no lady or gentleman ever did,—
was still far from decided as to the kind of cravat Colonel Lapham

ought to wear: shaken on other points, Lapham had begun to waver also concerning the black cravat. As to the question of gloves for the Colonel, which suddenly flashed upon him one evening, it appeared never to have entered the thoughts of the etiquette man, as Lapham called him. Other authors on the same subject were equally silent, and Irene could only remember having heard, in some vague sort of way, that gentlemen did not wear gloves so much any more.

Drops of perspiration gathered on Lapham's forehead in the anxiety of the debate; he groaned, and he swore a little in the compromise profanity which he used.

"I declare," said Penelope, where she sat purblindly sewing on a bit of dress for Irene, "the Colonel's clothes are as much trouble as anybody's. Why don't you go to Jordan & Marsh's and order one of the imported dresses for yourself, father?" That gave them all the relief of a laugh over it, the Colonel joining in piteously.

He had an awful longing to find out from Corey how he ought to go. He formulated and repeated over to himself an apparently careless question, such as, "Oh, by the way, Corey, where do you get your gloves?" This would naturally lead to some talk on the subject, which would, if properly managed, clear up the whole trouble. But Lapham found that he would rather die than ask this question, or any question that would bring up the dinner again. Corey did not recur to it, and Lapham avoided the matter with positive fierceness. He shunned talking with Corey at all, and suffered in grim silence.

One night, before they fell asleep, his wife said to him, "I was reading in one of those books to-day, and I don't believe but what we've made a mistake if Pen holds out that she won't go."

"Why?" demanded Lapham, in the dismay which beset him at every fresh recurrence to the subject.

"The book says that it's very impolite not to answer a dinner invitation promptly. Well, we've done that all right,—at first I didn't know but what we had been a little too quick, may be,—but then it says if you're not going, that it's the height of rudeness not to let them know at once, so that they can fill your place at the table."

The Colonel was silent for a while. "Well, I'm dumned," he said finally, "if there seems to be any end to this thing. If it was to do over again, I'd say no for all of us."

"I've wished a hundred times they hadn't asked us; but it's too late to think about that now. The question is, what are we going to do about Penelope?"

"Oh, I guess she'll go, at the last moment."

"She says she won't. She took a prejudice against Mrs. Corey that day, and she can't seem to get over it."

"Well, then, hadn't you better write in the morning, as soon as you're up, that she ain't coming?"

Mrs. Lapham sighed helplessly. "I shouldn't know how to get it in. It's so late now; I don't see how I could have the face."

"Well, then, she's got to go, that's all."

"She's set she won't."

"And I'm set she shall," said Lapham, with the loud obstinacy of a man whose women always have their way.

Mrs. Lapham was not supported by the sturdiness of his proclamation.

But she did not know how to do what she knew she ought to do about Penelope, and she let matters drift. After all, the child had a right to stay at home if she did not wish to go. That was what Mrs. Lapham felt, and what she said to her husband next morning, bidding him let Penelope alone, unless she chose herself to go. She said it was too late now to do anything, and she must make the best excuse she could when she saw Mrs. Corey. She began to wish that Irene and her father would go and excuse her too. She could not help saying this, and then she and Lapham had some unpleasant words.

"Look here!" he cried. "Who wanted to go in for these people in the first place? Didn't you come home full of 'em last year, and want me to sell out here and move somewheres else because it didn't seem to suit 'em? And now you want to put it all on me! I ain't going to stand it."

"Hush!" said his wife. "Do you want to raise the house? I didn't put it on you, as you say. You took it on yourself. Ever since that fellow happened to come into the new house that day, you've been perfectly crazy to get in with them. And now you're so afraid you shall do something wrong before 'em, you don't hardly dare to say your life's your own. I declare, if you pester me any more about those gloves, Silas Lapham, I won't go."

"Do you suppose I want to go on my own account?" he demanded furiously.

"No," she admitted. "Of course I don't. I know very well that you're doing it for Irene; but, for goodness gracious sake, don't worry our lives out, and make yourself a perfect laughing-stock before the children."

With this modified concession from her, the quarrel closed in sullen silence on Lapham's part. The night before the dinner came, and the question of his gloves was still unsettled, and in a fair way to remain so. He had bought a pair, so as to be on the safe side, perspiring in company with the young lady who sold them, and who helped him try them on at the shop; his nails were still full of the powder which she had plentifully peppered into them in order to overcome the resistance of his blunt fingers. But he was uncertain whether he should wear them. They had found a book at last that said the ladies removed their gloves on sitting down at table, but it said nothing about gentlemen's gloves. He left his wife where she stood half hook-and-eyed at her glass in her new dress, and went down to his own den beyond the parlor. Before he shut his door he caught a glimpse of Irene trailing up and down before the long mirror in her new dress, followed by the seamstress on her knees; the woman had her mouth full of pins, and from time to time she made Irene stop till she could put one of the pins into her train; Penelope sat in a corner criticising and counseling. It made Lapham sick, and he despised himself and all his brood for the trouble they were taking. But another glance gave him a sight of the young girl's face in the mirror, beautiful and radiant with happiness; and his heart melted again with paternal tenderness and pride. It was going to be a great pleasure to Irene, and Lapham felt that she was bound to cut out anything there. He was vexed with Penelope that she was not going, too; he would have liked to have those people hear her talk. He held his door a little open, and listened to the things she was "getting off" there to Irene. He showed that he felt really hurt and disappointed about Penelope, and the girl's mother made her console him the next evening before they all drove away without her. "You try to look on the bright side of it, father. I guess you'll see that it's best I didn't go when you get there. Irene needn't open her lips, and they can all see how pretty she is; but they wouldn't know how smart I was unless I talked, and may be then they wouldn't."

This thrust at her father's simple vanity in her made him laugh; and then they drove away, and Penelope shut the door, and went upstairs with her lips firmly shutting in a sob.

XIV

The Coreys were one of the few old families who lingered in Bellingham Place, the handsome, quiet old street which the sympathetic observer must grieve to see abandoned to boarding-houses. The dwellings are stately and tall, and the whole place wears an air of aristocratic seclusion, which Mrs. Corey's father might well have thought assured when he left her his house there at his death. It is one of two evidently designed by the same architect who built some houses in a characteristic taste on Beacon street opposite the Common. It has a wooden portico, with slender fluted columns, which have always been painted white, and which, with the delicate moldings of the cornice, form the sole and sufficient decoration of the street front; nothing could be simpler, and nothing could be better. Within, the architect has again indulged his preference for the classic; the roof of the vestibule, wide and low, rests on marble columns, slim and fluted like the wooden columns without, and an ample staircase climbs in a graceful, easy curve from the tessellated pavement. Some carved Venetian *scrigni** stretched along the wall; a rug lay at the foot of the stairs; but otherwise the simple adequacy of the architectural intention had been respected, and the place looked bare to the eyes of the Laphams when they entered. The Coreys had once kept a man, but when young Corey began his retrenchments the man had yielded to the neat maid who showed the Colonel into the reception-room and asked the ladies to walk up two flights.

He had his charges from Irene not to enter the drawing-room without her mother, and he spent five minutes in getting on his gloves, for he had desperately resolved to wear them at last. When he had them on, and let his large fists hang down on either side, they looked, in the saffron tint which the shop-girl said his gloves should be of, like canvased hams. He perspired with doubt as he climbed the stairs, and while he waited on the landing for Mrs. Lapham and Irene to come down from above, before going into the drawing-room, he stood staring at his hands, now open and now shut, and

*Chests for valuables, strongboxes (Italian).

breathing hard. He heard quiet talking beyond the *portière** within, and presently Tom Corey came out.

"Ah, Colonel Lapham! Very glad to see you."

Lapham shook hands with him and gasped, "Waiting for Mis' Lapham," to account for his presence. He had not been able to button his right glove, and he now began, with as much indifference as he could assume, to pull them both off, for he saw that Corey wore none. By the time he had stuffed them into the pocket of his coat-skirt his wife and daughter descended.

Corey welcomed them very cordially too, but looked a little mystified. Mrs. Lapham knew that he was silently inquiring for Penelope, and she did not know whether she ought to excuse her to him first or not. She said nothing, and after a glance toward the regions where Penelope might conjecturably be lingering, he held aside the *portière* for the Laphams to pass, and entered the room with them.

Mrs. Lapham had decided against low-necks on her own responsibility, and had intrenched herself in the safety of a black silk, in which she looked very handsome. Irene wore a dress of one of those shades which only a woman or an artist can decide to be green or blue, and which to other eyes looks both or neither, according to their degrees of ignorance. If it was more like a ball dress than a dinner dress, that might be excused to the exquisite effect. She trailed, a delicate splendor, across the carpet in her mother's somber wake, and the consciousness of success brought a vivid smile to her face. Lapham, pallid with anxiety lest he should somehow disgrace himself, giving thanks to God that he should have been spared the shame of wearing gloves where no one else did, but at the same time despairing that Corey should have seen him in them, had an unwonted aspect of almost pathetic refinement.

Mrs. Corey exchanged a quick glance of surprise and relief with her husband as she started across the room to meet her guests, and in her gratitude to them for being so irreproachable, she threw into her manner a warmth that people did not always find there. "General Lapham?" she said, shaking hands in quick succession with Mrs. Lapham and Irene, and now addressing herself to him.

---

*Door curtain (French).

"No, ma'am, only Colonel," said the honest man, but the lady did not hear him. She was introducing her husband to Lapham's wife and daughter, and Bromfield Corey was already shaking his hand and saying he was very glad to see him again, while he kept his artistic eye on Irene, and apparently could not take it off. Lily Corey gave the Lapham ladies a greeting which was physically rather than socially cold, and Nanny stood holding Irene's hand in both of hers a moment, and taking in her beauty and her style with a generous admiration which she could afford, for she was herself faultlessly dressed in the quiet taste of her city, and looking very pretty. The interval was long enough to let every man present confide his sense of Irene's beauty to every other; and then, as the party was small, Mrs. Corey made everybody acquainted. When Lapham had not quite understood, he held the person's hand, and, leaning urbanely forward, inquired, "What name?" He did that because a great man to whom he had been presented on the platform at a public meeting had done so to him, and he knew it must be right.

A little lull ensued upon the introductions, and Mrs. Corey said quietly to Mrs. Lapham, "Can I send any one to be of use to Miss Lapham?" as if Penelope must be in the dressing-room.

Mrs. Lapham turned fire-red, and the graceful forms in which she had been intending to excuse her daughter's absence went out of her head. "She isn't upstairs," she said, at her bluntest, as country people are when embarrassed. "She didn't feel just like coming tonight. I don't know as she's feeling very well."

Mrs. Corey emitted a very small "O!"—very small, very cold,—which began to grow larger and hotter and to burn into Mrs. Lapham's soul before Mrs. Corey could add, "I'm very sorry. It's nothing serious, I hope?"

Robert Chase, the painter, had not come, and Mrs. James Bellingham was not there, so that the table really balanced better without Penelope; but Mrs. Lapham could not know this, and did not deserve to know it. Mrs. Corey glanced round the room, as if to take account of her guests, and said to her husband, "I think we are all here, then," and he came forward and gave his arm to Mrs. Lapham. She perceived then that in their determination not to be the first to come, they had been the last, and must have kept the others waiting for them.

Lapham had never seen people go down to dinner arm-in-arm before, but he knew that his wife was distinguished in being taken out by the host, and he waited in jealous impatience to see if Tom Corey would offer his arm to Irene. He gave it to that big girl they called Miss Kingsbury, and the handsome old fellow whom Mrs. Corey had introduced as her cousin took Irene out. Lapham was startled from the misgiving in which this left him by Mrs. Corey's passing her hand through his arm, and he made a sudden movement forward, but felt himself gently restrained. They went out the last of all; he did not know why, but he submitted, and when they sat down he saw that Irene, although she had come in with that Mr. Bellingham, was seated beside young Corey, after all.

He fetched a long sigh of relief when he sank into his chair and felt himself safe from error if he kept a sharp lookout and did only what the others did. Bellingham had certain habits which he permitted himself, and one of these was tucking the corner of his napkin into his collar; he confessed himself an uncertain shot with a spoon, and defended his practice on the ground of neatness and common sense. Lapham put his napkin into his collar too, and then, seeing that no one but Bellingham did it, became alarmed and took it out again slyly. He never had wine on his table at home, and on principle he was a prohibitionist; but now he did not know just what to do about the glasses at the right of his plate. He had a notion to turn them all down, as he had read of a well-known politician's doing at a public dinner, to show that he did not take wine; but, after twiddling with one of them a moment, he let them be, for it seemed to him that would be a little too conspicuous, and he felt that every one was looking. He let the servant fill them all, and he drank out of each, not to appear odd. Later, he observed that the young ladies were not taking wine, and he was glad to see that Irene had refused it, and that Mrs. Lapham was letting it stand untasted. He did not know but he ought to decline some of the dishes, or at least leave most of some on his plate, but he was not able to decide; he took everything and ate everything.

He noticed that Mrs. Corey seemed to take no more trouble about the dinner than anybody, and Mr. Corey rather less; he was talking busily to Mrs. Lapham, and Lapham caught a word here and there that convinced him she was holding her own. He was getting on famously himself with Mrs. Corey, who had begun with him about his new house; he was telling her all about it, and giving her his ideas. Their conversation naturally included his architect across the table; Lapham had been delighted and secretly surprised to find the fellow there; and at something Seymour said the talk spread suddenly, and the pretty house he was building for Colonel Lapham became the general theme. Young Corey testified to its loveliness, and the architect said laughingly that if he had been able to make a nice thing of it, he owed it to the practical sympathy of his client.

"Practical sympathy is good," said Bromfield Corey; and, slanting his head confidentially to Mrs. Lapham, he added, "Does he bleed your husband, Mrs. Lapham? He's a terrible fellow for appropriations!"

Mrs. Lapham laughed, reddening consciously, and said she guessed the Colonel knew how to take care of himself. This struck Lapham, then draining his glass of sauterne, as wonderfully discreet in his wife.

Bromfield Corey leaned back in his chair a moment. "Well, after all, you can't say, with all your modern fuss about it, that you do much better now than the old fellows who built such houses as this."

"Ah," said the architect, "nobody can do better than well. Your house is in perfect taste; you know I've always admired it; and I don't think it's at all the worse for being old-fashioned. What we've done is largely to go back of the hideous style that raged after they forgot how to make this sort of house. But I think we may claim a better feeling for structure. We use better material, and more wisely; and by and by we shall work out something more characteristic and original."

"With your chocolates and olives, and your clutter of bric-à-brac?"

"All that's bad, of course, but I don't mean that. I don't wish to make you envious of Colonel Lapham, and modesty prevents my saying that his house is prettier,—though I may have my convictions,—but it's better built. All the new houses are better built. Now, your house———"

"Mrs. Corey's house," interrupted the host, with a burlesque haste in disclaiming responsibility for it that made them all laugh.

"My ancestral halls are in Salem, and I'm told you couldn't drive a nail into their timbers; in fact, I don't know that you would want to do it."

"I should consider it a species of sacrilege," answered Seymour, "and I shall be far from pressing the point I was going to make against a house of Mrs. Corey's."

This won Seymour the easy laugh, and Lapham silently wondered that the fellow never got off any of those things to him.

"Well," said Corey, "you architects and the musicians are the true and only artistic creators. All the rest of us, sculptors, painters, novelists, and tailors, deal with forms that we have before us; we try to imitate, we try to represent. But you two sorts of artists create form. If you represent, you fail. Somehow or other you do evolve the camel out of your inner consciousness."

"I will not deny the soft impeachment," said the architect, with a modest air.

"I dare say. And you'll own that it's very handsome of me to say this, after your unjustifiable attack on Mrs. Corey's property."

Bromfield Corey addressed himself again to Mrs. Lapham, and the talk subdivided itself as before. It lapsed so entirely away from the subject just in hand, that Lapham was left with rather a good idea, as he thought it, to perish in his mind, for want of a chance to express it. The only thing like a recurrence to what they had been saying was Bromfield Corey's warning Mrs. Lapham, in some connection that Lapham lost, against Miss Kingsbury. "She's worse," he was saying, "when it comes to appropriations than Seymour himself. Depend upon it, Mrs. Lapham, she will give you no peace of your mind, now she's met you, from this out. Her tender mercies are cruel; and I leave you to supply the context from your own scriptural knowledge. Beware of her, and all her works. She calls them works of charity; but heaven knows whether they are. It don't stand to reason that she gives the poor *all* the money she gets out of people. I have my own belief "—he gave it in a whisper for the whole table to hear—"that she spends it for champagne and cigars."

Lapham did not know about that kind of talking; but Miss Kingsbury seemed to enjoy the fun as much as anybody, and he laughed with the rest.

"You shall be asked to the very next debauch of the committee, Mr. Corey; then you won't dare expose us," said Miss Kingsbury.

"I wonder you haven't been down upon Corey to go to the Chardon street home and talk with your indigent Italians in their native tongue," said Charles Bellingham. "I saw in the 'Transcript' the other night that you wanted someone for the work."

"We did think of Mr. Corey," replied Miss Kingsbury; "but we reflected that he probably wouldn't talk with them at all; he would make them keep still to be sketched, and forget all about their wants."

Upon the theory that this was a fair return for Corey's pleasantry, the others laughed again.

"There is one charity," said Corey, pretending superiority to Miss Kingsbury's point, "that is so difficult I wonder it hasn't occurred to a lady of your courageous invention."

"Yes?" said Miss Kingsbury. "What is that?"

"The occupation, by deserving poor of neat habits, of all the beautiful, airy, wholesome houses that stand empty the whole summer long, while their owners are away in their lowly cots beside the sea."

"Yes, that is terrible," replied Miss Kingsbury, with quick earnestness, while her eyes grew moist. "I have often thought of our great, cool houses standing useless here, and the thousands of poor creatures stifling in their holes and dens, and the little children dying for wholesome shelter. How cruelly selfish we are!"

"That is a very comfortable sentiment, Miss Kingsbury," said Corey, "and must make you feel almost as if you had thrown open No. 931 to the whole North End. But I am serious about this matter. I spend my summers in town, and I occupy my own house, so that I can speak impartially and intelligently; and I tell you that in some of my walks on the Hill and down on the Back Bay, nothing but the surveillance of the local policeman prevents me from applying dynamite[7] to those long rows of close-shuttered, handsome, brutally insensible houses. If I were a poor man, with a sick child pining in some garret or cellar at the North End, I should break into one of them, and camp out on the grand piano."

"Surely, Bromfield," said his wife, "you don't consider what havoc such people would make with the furniture of a nice house!"

"That is true," answered Corey, with meek conviction. "I never thought of that."

"And if you were a poor man with a sick child, I doubt if you'd have so much heart for burglary as you have now," said James Bellingham.

"It's wonderful how patient they are," said the minister. "The spectacle of the hopeless comfort the hard-working poor man sees must be hard to bear."

Lapham wanted to speak up and say that he had been there himself, and knew how such a man felt. He wanted to tell them that generally a poor man was satisfied if he could make both ends meet; that he didn't envy any one his good luck, if he had earned it, so long as he wasn't running under himself. But before he could get the courage to address the whole table, Sewell added, "I suppose he don't always think of it."

"But some day he will think about it," said Corey. "In fact, we rather invite him to think about it, in this country."

"My brother-in-law," said Charles Bellingham, with the pride a man feels in a mentionably remarkable brother-in-law, "has no end of fellows at work under him out there at Omaha, and he says it's the fellows from countries where they've been kept from thinking about it that are discontented. The Americans never make any trouble. They seem to understand that so long as we give unlimited opportunity, nobody has a right to complain."

"What do you hear from Leslie?" asked Mrs. Corey, turning from these profitless abstractions to Mrs. Bellingham.

"You know," said that lady in a lower tone, "that there is another baby?"

"No! I hadn't heard of it!"

"Yes; a boy. They have named him after his uncle."

"Yes," said Charles Bellingham, joining in. "He is said to be a noble boy and to resemble me."

"All boys of that tender age are noble," said Corey, "and look like anybody you wish them to resemble. Is Leslie still homesick for the bean-pots of her native Boston?"

"She is getting over it, I fancy," replied Mrs. Bellingham. "She's very much taken up with Mr. Blake's enterprises, and leads a very exciting life. She says she's like people who have been home from Europe three years; she's past the most poignant stage of regret, and hasn't reached the second, when they feel that they must go again."

Lapham leaned a little toward Mrs. Corey, and said of a picture which he saw on the wall opposite, "Picture of your daughter, I presume?"

"No; my daughter's grandmother. It's a Stuart Newton;* he painted a great many Salem beauties. She was a Miss Polly Burroughs. My daughter is like her, don't you think?" They both looked at Nanny Corey and then at the portrait. "Those pretty old-fashioned dresses are coming in again. I'm not surprised you took it for her. The others"—she referred to the other portraits more or less darkling on the walls—"are my people; mostly Copleys."†

These names, unknown to Lapham, went to his head like the wine he was drinking; they seemed to carry light for the moment, but a film of deeper darkness followed. He heard Charles Bellingham telling funny stories to Irene and trying to amuse the girl; she was laughing and seemed very happy. From time to time Bellingham took part in the general talk between the host and James Bellingham and Miss Kingsbury and that minister, Mr. Sewell. They talked of people mostly; it astonished Lapham to hear with what freedom they talked. They discussed these persons unsparingly; James Bellingham spoke of a man known to Lapham for his business success and great wealth as not a gentleman; his cousin Charles said he was surprised that the fellow had kept from being governor so long.

When the latter turned from Irene to make one of these excursions into the general talk, young Corey talked to her; and Lapham caught some words from which it seemed that they were speaking of Penelope. It vexed him to think she had not come; she could have talked as well as any of them; she was just as bright; and Lapham was aware that Irene was not as bright, though when he looked at her face, triumphant in its young beauty and fondness, he said to himself that it did not make any difference. He felt that he was not holding up his end of the line, however. When someone spoke to him he could only summon a few words of reply, that

<hr/>

*Gilbert Stuart Newton (1794–1835), fashionable portrait painter, nephew of Gilbert Stuart, the portrait painter best known for his images of George Washington.
†John Singleton Copley (1738–1815), celebrated Boston painter.

seemed to lead to nothing; things often came into his mind appropriate to what they were saying, but before he could get them out they were off on something else; they jumped about so, he could not keep up; but he felt, all the same, that he was not doing himself justice.

At one time the talk ran off upon a subject that Lapham had never heard talked of before; but again he was vexed that Penelope was not there, to have her say; he believed that her say would have been worth hearing.

Miss Kingsbury leaned forward and asked Charles Bellingham if he had read "Tears, Idle Tears,"* the novel that was making such a sensation; and when he said no, she said she wondered at him. "It's perfectly heart-breaking, as you'll imagine from the name; but there's such a dear old-fashioned hero and heroine in it, who keep dying for each other all the way through and making the most wildly satisfactory and unnecessary sacrifices for each other. You feel as if you'd done them yourself."

"Ah, that's the secret of its success," said Bromfield Corey. "It flatters the reader by painting the characters colossal, but with his limp and stoop, so that he feels himself of their supernatural proportions. You've read it, Nanny?"

"Yes," said his daughter. "It ought to have been called 'Slop, Silly Slop.'"

"Oh, not quite *slop*, Nanny," pleaded Miss Kingsbury.

"It's astonishing," said Charles Bellingham, "how we do like the books that go for our heart-strings. And I really suppose that you can't put a more popular thing than self-sacrifice into a novel. We do like to see people suffering sublimely."

"There was talk some years ago," said James Bellingham, "about novels going out."

"They're just coming in!" cried Miss Kingsbury.

"Yes," said Mr. Sewell, the minister. "And I don't think there ever was a time when they formed the whole intellectual experience of more people. They do greater mischief than ever."

"Don't be envious, parson," said the host.

---

*Imaginary example of a popular sentimental novel, from the title of a well-known Tennyson poem.

"No," answered Sewell. "I should be glad of their help. But those novels with old-fashioned heroes and heroines in them—excuse me, Miss Kingsbury—are ruinous!"

"Don't you feel like a moral wreck, Miss Kingsbury?" asked the host.

But Sewell went on: "The novelists might be the greatest possible help to us if they painted life as it is, and human feelings in their true proportion and relation, but for the most part they have been and are altogether noxious."

This seemed sense to Lapham; but Bromfield Corey asked: "But what if life as it is isn't amusing? Aren't we to be amused?"

"Not to our hurt," sturdily answered the minister. "And the self-sacrifice painted in most novels like this————"

"Slop, Silly Slop?" suggested the proud father of the inventor of the phrase.

"Yes—is nothing but psychical suicide, and is as wholly immoral as the spectacle of a man falling upon his sword."

"Well, I don't know but you're right, parson," said the host; and the minister, who had apparently got upon a battle-horse of his, careered onward in spite of some tacit attempts of his wife to seize the bridle.

"Right? To be sure I am right. The whole business of love, and love-making and marrying, is painted by the novelists in a monstrous disproportion to the other relations of life. Love is very sweet, very pretty————"

"Oh, thank you, Mr. Sewell," said Nanny Corey in a way that set them all laughing.

"But it's the affair, commonly, of very young people, who have not yet character and experience enough to make them interesting. In novels it's treated, not only as if it were the chief interest of life, but the sole interest of the lives of two ridiculous young persons; and it is taught that love is perpetual, that the glow of a true passion lasts forever; and that it is sacrilege to think or act otherwise."

"Well, but isn't that true, Mr. Sewell?" pleaded Miss Kingsbury.

"I have known some most estimable people who had married a second time," said the minister, and then he had the applause with him. Lapham wanted to make some open recognition of his good sense, but could not.

"I suppose the passion itself has been a good deal changed," said Bromfield Corey, "since the poets began to idealize it in the days of chivalry."

"Yes; and it ought to be changed again," said Mr. Sewell.

"What! Back?"

"I don't say that. But it ought to be recognized as something natural and mortal, and divine honors, which belong to righteousness alone, ought not to be paid it."

"Oh, you ask too much, parson," laughed his host, and the talk wandered away to something else.

It was not an elaborate dinner; but Lapham was used to having everything on the table at once, and this succession of dishes bewildered him; he was afraid perhaps he was eating too much. He now no longer made any pretense of not drinking his wine, for he was thirsty, and there was no more water, and he hated to ask for any. The ice-cream came, and then the fruit. Suddenly Mrs. Corey rose and said across the table to her husband, "I suppose you will want your coffee here." And he replied, "Yes; we'll join you at tea."

The ladies all rose, and the gentlemen got up with them. Lapham started to follow Mrs. Corey, but the other men merely stood in their places, except young Corey, who ran and opened the door for his mother. Lapham thought with shame that it was he who ought to have done that; but no one seemed to notice, and he sat down again gladly, after kicking out one of his legs which had gone to sleep.

They brought in cigars with coffee, and Bromfield Corey advised Lapham to take one that he chose for him. Lapham confessed that he liked a good cigar about as well as anybody, and Corey said: "These are new. I had an Englishman here the other day who was smoking old cigars in the superstition that tobacco improved with age, like wine."

"Ah," said Lapham, "anybody who had ever lived off a tobacco country could tell him better than that." With the fuming cigar between his lips he felt more at home than he had before. He turned sidewise in his chair and, resting one arm on the back, intertwined the fingers of both hands, and smoked at large ease.

James Bellingham came and sat down by him. "Colonel Lapham,

weren't you with the 96th Vermont when they charged across the river in front of Pickensburg, and the rebel battery opened fire on them in the water?"

Lapham slowly shut his eyes and slowly dropped his head for assent, letting out a white volume of smoke from the corner of his mouth.

"I thought so," said Bellingham. "I was with the 85th Massachusetts, and I sha'n't forget that slaughter. We were all new to it still. Perhaps that's why it made such an impression."

"I don't know," suggested Charles Bellingham. "Was there anything much more impressive afterward? I read of it out in Missouri, where I was stationed at the time, and I recollect the talk of some old army men about it. They said that death-rate couldn't be beaten. I don't know that it ever was."

"About one in five of us got out safe," said Lapham, breaking his cigar-ash off on the edge of a plate. James Bellingham reached him a bottle of Apollinaris. He drank a glass, and then went on smoking.

They all waited, as if expecting him to speak, and then Corey said: "How incredible those things seem already! You gentlemen know that they happened; but are you still able to believe it?"

"Ah, nobody feels that anything happened," said Charles Bellingham. "The past of one's experience doesn't differ a great deal from the past of one's knowledge. It isn't much more probable; it's really a great deal less vivid than some scenes in a novel that one read when a boy."

"I'm not sure of that," said James Bellingham.

"Well, James, neither am I," consented his cousin, helping himself from Lapham's Apollinaris bottle. "There would be very little talking at dinner if one only said the things that one was sure of."

The others laughed, and Bromfield Corey remarked thoughtfully, "What astonishes the craven civilian in all these things is the abundance—the superabundance—of heroism. The cowards were the exception; the men that were ready to die, the rule."

"The woods were full of them," said Lapham, without taking his cigar from his mouth.

"That's a nice little touch in 'School,' " interposed Charles

Bellingham, "where the girl says to the fellow who was at Inkerman,* 'I should think you would be so proud of it,' and he reflects
awhile, and says, 'Well, the fact is, you know, there were so many of
us.'"

"Yes, I remember that," said James Bellingham, smiling for pleasure in it. "But I don't see why you claim the credit of being a craven
civilian, Bromfield," he added, with a friendly glance at his brother-
in-law, and with the willingness Boston men often show to turn one
another's good points to the light in company; bred so intimately
together at school and college and in society, they all know these
points. "A man who was out with Garibaldi† in '48," continued James
Bellingham.

"Oh, a little amateur red-shirting," Corey interrupted in deprecation. "But even if you choose to dispute my claim, what has become of all the heroism? Tom, how many club men do you know
who would think it sweet and fitting to die for their country?"

"I can't think of a great many at the moment, sir," replied the
son, with the modesty of his generation.

"And I couldn't in '61," said his uncle. "Nevertheless they were
there."

"Then your theory is that it's the occasion that is wanting," said
Bromfield Corey. "But why shouldn't civil-service reform, and the
resumption of specie payment, and a tariff for revenue only, inspire
heroes? They are all good causes."

"It's the occasion that's wanting," said James Bellingham, ignoring the *persiflage*.‡ "And I'm very glad of it."

"So am I," said Lapham, with a depth of feeling that expressed
itself in spite of the haze in which his brain seemed to float. There
was a great deal of the talk that he could not follow; it was too quick
for him; but here was something he was clear of. "I don't want to see
any more men killed in my time." Something serious, something

---

School was an 1869 play by the popular British playwright Thomas William Robert-
son. Inkerman was the site near Savastopol of an 1854 battle in the Crimean War.
†Patriotic rebel leader Giuseppe Garibaldi (1807–1882) liberated Italy from Austrian
rule.
‡Light, mocking banter (French).

somber must lurk behind these words, and they waited for Lapham to say more; but the haze closed round him again, and he remained silent, drinking Apollinaris.

"We non-combatants were notoriously reluctant to give up fighting," said Mr. Sewell, the minister; "but I incline to think Colonel Lapham and Mr. Bellingham may be right. I dare say we shall have the heroism again if we have the occasion. Till it comes, we must content ourselves with the every-day generosities and sacrifices. They make up in quantity what they lack in quality, perhaps."

"They're not so picturesque," said Bromfield Corey. "You can paint a man dying for his country, but you can't express on canvas a man fulfilling the duties of a good citizen."

"Perhaps the novelists will get at him by and by," suggested Charles Bellingham. "If I were one of these fellows, I shouldn't propose to myself anything short of that."

"What: the commonplace?" asked his cousin.

"Commonplace? The commonplace is just that light, impalpable, aërial essence which they've never got into their confounded books yet. The novelist who could interpret the common feelings of commonplace people would have the answer to 'the riddle of the painful earth'* on his tongue."

"Oh, not so bad as that, I hope," said the host; and Lapham looked from one to the other, trying to make out what they were at. He had never been so up a tree before.

"I suppose it isn't well for us to see human nature at white heat habitually," continued Bromfield Corey, after a while. "It would make us vain of our species. Many a poor fellow in that war and in many another has gone into battle simply and purely for his country's sake, not knowing whether, if he laid down his life, he should ever find it again, or whether, if he took it up hereafter, he should take it up in heaven or hell. Come, parson!" he said, turning to the minister, "what has ever been conceived of omnipotence, of omniscience, so sublime, so divine as that?"

"Nothing," answered the minister, quietly. "God has never been imagined at all. But if you suppose such a man as that

*From Tennyson's poem "The Palace of Art" (l. 213).

was Authorized, I think it will help you to imagine what God must be."

"There's sense in that," said Lapham. He took his cigar out of his mouth, and pulled his chair a little toward the table, on which he placed his ponderous fore-arms. "I want to tell you about a fellow I had in my own company when we first went out. We were all privates to begin with; after a while they elected me captain— I'd had the tavern stand, and most of 'em knew me. But Jim Millon never got to be anything more than corporal; corporal when he was killed." The others arrested themselves in various attitudes of attention, and remained listening to Lapham with an interest that profoundly flattered him. Now, at last, he felt that he was holding up his end of the rope. "I can't say he went into the thing from the highest motives, altogether; our motives are always pretty badly mixed, and when there's such a hurrah-boys as there was then, you can't tell which is which. I suppose Jim Millon's wife was enough to account for his going, herself. She was a pretty bad assortment," said Lapham, lowering his voice and glancing round at the door to make sure that it was shut, "and she used to lead Jim *one* kind of life. Well, sir," continued Lapham, synthetizing his auditors in that form of address, "that fellow used to save every cent of his pay and send it to that woman. Used to get me to do it for him. I tried to stop him. 'Why, Jim,' said I, 'you know what she'll do with it.' 'That's so, Cap,' says he, 'but I don't know what she'll do without it.' And it did keep her straight—straight as a string—as long as Jim lasted. Seemed as if there was something mysterious about it. They had a little girl,—about as old as my oldest girl,— and Jim used to talk to me about her. Guess he done it as much for her as for the mother; and he said to me before the last action we went into, 'I should like to turn tail and run, Cap. I ain't comin' out o' this one. But I don't suppose it would do.' 'Well, not for you, Jim,' said I. 'I want to live,' he says; and he bust out crying right there in my tent. 'I want to live for poor Molly and Zerrilla'—that's what they called the little one; I dunno where they got the name. 'I ain't ever had half a chance; and now she's doing better, and I believe we should get along after this.' He set there cryin' like a baby. But he wa'n't no baby when he went into action. I hated to look at him after it was over, not so much because he'd got a ball that was meant for me by a sharp-shooter—he saw the devil takin' aim, and he jumped to warn me—as because he didn't look like Jim; he looked like—fun; all desperate and savage. I guess he died hard."

The story made its impression, and Lapham saw it. "Now I say," he resumed, as if he felt that he was going to do himself justice, and say something to heighten the effect his story had produced. At the same time, he was aware of a certain want of clearness. He had the idea, but it floated vague, elusive, in his brain. He looked about as if for something to precipitate it in tangible shape.

"Apollinaris?" asked Charles Bellingham, handing the bottle from the other side. He had drawn his chair closer than the rest to Lapham's, and was listening with great interest. When Mrs. Corey asked him to meet Lapham he accepted gladly. "You know I go in for that sort of thing, Anna. Since Leslie's affair we're rather bound to do it. And I think we meet these practical fellows too little. There's always something original about them." He might naturally have believed that the reward of his faith was coming.

"Thanks, I will take some of this wine," said Lapham, pouring himself a glass of Madeira from a black and dusty bottle caressed by a label bearing the date of the vintage. He tossed off the wine, unconscious of its preciousness, and waited for the result. That cloudiness in his brain disappeared before it, but a mere blank remained. He not only could not remember what he was going to say, but he could not recall what they had been talking about. They waited, looking at him, and he stared at them in return. After a while he heard the host saying, "Shall we join the ladies?"

Lapham went, trying to think what had happened. It seemed to him a long time since he had drunk that wine.

Miss Corey gave him a cup of tea, where he stood aloof from his wife, who was talking with Miss Kingsbury and Mrs. Sewell; Irene was with Miss Nanny Corey. He could not hear what they were talking about; but if Penelope had come he knew that she would have done them all credit. He meant to let her know how he felt about her behavior when he got home. It was a shame for her to miss such a chance. Irene was looking beautiful, as pretty as all

the rest of them put together, but she was not talking, and Lapham
perceived that at a dinner party you ought to talk. He was himself
conscious of having talked very well. He now wore an air of great
dignity and, in conversing with the other gentlemen, he used a
grave and weighty deliberation. Some of them wanted him to go
into the library. There he gave his ideas of books. He said he had
not much time for anything but the papers; but he was going to
have a complete library in his new place. He made an elaborate acknowledgment to Bromfield Corey of his son's kindness in suggesting books for his library; he said that he had ordered them all,
and that he meant to have pictures. He asked Mr. Corey who was
about the best American painter going now. "I don't set up to be a
judge of pictures, but I know what I like," he said. He lost the re-
serve which he had maintained earlier, and began to boast. He
himself introduced the subject of his paint, in a natural transition
from pictures; he said Mr. Corey must take a run up to Lapham
with him some day, and see the Works; they would interest him,
and he would drive him round the country; he kept most of his
horses up there, and he could show Mr. Corey some of the finest
Jersey grades in the country. He told about his brother William, the
judge at Dubuque; and a farm he had out there that paid for itself
every year in wheat. As he cast off all fear, his voice rose, and he
hammered his arm-chair with the thick of his hand for emphasis.
Mr. Corey seemed impressed; he sat perfectly quiet, listening, and
Lapham saw the other gentlemen stop in their talk every now and
then to listen. After this proof of his ability to interest them, he
would have liked to have Mrs. Lapham suggest again that he was
unequal to their society, or to the society of anybody else. He surprised himself by his ease among men whose names had hitherto
overawed him. He got to calling Bromfield Corey by his surname
alone. He did not understand why young Corey seemed so preoccupied, and he took occasion to tell the company how he had said
to his wife the first time he saw that fellow that he could make a
man of him if he had him in the business; and he guessed he was
not mistaken. He began to tell stories of the different young men
he had had in his employ. At last he had the talk altogether to himself; no one else talked, and he talked unceasingly. It was a great
time; it was a triumph.

He was in this successful mood when word came to him that Mrs. Lapham was going; Tom Corey seemed to have brought it, but he was not sure. Anyway, he was not going to hurry. He made cordial invitations to each of the gentlemen to drop in and see him at his office, and would not be satisfied till he had exacted a promise from each. He told Charles Bellingham that he liked him, and assured James Bellingham that it had always been his ambition to know him, and that if any one had said when he first came to Boston that in less than ten years he should be hobnobbing with Jim Bellingham, he should have told that person he lied. He would have told anybody he lied that had told him ten years ago that a son of Bromfield Corey would have come and asked him to take him into the business. Ten years ago he, Silas Lapham, had come to Boston, a little worse off than nothing at all, for he was in debt for half the money that he had bought out his partner with, and here he was now worth a million, and meeting you gentlemen like one of you. And every cent of that was honest money,—no speculation,—every copper of it for value received. And here, only the other day, his old partner, who had been going to the dogs ever since he went out of the business, came and borrowed twenty thousand dollars of him! Lapham lent it because his wife wanted him to: she had always felt bad about the fellow's having to go out of the business.

He took leave of Mr. Sewell with patronizing affection, and bade him come to him if he ever got into a tight place with his parish work; he would let him have all the money he wanted; he had more money than he knew what to do with. "Why, when your wife sent to mine last fall," he said, turning to Mr. Corey, "I drew my check for five hundred dollars, but my wife wouldn't take more than one hundred; said she wasn't going to show off before Mrs. Corey. I call that a pretty good joke on Mrs. Corey. I must tell her how Mrs. Lapham done her out of a cool four hundred dollars."

He started toward the door of the drawing-room to take leave of the ladies; but Tom Corey was at his elbow, saying, "I think Mrs. Lapham is waiting for you below, sir," and in obeying the direction Corey gave him toward another door he forgot all about his purpose, and came away without saying good-night to his hostess.

Mrs. Lapham had not known how soon she ought to go, and had no idea that in her quality of chief guest she was keeping the others. She staid till eleven o'clock, and was a little frightened when she found what time it was; but Mrs. Corey, without pressing her to stay longer, had said it was not at all late. She and Irene had had a perfect time. Everybody had been very polite; on the way home they celebrated the amiability of both the Miss Coreys and of Miss Kingsbury. Mrs. Lapham thought that Mrs. Bellingham was about the pleasantest person she ever saw; she had told her all about her married daughter who had married an inventor and gone to live in Omaha—a Mrs. Blake.

"If it's that car-wheel Blake," said Lapham, proudly, "I know all about him. I've sold him tons of the paint."

"Pooh, papa! How you do smell of smoking!" cried Irene.

"Pretty strong, eh?" laughed Lapham, letting down a window of the carriage. His heart was throbbing wildly in the close air, and he was glad of the rush of cold that came in, though it stopped his tongue, and he listened more and more drowsily to the rejoicings that his wife and daughter exchanged. He meant to have them wake Penelope up and tell her what she had lost; but when he reached home he was too sleepy to suggest it. He fell asleep as soon as his head touched the pillow, full of supreme triumph.

But in the morning his skull was sore with the unconscious, night-long ache; and he rose cross and taciturn. They had a silent breakfast. In the cold gray light of the morning the glories of the night before showed poorer. Here and there a painful doubt obtruded itself and marred them with its awkward shadow. Penelope sent down word that she was not well, and was not coming to breakfast, and Lapham was glad to go to his office without seeing her.

He was severe and silent all day with his clerks, and peremptory with customers. Of Corey he was slyly observant, and as the day wore away he grew more restively conscious. He sent out word by his office-boy that he would like to see Mr. Corey for a few minutes after closing. The type-writer girl had lingered too, as if she wished to speak with him, and Corey stood in abeyance as she went toward Lapham's door.

"Can't see you to-night, Zerrilla," he said bluffly, but not unkindly. "Perhaps I'll call at the house, if it's important."

"It is," said the girl, with a spoiled air of insistence.

"Well," said Lapham; and, nodding to Corey to enter, he closed the door upon her. Then he turned to the young man and demanded: "Was I drunk last night?"

XV

Lapham's strenuous face was broken up with the emotions that had forced him to this question: shame, fear of the things that must have been thought of him, mixed with a faint hope that he might be mistaken, which died out at the shocked and pitying look in Corey's eyes.

"Was I drunk?" he repeated. "I ask you, because I was never touched by drink in my life before, and I don't know." He stood with his huge hands trembling on the back of his chair, and his dry lips apart, as he stared at Corey.

"That is what every one understood, Colonel Lapham," said the young man. "Every one saw how it was. Don't————"

"Did they talk it over after I left?" asked Lapham, vulgarly.

"Excuse me," said Corey, blushing, "my father doesn't talk his guests over with one another." He added, with youthful superfluity, "You were among gentlemen."

"I was the only one that wasn't a gentleman there!" lamented Lapham. "I disgraced you! I disgraced my family! I mortified your father before his friends!" His head dropped. "I showed that I wasn't fit to go with you. I'm not fit for any decent place. What did I say? What did I do?" he asked, suddenly lifting his head and confronting Corey. "Out with it! If you could bear to see it and hear it, I had ought to bear to know it!"

"There was nothing—really nothing," said Corey. "Beyond the fact that you were not quite yourself, there was nothing whatever. My father *did* speak of it to me," he confessed, "when we were alone. He said that he was afraid we had not been thoughtful of you, if you were in the habit of taking only water; I told him I had not seen wine at your table. The others said nothing about you."

"Ah, but what did they think!"

"Probably what we did: that it was purely a misfortune—an accident."

"I wasn't fit to be there," persisted Lapham. "Do you want to leave?" he asked, with savage abruptness.

"Leave?" faltered the young man.

"Yes; quit the business? Cut the whole connection?"

"I haven't the remotest idea of it!" cried Corey in amazement. "Why in the world should I?"

"Because you're a gentleman, and I'm not, and it ain't right I should be over you. If you want to go, I know some parties that would be glad to get you. I will give you up if you want to go before anything worse happens, and I sha'n't blame you. I can help you to something better than I can offer you here, and I will."

"There's no question of my going, unless you wish it," said Corey. "If you do————"

"Will you tell your father," interrupted Lapham, "that I had a notion all the time that I was acting the drunken blackguard, and that I've suffered for it all day? Will you tell him I don't want him to notice me if we ever meet, and that I know I'm not fit to associate with gentlemen in anything but a business way, if I am that?"

"Certainly, I shall do nothing of the kind," retorted Corey. "I can't listen to you any longer. What you say is shocking to me—shocking in a way you can't think."

"Why, man!" exclaimed Lapham, with astonishment; "if I can stand it, you can!"

"No," said Corey, with a sick look, "that doesn't follow. You may denounce yourself, if you will; but I have my reasons for refusing to hear you—my reasons why I can't hear you. If you say another word I must go away."

"I don't understand you," faltered Lapham, in bewilderment, which absorbed even his shame.

"You exaggerate the effect of what has happened," said the young man. "It's enough, more than enough, for you to have mentioned the matter to me, and I think it's unbecoming in me to hear you."

He made a movement toward the door, but Lapham stopped him with the tragic humility of his appeal. "Don't go yet! I can't let you. I've disgusted you,—I see that; but I didn't mean to. I—I take it back."

"Oh, there's nothing to take back," said Corey, with a repressed shudder for the abasement which he had seen. "But let us say no more about it—think no more. There wasn't one of the gentlemen present last night who didn't understand the matter precisely as my father and I did, and that fact must end it between us two."

He went out into the larger office beyond, leaving Lapham helpless to prevent his going. It had become a vital necessity with him to
think the best of Lapham, but his mind was in a whirl of whatever
thoughts were most injurious. He thought of him the night before
in the company of those ladies and gentlemen, and he quivered in
resentment of his vulgar, braggart, uncouth nature. He recognized
his own allegiance to the exclusiveness to which he was born and
bred, as a man perceives his duty to his country when her rights are
invaded. His eye fell on the porter going about in his shirt-sleeves to
make the place fast for the night, and he said to himself that Dennis
was not more plebeian than his master; that the gross appetites, the
blunt sense, the purblind ambition, the stupid arrogance were the
same in both, and the difference was in a brute will that probably
left the porter the gentler man of the two. The very innocence of
Lapham's life in the direction in which he had erred wrought against
him in the young man's mood: it contained the insult of clownish
inexperience. Amidst the stings and flashes of his wounded pride, all
the social traditions, all the habits of feeling, which he had silenced
more and more by force of will during the past months, asserted
their natural sway, and he rioted in his contempt of the offensive
boor, who was even more offensive in his shame than in his trespass.
He said to himself that he was a Corey, as if that were somewhat; yet
he knew that at the bottom of his heart all the time was that which
must control him at last, and which seemed sweetly to be suffering
his rebellion, secure of his submission in the end. It was almost with
the girl's voice that it seemed to plead with him, to undo in him, effect by effect, the work of his indignant resentment, to set all things
in another and fairer light, to give him hopes, to suggest palliations,
to protest against injustices. It *was* in Lapham's favor that he was so
guiltless in the past, and now Corey asked himself if it were the first
time he could have wished a guest at his father's table to have taken
less wine; whether Lapham was not rather to be honored for not
knowing how to contain his folly where a veteran transgressor might
have held his tongue. He asked himself, with a thrill of sudden remorse, whether, when Lapham humbled himself in the dust so
shockingly, he had shown him the sympathy to which such *abandon*
had the right; and he had to own that he had met him on the gentlemanly ground, sparing himself and asserting the superiority of his

sort, and not recognizing that Lapham's humiliation came from the sense of wrong, which he had helped to accumulate upon him by superfinely standing aloof and refusing to touch him.

He shut his desk and hurried out into the early night, not to go anywhere, but to walk up and down, to try to find his way out of the chaos, which now seemed ruin, and now the materials out of which fine actions and a happy life might be shaped. Three hours later he stood at Lapham's door.

At times what he now wished to do had seemed forever impossible, and again it had seemed as if he could not wait a moment longer. He had not been careless, but very mindful of what he knew must be the feelings of his own family in regard to the Laphams, and he had not concealed from himself that his family had great reason and justice on their side in not wishing him to alienate himself from their common life and associations. The most that he could urge to himself was that they had not all the reason and justice; but he had hesitated and delayed because they had so much. Often he could not make it appear right that he should merely please himself in what chiefly concerned himself. He perceived how far apart in all their experiences and ideals the Lapham girls and his sisters were; how different Mrs. Lapham was from his mother; how grotesquely unlike were his father and Lapham; and the disparity had not always amused him.

He had often taken it very seriously, and sometimes he said that he must forego the hope on which his heart was set. There had been many times in the past months when he had said that he must go no further, and as often as he had taken this stand he had yielded it, upon this or that excuse, which he was aware of trumping up. It was part of the complication that he should be unconscious of the injury he might be doing to someone besides his family and himself; this was the defect of his diffidence; and it had come to him in a pang for the first time when his mother said that she would not have the Laphams think she wished to make more of the acquaintance than he did; and then it had come too late. Since that he had suffered quite as much from the fear that it might not be as that it might be so; and now, in the mood, romantic and exalted, in which he found himself concerning Lapham, he was as far as might be from vain confidence. He ended the question in his own mind by affirming to himself that he was there, first of all, to see Lapham and give him an ultimate proof of his own perfect faith and unabated respect, and to offer him what reparation this involved for that want of sympathy—of humanity—which he had shown.

XVI

The Nova Scotia second-girl who answered Corey's ring said that Lapham had not come home yet.

"Oh," said the young man, hesitating on the outer step.

"I guess you better come in," said the girl. "I'll go and see when they're expecting him."

Corey was in the mood to be swayed by any chance. He obeyed the suggestion of the second-girl's patronizing friendliness, and let her shut him into the drawing-room, while she went upstairs to announce him to Penelope.

"Did you tell him father wasn't at home?"

"Yes. He seemed so kind of disappointed, I told him to come in, and I'd see when he would be in," said the girl, with the human interest which sometimes replaces in the American domestic the servile deference of other countries.

A gleam of amusement passed over Penelope's face, as she glanced at herself in the glass. "Well," she cried, finally, dropping from her shoulders the light shawl in which she had been huddled over a book when Corey rang, "I will go down."

"All right," said the girl, and Penelope began hastily to amend the disarray of her hair, which she tumbled into a mass on the top of her little head, setting off the pale dark of her complexion with a flash of crimson ribbon at her throat. She moved across the carpet once or twice with the quaint grace that belonged to her small figure, made a dissatisfied grimace at it in the glass, caught a handkerchief out of a drawer and slid it into her pocket, and then descended to Corey.

The Lapham drawing-room in Nankeen Square was in the particolored paint which the Colonel had hoped to repeat in his new house: the trim of the doors and windows was in light green and the panels in salmon; the walls were a plain tint of French gray paper, divided by gilt moldings into broad panels with a wide stripe of red velvet paper running up the corners; the chandelier was of massive imitation bronze; the mirror over the mantel rested on a fringed mantel-cover of green reps, and heavy curtains of that stuff hung from gilt lambrequin* frames at the window; the carpet was of a small pattern in crude green, which, at the time Mrs. Lapham bought it, covered half the new floors in Boston. In the paneled spaces on the walls were some stone-colored landscapes, representing the mountains and cañons of the West, which the Colonel and his wife had visited on one of the early official railroad excursions. In front of the long windows looking into the square were statues, kneeling figures which turned their backs upon the company within doors, and represented allegories of Faith and Prayer to people without. A white marble group of several figures, expressing an Italian conception of Lincoln Freeing the Slaves,—a Latin negro and his wife,—with our Eagle flapping his wings in approval, at Lincoln's feet, occupied one corner, and balanced the what-not† of an earlier period in another. These phantasms added their chill to that imparted by the tone of the walls, the landscapes, and the carpets, and contributed to the violence of the contrast when the chandelier was lighted up full glare, and the heat of the whole furnace welled up from the registers into the quivering atmosphere on one of the rare occasions when the Laphams invited company.

Corey had not been in this room before; the family had always received him in what they called the sitting-room. Penelope looked into this first, and then she looked into the parlor, with a smile that broke into a laugh as she discovered him standing under the single burner, which the second-girl had lighted for him in the chandelier.

"I don't understand how you came to be put in there," she said, as she led the way to the cozier place, "unless it was because Alice thought you were only here on probation, anyway. Father hasn't got home yet, but I'm expecting him every moment; I don't know what's keeping him. Did the girl tell you that mother and Irene were out?"

"No, she didn't say. It's very good of you to see me." She had not seen the exaltation which he had been feeling, he perceived with half a sigh; it must all be upon this lower level; perhaps it was best so. "There was something I wished to say to your father————I hope," he broke off, "you're better to-night."

"Oh, yes, thank you," said Penelope, remembering that she had not been well enough to go to dinner the night before.

---

*Short ornamental drapery, or an imitation of it.
†Open shelves for knickknacks.

"We all missed you very much."

"Oh, thank you! I'm afraid you wouldn't have missed me if I had been there."

"Oh, yes, we should," said Corey, "I assure you."

They looked at each other.

"I really think I believed I was saying something," said the girl.

"And so did I," replied the young man. They laughed rather wildly, and then they both became rather grave.

He took the chair she gave him, and looked across at her, where she sat on the other side of the hearth, in a chair lower than his, with her hands dropped in her lap, and the back of her head on her shoulders as she looked up at him. The soft-coal fire in the grate purred and flickered; the drop-light cast a mellow radiance on her face. She let her eyes fall, and then lifted them for an irrelevant glance at the clock on the mantel.

"Mother and Irene have gone to the Spanish Students' concert."

"Oh, have they?" asked Corey; and he put his hat, which he had been holding in his hand, on the floor beside his chair.

She looked down at it for no reason, and then looked up at his face for no other, and turned a little red. Corey turned a little red himself. She who had always been so easy with him now became a little constrained.

"Do you know how warm it is out-of-doors?" he asked.

"No; is it warm? I haven't been out all day."

"It's like a summer night."

She turned her face towards the fire, and then started abruptly. "Perhaps it's too warm for you here?"

"Oh, no, it's very comfortable."

"I suppose it's the cold of the last few days that's still in the house. I was reading with a shawl on when you came."

"I interrupted you."

"Oh, no. I had finished the book. I was just looking over it again."

"Do you like to read books over?"

"Yes; books that I like at all."

"What was it?" asked Corey.

The girl hesitated. "It has rather a sentimental name. Did you ever read it?—'Tears, Idle Tears.' "

"Oh, yes; they were talking of that last night; it's a famous book with ladies. They break their hearts over it. Did it make you cry?"

"Oh, it's pretty easy to cry over a book," said Penelope, laughing; "and that one is very natural till you come to the main point. Then the naturalness of all the rest makes that seem natural too; but I guess it's rather forced."

"Her giving him up to the other one?"

"Yes; simply because she happened to know that the other one had cared for him first. Why should she have done it? What right had she?"

"I don't know. I suppose that the self-sacrifice————"

"But it wasn't self-sacrifice—or not self-sacrifice alone. She was sacrificing him, too; and for someone who couldn't appreciate him half as much as she could. I'm provoked with myself when I think how I cried over that book—for I did cry. It's silly—it's wicked for any one to do what that girl did. Why can't they let people have a chance to behave reasonably in stories?"

"Perhaps they couldn't make it so attractive," suggested Corey, with a smile.

"It would be novel, at any rate," said the girl. "But so it would in real life, I suppose," she added.

"I don't know. Why shouldn't people in love behave sensibly?"

"That's a very serious question," said Penelope, gravely. "I couldn't answer it," and she left him the embarrassment of supporting an inquiry which she had certainly instigated herself. She seemed to have finally recovered her own ease in doing this. "Do you admire our autumnal display, Mr. Corey?"

"Your display?"

"The trees in the square. We think it's quite equal to an opening at Jordan & Marsh's."

"Ah, I'm afraid you wouldn't let me be serious even about your maples."

"Oh, yes, I should—if you like to be serious."

"Don't you?"

"Well, not about serious matters. That's the reason that book made me cry."

"You make fun of everything. Miss Irene was telling me last night about you."

"Then it's no use for me to deny it so soon. I must give Irene a talking to."

"I hope you won't forbid her to talk about you!"

She had taken up a fan from the table, and held it, now between her face and the fire, and now between her face and him. Her little visage, with that arch, lazy look in it, topped by its mass of dusky hair, and dwindling from the full cheeks to the small chin, had a Japanese effect in the subdued light, and it had the charm which comes to any woman with happiness. It would be hard to say how much of this she perceived that he felt. They talked about other things awhile, and then she came back to what he had said. She glanced at him obliquely round her fan, and stopped moving it. "Does Irene talk about me?" she asked.

"I think so—yes. Perhaps it's only I who talk about you. You must blame me if it's wrong," he returned.

"Oh, I didn't say it was wrong," she replied. "But I hope if you said anything very bad of me, you'll let me know what it was, so that I can reform————"

"No, don't change, please!" cried the young man.

Penelope caught her breath, but went on resolutely, "Or rebuke you for speaking evil of dignities." She looked down at the fan, now flat in her lap, and tried to govern her head, but it trembled, and she remained looking down. Again they let the talk stray, and then it was he who brought it back to themselves, as if it had not left them.

"I have to talk of you," said Corey, "because I get to talk to you so seldom."

"You mean that I do all the talking, when we're—together?" She glanced sidewise at him; but she reddened after speaking the last word.

"We're so seldom together," he pursued.

"I don't know what you mean————"

"Sometimes I've thought—I've been afraid—that you avoided me."

"Avoided you?"

"Yes! Tried not to be alone with me."

She might have told him that there was no reason why she should be alone with him, and that it was very strange he should make this complaint of her. But she did not. She kept looking down at the fan, and then she lifted her burning face and looked at the clock again. "Mother and Irene will be sorry to miss you," she gasped.

He instantly rose and came towards her. She rose too, and mechanically put out her hand. He took it as if to say good-night. "I didn't mean to send you away," she besought him.

"Oh, I'm not going," he answered, simply. "I wanted to say—to say that it's I who make her talk about you. To say I— There is something I want to say to you; I've said it so often to myself that I feel as if you must know it." She stood quite still, letting him keep her hand, and questioning his face with a bewildered gaze. "You must know— she must have told you—she must have guessed————" Penelope turned white, but outwardly quelled the panic that sent the blood to her heart. "I—I didn't expect—I hoped to have seen your father— but I must speak now, whatever————I love you!"

She freed her hand from both of those he had closed upon it, and went back from him across the room with a sinuous spring. "*Me!*" Whatever potential complicity had lurked in her heart, his words brought her only immeasurable dismay.

He came towards her again. "Yes, you. Who else?"

She fended him off with an imploring gesture. "I thought—I— it was————"

She shut her lips tight, and stood looking at him where he remained in silent amaze. Then her words came again, shudderingly. "Oh, what have you done?"

"Upon my soul," he said, with a vague smile, "I don't know. I hope no harm?"

"Oh, don't laugh!" she cried, laughing hysterically herself. "Unless you want me to think you the greatest wretch in the world!"

"I?" he responded. "For heaven's sake tell me what you mean!"

"You know I can't tell you. Can you say—can you put your hand on your heart and say that—you—say you never meant—that you meant me—all along?"

"Yes!— Yes! Who else? I came here to see your father, and to tell him that I wished to tell you this—to ask him———— But what does it matter? You must have known it—you must have seen—and it's for you to answer me. I've been abrupt, I know, and I've startled you; but if you love me, you can forgive that to my loving you so long before I spoke."

She gazed at him with parted lips.

"Oh, mercy! What shall I do? If it's true—what you say—you must go!" she said. "And you must never come any more. Do you promise that?"

"Certainly not," said the young man. "Why should I promise such a thing—so abominably wrong? I could obey if you didn't love me————"

"Oh, I don't! Indeed I don't! Now will you obey?"

"No. I don't believe you."

"Oh!"

He possessed himself of her hand again.

"My love—my dearest! What is this trouble, that you can't tell it? It can't be anything about yourself. If it is anything about any one else, it wouldn't make the least difference in the world, no matter what it was. I would be only too glad to show by any act or deed I could that nothing could change me towards you."

"Oh, you don't understand!"

"No, I don't. You must tell me."

"I will never do that."

"Then I will stay here till your mother comes, and ask her what it is."

"Ask her?"

"Yes! Do you think I will give you up till I know why I must?"

"You force me to it! Will you go if I tell you, and never let any human creature know what you have said to me?"

"Not unless you give me leave."

"That will be never. Well, then————" She stopped, and made two or three ineffectual efforts to begin again. "No, no! I can't. You must go!"

"I will not go!"

"You said you—loved me. If you do, you will go."

He dropped the hands he had stretched towards her, and she hid her face in her own.

"There!" she said, turning it suddenly upon him. "Sit down there. And will you promise me—on your honor—not to speak—not to try to persuade me—not to—touch me? You won't touch me?"

"I will obey you, Penelope."

"As if you were never to see me again? As if I were dying?"

"I will do what you say. But I shall see you again; and don't talk of dying. This is the beginning of life————"

"No. It's the end," said the girl, resuming at last something of the hoarse drawl which the tumult of her feeling had broken into those half-articulate appeals. She sat down too, and lifted her face towards him. "It's the end of life for me, because I know now that I must have been playing false from the beginning. You don't know what I mean, and I can never tell you. It isn't my secret—it's someone else's. You—you must never come here again. I can't tell you why, and you must never try to know. Do you promise?"

"You can forbid me. I must do what you say."

"I do forbid you, then. And you shall not think I am cruel————"

"How could I think that?"

"Oh, how hard you make it!"

Corey laughed for very despair. "Can I make it easier by disobeying you?"

"I know I am talking crazily. But I'm not crazy."

"No, no," he said, with some wild notion of comforting her; "but try to tell me this trouble! There is nothing under heaven—no calamity, no sorrow—that I wouldn't gladly share with you, or take all upon myself if I could!"

"I know! But this you can't. Oh, my————"

"Dearest! Wait! Think! Let me ask your mother—your father————"

She gave a cry.

"No! If you do that, you will make me hate you! Will you————"

The rattling of a latch-key was heard in the outer door.

"Promise!" cried Penelope.

"Oh, I promise!"

"Good-bye!" She suddenly flung her arms round his neck, and, pressing her cheek tight against his, flashed out of the room by one door as her father entered it by another.

Corey turned to him in a daze. "I—I called to speak with you—about a matter————But it's so late now. I'll—I'll see you tomorrow."

"No time like the present," said Lapham, with a fierceness that did not seem referable to Corey. He had his hat still on, and he glared at the young man out of his blue eyes with a fire that something else must have kindled there.

"I really can't, now," said Corey, weakly. "It will do quite as well to-morrow. Good-night, sir."

"Good-night," answered Lapham abruptly, following him to the door, and shutting it after him. "I think the devil must have got into pretty much everybody to-night," he muttered, coming back to the room, where he put down his hat. Then he went to the kitchen-stairs and called down, "Hello, Alice! I want something to eat!"

XVII

W hat's the reason the girls never get down to breakfast any more?" asked Lapham when he met his wife at the table in the morning. He had been up an hour and a half, and he spoke with the severity of a hungry man. "It seems to me they don't amount to anything. Here I am, at my time of life, up the first one in the house. I ring the bell for the cook at quarter-past six every morning, and the breakfast is on the table at half-past seven right along, like clock-work, but I never see anybody but you till I go to the office."

"Oh, yes, you do, Si," said his wife, soothingly. "The girls are nearly always down. But they're young, and it tires them more than it does us to get up early."

"They can rest afterwards. They don't do anything after they *are* up," grumbled Lapham.

"Well, that's your fault, ain't it? You oughtn't to have made so much money, and then they'd have had to work." She laughed at Lapham's Spartan mood, and went on to excuse the young people. "Irene's been up two nights hand running, and Penelope says she ain't well. What makes you so cross about the girls? Been doing something you're ashamed of?"

"I'll tell you when I've been doing anything to be ashamed of," growled Lapham.

"Oh, no, you won't!" said his wife, jollily. "You'll only be hard on the rest of us. Come, now, Si; what is it?"

Lapham frowned into his coffee with sulky dignity, and said, without looking up, "I wonder what that fellow wanted here last night?"

"What fellow?"

"Corey. I found him here when I came home, and he said he wanted to see me; but he wouldn't stop."

"Where was he?"

"In the sitting-room."

"Was Pen there?"

"I didn't see her."

Mrs. Lapham paused, with her hand on the cream-jug. "Why, what in the land *did* he want? Did he say he wanted you?"

210

"That's what he said."

"And then he wouldn't stay?"

"No."

"Well, then, I'll tell you just what it is, Silas Lapham. He came here"—she looked about the room and lowered her voice—"to see you about Irene, and then he hadn't the courage."

"I guess he's got courage enough to do pretty much what he wants to," said Lapham, glumly. "All I know is, he was here. You better ask Pen about it, if she ever gets down."

"I guess I sha'n't wait for her," said Mrs. Lapham; and, as her husband closed the front door after him, she opened that of her daughter's room and entered abruptly.

The girl sat at the window, fully dressed, and as if she had been sitting there a long time. Without rising, she turned her face towards her mother. It merely showed black against the light, and revealed nothing till her mother came close to her with successive questions. "Why, how long have you been up, Pen? Why don't you come to your breakfast? Did you see Mr. Corey when he called last night? Why, what's the matter with you? What have you been crying about?"

"Have I been crying?"

"Yes! Your cheeks are all wet!"

"I thought they were on fire. Well, I'll tell you what's happened." She rose and then fell back in her chair. "Lock the door!" she ordered, and her mother mechanically obeyed. "I don't want Irene in here. There's nothing the matter. Only, Mr. Corey offered himself to me last night."

Her mother remained looking at her, helpless, not so much with amaze, perhaps, as dismay.

"Oh, I'm not a ghost! I wish I was! You had better sit down, mother. You have got to know all about it."

Mrs. Lapham dropped nervelessly into the chair at the other window, and while the girl went slowly but briefly on, touching only the vital points of the story, and breaking at times into a bitter drollery, she sat as if without the power to speak or stir.

"Well, that's all, mother. I should say I had dreamt it, if I had slept any last night; but I guess it really happened."

The mother glanced round at the bed, and said, glad to occupy herself delayingly with the minor care: "Why, you have been sitting up all night! You will kill yourself."

"I don't know about killing myself, but I've been sitting up all night," answered the girl. Then, seeing that her mother remained blankly silent again, she demanded, "Why don't you blame me, mother? Why don't you say that I led him on, and tried to get him away from her? Don't you believe I did?"

Her mother made her no answer, as if these ravings of self-accusal needed none. "Do you think," she asked, simply, "that he got the idea you cared for him?"

"He knew it! How could I keep it from him? I said I didn't—at first!"

"It was no use," sighed the mother. "You might as well said you did. It couldn't help Irene any, if you didn't."

"I always tried to help her with him, even when I———"

"Yes, I know. But she never was equal to him. I saw that from the start; but I tried to blind myself to it. And when he kept coming———"

"You never thought of me!" cried the girl, with a bitterness that reached her mother's heart. "I was nobody! I couldn't feel! No one could care for me!" The turmoil of despair, of triumph, of remorse and resentment, which filled her soul, tried to express itself in the words.

"No," said the mother humbly. "I didn't think of you. Or I didn't think of you enough. It did come across me sometimes that maybe——— But it didn't seem as if——— And your going on so for Irene———"

"You let me go on. You made me always go and talk with him for her, and you didn't think I would talk to him for myself. Well, I didn't!"

"I'm punished for it. When did you—begin to care for him?"

"How do I know? What difference does it make? It's all over now, no matter when it began. He won't come here any more, unless I let him." She could not help betraying her pride in this authority of hers, but she went on anxiously enough: "What will you say to Irene? She's safe as far as I'm concerned; but if he don't care for her, what will you do?"

"I don't know what to do," said Mrs. Lapham. She sat in an

apathy from which she apparently could not rouse herself. "I don't see as anything can be done."

Penelope laughed in a pitying derision.

"Well, let things go on then. But they won't go on."

"No, they won't go on," echoed her mother. "She's pretty enough, and she's capable; and your father's got the money—I don't know what I'm saying! She ain't equal to him, and she never was. I kept feeling it all the time, and yet I kept blinding myself."

"If he had ever cared for her," said Penelope, "it wouldn't have mattered whether she was equal to him or not. I'm not equal to him either."

Her mother went on: "I might have thought it was you; but I had got set———— Well! I can see it all clear enough, now it's too late. I don't know what to do."

"And what do you expect me to do?" demanded the girl. "Do you want me to go to Irene and tell her that I've got him away from her?"

"Oh, good Lord!" cried Mrs. Lapham. "What shall I do? What do you want I should do, Pen?"

"Nothing for me," said Penelope. "I've had it out with myself. Now do the best you can for Irene."

"I couldn't say you had done wrong, if you was to marry him to-day."

"Mother!"

"No, I couldn't. I couldn't say but what you had been good and faithful all through, and you had a perfect right to do it. There ain't any one to blame. He's behaved like a gentleman, and I can see now that he never thought of her, and that it was you all the while. Well, marry him, then! He's got the right, and so have you."

"What about Irene? I don't want you to talk about me. I can take care of myself."

"She's nothing but a child. It's only a fancy with her. She'll get over it. She hain't really got her heart set on him."

"She's got her heart set on him, mother. She's got her whole life set on him. You know that."

"Yes, that's so," said the mother, as promptly as if she had been arguing to that rather than the contrary effect.

"If I could give him to her, I would. But he isn't mine to give." She added in a burst of despair, "He isn't mine to keep!"

"Well," said Mrs. Lapham, "she has got to bear it. I don't know what's to come of it all. But she's got to bear her share of it." She rose and went toward the door.

Penelope ran after her in a sort of terror. "You're not going to tell Irene?" she gasped, seizing her mother by either shoulder.

"Yes, I am," said Mrs. Lapham. "If she's a woman grown, she can bear a woman's burden."

"I can't let you tell Irene," said the girl, letting fall her face on her mother's neck. "Not Irene," she moaned. "I'm afraid to let you. How can I ever look at her again?"

"Why, you haven't done anything, Pen," said her mother, soothingly.

"I wanted to! Yes, I must have done something. How could I help it? I did care for him from the first, and I must have tried to make him like me. Do you think I did? No, no! You mustn't tell Irene! Not—not—yet! Mother! Yes! I did try to get him from her!" she cried, lifting her head, and suddenly looking her mother in the face with those large dim eyes of hers. "What do you think? Even last night! It was the first time I ever had him all to myself, for myself, and I know now that I tried to make him think that I was pretty and—funny. And I didn't try to make him think of her. I knew that I pleased him, and I tried to please him more. Perhaps I could have kept him from saying that he cared for me; but when I saw he did— I must have seen it—I couldn't. I had never had him to myself, and for myself, before. I needn't have seen him at all, but I wanted to see him; and when I was sitting there alone with him, how do I know what I did to let him feel that I cared for him? Now, will you tell Irene? I never thought he did care for me, and never expected him to. But I liked him. Yes—I did like him! Tell her that! Or else I will."

"If it was to tell her he was dead," began Mrs. Lapham, absently.

"How easy it would be!" cried the girl in self-mockery. "But he's worse than dead to her; and so am I. I've turned it over a million ways, mother; I've looked at it in every light you can put it in, and I can't make anything but misery out of it. You can see the misery at the first glance, and you can't see more or less if you spend your life looking at it." She laughed again, as if the hopelessness of the thing amused her. Then she flew to the extreme of self-assertion. "Well, I *have* a right to him, and he has a right to me. If he's never done anything to make her think he cared for her,—and I know he hasn't; it's all been our doing,—then he's free and I'm free. We can't make her happy, whatever we do; and why shouldn't I——— No, that won't do! I reached that point before!" She broke again into her desperate laugh. "You may try now, mother!"

"I'd best speak to your father first———"

Penelope smiled a little more forlornly than she had laughed.

"Well, yes; the Colonel will have to know. It isn't a trouble that I can keep to myself exactly. It seems to belong to too many other people."

Her mother took a crazy encouragement from her return to her old way of saying things. "Perhaps he can think of something."

"Oh, I don't doubt but the Colonel will know just what to do!"

"You mustn't be too down-hearted about it. It—it'll all come right———"

"You tell Irene that, mother."

Mrs. Lapham had put her hand on the door-key; she dropped it, and looked at the girl with a sort of beseeching appeal for the comfort she could not imagine herself. "Don't look at me, mother," said Penelope, shaking her head. "You know that if Irene were to die without knowing it, it wouldn't come right for me."

"Pen!"

"I've read of cases where a girl gives up the man that loves her so as to make some other girl happy that the man doesn't love. That might be done."

"Your father would think you were a fool," said Mrs. Lapham, finding a sort of refuge in her strong disgust for the pseudo-heroism. "No! If there's to be any giving up, let it be by the one that sha'n't make anybody but herself suffer. There's trouble and sorrow enough in the world, without making it on purpose!"

She unlocked the door, but Penelope slipped round and set herself against it. "Irene shall not give up!"

"I will see your father about it," said the mother. "Let me out now———"

"Don't let Irene come here!"

"No. I will tell her that you haven't slept. Go to bed now, and try to get some rest. She isn't up herself yet. You must have some breakfast."

"No; let me sleep if I can. I can get something when I wake up. I'll come down if I can't sleep. Life has got to go on. It does when there's a death in the house, and this is only a little worse."

"Don't you talk nonsense!" cried Mrs. Lapham, with angry authority.

"Well, a little better, then," said Penelope, with meek concession.

Mrs. Lapham attempted to say something, and could not. She went out and opened Irene's door. The girl lifted her head drowsily from her pillow. "Don't disturb your sister when you get up, Irene. She hasn't slept well————"

"*Please* don't talk! I'm almost *dead* with sleep!" returned Irene. "Do go, mamma! I sha'n't disturb her." She turned her face down in the pillow, and pulled the covering up over her ears.

The mother slowly closed the door and went down-stairs, feeling bewildered and baffled almost beyond the power to move. The time had been when she would have tried to find out why this judgment had been sent upon her. But now she could not feel that the innocent suffering of others was inflicted for her fault; she shrank instinctively from that cruel and egotistic misinterpretation of the mystery of pain and loss. She saw her two children, equally if differently dear to her, destined to trouble that nothing could avert, and she could not blame either of them; she could not blame the means of this misery to them; he was as innocent as they, and though her heart was sore against him in this first moment, she could still be just to him in it. She was a woman who had been used to seek the light by striving; she had hitherto literally worked to it. But it is the curse of prosperity that it takes work away from us, and shuts that door to hope and health of spirit. In this house, where everything had come to be done for her, she had no tasks to interpose between her and her despair. She sat down in her own room and let her hands fall in her lap,—the hands that had once been so helpful and busy,—and tried to think it all out. She had never heard of the fate that was once supposed to appoint the sorrows of men irrespective of their blamelessness or blame,* before the time when it came to be believed that sorrows were penalties; but in her simple way she recognized

---

*Most likely the classical notion of Fate rather than the Calvinist belief in predestination.

something like that mythic power when she rose from her struggle with the problem, and said aloud to herself, "Well, the witch is in it." Turn which way she would, she saw no escape from the misery to come—the misery which had come already to Penelope and herself, and that must come to Irene and her father. She started when she definitely thought of her husband, and thought with what violence it would work in every fiber of his rude strength. She feared that, and she feared something worse—the effect which his pride and ambition might seek to give it; and it was with terror of this, as well as the natural trust with which a woman must turn to her husband in any anxiety at last, that she felt she could not wait for evening to take counsel with him. When she considered how wrongly he might take it all, it seemed as if it were already known to him, and she was impatient to prevent his error.

She sent out for a messenger, whom she dispatched with a note to his place of business: "Silas, I should like to ride with you this afternoon. Can't you come home early? Persis." And she was at dinner with Irene, evading her questions about Penelope, when answer came that he would be at the house with the buggy at half-past two. It is easy to put off a girl who has but one thing in her head; but, though Mrs. Lapham could escape without telling anything of Penelope, she could not escape seeing how wholly Irene was engrossed with hopes now turned so vain and impossible. She was still talking of that dinner, of nothing but that dinner, and begging for flattery of herself and praise of him, which her mother had till now been so ready to give.

"Seems to me you don't take very much interest, mamma!" she said, laughing and blushing, at one point.

"Yes,—yes, I do," protested Mrs. Lapham, and then the girl prattled on.

"I guess I shall get one of those pins that Nanny Corey had in her hair. I think it would become me, don't you?"

"Yes; but, Irene—I don't like to have you go on so, till—unless he's said something to show— You oughtn't to give yourself up to thinking———" But at this the girl turned so white, and looked such reproach at her, that she added, frantically: "Yes, get the pin. It is just the thing for you! But don't disturb Penelope. Let her alone till I get back. I'm going out to ride with your father. He'll be here in half an hour. Are you through? Ring, then. Get yourself that fan you saw the other day. Your father won't say anything; he likes to have you look well. I could see his eyes on you half the time the other night."

"I should have liked to have Pen go with me," said Irene, restored to her normal state of innocent selfishness by these flatteries. "Don't you suppose she'll be up in time? What's the matter with her that she didn't sleep?"

"I don't know. Better let her alone."

"Well," submitted Irene.

XVIII

Mrs. Lapham went away to put on her bonnet and cloak, and she was waiting at the window when her husband drove up. She opened the door and ran down the steps. "Don't get out; I can help myself in," and she clambered to his side, while he kept the fidgeting mare still with voice and touch.

"Where do you want I should go?" he asked, turning the buggy.

"Oh, I don't care. Out Brookline way, I guess. I wish you hadn't brought this fool of a horse," she gave way, petulantly. "I wanted to have a talk."

"When I can't drive this mare and talk too, I'll sell out altogether," said Lapham. "She'll be quiet enough when she's had her spin."

"Well," said his wife; and while they were making their way across the city to the Milldam she answered certain questions he asked about some points in the new house.

"I should have liked to have you stop there," he began; but she answered so quickly, "Not to-day," that he gave it up and turned his horse's head westward, when they struck Beacon street.

He let the mare out, and he did not pull her in till he left the Brighton road and struck off under the low boughs that met above one of the quiet streets of Brookline, where the stone cottages, with here and there a patch of determined ivy on their northern walls, did what they could to look English amid the glare of the autumnal foliage. The smooth earthen track under the mare's hoofs was scattered with flakes of the red and yellow gold that made the air luminous around them, and the perspective was gay with innumerable tints and tones.

"Pretty sightly," said Lapham, with a long sigh, letting the reins lie loose in his vigilant hand, to which he seemed to relegate the whole charge of the mare. "I want to talk with you about Rogers, Persis. He's been getting in deeper and deeper with me; and last night he pestered me half to death to go in with him in one of his schemes. I ain't going to blame anybody, but I hain't got very much confidence in Rogers. And I told him so last night."

"Oh, don't talk to me about Rogers!" his wife broke in. "There's something a good deal more important than Rogers in the world, and more important than your business. It seems as if you couldn't think of anything else—that and the new house. Did you suppose I wanted to ride so as to talk Rogers with you?" she demanded, yielding to the necessity a wife feels of making her husband pay for her suffering, even if he has not inflicted it. "I declare————"

"Well, hold on, now!" said Lapham. "What *do* you want to talk about? I'm listening."

His wife began, "Why, it's just this, Silas Lapham!" and then she broke off to say, "Well, you may wait, now—starting me wrong, when it's hard enough anyway."

Lapham silently turned his whip over and over in his hand and waited.

"Did you suppose," she asked at last, "that that young Corey had been coming to see Irene?"

"I don't know what I supposed," replied Lapham sullenly. "You always said so." He looked sharply at her under his lowering brows.

"Well, he hasn't," said Mrs. Lapham; and she replied to the frown that blackened on her husband's face, "And I can tell you what, if you take it in that way I sha'n't speak another word."

"Who's takin' it what way?" retorted Lapham savagely. "What are you drivin' at?"

"I want you should promise that you'll hear me out quietly."

"I'll hear you out if you'll give me a chance. I haven't said a word yet."

"Well, I'm not going to have you flying into forty furies, and looking like a perfect thunder-cloud at the very start. I've had to bear it, and you've got to bear it too."

"Well, let me have a chance at it, then."

"It's nothing to blame anybody about, as I can see, and the only question is, what's the best thing to do about it. There's only one thing we can do; for if he don't care for the child, nobody wants to make him. If he hasn't been coming to see her, he hasn't, and that's all there is to it."

"No, it ain't!" exclaimed Lapham.

"There!" protested his wife.

"If he hasn't been coming to see her, what *has* he been coming for?"

"He's been coming to see Pen!" cried the wife. "Now are you satisfied?" Her tone implied that he had brought it all upon them; but at the sight of the swift passions working in his face to a perfect comprehension of the whole trouble, she fell to trembling, and her broken voice lost all the spurious indignation she had put into it. "Oh, Silas! what are we going to do about it? I'm afraid it'll kill Irene."

Lapham pulled off the loose driving-glove from his right hand with the fingers of his left, in which the reins lay. He passed it over his forehead, and then flicked from it the moisture it had gathered there. He caught his breath once or twice, like a man who meditates a struggle with superior force and then remains passive in its grasp.

His wife felt the need of comforting him, as she had felt the need of afflicting him. "I don't say but what it can be made to come out all right in the end. All I say is, I don't see my way clear yet."

"What makes you think he likes Pen?" he asked, quietly.

"He told her so last night, and she told me this morning. Was he at the office to-day?"

"Yes, he was there. I haven't been there much myself. He didn't say anything to me. Does Irene know?"

"No; I left her getting ready to go out shopping. She wants to get a pin like the one Nanny Corey had on."

"Oh, my Lord!" groaned Lapham.

"It's been Pen from the start, I guess, or almost from the start. I don't say but what he was attracted some by Irene at the very first; but I guess it's been Pen ever since he saw her; and we've taken up with a notion, and blinded ourselves with it. Time and again I've had my doubts whether he cared for Irene any; but I declare to goodness, when he kept coming, I never hardly thought of Pen, and I couldn't help believing at last he did care for Irene. Did it ever strike you he might be after Pen?"

"No. I took what you said. I supposed you knew."

"Do you blame me, Silas?" she asked timidly.

"No. What's the use of blaming? We don't either of us want anything but the children's good. What's it all of it for, if it ain't for that? That's what we've both slaved for all our lives."

"Yes, I know. Plenty of people lose their children," she suggested.

"Yes, but that don't comfort me any. I never was one to feel good because another man felt bad. How would you have liked it if someone had taken comfort because his boy lived when ours died? No, I can't do it. And this is worse than death, someways. That comes and it goes; but this looks as if it was one of those things that had come to stay. The way I look at it, there ain't any hope for anybody. Suppose we don't want Pen to have him; will that help Irene any, if he don't want her? Suppose we don't want to let him have either; does that help either?"

"You talk," exclaimed Mrs. Lapham, "as if our say was going to settle it. Do you suppose that Penelope Lapham is a girl to take up with a fellow that her sister is in love with, and that she always thought was in love with her sister, and go off and be happy with him? Don't you believe but what it would come back to her, as long as she breathed the breath of life, how she'd teased her about him, as I've heard Pen tease Irene, and helped to make her think he was in love with her, by showing that she thought so herself? It's ridiculous!"

Lapham seemed quite beaten down by this argument. His huge head hung forward over his breast; the reins lay loose in his moveless hand; the mare took her own way. At last he lifted his face and shut his heavy jaws.

"Well?" quavered his wife.

"Well," he answered, "if he wants her, and she wants him, I don't see what that's got to do with it." He looked straight forward, and not at his wife.

She laid her hands on the reins. "Now, you stop right here, Silas Lapham! If I thought that—if I really believed you could be willing to break that poor child's heart, and let Pen disgrace herself by marrying a man that had as good as killed her sister, just because you wanted Bromfield Corey's son for a son-in-law————"

Lapham turned his face now, and gave her a look. "You had better not believe that, Persis! Get up!" he called to the mare, without glancing at her, and she sprang forward. "I see you've got past being any use to yourself on this subject."

"Hello!" shouted a voice in front of him. "Where the devil you goin' to?"

"Do you want to kill somebody?" shrieked his wife.

There was a light crash, and the mare recoiled her length, and separated their wheels from those of the open buggy in front which

Lapham had driven into. He made his excuses to the occupant; and the accident relieved the tension of their feelings and left them far from the point of mutual injury which they had reached in their common trouble and their unselfish will for their children's good.

It was Lapham who resumed the talk. "I'm afraid we can't either of us see this thing in the right light. We're too near to it. I wish to the Lord there was somebody to talk to about it."

"Yes," said his wife; "but there ain't anybody."

"Well, I dunno," suggested Lapham, after a moment; "why not talk to the minister of your church? May be he could see some way out of it."

Mrs. Lapham shook her head hopelessly. "It wouldn't do. I've never taken up my connection with the church, and I don't feel as if I'd got any claim on him."

"If he's anything of a man, or anything of a preacher, you *have* got a claim on him," urged Lapham; and he spoiled his argument by adding, "I've contributed enough *money* to his church."

"Oh, that's nothing," said Mrs. Lapham. "I ain't well enough acquainted with Dr. Langworthy, or else I'm *too* well. No; if I was to ask any one, I should want to ask a total stranger. But what's the use, Si? Nobody could make us see it any different from what it is, and I don't know as I should want they should."

It blotted out the tender beauty of the day and weighed down their hearts ever more heavily within them. They ceased to talk of it a hundred times, and still came back to it. They drove on and on. It began to be late. "I guess we better go back, Si," said his wife; and as he turned without speaking, she pulled her veil down and began to cry softly behind it, with low little broken sobs.

Lapham started the mare up and drove swiftly homeward. At last his wife stopped crying and began trying to find her pocket. "Here, take mine, Persis," he said kindly, offering her his handkerchief, and she took it and dried her eyes with it. "There was one of those fellows there the other night," he spoke again, when his wife leaned back against the cushions in peaceful despair, "that I liked the looks of about as well as any man I ever saw. I guess he was a pretty good man. It was that Mr. Sewell." He looked at his wife, but she did not say anything. "Persis," he resumed, "I can't bear to go back with nothing settled in our minds. I can't bear to let you."

"We must, Si," returned his wife, with gentle gratitude. Lapham
groaned. "Where does he live?" she asked.

"On Bolingbroke street. He gave me his number."

"Well, it wouldn't do any good. What could he say to us?"

"Oh, I don't know as he could say anything," said Lapham hopelessly; and neither of them said anything more till they crossed the
Milldam and found themselves between the rows of city houses.

"Don't drive past the new house, Si," pleaded his wife. "I
couldn't bear to see it. Drive—drive up Bolingbroke street. We might
as well see where he *does* live."

"Well," said Lapham. He drove along slowly. "That's the place,"
he said finally, stopping the mare and pointing with his whip.

"It wouldn't do any good," said his wife, in a tone which he understood as well as he understood her words. He turned the mare up
to the curbstone.

"You take the reins a minute," he said, handing them to his wife.

He got down and rang the bell, and waited till the door opened;
then he came back and lifted his wife out. "He's in," he said.

He got the hitching-weight from under the buggy-seat and
made it fast to the mare's bit.

"Do you think she'll stand with that?" asked Mrs. Lapham.

"I guess so. If she don't, no matter."

"Ain't you afraid she'll take cold," she persisted, trying to make
delay.

"Let her!" said Lapham. He took his wife's trembling hand under
his arm, and drew her to the door.

"He'll think we're crazy," she murmured, in her broken pride.

"Well, we *are*," said Lapham. "Tell him we'd like to see him alone
awhile," he said to the girl who was holding the door ajar for him,
and she showed him into the reception-room, which had been the
Protestant confessional for many burdened souls before their time,
coming, as they did, with the belief that they were bowed down with
the only misery like theirs in the universe; for each one of us must
suffer long to himself before he can learn that he is but one in a great
community of wretchedness which has been pitilessly repeating itself from the foundation of the world.

They were as loath to touch their trouble when the minister
came in as if it were their disgrace; but Lapham did so at last, and,

with a simple dignity which he had wanted in his bungling and apologetic approaches, he laid the affair clearly before the minister's compassionate and reverent eye. He spared Corey's name, but he did not pretend that it was not himself and his wife and their daughters who were concerned.

"I don't know as I've got any right to trouble you with this thing," he said, in the moment while Sewell sat pondering the case, "and I don't know as I've got any warrant for doing it. But, as I told my wife here, there was something about you—I don't know whether it was anything you *said* exactly—that made me feel as if you could help us. I guess I didn't say so much as that to her; but that's the way I felt. And here we are. And if it ain't all right————"

"Surely," said Sewell, "it's all right. I thank you for coming—for trusting your trouble to me. A time comes to every one of us when we can't help ourselves, and then we must get others to help us. If people turn to me at such a time, I feel sure that I was put into the world for something—if nothing more than to give my pity, my sympathy."

The brotherly words, so plain, so sincere, had a welcome in them that these poor outcasts of sorrow could not doubt.

"Yes," said Lapham huskily, and his wife began to wipe the tears again under her veil.

Sewell remained silent, and they waited till he should speak. "We can be of use to one another here, because we can always be wiser for someone else than we can for ourselves. We can see another's sins and errors in a more merciful light—and that is always a fairer light—than we can our own; and we can look more sanely at others' afflictions." He had addressed these words to Lapham; now he turned to his wife. "If someone had come to you, Mrs. Lapham, in just this perplexity, what would you have thought?"

"I don't know as I understand you," faltered Mrs. Lapham.

Sewell repeated his words, and added, "I mean, what do you think someone else ought to do in your place?"

"Was there ever any poor creatures in such a strait before?" she asked, with pathetic incredulity.

"There's no new trouble under the sun," said the minister.

"Oh, if it was any one else, I should say—I should say—Why, of course! I should say that their duty was to let————" She paused.

William Dean Howells

"One suffer instead of three, if none is to blame?" suggested Sewell. "That's sense, and that's justice. It's the economy of pain which naturally suggests itself, and which would insist upon itself, if we were not all perverted by traditions which are the figment of the shallowest sentimentality. Tell me, Mrs. Lapham, didn't this come into your mind when you first learned how matters stood?"

"Why, yes, it flashed across me. But I didn't think it could be right."

"And how was it with you, Mr. Lapham?"

"Why, that's what I thought, of course. But I didn't see my way———"

"No," cried the minister, "we are all blinded, we are all weakened by a false ideal of self-sacrifice. It wraps us round with its meshes, and we can't fight our way out of it. Mrs. Lapham, what made you feel that it might be better for three to suffer than one?"

"Why, she did herself. I know she would die sooner than take him away from her."

"I supposed so!" cried the minister bitterly. "And yet she is a sensible girl, your daughter?"

"She has more common sense———"

"Of course! But in such a case we somehow think it must be wrong to use our common sense. I don't know where this false ideal comes from, unless it comes from the novels that befool and debauch almost every intelligence in some degree. It certainly doesn't come from Christianity, which instantly repudiates it when confronted with it. Your daughter believes, in spite of her common sense, that she ought to make herself and the man who loves her unhappy, in order to assure the lifelong wretchedness of her sister, whom he doesn't love, simply because her sister saw him and fancied him first! And I'm sorry to say that ninety-nine young people out of a hundred—oh, nine hundred and ninety-nine out of a thousand!—would consider that noble and beautiful and heroic; whereas you know at the bottom of your hearts that it would be foolish and cruel and revolting. You know what marriage is! And what it must be without love on both sides."

The minister had grown quite heated and red in the face.

"I lose all patience!" he went on vehemently. "This poor child of yours has somehow been brought to believe that it will kill her sister if her sister does not have what does not belong to her, and what it is not in the power of all the world, or any soul in the world, to give her. Her sister will suffer—yes, keenly!—in heart and in pride; but she will not die. You will suffer, too, in your tenderness for her; but you must do your duty. You must help her to give up. You would be guilty if you did less. Keep clearly in mind that you are doing right, and the only possible good. And God be with you!"

XIX

He talked sense, Persis," said Lapham gently, as he mounted to his wife's side in the buggy and drove slowly homeward through the dusk.

"Yes, he talked sense," she admitted. But she added, bitterly, "I guess, if he had it to do! Oh, he's right, and it's got to be done. There ain't any other way for it. It's sense; and, yes, it's justice." They walked to their door after they left the horse at the livery stable around the corner, where Lapham kept it. "I want you should send Irene up to our room as soon as we get in, Silas."

"Why, ain't you going to have any supper first?" faltered Lapham, with his latch-key in the lock.

"No. I can't lose a minute. If I do, I sha'n't do it at all."

"Look here, Persis," said her husband tenderly, "let me do this thing."

"Oh, you!" said his wife, with a woman's compassionate scorn for a man's helplessness in such a case. "Send her right up. And I shall feel—" She stopped, to spare him.

Then she opened the door, and ran up to her room, without waiting to speak to Irene, who had come into the hall at the sound of her father's key in the door.

"I guess your mother wants to see you upstairs," said Lapham, looking away.

Her mother turned round and faced the girl's wondering look as Irene entered the chamber, so close upon her that she had not yet had time to lay off her bonnet; she stood with her wraps still on her arm.

"Irene!" she said harshly, "there is something you have got to bear. It's a mistake we've all made. He don't care anything for you. He never did. He told Pen so last night. He cares for her."

The sentences had fallen like blows. But the girl had taken them without flinching. She stood up immovable, but the delicate rose-light of her complexion went out and left her snow-white. She did not offer to speak.

"Why don't you say something?" cried her mother. "Do you want to kill me, Irene?"

"Why should I want to hurt *you*, mamma?" the girl replied steadily, but in an alien voice. "There's nothing to say. I want to see Pen a minute."

She turned and left the room. As she mounted the stairs that led to her own and her sister's rooms on the floor above, her mother helplessly followed. Irene went first to her own room at the front of the house, and then came out, leaving the door open and the gas flaring behind her. The mother could see that she had tumbled many things out of the drawers of her bureau upon the marble top.

She passed her mother, where she stood in the entry. "You can come too, if you want to, mamma," she said.

She opened Penelope's door without knocking, and went in. Penelope sat at the window, as in the morning. Irene did not go to her; but she went and laid a gold hair-pin on her bureau, and said, without looking at her, "There's a pin that I got today, because it was like his sister's. It won't become a dark person so well, but you can have it."

She stuck a scrap of paper in the side of Penelope's mirror. "There's that account of Mr. Stanton's ranch. You'll want to read it, I presume."

She laid a withered *boutonnière* on the bureau beside the pin. "There's his button-hole bouquet. He left it by his plate, and I stole it."

She had a pine-shaving, fantastically tied up with a knot of ribbon, in her hand. She held it a moment; then, looking deliberately at Penelope, she went up to her, and dropped it in her lap without a word. She turned, and, advancing a few steps, tottered and seemed about to fall.

Her mother sprang forward with an imploring cry, "Oh, 'Rene, 'Rene, 'Rene!"

Irene recovered herself before her mother could reach her. "Don't touch me," she said icily. "Mamma, I'm going to put on my things. I want papa to walk with me. I'm choking here."

"I—I can't let you go out, Irene, child," began her mother.

"You've got to," replied the girl. "Tell papa to hurry his supper."

"Oh, poor soul! He doesn't want any supper. *He* knows it too."

"I don't want to talk about that. Tell him to get ready."

She left them once more.

Mrs. Lapham turned a hapless glance upon Penelope.

"Go and tell him, mother," said the girl. "I would, if I could. If she can walk, let her. It's the only thing for her." She sat still; she did not even brush to the floor the fantastic thing that lay in her lap, and that sent up faintly the odor of the sachet powder with which Irene liked to perfume her boxes.

Lapham went out with the unhappy child, and began to talk with her, crazily, incoherently enough.

She mercifully stopped him. "Don't talk, papa. I don't want any one should talk with me."

He obeyed, and they walked silently on and on. In their aimless course they reached the new house on the water side of Beacon, and she made him stop, and stood looking up at it. The scaffolding which had so long defaced the front was gone, and in the light of the gas-lamp before it all the architectural beauty of the façade was suggested, and much of the finely felt detail was revealed. Seymour had pretty nearly satisfied himself in that rich façade; certainly Lapham had not stinted him of the means.

"Well," said the girl, "I shall never live in it," and she began to walk on.

Lapham's sore heart went down, as he lumbered heavily after her. "Oh, yes, you will, Irene. You'll have lots of good times there yet."

"No," she answered, and said nothing more about it. They had not talked of their trouble at all, and they did not speak of it now. Lapham understood that she was trying to walk herself weary, and he was glad to hold his peace and let her have her way. She halted him once more before the red and yellow lights of an apothecary's window.

"Isn't there something they give you to make you sleep?" she asked vaguely. "I've got to sleep to-night!"

Lapham trembled. "I guess you don't want anything, Irene."

"Yes, I do! Get me something!" she retorted willfully. "If you don't, I shall die. I must sleep."

They went in, and Lapham asked for something to make a nervous person sleep. Irene stood poring over the show-case full of brushes and trinkets, while the apothecary put up the bromide, which he guessed would be about the best thing. She did not show any emotion; her face was like a stone, while her father's expressed the anguish of his sympathy. He looked as if he had not slept for a week; his fat eyelids drooped over his glassy eyes, and his cheeks and throat hung flaccid. He started as the apothecary's cat stole smoothly up and rubbed itself against his leg; and it was to him that the man said, "You want to take a tablespoonful of that as long as you're awake. I guess it won't take a great many to fetch you."

"All right," said Lapham, and paid and went out. "I don't know but I *shall* want some of it," he said, with a joyless laugh.

Irene came closer up to him and took his arm. He laid his heavy paw on her gloved fingers. After a while she said, "I want you should let me go up to Lapham to-morrow."

"To Lapham? Why, to-morrow's Sunday, Irene! You can't go to-morrow."

"Well, Monday, then. I can live through one day here."

"Well," said the father passively. He made no pretense of asking her why she wished to go, nor any attempt to dissuade her.

"Give me that bottle," she said, when he opened the door at home for her, and she ran up to her own room.

The next morning Irene came to breakfast with her mother; the Colonel and Penelope did not appear, and Mrs. Lapham looked sleep-broken and careworn.

The girl glanced at her. "Don't you fret about me, mamma," she said. "I shall get along." She seemed herself as steady and strong as rock.

"I don't like to see you keeping up so, Irene," replied her mother. "It'll be all the worse for you when you do break. Better give way a little at the start."

"I sha'n't break, and I've given way all I'm going to. I'm going to Lapham to-morrow,—I want you should go with me, mamma,—and I guess I can keep up one day here. All about it is, I don't want you should say anything, or *look* anything. And, whatever I do, I don't want you should try to stop me. And, the first thing, I'm going to take her breakfast up to her. Don't!" she cried, intercepting the protest on her mother's lips. "I shall not let it hurt Pen, if I can help it. She's never done a thing nor thought a thing to wrong me. I had to fly out at her last night; but that's all over now, and I know just what I've got to bear."

She had her way unmolested. She carried Penelope's breakfast to her, and omitted no care or attention that could make the sacrifice

complete, with an heroic pretense that she was performing no unusual service. They did not speak, beyond her saying, in a clear, dry
note, "Here's your breakfast, Pen," and her sister's answering,
hoarsely and tremulously, "Oh, thank you, Irene." And, though two
or three times they turned their faces toward each other while Irene
remained in the room, mechanically putting its confusion to rights,
their eyes did not meet. Then Irene descended upon the other
rooms, which she set in order, and some of which she fiercely swept
and dusted. She made the beds; and she sent the two servants away
to church as soon as they had eaten their breakfast, telling them that
she would wash their dishes. Throughout the morning her father
and mother heard her about the work of getting dinner, with certain
silences which represented the moments when she stopped and
stood stock-still, and then, readjusting her burden, forced herself
forward under it again.

They sat alone in the family-room, out of which their two girls
seemed to have died. Lapham could not read his Sunday papers, and
she had no heart to go to church, as she would have done earlier in
life when in trouble. Just then she was obscurely feeling that the
church was somehow to blame for that counsel of Mr. Sewell's on
which they had acted.

"I should like to know," she said, having brought the matter up,
"whether he would have thought it was such a light matter if it had
been his own children. Do you suppose he'd have been so ready to
act on his own advice if it *had* been?"

"He told us the right thing to do, Persis,—the only thing. We
couldn't let it go on," urged her husband gently.

"Well, it makes me despise Pen! Irene's showing twice the character that she is, this very minute."

The mother said this so that the father might defend her daughter to her. He did not fail. "Irene's got the easiest part, the way I look
at it. And you'll see that Pen'll know how to behave when the time
comes."

"What do you want she should do?"

"I haven't got so far as that yet. What are we going to do about
Irene?"

"What do you want Pen should do," repeated Mrs. Lapham,
"when it comes to it?"

"Well, I don't want she should take him, for one thing," said Lapham.

This seemed to satisfy Mrs. Lapham as to her husband, and she said, in defense of Corey, "Why, I don't see what he's done. It's all been our doing."

"Never mind that now. What about Irene?"

"She says she's going to Lapham to-morrow. She feels that she's got to get away somewhere. It's natural she should."

"Yes. And I presume it will be about the best thing for her. Shall you go with her?"

"Yes."

"Well." He comfortlessly took up a newspaper again, and she rose with a sigh, and went to her room to pack some things for the morrow's journey.

After dinner, when Irene had cleared away the last trace of it in kitchen and dining-room with unsparing punctilio, she came downstairs, dressed to go out, and bade her father come to walk with her again. It was a repetition of the aimlessness of the last night's wanderings. They came back, and she got tea for them, and after that they heard her stirring about in her own room, as if she were busy about many things; but they did not dare to look in upon her, even after all the noises had ceased, and they knew she had gone to bed.

"Yes; it's a thing she's got to fight out by herself," said Mrs. Lapham.

"I guess she'll get along," said Lapham. "But I don't want you should misjudge Pen either. She's all right too. She ain't to blame."

"Yes, I know. But I can't work round to it all at once. I sha'n't misjudge her, but you can't expect me to get over it right away."

"Mamma," said Irene, when she was hurrying their departure the next morning, "what did she tell him when he asked her?"

"Tell him?" echoed the mother; and after a while she added, "She didn't tell him anything."

"Did she say anything about me?"

"She said he mustn't come here any more."

Irene turned and went into her sister's room. "Good-bye, Pen," she said, kissing her with an effect of not seeing or touching her. "I want you should tell him all about it. If he's half a man, he won't give up till he knows why you won't have him; and he has a right to know."

"It wouldn't make any difference. I couldn't have him after—"

"That's for you to say. But if you don't tell him about me, I will."

" 'Rene!"

"Yes! You needn't say I cared for him. But you can say that you all thought he—cared for—me."

"Oh, Irene————"

"Don't!" Irene escaped from the arms that tried to cast themselves about her. "You are all right, Pen. You haven't done anything. You've helped me all you could. But I can't—yet."

She went out of the room and summoned Mrs. Lapham with a sharp "Now, mamma!" and went on putting the last things into her trunks.

The Colonel went to the station with them, and put them on the train. He got them a little compartment to themselves in the Pullman car; and as he stood leaning with his lifted hands against the sides of the doorway, he tried to say something consoling and hopeful: "I guess you'll have an easy ride, Irene. I don't believe it'll be dusty, any, after the rain last night."

"Don't you stay till the train starts, papa," returned the girl, in rigid rejection of his futilities. "Get off now."

"Well, if you want I should," he said, glad to be able to please her in anything. He remained on the platform till the cars started. He saw Irene bustling about in the compartment, making her mother comfortable for the journey; but Mrs. Lapham did not lift her head. The train moved off, and he went heavily back to his business.

From time to time during the day, when he caught a glimpse of him, Corey tried to make out from his face whether he knew what had taken place between him and Penelope. When Rogers came in about time of closing, and shut himself up with Lapham in his room, the young man remained till the two came out together and parted in their salutationless fashion.

Lapham showed no surprise at seeing Corey still there, and merely answered, "Well!" when the young man said that he wished to speak with him, and led the way back to his room.

Corey shut the door behind them. "I only wish to speak to you in case you know of the matter already; for otherwise I'm bound by a promise."

"I guess I know what you mean. It's about Penelope."

"Yes, it's about Miss Lapham. I am greatly attached to her—you'll excuse my saying it; I couldn't excuse myself if I were not."

"Perfectly excusable," said Lapham. "It's all right."

"Oh, I'm glad to hear you say that!" cried the young fellow joyfully. "I want you to believe that this isn't a new thing or an unconsidered thing with me—though it seemed so unexpected to her."

Lapham fetched a deep sigh. "It's all right as far as I'm concerned—or her mother. We've both liked you first-rate."

"Yes?"

"But there seems to be something in Penelope's mind—I don't know————" The Colonel consciously dropped his eyes.

"She referred to something—I couldn't make out what—but I hoped—I hoped—that with your leave I might overcome it—the barrier—whatever it was. Miss Lapham—Penelope—gave me the hope—that I was—wasn't—indifferent to her————"

"Yes, I guess that's so," said Lapham. He suddenly lifted his head, and confronted the young fellow's honest face with his own face, so different in its honesty. "Sure you never made up to any one else at the same time?"

"*Never!* Who could imagine such a thing? If that's all, I can easily————"

"I don't say that's all, nor that that's it. I don't want you should go upon that idea. I just thought, may be—you hadn't thought of it."

"No, I certainly hadn't thought of it! Such a thing would have been so impossible to me that I *couldn't* have thought of it; and it's so shocking to me now that I don't know what to say to it."

"Well, don't take it too much to heart," said Lapham, alarmed at the feeling he had excited; "I don't say she thought so. I was trying to guess—trying to————"

"If there is *anything* I can say or do to convince you————"

"Oh, it ain't necessary to say anything. I'm all right."

"But Miss Lapham! I may see her again? I may try to convince her that————"

He stopped in distress, and Lapham afterwards told his wife that he kept seeing the face of Irene as it looked when he parted with her in the car; and whenever he was going to say yes, he could not open his lips. At the same time he could not help feeling that Penelope had a right to what was her own, and Sewell's words came back to him. Besides, they had already put Irene to the worst suffering. Lapham compromised, as he imagined.

"You can come round to-night and see *me*, if you want to," he said; and he bore grimly the gratitude that the young man poured out upon him.

Penelope came down to supper and took her mother's place at the head of the table.

Lapham sat silent in her presence as long as he could bear it. Then he asked, "How do you feel to-night, Pen?"

"Oh, like a thief," said the girl. "A thief that hasn't been arrested yet."

Lapham waited awhile before he said, "Well, now, your mother and I want you should hold up on that awhile."

"It isn't for you to say. It's something I *can't* hold up on."

"Yes, I guess you can. If I know what's happened, then what's happened is a thing that nobody is to blame for. And we want you should make the best of it, and not the worst. Heigh? It ain't going to help Irene any for you to hurt yourself—or anybody else; and I don't want you should take up with any such crazy notion. As far as heard from, you haven't stolen anything, and whatever you've got belongs to you."

"Has he been speaking to you, father?"

"Your mother's been speaking to me."

"Has *he* been speaking to you?"

"That's neither here nor there."

"Then he's broken his word, and I will never speak to him again!"

"If he was any such fool as to promise that he wouldn't talk to me on a subject"—Lapham drew a deep breath, and then made the plunge—"that I brought up————"

"Did you bring it up?"

"The same as brought up—the quicker he broke his word the better; and I want you should act upon that idea. Recollect that it's my

business, and your mother's business, as well as yours, and we're going
to have our say. He hain't done anything wrong, Pen, nor anything that
he's going to be punished for. Understand that. He's got to have a
reason, if you're not going to have him. I don't say you've got to have
him; I want you should feel perfectly free about that; but I *do* say
you've got to give him a reason."

"Is he coming here?"

"I don't know as you'd call it coming————"

"Yes, you do, father!" said the girl, in forlorn amusement at his
shuffling.

"He's coming here to see *me*————"

"When's he coming?"

"I don't know but he's coming to-night."

"And you want I should see him?"

"I don't know but you'd better."

"All right. I'll see him."

Lapham drew a long, deep breath of suspicion inspired by this
acquiescence. "What you going to do?" he asked presently.

"I don't know yet," answered the girl sadly. "It depends a good
deal upon what *he* does."

"Well," said Lapham, with the hungriness of unsatisfied anxiety
in his tone. When Corey's card was brought into the family-room
where he and Penelope were sitting, he went into the parlor to find
him. "I guess Penelope wants to see you," he said; and, indicating the
family-room, he added, "She's in there," and did not go back himself.

Corey made his way to the girl's presence with open trepidation, which was not allayed by her silence and languor. She sat in the
chair where she had sat the other night, but she was not playing
with a fan now.

He came toward her, and then stood faltering. A faint smile
quivered over her face at the spectacle of his subjection. "Sit down,
Mr. Corey," she said. "There's no reason why we shouldn't talk it over
quietly; for I know you will think I'm right."

"I'm sure of that," he answered hopefully. "When I saw that your
father knew of it to-day, I asked him to let me see you again. I'm
afraid that I broke my promise to you—technically————"

"It had to be broken."

He took more courage at her words. "But I've only come to do whatever you say, and not to be an—annoyance to you————"

"Yes, you have to know; but I couldn't tell you before. Now they all think I should."

A tremor of anxiety passed over the young man's face, on which she kept her eyes steadily fixed.

"We supposed it—it was—Irene————"

He remained blank a moment, and then he said with a smile of relief, of deprecation, of protest, of amazement, of compassion:

"*Oh!* Never! Never for an instant! How could you think such a thing? It was impossible! I never thought of her. But I see—I see! I can explain—no, there's nothing to explain! I have never knowingly done or said a thing from first to last to make you think that. I see how terrible it is!" he said; but he still smiled, as if he could not take it seriously. "I admired her beauty—who could help doing that?— and I thought her very good and sensible. Why, last winter in Texas, I told Stanton about our meeting in Canada, and we agreed—I only tell you to show you how far I always was from what you thought— that he must come North and try to see her, and—and—of course, it all sounds very silly!—and he sent her a newspaper with an account of his ranch in it————"

"She thought it came from you."

"Oh, good heavens! He didn't tell me till after he'd done it. But he did it for a part of our foolish joke. And when I met your sister again, I only admired her as before. I can see, now, how I must have seemed to be seeking her out; but it was to talk of you with her— I never talked of anything else if I could help it, except when I changed the subject because I was ashamed to be always talking of you. I see how distressing it is for all of you. But tell me that you believe me!"

"Yes, I must. It's all been our mistake————"

"It has indeed! But there's no mistake about my loving *you*, Penelope," he said; and the old-fashioned name, at which she had often mocked, was sweet to her from his lips.

"That only makes it worse!" she answered.

"Oh, no!" he gently protested. "It makes it better. It makes it right. How is it worse? How is it wrong?"

"Can't you see? You must understand all now! Don't you see that if she believed so too, and if she————" She could not go on.

"Did she—did your sister—think that too?" gasped Corey.

"She used to talk with me about you; and when you say you care for me now, it makes me feel like the vilest hypocrite in the world. That day you gave her the list of books, and she came down to Nantasket, and went on about you, I helped her to flatter herself—oh! I don't see how she can forgive me. But she knows I can never forgive myself! That's the reason she can do it. I can see now," she went on, "how I must have been trying to get you from her. I can't endure it! The only way is for me never to see you or speak to you again!" She laughed forlornly. "That would be pretty hard on you, if you cared."

"I do care—all the world!"

"Well, then, it would if you were going to keep on caring. You won't long, if you stop coming now."

"Is this all, then? Is it the end?"

"It's—whatever it is. I can't get over the thought of her. Once I thought I could, but now I see that I can't. It seems to grow worse. Sometimes I feel as if it would drive me crazy."

He sat looking at her with lack-luster eyes. The light suddenly came back into them. "Do you think I could love you if you had been false to her? I know you have been true to her, and truer still to yourself. I never tried to see her, except with the hope of seeing you too. I supposed she must know that I was in love with you. From the first time I saw you there that afternoon, you filled my fancy. Do you think I was flirting with the child, or—no, you don't think that! We have not done wrong. We have not harmed any one knowingly. We have a right to each other————"

"No! no! you must never speak to me of this again. If you do, I shall know that you despise me."

"But how will that help her? I don't love her."

"Don't say that to me! I have said that to myself too much."

"If you forbid me to love you, it won't make me love her," he persisted.

She was about to speak, but she caught her breath without doing so, and merely stared at him.

"I must do what you say," he continued. "But what good will it do her? You can't make her happy by making yourself unhappy."

"Do you ask me to profit by a wrong?"

"Not for the world. But there is no wrong!"

"There is something—I don't know what. There's a wall between us. I shall dash myself against it as long as I live; but that won't break it."

"Oh!" he groaned. "We have done no wrong. Why should we suffer from another's mistake as if it were our sin?"

"I don't know. But we must suffer."

"Well, then, I will not, for my part, and I will not let you. If you care for me——"

"You had no right to know it."

"You make it my privilege to keep you from doing wrong for the right's sake. I'm sorry, with all my heart and soul, for this error; but I can't blame myself, and I won't deny myself the happiness I haven't done anything to forfeit. I will never give you up. I will wait as long as you please for the time when you shall feel free from this mistake; but you shall be mine at last. Remember that. I might go away for months—a year, even; but that seems a cowardly and guilty thing, and I'm not afraid, and I'm not guilty, and I'm going to stay here and try to see you."

She shook her head. "It won't change anything. Don't you see that there's no hope for us?"

"When is she coming back?" he asked.

"I don't know. Mother wants father to come and take her out West for a while."

"She's up there in the country with your mother yet?"

"Yes."

He was silent; then he said, desperately:

"Penelope, she is very young; and perhaps—perhaps she might meet——"

"It would make no difference. It wouldn't change it for me."

"You are cruel—cruel to yourself, if you love me, and cruel to me. Don't you remember that night—before I spoke—you were talking of that book; and you said it was foolish and wicked to do as that girl did. Why is it different with you, except that you give me nothing, and can never give me anything when you take yourself away? If it were anybody else, I am sure you would say————"

"But it isn't anybody else, and that makes it impossible. Sometimes I think it might be if I would only say so to myself, and then all that I said to her about you comes up————"

"I will wait. It can't always come up. I won't urge you any longer now. But you will see it differently—more clearly. Good-bye—no! Good-night! I shall come again to-morrow. It will surely come right, and, whatever happens, you have done no wrong. Try to keep that in mind. I am so happy, in spite of all!"

He tried to take her hand, but she put it behind her. "No, no! I can't let you—yet!"

XX

After a week Mrs. Lapham returned, leaving Irene alone at the old homestead in Vermont. "She's comfortable there—as comfortable as she can be anywheres, I guess," she said to her husband, as they drove together from the station, where he had met her in obedience to her telegraphic summons. "She keeps herself busy helping about the house; and she goes round amongst the hands in their houses. There's sickness, and you know how helpful she is where there's sickness. She don't complain any. I don't know as I've heard a word out of her mouth since we left home; but I'm afraid it'll wear on her, Silas."

"You don't look over and above well yourself, Persis," said her husband kindly.

"Oh, don't talk about me. What I want to know is whether you can't get the time to run off with her somewhere? I wrote to you about Dubuque. She'll work herself down, I'm afraid; and *then* I don't know as she'll be over it. But if she could go off, and be amused—see new people————"

"I could *make* the time," said Lapham, "if I had to. But, as it happens, I've got to go out West on business,—I'll tell you about it,—and I'll take Irene along."

"Good!" said his wife. "That's about the best thing I've heard yet. Where you going?"

"Out Dubuque way."

"Anything the matter with Bill's folks?"

"No. It's business."

"How's Pen?"

"I guess she ain't much better than Irene."

"He been about any?"

"Yes. But I can't see as it helps matters much."

"Tchk!" Mrs. Lapham fell back against the carriage cushions. "I declare, to see her willing to take the man that we all thought wanted her sister! I can't make it seem right."

"It's right," said Lapham stoutly; "but I guess she ain't willing; I wish she was. But there don't seem to be any way out of the thing,

242

anywhere. It's a perfect snarl. But I don't want you should be anyways ha'sh with Pen."

Mrs. Lapham answered nothing; but when she met Penelope she gave the girl's wan face a sharp look, and began to whimper on her neck.

Penelope's tears were all spent. "Well, mother," she said, "you come back almost as cheerful as you went away. I needn't ask if 'Rene's in good spirits. We all seem to be overflowing with them. I suppose this is one way of congratulating me. Mrs. Corey hasn't been round to do it yet."

"Are you—are you engaged to him, Pen?" gasped her mother.

"Judging by my feelings, I should say not. I feel as if it was a last will and testament. But you'd better ask him when he comes."

"I can't bear to look at him."

"I guess he's used to that. He don't seem to expect to be looked at. Well! we're all just where we started. I wonder how long it will keep up?"

Mrs. Lapham reported to her husband when he came home at night—he had left his business to go and meet her, and then, after a desolate dinner at the house, had returned to the office again—that Penelope was fully as bad as Irene. "And she don't know how to work it off. Irene keeps doing; but Pen just sits in her room and mopes. She don't even read. I went up this afternoon to scold her about the state the house was in—you can see that Irene's away by the perfect mess; but when I saw her through the crack of the door I hadn't the heart. She sat there with her hands in her lap, just staring. And, my goodness! she jumped so when she saw me; and then she fell back, and began to laugh, and said she, 'I thought it was my ghost, mother!' I felt as if I should give way."

Lapham listened jadedly, and answered far from the point. "I guess I've got to start out there pretty soon, Persis."

"How soon?"

"Well, to-morrow morning."

Mrs. Lapham sat silent. Then, "All right," she said. "I'll get you ready."

"I shall run up to Lapham for Irene, and then I'll push on through Canada. I can get there about as quick."

"Is it anything you can tell me about, Silas?"

"Yes," said Lapham. "But it's a long story, and I guess you've got your hands pretty full as it is. I've been throwing good money after bad,—the usual way,—and now. I've got to see if I can save the pieces."

After a moment Mrs. Lapham asked, "Is it—Rogers?"

"It's Rogers."

"I didn't want you should get in any deeper with him."

"No. You didn't want I should press him either; and I had to do one or the other. And so I got in deeper."

"Silas," said his wife, "I'm afraid I made you!"

"It's all right, Persis, as far forth as that goes. I was glad to make it up with him—I jumped at the chance. I guess Rogers saw that he had a soft thing in me, and he's worked it for all it was worth. But it'll all come out right in the end."

Lapham said this as if he did not care to talk any more about it. He added, casually, "Pretty near everybody but the fellows that owe *me* seem to expect me to do a cash business, all of a sudden."

"Do you mean that you've got payments to make, and that people are not paying *you*?"

Lapham winced a little. "Something like that," he said, and he lighted a cigar. "But when I tell you it's all right, I mean it, Persis. I ain't going to let the grass grow under my feet, though,—especially while Rogers digs the ground away from the roots."

"What are you going to do?"

"If it has to come to that, I'm going to squeeze him." Lapham's countenance lighted up with greater joy than had yet visited it since the day they had driven out to Brookline. "Milton K. Rogers is a rascal, if you want to know; or else all the signs fail. But I guess he'll find he's got his come-uppance." Lapham shut his lips so that the short, reddish-gray beard stuck straight out on them.

"What's he done?"

"What's he done? Well, now, I'll tell you what he's done, Persis, since you think Rogers is such a saint, and that I used him so badly in getting him out of the business. He's been dabbling in every sort of fool thing you can lay your tongue to,—wild-cat stocks, patent-rights, land speculations, oil claims,—till he's run through about everything. But he did have a big milling property out on the line of the P. Y. & X.,—saw-mills and grist-mills and lands,—and for the last eight years he's been doing a land-office business with 'em— business that would have made anybody else rich. But you can't make Milton K. Rogers rich, any more than you can fat a hide-bound colt. It ain't in him. He'd run through Vanderbilt, Jay Gould, and Tom Scott* rolled into one, in less than six months, give him a chance, and come out and want to borrow money of you. Well, he won't borrow any more money of me; and if he thinks I don't know as much about that milling property as he does, he's mistaken. I've taken his mills, but I guess I've got the inside track; Bill's kept me posted; and now I'm going out there to see how I can unload; and I sha'n't mind a great deal if Rogers is under the load when it's off, once."

"I don't understand you, Silas."

"Why, it's just this. The Great Lacustrine & Polar Railroad has leased the P. Y. & X.† for ninety-nine years,—bought it, practically,— and it's going to build car-works right by those mills, and it may want them. And Milton K. Rogers knew it when he turned 'em in on me."

"Well, if the road wants them, don't that make the mills valu-able? You can get what you ask for them!"

"Can I? The P. Y. & X. is the only road that runs within fifty miles of the mills, and you can't get a foot of lumber nor a pound of flour to market any other way. As long as he had a little local road like the P. Y. & X. to deal with, Rogers could manage; but when it come to a big through line like the G. L. & P., he couldn't stand any chance at all. If such a road as that took a fancy to his mills, do you think it would pay what he asked? No, sir! He would take what the road of-fered, or else the road would tell him to carry his flour and lumber to market himself."

"And do you suppose he knew the G. L. & P. wanted the mills when he turned them in on you?" asked Mrs. Lapham, aghast, and falling helplessly into his alphabetical parlance.

The Colonel laughed scoffingly. "Well, when Milton K. Rogers

---

*Cornelius Vanderbilt (1794–1877), Jay Gould (1836–1892), and Thomas Scott (1823–1881) were fabulously wealthy robber barons of the Gilded Age.
†All fictitious railroad companies.

don't know which side his bread's buttered on! I don't understand," he added thoughtfully, "how he's always letting it fall on the buttered side. But such a man as that is sure to have a screw loose in him somewhere."

Mrs. Lapham sat discomfited. All that she could say was, "Well, I want you should ask yourself whether Rogers would ever have gone wrong, or got into these ways of his, if it hadn't been for your forcing him out of the business when you did. I want you should think whether you're not responsible for everything he's done since."

"You go and get that bag of mine ready," said Lapham sullenly. "I guess I can take care of myself. And Milton K. Rogers too," he added.

That evening Corey spent the time after dinner in his own room, with restless excursions to the library, where his mother sat with his father and sisters, and showed no signs of leaving them. At last, in coming down, he encountered her on the stairs, going up. They both stopped consciously.

"I would like to speak with you, mother. I have been waiting to see you alone."

"Come to my room," she said.

"I have a feeling that you know what I want to say," he began there.

She looked up at him where he stood by the chimney-piece, and tried to put a cheerful note into her questioning "Yes?"

"Yes; and I have a feeling that you won't like it—that you won't approve of it. I wish you did—I wish you could!"

"I'm used to liking and approving everything you do, Tom. If I don't like this at once, I shall try to like it—you know that—for your sake, whatever it is."

"I'd better be short," he said, with a quick sigh. "It's about Miss Lapham." He hastened to add, "I hope it isn't surprising to you. I'd have told you before, if I could."

"No, it isn't surprising. I was afraid—I suspected something of the kind."

They were both silent in a painful silence.

"Well, mother?" he asked at last.

"If it's something you've quite made up your mind to———"

"It is!"

"And if you've already spoken to her————"

"I had to do that first, of course."

"There would be no use of my saying anything, even if I disliked it."

"You do dislike it!"

"No—no! I can't say that. Of course, I should have preferred it if you had chosen some nice girl among those that you had been brought up with—some friend or associate of your sisters, whose people we had known————"

"Yes, I understand that, and I can assure you that I haven't been indifferent to your feelings. I have tried to consider them from the first, and it kept me hesitating in a way that I'm ashamed to think of; for it wasn't quite right towards—others. But your feelings and my sisters' have been in my mind, and if I couldn't yield to what I supposed they must be, entirely————"

Even so good a son and brother as this, when it came to his love affair, appeared to think that he had yielded much in considering the feelings of his family at all.

His mother hastened to comfort him. "I know—I know. I've seen for some time that this might happen, Tom, and I have prepared myself for it. I have talked it over with your father, and we both agreed from the beginning that you were not to be hampered by our feeling. Still—it is a surprise. It must be."

"I know it. I can understand your feeling. But I'm sure that it's one that will last only while you don't know her well."

"Oh, I'm sure of that, Tom. I'm sure that we shall all be fond of her,—for your sake at first, even,—and I hope she'll like us."

"I am quite certain of that," said Corey, with that confidence which experience does not always confirm in such cases. "And your taking it as you do lifts a tremendous load off me."

But he sighed so heavily, and looked so troubled, that his mother said, "Well, now, you mustn't think of that any more. We wish what is for your happiness, my son, and we will gladly reconcile ourselves to anything that might have been disagreeable. I suppose we needn't speak of the family. We must both think alike about them. They have their—drawbacks, but they are thoroughly good people, and I satisfied myself the other night that they were not to be dreaded." She rose, and put her arm round his neck. "And I wish you joy, Tom! If she's half as good as you are, you will both be very happy." She was going to kiss him, but something in his looks stopped her—an absence, a trouble, which broke out in his words.

"I must tell you, mother! There's been a complication—a mistake—that's a blight on me yet, and that it sometimes seems as if we couldn't escape from. I wonder if you can help us! They all thought I meant—the other sister."

"Oh, Tom! But how could they?"

"I don't know. It seemed so glaringly plain—I was ashamed of making it so outright from the beginning. But they did. Even she did, herself!"

"But where could they have thought your eyes were—your taste? It wouldn't be surprising if any one were taken with that wonderful beauty; and I'm sure she's good too. But I'm astonished at them! To think you could prefer that little, black, odd creature, with her joking and————"

"Mother!" cried the young man, turning a ghastly face of warning upon her.

"What do you mean, Tom?"

"Did you—did—did you think so, too,—that it was Irene I meant?"

"Why, of course!"

He stared at her hopelessly.

"Oh, my son!" she said, for all comment on the situation.

"Don't reproach me, mother! I couldn't stand it."

"No. I didn't mean to do that. But how—how could it happen?"

"I don't know. When she first told me that they had understood it so, I laughed—almost—it was so far from me. But now, when you seem to have had the same idea— Did you all think so?"

"Yes."

They remained looking at each other. Then Mrs. Corey began: "It did pass through my mind once—that day I went to call upon them—that it might not be as we thought; but I knew so little of— of————"

"Penelope," Corey mechanically supplied.

"Is that her name?—I forgot—that I only thought of you in relation to her long enough to reject the idea; and it was natural, after our seeing something of the other one last year, that I might suppose you had formed some—attachment————"

"Yes; that's what they thought too. But I never thought of her as anything but a pretty child. I was civil to her because you wished it; and when I met her here again, I only tried to see her so that I could talk with her about her sister."

"You needn't defend yourself to *me*, Tom," said his mother, proud to say it to him in his trouble. "It's a terrible business for them, poor things," she added. "I don't know how they could get over it. But, of course, sensible people must see————"

"They haven't got over it. At least *she* hasn't. Since it's happened, there's been nothing that hasn't made me prouder and fonder of her! At first I *was* charmed with her—my fancy was taken; she delighted me—I don't know how; but she was simply the most fascinating person I ever saw. Now I never think of that. I only think how good she is—how patient she is with me, and how unsparing she is of herself. If she were concerned alone—if I were not concerned too—it would soon end. She's never had a thought for anything but her sister's feeling and mine from the beginning. I go there,—I know that I oughtn't, but I can't help it,—and she suffers it, and tries not to let me see that she is suffering it. There never was any one like her—so brave, so true, so noble. I won't give her up—I can't. But it breaks my heart when she accuses herself of what was all my doing. We spend our time trying to reason out of it, but we always come back to it at last, and I have to hear her morbidly blaming herself. Oh!"

Doubtless Mrs. Corey imagined some reliefs to this suffering, some qualifications of this sublimity in a girl she had disliked so distinctly; but she saw none in her son's behavior, and she gave him her further sympathy. She tried to praise Penelope, and said that it was not to be expected that she could reconcile herself at once to everything. "I shouldn't have liked it in her if she had. But time will bring it all right. And if she really cares for you————"

"I extorted that from her."

"Well, then, you must look at it in the best light you can. There is no blame anywhere, and the mortification and pain is something that must be lived down. That's all. And don't let what I said grieve you, Tom. You know I scarcely knew her, and I—I shall be sure to like any one you like, after all."

"Yes, I know," said the young man drearily. "Will you tell father?"

"If you wish."

"He must know. And I couldn't stand any more of this, just yet—any more mistake."

"I will tell him," said Mrs. Corey; and it was naturally the next thing for a woman who dwelt so much on decencies to propose: "We must go to call on her—your sisters and I. They have never seen her even; and she mustn't be allowed to think we're indifferent to her, especially under the circumstances."

"Oh, no! Don't go—not yet," cried Corey, with an instinctive perception that nothing could be worse for him. "We must wait—we must be patient. I'm afraid it would be painful to her now."

He turned away without speaking further; and his mother's eyes followed him wistfully to the door. There were some questions that she would have liked to ask him; but she had to content herself with trying to answer them when her husband put them to her.

There was this comfort for her always in Bromfield Corey, that he never was much surprised at anything, however shocking or painful. His standpoint in regard to most matters was that of the sympathetic humorist who would be glad to have the victim of circumstance laugh with him, but was not too much vexed when the victim could not. He laughed now when his wife, with careful preparation, got the facts of his son's predicament fully under his eye.

"Really, Bromfield," she said, "I don't see how you *can* laugh. Do you see any way out of it?"

"It seems to me that the way has been found already. Tom has told his love to the right one, and the wrong one knows it. Time will do the rest."

"If I had so low an opinion of them all as that, it would make me very unhappy. It's shocking to think of it."

"It is, upon the theory of ladies and all young people," said her husband, with a shrug, feeling his way to the matches on the mantel, and then dropping them with a sigh, as if recollecting that he must not smoke there. "I've no doubt Tom feels himself an awful sinner. But apparently he's resigned to his sin; he isn't going to give her up."

"I'm glad to say, for the sake of human nature, that she isn't resigned—little as I like her," cried Mrs. Corey.

Her husband shrugged again. "Oh, there mustn't be any indecent haste. She will instinctively observe the proprieties. But come, now, Anna! you mustn't pretend to me here, in the sanctuary of home, that practically the human affections don't reconcile themselves to any situation that the human sentiments condemn. Suppose the wrong sister had died: would the right one have had any scruple in marrying Tom, after they had both 'waited a proper time,' as the phrase is?"

"Bromfield, you're shocking!"

"Not more shocking than reality. You may regard this as a second marriage." He looked at her with twinkling eyes, full of the triumph the spectator of his species feels in signal exhibitions of human nature. "Depend upon it, the right sister will be reconciled; the wrong one will be consoled; and all will go merry as a marriage bell—a second marriage bell. Why, it's quite like a romance!" Here he laughed outright again.

"Well," sighed the wife, "I could almost wish the right one, as you call her, would reject Tom. I dislike her so much."

"Ah, now you're talking business, Anna," said her husband, with his hands spread behind the back he turned comfortably to the fire. "The whole Lapham tribe is distasteful to me. As I don't happen to have seen our daughter-in-law elect, I have still the hope—which you're disposed to forbid me—that she may not be quite so unacceptable as the others."

"Do you really feel so, Bromfield?" anxiously inquired his wife.

"Yes—I think I do"; and he sat down, and stretched out his long legs toward the fire.

"But it's very inconsistent of you to oppose the matter now, when you've shown so much indifference up to this time. You've told me, all along, that it was of no use to oppose it."

"So I have. I was convinced of that at the beginning, or my reason was. You know very well that I am equal to any trial, any sacrifice, day after to-morrow; but when it comes to-day it's another
thing. As long as this crisis decently kept its distance, I could look at
it with an impartial eye; but now that it seems at hand, I find that,
while my reason is still acquiescent, my nerves are disposed to—
excuse the phrase—kick. I ask myself, what have I done nothing for,
all my life, and lived as a gentleman should, upon the earnings of
somebody else, in the possession of every polite taste and feeling that
adorns leisure, if I'm to come to this at last? And I find no satisfactory answer. I say to myself that I might as well have yielded to the
pressure all round me, and gone to work, as Tom has."

Mrs. Corey looked at him forlornly, divining the core of real re-
pugnance that existed in his self-satire.

"I assure you, my dear," he continued, "that the recollection of
what I suffered from the Laphams at that dinner of yours is an anguish still. It wasn't their behavior,—they behaved well enough—
or ill enough; but their conversation was terrible. Mrs. Lapham's
range was strictly domestic; and when the Colonel got me in the
library, he poured mineral paint all over me, till I could have been
safely warranted not to crack or scale in any climate. I suppose we
shall have to see a good deal of them. They will probably come here
every Sunday night to tea. It's a perspective without a vanishing-
point."

"It may not be so bad, after all," said his wife; and she suggested for his consolation that he knew very little about the
Laphams yet.

He assented to the fact. "I know very little about them, and about
my other fellow-beings. I dare say that I should like the Laphams better if I knew them better. But in any case, I resign myself. And we
must keep in view the fact that this is mainly Tom's affair, and if his
affections have regulated it to his satisfaction, we must be content."

"Oh, yes," sighed Mrs. Corey. "And perhaps it won't turn out so
badly. It's a great comfort to know that you feel just as I do about it."

"I do," said her husband, "and more too."

It was she and her daughters who would be chiefly annoyed by
the Lapham connection; she knew that. But she had to begin to bear

the burden by helping her husband to bear his light share of it. To see him so depressed dismayed her, and she might well have reproached him more sharply than she did for showing so much indifference, when she was so anxious, at first. But that would not have served any good end now. She even answered him patiently when he asked her, "What did you say to Tom when he told you it was the other one?"

"What could I say? I could do nothing, but try to take back what I had said against her."

"Yes, you had quite enough to do, I suppose. It's an awkward business. If it had been the pretty one, her beauty would have been our excuse. But the plain one—what do you suppose attracted him in her?"

Mrs. Corey sighed at the futility of the question. "Perhaps I did her injustice. I only saw her a few moments. Perhaps I got a false impression. I don't think she's lacking in sense, and that's a great thing. She'll be quick to see that we don't mean unkindness, and can't, by anything we say or do, when she's Tom's wife." She pronounced the distasteful word with courage, and went on: "The pretty one might not have been able to see that. She might have got it into her head that we were looking down on her; and those insipid people are terribly stubborn. We can come to some understanding with this one; I'm sure of that." She ended by declaring that it was now their duty to help Tom out of his terrible predicament.

"Oh, even the Lapham cloud has a silver lining," said Corey. "In fact, it seems really to have all turned out for the best, Anna; though it's rather curious to find you the champion of the Lapham side, at last. Confess, now, that the right girl has secretly been your choice all along, and that while you sympathize with the wrong one, you rejoice in the tenacity with which the right one is clinging to her own!" He added with final seriousness, "It's just that she should, and, so far as I understand the case, I respect her for it."

"Oh, yes," sighed Mrs. Corey. "It's natural, and it's right." But she added, "I suppose they're glad of him on any terms."

"That is what I have been taught to believe," said her husband. "When shall we see our daughter-in-law elect? I find myself rather impatient to have that part of it over."

Mrs. Corey hesitated. "Tom thinks we had better not call, just yet."

"She has told him of your terrible behavior when you called before?"

"No, Bromfield! She couldn't be so vulgar as *that*?"

"But anything short of it?"

XXI

Lapham was gone a fortnight. He was in a sullen humor when he came back, and kept himself shut close within his own den at the office the first day. He entered it in the morning without a word to his clerks as he passed through the outer room, and he made no sign throughout the forenoon, except to strike savagely on his desk-bell from time to time, and send out to Walker for some book of accounts or a letter-file. His boy confidentially reported to Walker that the old man seemed to have got a lot of papers round; and at lunch the book-keeper said to Corey, at the little table which they had taken in a corner together, in default of seats at the counter, "Well, sir, I guess there's a cold wave coming."

Corey looked up innocently, and said, "I haven't read the weather report."

"Yes, sir," Walker continued, "it's coming. Areas of rain along the whole coast, and increased pressure in the region of the private office. Storm-signals up at the old man's door now."

Corey perceived that he was speaking figuratively, and that his meteorology was entirely personal to Lapham. "What do you mean?" he asked, without vivid interest in the allegory, his mind being full of his own tragi-comedy.

"Why, just this: I guess the old man's takin' in sail. And I guess he's got to. As I told you the first time we talked about him, there don't any one know one-quarter as much about the old man's business as the old man does himself; and I ain't betraying any confidence when I say that I guess that old partner of his has got pretty deep into his books. I guess he's over head and ears in 'em, and the old man's gone in after him, and he's got a drownin' man's grip round his neck. There seems to be a kind of a lull—kind of a dead calm, I call it—in the paint market just now; and then again a ten-hundred-thousand-dollar man don't build a hundred-thousand-dollar house without feeling the drain, unless there's a regular boom. And just now there ain't any boom at all. Oh, I don't say but what the old man's got anchors to windward; guess he *has*; but if he's *goin'* to leave me his money, I wish he'd left it six weeks ago. Yes, sir, I guess there's a cold wave comin'; but you can't generally 'most always tell, as a usual thing, where the old man's concerned, and it's only a guess." Walker began to feed in his breaded chop with the same nervous excitement with which he abandoned himself to the slangy and figurative excesses of his talks. Corey had listened with a miserable curiosity and compassion up to a certain moment, when a broad light of hope flashed upon him. It came from Lapham's potential ruin; and the way out of the labyrinth that had hitherto seemed so hopeless was clear enough, if another's disaster would befriend him, and give him the opportunity to prove the unselfishness of his constancy. He thought of the sum of money that was his own, and that he might offer to lend, or practically give, if the time came; and with his crude hopes and purposes formlessly exulting in his heart, he kept on listening with an unchanged countenance.

Walker could not rest till he had developed the whole situation, so far as he knew it. "Look at the stock we've got on hand. There's going to be an awful shrinkage on that, now! And when everybody is shutting down, or running half time, the works up at Lapham are going full chip, just the same as ever. Well, it's his pride. I don't say but what it's a good sort of pride, but he likes to make his brags that the fire's never been out in the works since they started, and that no man's work or wages has ever been cut down yet at Lapham, it don't matter *what* the times are. Of course," explained Walker, "I shouldn't talk so to everybody; don't know as I should talk so to *any*body but you, Mr. Corey."

"Of course," assented Corey.

"Little off your feed to-day," said Walker, glancing at Corey's plate.

"I got up with a headache."

"Well, sir, if you're like me you'll carry it round all day, then. I don't know a much meaner thing than a headache—unless it's earache, or toothache, or some other kind of ache. I'm pretty hard to suit, when it comes to diseases. Notice how yellow the old man looked when he came in this morning? I don't like to see a man of his build look yellow—much."

About the middle of the afternoon the dust-colored face of Rogers, now familiar to Lapham's clerks, showed itself among them. "Has Colonel Lapham returned yet?" he asked, in his dry, wooden tones, of Lapham's boy.

"Yes, he's in his office," said the boy; and as Rogers advanced, he rose and added, "I don't know as you can see him to-day. His orders are not to let anybody in."

"Oh, indeed!" said Rogers; "I think he will see *me!*" and he pressed forward.

"Well, I'll have to ask," returned the boy; and hastily preceding Rogers, he put his head in at Lapham's door, and then withdrew it. "Please to sit down," he said; "he'll see you pretty soon;" and, with an air of some surprise, Rogers obeyed. His sere, dull-brown whiskers and the mustache closing over both lips were incongruously and illogically clerical in effect, and the effect was heightened for no reason by the parchment texture of his skin; the baldness extending to the crown of his head was like a baldness made up for the stage. What his face expressed chiefly was a bland and beneficent caution. Here, you must have said to yourself, is a man of just, sober, and prudent views, fixed purposes, and the good citizenship that avoids debt and hazard of every kind.

"What do you want?" asked Lapham, wheeling round in his swivel-chair as Rogers entered his room, and pushing the door shut with his foot, without rising.

Rogers took the chair that was not offered him, and sat with his hat-brim on his knees, and its crown pointed towards Lapham. "I want to know what you are going to do," he answered, with sufficient self-possession.

"I'll tell you, first, what I've *done,*" said Lapham. "I've been to Dubuque, and I've found out all about that milling property you turned in on me. Did you know that the G. L. & P. had leased the P. Y. & X.?"

"I some suspected that it might."

"Did you know it when you turned the property in on me? Did you know that the G. L. & P. wanted to buy the mills?"

"I presumed the road would give a fair price for them," said Rogers, winking his eyes in outward expression of inwardly blinking the point.

"You lie," said Lapham, as quietly as if correcting him in a slight error; and Rogers took the word with equal *sang* froid. "You knew the road wouldn't give a fair price for the mills. You knew it would give what it chose, and that I couldn't help myself, when you let me take them. You're a thief, Milton K. Rogers, and you stole money

I lent you." Rogers sat listening, as if respectfully considering the statements. "You knew how I felt about that old matter—or my wife did; and that I wanted to make it up to you, if you felt anyway badly used. And you took advantage of it. You've got money out of me, in the first place, on securities that wa'n't worth thirty-five cents on the dollar, and you've let me in for this thing, and that thing, and you've bled me every time. And all I've got to show for it is a milling property on a line of road that can squeeze me, whenever it wants to, as dry as it pleases. And you want to know what I'm going to do? I'm going to squeeze *you*. I'm going to sell these collaterals of yours,"— he touched a bundle of papers among others that littered his desk,— "and I'm going to let the mills go for what they'll fetch. I ain't going to fight the G. L. & P."

Lapham wheeled about in his chair and turned his burly back on his visitor, who sat wholly unmoved.

"There are some parties," he began, with a dry tranquillity ignoring Lapham's words, as if they had been an outburst against some third person, who probably merited them, but in whom he was so little interested that he had been obliged to use patience in listening to his condemnation,—"there are some English parties who have been making inquiries in regard to those mills."

"I guess you're lying, Rogers," said Lapham, without looking round.

"Well, all that I have to ask is that you will not act hastily."

"I see you don't think I'm in earnest!" cried Lapham, facing fiercely about. "You think I'm fooling, do you?" He struck his bell, and "William," he ordered the boy who answered it, and who stood waiting while he dashed off a note to the brokers and inclosed it with the bundle of securities in a large envelope, "take these down to Gallop & Paddock's, in State street, right away. Now go!" he said to Rogers, when the boy had closed the door after him; and he turned once more to his desk.

Rogers rose from his chair, and stood with his hat in his hand. He was not merely dispassionate in his attitude and expression, he was impartial. He wore the air of a man who was ready to return to business whenever the wayward mood of his interlocutor permitted. "Then I understand," he said, "that you will take no action in regard to the mills till I have seen the parties I speak of."

Lapham faced about once more, and sat looking up into the visage of Rogers in silence. "I wonder what you're up to," he said at last; "I should like to know." But as Rogers made no sign of gratifying his curiosity, and treated this last remark of Lapham's as of the irrelevance of all the rest, he said, frowning, "You bring me a party that will give me enough for those mills to clear me of you, and I'll talk to you. But don't you come here with any man of straw. And I'll give you just twenty-four hours to prove yourself a swindler again."

Once more Lapham turned his back, and Rogers, after looking thoughtfully into his hat a moment, cleared his throat, and quietly withdrew, maintaining to the last his unprejudiced demeanor.

Lapham was not again heard from, as Walker phrased it, during the afternoon, except when the last mail was taken in to him; then the sound of rending envelopes, mixed with that of what seemed suppressed swearing, penetrated to the outer office. Somewhat earlier than the usual hour for closing, he appeared there with his hat on and his overcoat buttoned about him. He said briefly to his boy, "William, I sha'n't be back again this afternoon," and then went to Miss Dewey and left a number of letters on her table to be copied, and went out. Nothing had been said, but a sense of trouble subtly diffused itself through those who saw him go out.

That evening, as he sat down with his wife alone at tea, he asked, "Ain't Pen coming to supper?"

"No, she ain't," said his wife. "I don't know as I like the way she's going on, any too well. I'm afraid, if she keeps on, she'll be down sick. She's got deeper feelings than Irene."

Lapham said nothing, but, having helped himself to the abundance of his table in his usual fashion, he sat and looked at his plate with an indifference that did not escape the notice of his wife. "What's the matter with you?" she asked.

"Nothing. I haven't got any appetite."

"What's the matter?" she persisted.

"Trouble's the matter; bad luck and lots of it's the matter," said Lapham. "I haven't ever hid anything from you, Persis, when you asked me, and it's too late to begin now. I'm in a fix. I'll tell you what kind of a fix, if you think it'll do you any good; but I guess you'll be satisfied to know that it's a fix."

"How much of a one?" she asked, with a look of grave, steady courage in her eyes.

"Well, I don't know as I can tell, just yet," said Lapham, avoiding this look. "Things have been dull all the fall, but I thought they'd brisk up, come winter. They haven't. There have been a lot of failures, and some of 'em owed me, and some of 'em had me on their paper; and————" Lapham stopped.

"And what?" prompted his wife.

He hesitated before he added, "And then—Rogers."

"I'm to blame for that," said Mrs. Lapham. "I forced you to it."

"No; I was as willing to go into it as what you were," answered Lapham. "I don't want to blame anybody."

Mrs. Lapham had a woman's passion for fixing responsibility; she could not help saying, as soon as acquitted, "I warned you against him, Silas. I told you not to let him get in any deeper with you."

"Oh, yes. I had to help him to try to get my money back. I might as well poured water into a sieve. And now————" Lapham stopped.

"Don't be afraid to speak out to me, Silas Lapham. If it comes to the worst, I want to know it—I've got to know it. What did I ever care for the money? I've had a happy home with you ever since we were married, and I guess I shall have as long as you live, whether we go on to the Back Bay, or go back to the old house at Lapham. I know who's to blame, and I blame myself. It was my forcing Rogers on to you." She came back to this, with her helpless longing, inbred in all Puritan souls, to have some one specifically suffer for the evil in the world, even if it must be herself.

"It hasn't come to the worst yet, Persis," said her husband. "But I shall have to hold up on the new house a little while, till I can see where I am."

"I shouldn't care if we had to sell it," cried his wife, in passionate self-condemnation. "I should be *glad* if we had to, as far as I'm concerned."

"I shouldn't," said Lapham.

"I know!" said his wife; and she remembered ruefully how his heart was set on it.

He sat musing. "Well, I guess it's going to come out all right in the end. Or, if it ain't," he sighed, "we can't help it. May be Pen needn't worry so much about Corey, after all," he continued, with a bitter irony new to him. "It's an ill wind that blows nobody good. And there's a chance," he ended, with a still bitterer laugh, "that Rogers will come to time, after all."

"I don't believe it!" exclaimed Mrs. Lapham, with a gleam of hope in her eyes. "What chance?"

"One in ten million," said Lapham; and her face fell again. "He says there are some English parties after him to buy these mills."

"Well?"

"Well, I gave him twenty-four hours to prove himself a liar."

"You don't believe there are any such parties?"

"Not in this world."

"But if there were?"

"Well, if there were, Persis——— But pshaw!"

"No, no!" she pleaded eagerly. "It don't seem as if he could be such a villain. What would be the use of his pretending? If he brought the parties to you———"

"Well," said Lapham scornfully, "I'd let them have the mills at the price Rogers turned 'em in on me at. I don't want to make anything on 'em. But guess I shall hear from the G. L. & P. first. And when they make their offer, I guess I'll have to accept it, whatever it is. I don't think they'll have a great many competitors."

Mrs. Lapham could not give up her hope. "If you could get your price from those English parties before they knew that the G. L. & P. wanted to buy the mills, would it let you out with Rogers?"

"Just about," said Lapham.

"Then I know he'll move heaven and earth to bring it about. I know you won't be allowed to suffer for doing him a kindness, Silas. He can't be so ungrateful! Why, why should he pretend to have any such parties in view when he hasn't? Don't you be down-hearted, Si. You'll see that he'll be round with them to-morrow."

Lapham laughed, but she urged so many reasons for her belief in Rogers that Lapham began to rekindle his own faith a little. He ended by asking for a hot cup of tea; and Mrs. Lapham sent the pot out and had a fresh one steeped for him. After that he made a hearty supper in the revulsion from his entire despair; and they fell asleep that night talking hopefully of his affairs, which he laid before her fully, as he used to do when he first started in business. That brought the old times back, and he said: "If this had happened then, I shouldn't have cared much. I was young then, and I wasn't afraid of anything. But I noticed that after I passed fifty I began to get scared easier. I don't believe I could pick up, now, from a regular knock-down."

"Pshaw! You scared, Silas Lapham?" cried his wife, proudly. "I should like to see the thing that ever scared you; or the knockdown that you couldn't pick up from!"

"Is that so, Persis?" he asked, with the joy her courage gave him.

In the middle of the night she called to him, in a voice which the darkness rendered still more deeply troubled: "Are you awake, Silas?"

"Yes; I'm awake."

"I've been thinking about those English parties, Si————"

"So've I."

"And I can't make it out but what you'd be just as bad as Rogers, every bit and grain, if you were to let them have the mills————"

"And not tell 'em what the chances were with the G. L. & P.? I thought of that, and you needn't be afraid."

She began to bewail herself, and to sob convulsively: "Oh, Silas! Oh, Silas!" Heaven knows in what measure the passion of her soul was mixed with pride in her husband's honesty, relief from an apprehended struggle, and pity for him.

"Hush, hush, Persis!" he besought her. "You'll wake Pen if you keep on that way. Don't cry any more! You mustn't."

"Oh, let me cry, Silas! It'll help me. I shall be all right in a minute. Don't you mind." She sobbed herself quiet. "It does seem too hard," she said, when she could speak again, "that you have to give up this chance when Providence had fairly raised it up for you."

"I guess it wa'n't Providence raised it up," said Lapham. "Any rate, it's got to go. Most likely Rogers was lyin', and there ain't any such parties; but if there were, they couldn't have the mills from me without the whole story. Don't you be troubled, Persis. I'm going to pull through all right."

"Oh, I ain't afraid. I don't suppose but what there's plenty would help you, if they knew you needed it, Si."

"They would if they knew I didn't need it," said Lapham sardonically.

"Did you tell Bill how you stood?"

"No, I couldn't bear to. I've been the rich one so long, that I couldn't bring myself to own up that I was in danger."

"Yes."

"Besides, it didn't look so ugly till today. But I guess we sha'n't let ugly looks scare us."

"No."

XXII

The morning postman brought Mrs. Lapham a letter from Irene, which was chiefly significant because it made no reference whatever to the writer or her state of mind. It gave the news of her uncle's family; it told of their kindness to her; her cousin Will was going to take her and his sisters ice-boating on the river, when it froze.

By the time this letter came, Lapham had gone to his business, and the mother carried it to Penelope to talk over. "What do you make out of it?" she asked; and without waiting to be answered, she said, "I don't know as I believe in cousins marrying, a great deal; but if Irene and Will were to fix it up between 'em—" She looked vaguely at Penelope.

"It wouldn't make any difference as far as I was concerned," replied the girl, listlessly.

Mrs. Lapham lost her patience.

"Well, then, I'll tell you what, Penelope!" she exclaimed. "Perhaps it'll make a difference to you if you know that your father's in *real* trouble. He's harassed to death, and he was awake half the night, talking about it. That abominable old Rogers has got a lot of money away from him; and he's lost by others that he's helped,"—Mrs. Lapham put it in this way because she had no time to be explicit,— "and I want you should come out of your room now, and try to be of some help and comfort to him when he comes home to-night. I guess Irene wouldn't mope round much, if she was here," she could not help adding.

The girl lifted herself on her elbow. "What's that you say about father?" she demanded, eagerly. "Is he in trouble? Is he going to lose his money? Shall we have to stay in this house?"

"We may be very *glad* to stay in this house," said Mrs. Lapham, half angry with herself for having given cause for the girl's conjectures, and half with the habit of prosperity in her child, which could conceive no better of what adversity was. "And I want you should get up and show that you've got some feeling for somebody in the world besides yourself."

"Oh, I'll get up!" said the girl, promptly, almost cheerfully.

"I don't say it's as bad now as it looked a little while ago," said her mother, conscientiously hedging a little from the statement which she had based rather upon her feelings than her facts. "Your father thinks he'll pull through all right, and I don't know but what he will. But I want you should see if you can't do something to cheer him up and keep him from getting so perfectly down-hearted as he seems to get, under the load he's got to carry. And stop thinking about yourself awhile, and behave yourself like a sensible girl."

"Yes, yes," said the girl; "I will. You needn't be troubled about me any more."

Before she left her room she wrote a note, and when she came down she was dressed to go out-of-doors and post it herself. The note was to Corey:

"Do not come to see me any more till you hear from me. I have a reason which I cannot give you now; and you must not ask what it is."

All day she went about in a buoyant desperation, and she came down to meet her father at supper.

"Well, Persis," he said scornfully, as he sat down, "we might as well saved our good resolutions till they were wanted. I guess those English parties have gone back on Rogers."

"Do you mean he didn't come?"

"He hadn't come up to half-past five," said Lapham.

"Tchk!" uttered his wife.

"But I guess I shall pull through without Mr. Rogers," continued Lapham. "A firm that I didn't think could weather it is still afloat, and so far forth as the danger goes of being dragged under with it, I'm all right." Penelope came in. "Hello, Pen!" cried her father. "It ain't often I meet you nowadays." He put up his hand as she passed his chair, and pulled her down and kissed her.

"No," she said; "but I thought I'd come down to-night and cheer you up a little. I shall not talk; the sight of me will be enough."

Her father laughed out. "Mother been telling you? Well, I was pretty blue last night; but I guess I was more scared than hurt.

How'd you like to go to the theater to-night? Sellers* at the Park. Heigh?"

"Well, I don't know. Don't you think they could get along without me there?"

"No; couldn't work it at all," cried the Colonel. "Let's all go. Unless," he added, inquiringly, "there's somebody coming here?"

"There's nobody coming," said Penelope.

"Good! Then we'll go. Mother, don't you be late now."

"Oh, I sha'n't keep you waiting," said Mrs. Lapham. She had thought of telling what a cheerful letter she had got from Irene; but upon the whole it seemed better not to speak of Irene at all just then. After they returned from the theater, where the Colonel roared through the comedy, with continual reference of his pleasure to Penelope, to make sure that she was enjoying it too, his wife said, as if the whole affair had been for the girl's distraction rather than his, "I don't believe but what it's going to come out all right about the children;" and then she told him of the letter, and the hopes she had founded upon it.

"Well, perhaps you're right, Persis," he consented.

"I haven't seen Pen so much like herself since it happened. I declare, when I see the way she came out to-night, just to please you, I don't know as I want you should get over all your troubles right away."

"I guess there'll be enough to keep Pen going for a while yet," said the Colonel, winding up his watch.

But for a time there was a relief, which Walker noted, in the atmosphere at the office, and then came another cold wave, slighter than the first, but distinctly felt there, and succeeded by another relief. It was like the winter which was wearing on to the end of the year, with alternations of freezing weather, and mild days stretching to weeks, in which the snow and ice wholly disappeared. It was none the less winter, and none the less harassing for these fluctuations, and Lapham showed in his face and temper the effect of like fluctuations in his affairs. He grew thin and old, and both at home and at

---

* *Colonel Sellers* (1874), with Sellers as a grand speculator, was a popular play Mark Twain adapted from his satire *The Gilded Age* (1873). Twain and Howells collaborated on an unsuccessful sequel.

his office he was irascible to the point of offense. In these days Penelope shared with her mother the burden of their troubled home, and
united with her in supporting the silence or the petulance of the
gloomy, secret man who replaced the presence of jolly prosperity
there. Lapham had now ceased to talk of his troubles, and savagely re-
sented his wife's interference. "You mind your own business, Persis,"
he said one day, "if you've got any;" and after that she left him
mainly to Penelope, who did not think of asking him questions.

"It's pretty hard on you, Pen," she said.

"That makes it easier for me," returned the girl, who did not
otherwise refer to her own trouble. In her heart she had wondered a
little at the absolute obedience of Corey, who had made no sign since
receiving her note. She would have liked to ask her father if Corey
was sick; she would have liked him to ask her why Corey did not
come any more. Her mother went on:

"I don't believe your father knows where he stands. He works
away at those papers he brings home here at night, as if he didn't half
know what he was about. He always did have that close streak in him,
and I don't suppose but what he's been going into things he don't
want anybody else to know about, and he's kept these accounts of his
own."

Sometimes he gave Penelope figures to work at, which he would
not submit to his wife's nimbler arithmetic. Then she went to bed
and left them sitting up till midnight, struggling with problems in
which they were both weak. But she could see that the girl was a
comfort to her father, and that his troubles were a defense and shelter to her. Some nights she could hear them going out together, and
then she lay awake for their return from their long walk. When the
hour or day of respite came again, the home felt it first. Lapham
wanted to know what the news from Irene was; he joined his wife
in all her cheerful speculations, and tried to make her amends for his
sullen reticence and irritability. Irene was staying on at Dubuque.
There came a letter from her, saying that her uncle's people wanted
her to spend the winter there. "Well, let her," said Lapham. "It'll be
the best thing for her." Lapham himself had letters from his brother
at frequent intervals. His brother was watching the G. L. & P., which
as yet had made no offer for the mills. Once, when one of these letters came, he submitted to his wife whether, in the absence of any

positive information that the road wanted the property, he might not, with a good conscience, dispose of it to the best advantage to anybody who came along.

She looked wistfully at him; it was on the rise from a season of deep depression with him. "No, Si," she said; "I don't see how you could do that."

He did not assent and submit, as he had done at first, but began to rail at the unpracticality of women; and then he shut some papers he had been looking over into his desk, and flung out of the room.

One of the papers had slipped through the crevice of the lid, and lay upon the floor. Mrs. Lapham kept on at her sewing, but after a while she picked the paper up to lay it on the desk. Then she glanced at it, and saw that it was a long column of dates and figures, recording successive sums, never large ones, paid regularly to "Wm. M." The dates covered a year, and the sum amounted at least to several hundreds.

Mrs. Lapham laid the paper down on the desk, and then she took it up again and put it into her work-basket, meaning to give it to him. When he came in she saw him looking absentmindedly about for something, and then going to work upon his papers, apparently without it. She thought she would wait till he missed it definitely, and then give him the scrap she had picked up. It lay in her basket, and after some days it found its way under the work in it, and she forgot it.

XXIII

Since New Year's there had scarcely been a mild day, and the streets were full of snow, growing foul under the city feet and hoofs, and renewing its purity from the skies with repeated falls, which in turn lost their whiteness, beaten down, and beaten black and hard into a solid bed like iron. The sleighing was incomparable, and the air was full of the din of bells; but Lapham's turnout was not of those that thronged the Brighton road every afternoon; the man at the livery-stable sent him word that the mare's legs were swelling.

He and Corey had little to do with each other. He did not know how Penelope had arranged it with Corey; his wife said she knew no more than he did, and he did not like to ask the girl herself, especially as Corey no longer came to the house. He saw that she was cheerfuller than she had been, and helpfuller with him and her mother. Now and then Lapham opened his troubled soul to her a little, letting his thought break into speech without preamble or conclusion. Once he said:

"Pen, I presume you know I'm in trouble."

"We all seem to be there," said the girl.

"Yes, but there's a difference between being there by your own fault and being there by somebody else's."

"I don't call it his fault," she said.

"I call it mine," said the Colonel.

The girl laughed. Her thought was of her own care, and her father's wholly of his. She must come to his ground. "What have you been doing wrong?"

"I don't know as you'd call it wrong. It's what people do all the time. But I wish I'd let stocks alone. It's what I always promised your mother I would do. But there's no use cryin' over spilt milk; or watered stock, either."

"I don't think there's much use crying about anything. If it could have been cried straight, it would have been all right from the start," said the girl, going back to her own affair; and if Lapham had not been so deeply engrossed in his, he might have seen how little she cared for all that money could do or undo. He did not observe her

269

enough to see how variable her moods were in those days, and how often she sank from some wild gayety into abject melancholy; how at times she was fiercely defiant of nothing at all, and at others inexplicably humble and patient. But no doubt none of these signs had passed unnoticed by his wife, to whom Lapham said one day, when he came home, "Persis, what's the reason Pen don't marry Corey?"

"You know as well as I do, Silas," said Mrs. Lapham, with an inquiring look at him for what lay behind his words.

"Well, I think it's all tomfoolery, the way she's going on. There ain't any rhyme nor reason to it." He stopped, and his wife waited. "If she said the word, I could have some help from them." He hung his head, and would not meet his wife's eye.

"I guess you're in a pretty bad way, Si," she said pityingly, "or you wouldn't have come to that."

"I'm in a hole," said Lapham, "and I don't know where to turn. You won't let me do anything about those mills————"

"Yes, I'll let you," said his wife sadly.

He gave a miserable cry. "You know I can't do anything, if you do. Oh, my Lord!"

She had not seen him so low as that before. She did not know what to say. She was frightened, and could only ask, "Has it come to the worst?"

"The new house has got to go," he answered evasively.

She did not say anything. She knew that the work on the house had been stopped since the beginning of the year. Lapham had told the architect that he preferred to leave it unfinished till the spring, as there was no prospect of their being able to get into it that winter; and the architect had agreed with him that it would not hurt it to stand. Her heart was heavy for him, though she could not say so. They sat together at the table, where she had come to be with him at his belated meal. She saw that he did not eat, and she waited for him to speak again, without urging him to take anything. They were past that.

"And I've sent orders to shut down at the Works," he added.

"Shut down at the Works!" she echoed with dismay. She could not take it in. The fire at the Works had never been out before since it was first kindled. She knew how he had prided himself upon that; how he had bragged of it to every listener, and had always lugged the fact in as the last expression of his sense of success. "Oh, Silas!"

"What's the use?" he retorted. "I saw it was coming a month ago. There are some fellows out in West Virginia that have been running the paint as hard as they could. They couldn't do much; they used to put it on the market raw. But lately they got to baking it, and now they've struck a vein of natural gas right by their works, and they pay ten cents for fuel where I pay a dollar, and they make as good a paint. Anybody can see where it's going to end. Besides, the market's overstocked. It's glutted. There wa'n't anything to do but to shut down, and I've shut down."

"I don't know what's going to become of the hands in the middle of the winter, this way," said Mrs. Lapham, laying hold of one definite thought which she could grasp in the turmoil of ruin that whirled before her eyes.

"I don't care what becomes of the hands," cried Lapham. "They've shared my luck; now let 'em share the other thing. And if you're so very sorry for the hands, I wish you'd keep a little of your pity for me. Don't you know what shutting down the Works means?"

"Yes, indeed I do, Silas," said his wife tenderly.

"Well, then!" He rose, leaving his supper untasted, and went into the sitting-room, where she presently found him, with that everlasting confusion of papers before him on the desk. That made her think of the paper in her work-basket, and she decided not to make the careworn, distracted man ask her for it, after all. She brought it to him.

He glanced blankly at it and then caught it from her, turning red and looking foolish. "Where'd you get that?"

"You dropped it on the floor the other night, and I picked it up. Who is 'Wm. M.'?"

" 'Wm. M.'?" he repeated, looking confusedly at her, and then at the paper. "Oh,—it's nothing." He tore the paper into small pieces, and went and dropped them into the fire. When Mrs. Lapham came into the room in the morning, before he was down, she found a scrap of the paper, which must have fluttered to the hearth; and glancing at it she saw that the words were "Mrs. M." She wondered what dealings with a woman her husband could have, and she remembered the confusion he had shown about the paper, and which she had thought was because she had surprised one of his business secrets. She was still thinking of it when he came down to breakfast, heavy-eyed, tremulous, with deep seams and wrinkles in his face.

After a silence which he did not seem inclined to break, "Silas," she asked, "who is 'Mrs. M.'?"

He stared at her. "I don't know what you're talking about."

"Don't you?" she returned mockingly. "When you do, you tell me. Do you want any more coffee?"

"No."

"Well, then, you can ring for Alice when you've finished. I've got some things to attend to." She rose abruptly, and left the room. Lapham looked after her in a dull way, and then went on with his breakfast. While he still sat at his coffee, she flung into the room again, and dashed some papers down beside his plate. "Here are some more things of yours, and I'll thank you to lock them up in your desk and not litter my room with them, if you please." Now he saw that she was angry, and it must be with him. It enraged him that in such a time of trouble she should fly out at him in that way. He left the house without trying to speak to her.

That day Corey came just before closing, and, knocking at Lapham's door, asked if he could speak with him a few moments.

"Yes," said Lapham, wheeling round in his swivel-chair and kicking another towards Corey. "Sit down. I want to talk to you. I'd ought to tell you you're wasting your time here. I spoke the other day about your placin' yourself better, and I can help you to do it, yet. There ain't going to be the outcome for the paint in the foreign markets that we expected, and I guess you better give it up."

"I don't wish to give it up," said the young fellow, setting his lips. "I've as much faith in it as ever; and I want to propose now what I hinted at in the first place. I want to put some money into the business."

"Some money!" Lapham leaned towards him, and frowned as if he had not quite understood, while he clutched the arms of his chair.

"I've got about thirty thousand dollars that I could put in, and if you don't want to consider me a partner—I remember that you objected to a partner—you can let me regard it as an investment. But I think I see the way to doing something at once in Mexico, and

I should like to feel that I had something more than a drummer's interest in the venture."

The men sat looking into each other's eyes. Then Lapham leaned back in his chair, and rubbed his hand hard and slowly over his face. His features were still twisted with some strong emotion when he took it away. "Your family know about this?"

"My uncle James knows."

"He thinks it would be a good plan for you?"

"He thought that by this time I ought to be able to trust my own judgment."

"Do you suppose I could see your uncle at his office?"

"I imagine he's there."

"Well, I want to have a talk with him, one of these days." He sat pondering awhile, and then rose, and went with Corey to his door. "I guess I sha'n't change my mind about taking you into the business in that way," he said coldly. "If there was any reason why I shouldn't at first, there's more now."

"Very well, sir," answered the young man, and went to close his desk. The outer office was empty; but while Corey was putting his papers in order it was suddenly invaded by two women, who pushed by the protesting porter on the stairs and made their way towards Lapham's room. One of them was Miss Dewey, the type-writer girl, and the other was a woman whom she would resemble in face and figure twenty years hence, if she led a life of hard work varied by paroxysms of hard drinking.

"That his room, Z'rilla?" asked this woman, pointing towards Lapham's door with a hand that had not freed itself from the fringe of dirty shawl under which it had hung. She went forward without waiting for the answer, but before she could reach it the door opened, and Lapham stood filling its space.

"Look here, Colonel Lapham!" began the woman, in a high key of challenge. "I want to know if this is the way you're goin' back on me and Z'rilla?"

"What do you want?" asked Lapham.

"What do I want? What do you s'pose I want? I want the money to pay my month's rent; there ain't a bite to eat in the house; and I want some money to market."

Lapham bent a frown on the woman, under which she shrank back a step. "You've taken the wrong way to get it. Clear out!"

"I won't clear out!" said the woman, beginning to whimper.

"Corey!" said Lapham, in the peremptory voice of a master,—he had seemed so indifferent to Corey's presence that the young man thought he must have forgotten he was there,—"is Dennis anywhere round?"

"Yissor," said Dennis, answering for himself from the head of the stairs, and appearing in the wareroom.

Lapham spoke to the woman again. "Do you want I should call a hack, or do you want I should call an officer?"

The woman began to cry into an end of her shawl. "I don't know what we're goin' to do."

"You're going to clear out," said Lapham. "Call a hack, Dennis. If you ever come here again, I'll have you arrested. Mind that! Zer-rilla, I shall want you early to-morrow morning."

"Yes, sir," said the girl meekly; she and her mother shrank out after the porter.

Lapham shut his door without a word.

At lunch the next day Walker made himself amends for Corey's reticence by talking a great deal. He talked about Lapham, who seemed to have, more than ever since his apparent difficulties began, the fas-cination of an enigma for his book-keeper, and he ended by asking, "Did you see that little circus last night?"

"What little circus?" asked Corey in his turn.

"Those two women and the old man. Dennis told me about it. I told him if he liked his place he'd better keep his mouth shut."

"That was very good advice," said Corey.

"Oh, all right, if you don't want to talk. Don't know as I should in your place," returned Walker, in the easy security he had long felt that Corey had no intention of putting on airs with him. "But I'll tell you what: the old man can't expect it of everybody. If he keeps this thing up much longer, it's going to be talked about. You can't have a woman walking into your place of business, and trying to bulldoze you before your porter, without setting your porter to thinking. And the last thing you want a porter to do is to think; for when a porter thinks, he thinks wrong."

"I don't see why even a porter couldn't think right about that affair," replied Corey. "I don't know who the woman was, though I believe she was Miss Dewey's mother; but I couldn't see that Colonel Lapham showed anything but a natural resentment of her coming to him in that way. I should have said she was some rather worthless person whom he'd been befriending, and that she had presumed upon his kindness."

"Is that so? What do you think of his never letting Miss Dewey's name go on the books?"

"That it's another proof it's a sort of charity of his. That's the only way to look at it."

"Oh, I'm all right." Walker lighted a cigar and began to smoke, with his eyes closed to a fine straight line. "It won't do for a book-keeper to think wrong, any more than a porter, I suppose. But I guess you and I don't think very different about this thing."

"Not if you think as I do," replied Corey steadily; "and I know you would do that if you had seen the 'circus' yourself. A man doesn't treat people who have a disgraceful hold upon him as he treated them."

"It depends upon who he is," said Walker, taking his cigar from his mouth. "I never said the old man was afraid of anything."

"And character," continued Corey, disdaining to touch the matter further, except in generalities, "must go for something. If it's to be the prey of mere accident and appearance, then it goes for nothing."

"Accidents will happen in the best-regulated families," said Walker, with vulgar, good-humored obtuseness that filled Corey with indignation. Nothing, perhaps, removed his matter-of-fact nature further from the common-place than a certain generosity of instinct, which I should not be ready to say was always infallible.

That evening it was Miss Dewey's turn to wait for speech with Lapham after the others were gone. He opened his door at her knock, and stood looking at her with a worried air. "Well, what do you want, Zerrilla?" he asked, with a sort of rough kindness.

"I want to know what I'm going to do about Hen. He's back again; and he and mother have made it up, and they both got to drinking last night after I went home, and carried on so that the neighbors came in."

Lapham passed his hand over his red and heated face. "I don't know what I'm going to do. You're twice the trouble that my own family is, now. But I know what I'd do, mighty quick, if it wasn't for you, Zerrilla," he went on relentingly. "I'd shut your mother up somewheres, and if I could get that fellow off for a three years' voyage————"

"I declare," said Miss Dewey, beginning to whimper, "it seems as if he came back just so often to spite me. He's never gone more than a year at the furthest, and you can't make it out habitual drunkenness, either, when it's just sprees. I'm at my wit's end."

"Oh, well, you mustn't cry around here," said Lapham soothingly.

"I know it," said Miss Dewey. "If I could get rid of Hen, I could manage well enough with mother. Mr. Wemmel would marry me if I could get the divorce. He's said so over and over again."

"I don't know as I like that very well," said Lapham, frowning. "I don't know as I want you should get married in any hurry again. I don't know as I like your going with anybody else just yet."

"Oh, you needn't be afraid but what it'll be all right. It'll be the best thing all round, if I can marry him."

"Well!" said Lapham impatiently; "I can't think about it now. I suppose they've cleaned everything out again?"

"Yes, they have," said Zerrilla; "there isn't a cent left."

"You're a pretty expensive lot," said Lapham. "Well, here!" He took out his pocket-book and gave her a note. "I'll be round to-night and see what can be done."

He shut himself into his room again, and Zerrilla dried her tears, put the note into her bosom, and went her way.

Lapham kept the porter nearly an hour later. It was then six o'clock, the hour at which the Laphams usually had tea; but all custom had been broken up with him during the past months, and he did not go home now. He determined, perhaps in the extremity in which a man finds relief in combating one care with another, to keep his promise to Miss Dewey, and at the moment when he might otherwise have been sitting down at his own table he was climbing the stairs to her lodging in the old-fashioned dwelling which had been portioned off into flats. It was in a region of depots, and of the cheap hotels, and "ladies' and gents'" dining-rooms, and restaurants with bars, which abound near depots; and Lapham followed to Miss

Dewey's door a waiter from one of these, who bore on a salver before him a supper covered with a napkin. Zerrilla had admitted them, and at her greeting a young fellow in the shabby shore-suit of a sailor, buttoning imperfectly over the nautical blue flannel of his shirt, got up from where he had been sitting, on one side of the stove, and stood infirmly on his feet, in token of receiving the visitor. The woman who sat on the other side did not rise, but began a shrill, defiant apology.

"Well, I don't suppose but what you'll think we're livin' on the fat o' the land, right straight along, all the while. But it's just like this. When that child came in from her work, she didn't seem to have the spirit to go to cookin' anything, and I had such a bad night last night I was feelin' all broke up, and s'd I, what's the use, anyway? By the time the butcher's heaved in a lot o' bone, and made you pay for the suet he cuts away, it comes to the same thing, and why not git it from the rest'rant first off, and save the cost o' your fire? s'd I."

"What have you got there under your apron? A bottle?" demanded Lapham, who stood with his hat on and his hands in his pockets, indifferent alike to the ineffective reception of the sailor and the chair Zerrilla had set him.

"Well, yes, it's a bottle," said the woman, with an assumption of virtuous frankness. "It's whisky; I got to have something to rub my rheumatism with."

"Humph!" grumbled Lapham. "You've been rubbing his rheumatism too, I see."

He twisted his head in the direction of the sailor, now softly and rhythmically waving to and fro on his feet.

"He hain't had a drop today in this house!" cried the woman.

"What are you doing around here?" said Lapham, turning fiercely upon him. "You've got no business ashore. Where's your ship? Do you think I'm going to let you come here and eat your wife out of house and home, and then give money to keep the concern going?"

"Just the very words I said when he first showed his face here, yist'day. Didn't I, Z'rilla?" said the woman, eagerly joining in the rebuke of her late boon companion. "You got no business here, Hen, s'd I. You can't come here to live on me and Z'rilla, s'd I. You want to go back to your ship, s'd I. That's what I said."

The sailor mumbled, with a smile of tipsy amiability for Lapham, something about the crew being discharged.

"Yes," the woman broke in, "that's always the way with these coasters. Why don't you go off on some them long v'y'ges? s'd I. It's pretty hard, when Mr. Wemmel stands ready to marry Z'rilla and provide a comfortable home for us both,—I hain't got a great many years more to live, and I should like to get some satisfaction out of 'em and not be beholden and dependent all my days,—to have Hen, here, blockin' the way. I tell him there'd be more money for him in the end; but he can't seem to make up his mind to it."

"Well, now, look here," said Lapham. "I don't care anything about all that. It's your own business, and I'm not going to meddle with it. But it's my business who lives off me; and so I tell you all three, I'm willing to take care of Zerrilla, and I'm willing to take care of her mother————"

"I guess if it hadn't been for that child's father," the mother interpolated, "you wouldn't been here to tell the tale, Colonel Lapham."

"I know all about that," said Lapham. "But I'll tell you what, Mr. Dewey, I'm not going to support you."

"I don't see what Hen's done," said the old woman, impartially.

"He hasn't done anything, and I'm going to stop it. He's got to get a ship, and he's got to get out of this. And Zerrilla needn't come back to work till he does. I'm done with you all."

"Well, I vow," said the mother, "if I ever heard anything like it! Didn't that child's father lay down his life for you? Hain't you said it yourself a hundred times? And don't she work for her money, and slave for it mornin', noon, and night? You talk as if we was beholden to you for the very bread in our mouths. I guess if it hadn't been for Jim, you wouldn't been here crowin' over us."

"You mind what I say. I mean business this time," said Lapham, turning to the door.

The woman rose and followed him, with her bottle in her hand. "Say, Colonel! what should you advise Z'rilla to do about Mr. Wemmel? I tell her there ain't any use goin' to the trouble to git a divorce without she's sure about him. Don't you think we'd ought to git him to sign a paper, or something, that he'll marry her if she gits it? I don't like to have things going at loose ends the way they are. It ain't sense. It ain't right."

Lapham made no answer to the mother anxious for her child's future, and concerned for the moral questions involved. He went out and down the stairs, and on the pavement at the lower door he almost struck against Rogers, who had a bag in his hand, and seemed to be hurrying towards one of the depots. He halted a little, as if to speak to Lapham; but Lapham turned his back abruptly upon him, and took the other direction.

The days were going by in a monotony of adversity to him, from which he could no longer escape, even at home. He attempted once or twice to talk of his troubles to his wife, but she repulsed him sharply; she seemed to despise and hate him; but he set himself doggedly to make a confession to her, and he stopped her one night, as she came into the room where he sat—hastily upon some errand that was to take her directly away again.

"Persis, there's something I've got to tell you."

She stood still, as if fixed against her will, to listen.

"I guess you know something about it already, and I guess it's set you against me."

"Oh, I guess not, Colonel Lapham. You go your way, and I go mine. That's all."

She waited for him to speak, listening with a cold, hard smile on her face.

"I don't say it to make favor with you, because I don't want you to spare me, and I don't ask you; but I got into it through Milton K. Rogers."

"Oh!" said Mrs. Lapham contemptuously.

"I always felt the way I said about it—that it wa'n't any better than gambling, and I say so now. It's like betting on the turn of a card; and I give you my word of honor, Persis, that I never was in it at all till that scoundrel began to load me up with those wild-cat securities of his. Then it seemed to me as if I ought to try to do something to get somewhere even. I know it's no excuse; but watching the market to see what the infernal things were worth from day to day, and seeing it go up, and seeing it go down, was too much for me; and, to make a long story short, I began to buy and sell on a margin—just what I told you I never would do. I seemed to make something—I did make something; and I'd have stopped, I do believe, if I could have reached the figure I'd set in my own mind to start with; but I couldn't fetch it. I began to lose, and then I began to throw good money after bad, just as I always did with everything that Rogers ever came within a mile of. Well, what's the use? I lost the money that would have carried me out of this, and I shouldn't have had to shut down the Works, or sell the house, or———"

Lapham stopped. His wife, who at first had listened with mystification, and then dawning incredulity, changing into a look of relief that was almost triumph, lapsed again into severity. "Silas Lapham, if you was to die the next minute, is this what you started to tell me?"

"Why, of course it is. What did you suppose I started to tell you?"

"And—look me in the eyes!—you haven't got anything else on your mind now?"

"No! There's trouble enough, the Lord knows; but there's nothing else to tell you. I suppose Pen gave you a hint about it. I dropped something to her. I've been feeling bad about it, Persis, a good while, but I hain't had the heart to speak of it. I can't expect you to say you like it. I've been a fool, I'll allow, and I've been something worse, if you choose to say so; but that's all. I haven't hurt anybody but myself—and you and the children."

Mrs. Lapham rose and said, with her face from him, as she turned towards the door, "It's all right, Silas. I sha'n't ever bring it up against you."

She fled out of the room, but all that evening she was very sweet with him, and seemed to wish in all tacit ways to atone for her past unkindness.

She made him talk of his business, and he told her of Corey's offer, and what he had done about it. She did not seem to care for his part in it, however; at which Lapham was silently disappointed a little, for he would have liked her to praise him.

"He did it on account of Pen!"

"Well, he didn't insist upon it, anyway," said Lapham, who must have obscurely expected that Corey would recognize his own magnanimity by repeating his offer. If the doubt that follows a self-devoted action—the question whether it was not after all a needless folly—is mixed, as it was in Lapham's case, with the vague belief that we might have done ourselves a good turn without great risk of hurting any one else by being a little less unselfish, it becomes a regret that is hard to bear. Since Corey spoke to him, some things had happened that gave Lapham hope again.

"I'm going to tell her about it," said his wife, and she showed herself impatient to make up for the time she had lost. "Why didn't you tell me before, Silas?"

"I didn't know we were on speaking terms before," said Lapham sadly.

"Yes, that's true," she admitted, with a conscious flush. "I hope he won't think Pen's known about it all this while."

XXIV

That evening James Bellingham came to see Corey after dinner, and went to find him in his own room.

"I've come at the instance of Colonel Lapham," said the uncle. "He was at my office to-day, and I had a long talk with him. Did you know that he was in difficulties?"

"I fancied that he was in some sort of trouble. And I had the book-keeper's conjectures—he doesn't really know much about it."

"Well, he thinks it time—on all accounts—that you should know how he stands, and why he declined that proposition of yours. I must say he has behaved very well—like a gentleman."

"I'm not surprised."

"I am. It's hard to behave like a gentleman where your interest is vitally concerned. And Lapham doesn't strike me as a man who's in the habit of acting from the best in him always."

"Do any of us?" asked Corey.

"Not all of us, at any rate," said Bellingham. "It must have cost him something to say no to you, for he's just in that state when he believes that this or that chance, however small, would save him."

Corey was silent. "Is he really in such a bad way?"

"It's hard to tell just where he stands. I suspect that a hopeful temperament and fondness for round numbers have always caused him to set his figures beyond his actual worth. I don't say that he's been dishonest about it, but he's had a loose way of estimating his assets; he's reckoned his wealth on the basis of his capital, and some of his capital is borrowed. He's lost heavily by some of the recent failures, and there's been a terrible shrinkage in his values. I don't mean merely in the stock of paint on hand, but in a kind of competition which has become very threatening. You know about that West Virginia paint?"

Corey nodded.

"Well, he tells me that they've struck a vein of natural gas out there which will enable them to make as good a paint as his own at a cost of manufacturing so low that they can undersell him everywhere. If this proves to be the case, it will not only drive his paint out of the market, but will reduce the value of his Works—the whole plant—at Lapham to a merely nominal figure."

"I see," said Corey dejectedly. "I've understood that he had put a great deal of money into his Works."

"Yes, and he estimated his mine there at a high figure. Of course it will be worth little or nothing if the West Virginia paint drives his out. Then, besides, Lapham has been into several things outside of his own business, and, like a good many other men who try outside things, he's kept account of them himself; and he's all mixed up about them. He's asked me to look into his affairs with him, and I've promised to do so. Whether he can be tided over his difficulties remains to be seen. I'm afraid it will take a good deal of money to do it—a great deal more than he thinks, at least. He believes comparatively little would do it. I think differently. I think that anything less than a great deal would be thrown away on him. If it were merely a question of a certain sum—even a large sum—to keep him going, it might be managed; but it's much more complicated. And, as I say, it must have been a trial to him to refuse your offer."

This did not seem to be the way in which Bellingham had meant to conclude. But he said no more; and Corey made him no response.

He remained pondering the case, now hopefully, now doubtfully, and wondering, whatever his mood was, whether Penelope knew anything of the fact with which her mother went nearly at the same moment to acquaint her.

"Of course, he's done it on your account," Mrs. Lapham could not help saying.

"Then he was very silly. Does he think I would have let him give father money? And if father lost it for him, does he suppose it would make it any easier for me? I think father acted twice as well. It was very silly."

In repeating the censure, her look was not so severe as her tone; she even smiled a little, and her mother reported to her father that she acted more like herself than she had yet since Corey's offer.

"I think, if he was to repeat his offer, she would have him now," said Mrs. Lapham.

"Well, I'll let her know if he does," said the Colonel.

"I guess he won't do it to you!" she cried.

"Who else will he do it to?" he demanded.

They perceived that they had each been talking of a different offer.

After Lapham went to his business in the morning the postman brought another letter from Irene, which was full of pleasant things that were happening to her; there was a great deal about her cousin Will, as she called him. At the end she had written, "Tell Pen I don't want she should be foolish."

"There!" said Mrs. Lapham. "I guess it's going to come out right, all round;" and it seemed as if even the Colonel's difficulties were past. "When your father gets through this, Pen," she asked impulsively, "what shall you do?"

"What have you been telling Irene about me?"

"Nothing much. What should you do?"

"It would be a good deal easier to say what I should do if father didn't," said the girl.

"I know you think it was nice in him to make your father that offer," urged the mother.

"It was nice, yes; but it was silly," said the girl. "Most nice things are silly, I suppose," she added.

She went to her room and wrote a letter. It was very long, and very carefully written; and when she read it over, she tore it into small pieces. She wrote another one, short and hurried, and tore that up too. Then she went back to her mother, in the family room, and asked to see Irene's letter, and read it over to herself. "Yes, she seems to be having a good time," she sighed. "Mother, do you think I ought to let Mr. Corey know that I know about it?"

"Well, I should think it would be a pleasure to him," said Mrs. Lapham judicially.

"I'm not so sure of that—the way I should have to tell him. I should begin by giving him a scolding. Of course, he meant well by it, but can't you see that it wasn't very flattering? How did he expect it would change me?"

"I don't believe he ever thought of that."

"Don't you? Why?"

"Because you can see that he isn't one of that kind. He might want to please you without wanting to change you by what he did."

"Yes. He must have known that nothing would change me,—at

least, nothing that he could do. I thought of that. I shouldn't like him to feel that I couldn't appreciate it, even if I did think it was silly. Should you write to him?"

"I don't see why not."

"It would be too pointed. No, I shall just let it go. I wish he hadn't done it."

"Well, he has done it."

"And I've tried to write to him about it—two letters: one so humble and grateful that it couldn't stand up on its edge, and the other so pert and flippant. Mother, I wish you could have seen those two letters! I wish I had kept them to look at if I ever got to thinking I had any sense again. They would take the conceit out of me."

"What's the reason he don't come here any more?"

"Doesn't he come?" asked Penelope in turn, as if it were something she had not noticed particularly.

"You'd ought to know."

"Yes." She sat silent awhile. "If he doesn't come, I suppose it's because he's offended at something I did."

"What did you do?"

"Nothing. I—wrote to him—a little while ago. I suppose it was very blunt, but I didn't believe he would be angry at it. But this—this that he's done shows he was angry, and that he wasn't just seizing the first chance to get out of it."

"What have you done, Pen?" demanded her mother sharply.

"Oh, I don't know. All the mischief in the world, I suppose. I'll tell you. When you first told me that father was in trouble with his business, I wrote to him not to come any more till I let him. I said I couldn't tell him why, and he hasn't been here since. I'm sure I don't know what it means."

Her mother looked at her with angry severity. "Well, Penelope Lapham! For a sensible child, you *are* the greatest goose I ever saw. Did you think he would come here and *see* if you wouldn't let him come?"

"He might have written," urged the girl.

Her mother made that despairing "Tchk!" with her tongue, and fell back in her chair. "I should have *despised* him if he had written. He's acted just exactly right, and you—you've acted—I don't know *how* you've acted. I'm ashamed of you. A girl that could be so sensible for her sister, and always say and do just the right thing, and then when it comes to herself to be such a *disgusting* simpleton!"

"I thought I ought to break with him at once, and not let him suppose that there was any hope for him or me if father was poor. It was my one chance, in this whole business, to do anything heroic, and I jumped at it. You mustn't think, because I can laugh at it now, that I wasn't in earnest, mother! I *was*—dead! But the Colonel has gone to ruin so gradually, that he's spoilt everything. I expected that he would be bankrupt the next day, and that then *he* would understand what I meant. But to have it drag along for a fortnight seems to take all the heroism out of it, and leave it as flat!" She looked at her mother with a smile that shone through her tears, and a pathos that quivered round her jesting lips. "It's easy enough to be sensible for other people. But when it comes to myself, there I am! Especially, when I want to do what I oughtn't so much that it seems as if doing what I didn't want to do must be doing what I ought! But it's been a great success one way, mother. It's helped me to keep up before the Colonel. If it hadn't been for Mr. Corey's staying away, and my feeling so indignant with him for having been badly treated by me, I shouldn't have been worth anything at all."

The tears started down her cheeks, but her mother said, "Well, now, go along, and write to him. It don't matter what you say, much; and don't be so very particular."

Her third attempt at a letter pleased her scarcely better than the rest, but she sent it, though it seemed so blunt and awkward. She wrote:

DEAR FRIEND:

I expected when I sent you that note, that you would understand, almost the next day, why I could not see you any more. You must know now, and you must not think that if anything happened to my father, I should wish you to help him. But that is no reason why I should not thank you, and I do thank you, for offering. It was like you, I will say that.

Yours sincerely,
PENELOPE LAPHAM.

She posted her letter, and he sent his reply in the evening, by hand:

DEAREST:

What I did was nothing, till you praised it. Everything I have and am is yours. Won't you send a line by the bearer, to say that I may come to see you? I know how you feel; but I am sure that I can make you think differently. You must consider that I loved you without a thought of your father's circumstances, and always shall.

T. C.

The generous words were blurred to her eyes by the tears that sprang into them. But she could only write in answer:

"Please do not come; I have made up my mind. As long as this trouble is hanging over us, I cannot see you. And if father is unfortunate, all is over between us."

She brought his letter to her mother, and told her what she had written in reply. Her mother was thoughtful awhile before she said, with a sigh, "Well, I hope you've begun as you can carry out, Pen."

"Oh, I shall not have to carry out at all. I shall not have to do anything. That's one comfort—the only comfort." She went away to her own room, and when Mrs. Lapham told her husband of the affair, he was silent at first, as she had been. Then he said, "I don't know as I should have wanted her to done differently; I don't know as she could. If I ever come right again, she won't have anything to feel meeching about; and if I don't, I don't want she should be beholden to anybody. And I guess that's the way she feels."

The Coreys in their turn sat in judgment on the fact which their son felt bound to bring to their knowledge.

"She has behaved very well," said Mrs. Corey, to whom her son had spoken.

"My dear," said her husband, with his laugh, "she has behaved too well. If she had studied the whole situation with the most artful eye to its mastery, she could not possibly have behaved better."

The process of Lapham's financial disintegration was like the course of some chronic disorder, which has fastened itself upon the constitution, but advances with continual reliefs, with apparent amelioration, and at times seems not to advance at all, when it gives hope of final recovery not only to the sufferer, but to the eye of science itself. There were moments when James Bellingham, seeing Lapham pass this crisis and that, began to fancy that he might pull through altogether; and at these moments, when his adviser could not oppose anything but experience and probability to the evidence of the fact, Lapham was buoyant with courage, and imparted his hopefulness to his household. Our theory of disaster, of sorrow, of affliction, borrowed from the poets and novelists, is that it is incessant; but every passage in our own lives and in the lives of others, so far as we have witnessed them, teaches us that this is false. The house of mourning is decorously darkened to the world, but within itself it is also the house of laughing. Bursts of gayety, as heartfelt as its grief, relieve the gloom, and the stricken survivors have their jests together, in which the thought of the dead is tenderly involved, and a fond sense, not crazier than many others, of sympathy and enjoyment beyond the silence, justifies the sunnier mood before sorrow rushes back, deploring and despairing, and making it all up again with the conventional fitness of things. Lapham's adversity had this quality in common with bereavement. It was not always like the adversity we figure in allegory; it had its moments of being like prosperity, and if upon the whole it was continual, it was not incessant. Sometimes there was a week of repeated reverses, when he had to keep his teeth set and to hold on hard to all his hopefulness; and then days came of negative result or slight success, when he was full of his jokes at the tea-table, and wanted to go to the theater, or to do something to cheer Penelope up. In some miraculous way, by some enormous stroke of success which should eclipse the brightest of his past prosperity, he expected to do what would reconcile all difficulties, not only in his own affairs, but in hers too. "You'll see," he said to his wife; "it's going to come out all right. Irene'll fix it up with Bill's boy, and then she'll be off Pen's mind; and if things go on as they've been going for the last two days, I'm going to be in a position to do the favors myself, and Pen can feel that *she's* makin' a sacrifice, and then I guess may be she'll do it. If things turn out as I expect now, and times ever *do* get any better generally, I can show Corey that I appreciate his offer. I can offer him the partnership myself then."

Even in the other moods, which came when everything had been going wrong, and there seemed no way out of the net, there were points of consolation to Lapham and his wife. They rejoiced that Irene was safe beyond the range of their anxieties, and they had a proud satisfaction that there had been no engagement between Corey and Penelope, and that it was she who had forbidden it. In the closeness of interest and sympathy in which their troubles had reunited them, they confessed to each other that nothing would have been more galling to their pride than the idea that Lapham should not have been able to do everything for his daughter that the Coreys might have expected. Whatever happened now, the Coreys could not have it to say that the Laphams had tried to bring any such thing about.

Bellingham had lately suggested an assignment* to Lapham, as the best way out of his difficulties. It was evident that he had not the money to meet his liabilities at present, and that he could not raise it without ruinous sacrifices, that might still end in ruin after all. If he made the assignment, Bellingham argued, he could gain time and make terms; the state of things generally would probably improve, since it could not be worse, and the market, which he had glutted with his paint, might recover and he could start again. Lapham had not agreed with him. When his reverses first began, it had seemed easy for him to give up everything, to let the people he owed take all, so only they would let him go out with clean hands; and he had dramatized this feeling in his talk with his wife, when they spoke together of the mills on the G. L. & P. But ever since then it had been growing harder, and he could not consent even to seem to do it now in the proposed assignment. He had not found other men so very liberal or faithful with him; a good many of them appeared to have combined to hunt him down; a sense of enmity towards all his creditors asserted itself in him; he asked himself why they should not suffer a little too. Above all, he shrank from the publicity of the assignment. It was open confession that he had been a fool in some way; he could not bear to have his family—his brother the judge, especially, to whom he had always appeared the soul of business wisdom—think him imprudent or stupid. He would make any sacrifice before it came to that. He determined in parting with Bellingham

---

*"Assignment" refers to the transfer of control over his company to deal with creditors and protect his personal assets.

to make the sacrifice which he had oftenest in his mind, because it
was the hardest, and to sell his new house. That would cause the least
comment. Most people would simply think that he had got a splendid offer, and with his usual luck had made a very good thing of it;
others who knew a little more about him would say that he was haul-
ing in his horns, but they could not blame him; a great many other
men were doing the same in those hard times—the shrewdest and
safest men; it might even have a good effect.

He went straight from Bellingham's office to the real-estate broker in whose hands he meant to put his house, for he was not the
sort of man to shilly-shally when he had once made up his mind. But
he found it hard to get his voice up out of his throat, when he said
he guessed he would get the broker to sell that new house of his on
the water side of Beacon. The broker answered cheerfully, yes; he
supposed Colonel Lapham knew it was a pretty dull time in real estate? and Lapham said yes, he knew that, but he should not sell at a
sacrifice, and he did not care to have the broker name him or describe
the house definitely unless parties meant business. Again the broker
said yes; and he added, as a joke Lapham would appreciate, that he
had half a dozen houses on the water side of Beacon on the same
terms; that nobody wanted to be named or to have his property described.

It did, in fact, comfort Lapham a little to find himself in the same
boat with so many others; he smiled grimly, and said in his turn, yes,
he guessed that was about the size of it with a good many people.
But he had not the heart to tell his wife what he had done, and he
sat taciturn that whole evening, without even going over his accounts, and went early to bed, where he lay tossing half the night before he fell asleep. He slept at last only upon the promise he made
himself that he would withdraw the house from the broker's hands;
but he went heavily to his own business in the morning without
doing so. There was no such rush, anyhow, he reflected bitterly; there
would be time to do that a month later, probably.

It struck him with a sort of dismay when a boy came with a note
from the broker, saying that a party who had been over the house in
the fall had come to him to know whether it could be bought, and
was willing to pay the cost of the house up to the time he had seen
it. Lapham took refuge in trying to think who the party could be; he

concluded that it must have been somebody who had gone over it with the architect, and he did not like that; but he was aware that this was not an answer to the broker, and he wrote that he would give him an answer in the morning.

Now that it had come to the point, it did not seem to him that he could part with the house. So much of his hope for himself and his children had gone into it that the thought of selling it made him tremulous and sick. He could not keep about his work steadily, and with his nerves shaken by want of sleep, and the shock of this sudden and unexpected question, he left his office early, and went over to look at the house and try to bring himself to some conclusion there. The long procession of lamps on the beautiful street was flaring in the clear red of the sunset towards which it marched, and Lapham, with a lump in his throat, stopped in front of his house and looked at their multitude. They were not merely a part of the landscape; they were a part of his pride and glory, his success, his triumphant life's work which was fading into failure in his helpless hands. He ground his teeth to keep down that lump, but the moisture in his eyes blurred the lamps, and the keen, pale crimson against which it made them flicker. He turned and looked up, as he had so often done, at the window-spaces, neatly glazed for the winter with white linen, and recalled the night when he had stopped with Irene before the house, and she had said that she should never live there, and he had tried to coax her into courage about it. There was no such façade as that on the whole street, to his thinking. Through his long talks with the architect, he had come to feel almost as intimately and fondly as the architect himself the satisfying simplicity of the whole design and the delicacy of its detail. It appealed to him as an exquisite bit of harmony appeals to the unlearned ear, and he recognized the difference between this fine work and the obstreperous pretentiousness of the many overloaded house-fronts which Seymour had made him notice for his instruction elsewhere on the Back Bay. Now, in the depths of his gloom, he tried to think what Italian city it was where Seymour said he had first got the notion of treating brickwork in that way.

He unlocked the temporary door with the key he always carried, so that he could let himself in and out whenever he liked, and entered the house, dim and very cold with the accumulated frigidity of the whole winter in it, and looking as if the arrest of work upon it had taken place a thousand years before. It smelt of the unpainted woods and the clean, hard surfaces of the plaster, where the experiments in decoration had left it untouched; and mingled with these odors was that of some rank pigments and metallic compositions which Seymour had used in trying to realize a certain daring novelty of finish, which had not proved successful. Above all, Lapham detected the peculiar odor of his own paint, with which the architect had been greatly interested one day, when Lapham showed it to him at the office. He had asked Lapham to let him try the Persis Brand in realizing a little idea he had for the finish of Mrs. Lapham's room. If it succeeded, they could tell her what it was, for a surprise.

Lapham glanced at the bay-window in the reception-room, where he sat with his girls on the trestles when Corey first came by; and then he explored the whole house to the attic, in the light faintly admitted through the linen sashes. The floors were strewn with shavings and chips which the carpenters had left, and in the music-room these had been blown into long irregular windrows by the draughts through a wide rent in the linen sash. Lapham tried to pin it up, but failed, and stood looking out of it over the water. The ice had left the river, and the low tide lay smooth and red in the light of the sunset. The Cambridge flats showed the sad, sodden yellow of meadows stripped bare after a long sleep under snow; the hills, the naked trees, the spires and roofs had a black outline, as if they were objects in a landscape of the French school.

The whim seized Lapham to test the chimney in the music-room; it had been tried in the dining-room below, and in his girls' fire-places above, but here the hearth was still clean. He gathered some shavings and blocks together, and kindled them, and as the flame mounted gayly from them, he pulled up a nail-keg which he found there and sat down to watch it. Nothing could have been better; the chimney was a perfect success; and as Lapham glanced out of the torn linen sash he said to himself that that party, whoever he was, who had offered to buy his house might go to the devil; he would never sell it as long as he had a dollar. He said that he should pull through yet; and it suddenly came into his mind that, if he could raise the money to buy out those West Virginia fellows, he should be all right, and would have the whole game in his own hand. He slapped himself on the thigh, and wondered that he had never thought of that before; and then, lighting a cigar with a splinter from the fire, he sat down again to work the scheme out in his own mind.

He did not hear the feet heavily stamping up the stairs, and coming towards the room where he sat; and the policeman to whom the feet belonged had to call out to him, smoking at his chimney-corner, with his back turned to the door, "Hello! what are you doing here?"

"What's that to you?" retorted Lapham, wheeling half round on his nail-keg.

"I'll show you," said the officer, advancing upon him, and then stopping short as he recognized him. "Why, Colonel Lapham! I thought it was some tramp got in here!"

"Have a cigar?" said Lapham hospitably. "Sorry there ain't another nail-keg."

The officer took the cigar. "I'll smoke it outside. I've just come on, and I can't stop. Tryin' your chimney?"

"Yes, I thought I'd see how it would draw, in here. It seems to go first-rate."

The policeman looked about him with an eye of inspection. "You want to get that linen window, there, mended up."

"Yes, I'll speak to the builder about that. It can go for one night."

The policeman went to the window and failed to pin the linen together where Lapham had failed before. "I can't fix it." He looked round once more, and saying, "Well, good-night," went out and down the stairs.

Lapham remained by the fire till he had smoked his cigar; then he rose and stamped upon the embers that still burned with his heavy boots, and went home. He was very cheerful at supper. He told his wife that he guessed he had a sure thing of it now, and in another twenty-four hours he should tell her just how. He made Penelope go to the theater with him, and when they came out, after the play, the night was so fine that he said they must walk round by the new house and take a look at it in the starlight. He said he had been there before he came home, and tried Seymour's chimney in the music-room, and it worked like a charm.

As they drew near Beacon street they were aware of unwonted stir and tumult, and presently the still air transmitted a turmoil of sound, through which a powerful and incessant throbbing made itself felt. The sky had reddened above them, and turning the corner at the Public Garden, they saw a black mass of people obstructing the perspective of the brightly-lighted street, and out of this mass a half dozen engines, whose strong heart-beats had already reached them, sent up volumes of fire-tinged smoke and steam from their funnels. Ladders were planted against the façade of a building, from the roof of which a mass of flame burnt smoothly upward, except where here and there it seemed to pull contemptuously away from the heavy streams of water which the firemen, clinging like great beetles to their ladders, poured in upon it.

Lapham had no need to walk down through the crowd, gazing and gossiping, with shouts and cries and hysterical laughter, before the burning house, to make sure that it was his.

"I guess I done it, Pen," was all he said.

Among the people who were looking at it were a party who seemed to have run out from dinner in some neighboring house; the ladies were fantastically wrapped up, as if they had flung on the first things they could seize.

"Isn't it perfectly magnificent!" cried a pretty girl. "I wouldn't have missed it on any account. Thank you so much, Mr. Symington, for bringing us out!"

"Ah, I thought you'd like it," said this Mr. Symington, who must have been the host; "and you can enjoy it without the least compunction, Miss Delano, for I happen to know that the house belongs to a man who could afford to burn one up for you once a year."

"Oh, do you think he would, if I came again?"

"I haven't the least doubt of it. We don't do things by halves in Boston."

"He ought to have had a coat of his non-combustible paint on it," said another gentleman of the party.

Penelope pulled her father away toward the first carriage she could reach of a number that had driven up. "Here, father! get into this."

"No, no; I couldn't ride," he answered heavily, and he walked home in silence. He greeted his wife with, "Well, Persis, our house is gone! And I guess I set it on fire myself;" and while he rummaged among the papers in his desk, still with his coat and hat on, his wife got the facts as she could from Penelope. She did not reproach him.

Here was a case in which his self-reproach must be sufficiently sharp without any edge from her. Besides, her mind was full of a terrible thought.

"Oh, Silas," she faltered, "they'll think you set it on fire to get the insurance!"

Lapham was staring at a paper which he held in his hand. "I had a builder's risk on it, but it expired last week. It's a dead loss."

"Oh, thank the merciful Lord!" cried his wife.

"Merciful!" said Lapham. "Well, it's a queer way of showing it."

He went to bed, and fell into the deep sleep which sometimes follows a great moral shock. It was perhaps rather a torpor than a sleep.

XXV

Lapham awoke confused, and in a kind of remoteness from the loss of the night before, through which it loomed mistily. But before he lifted his head from the pillow, it gathered substance and weight against which it needed all his will to bear up and live. In that moment he wished that he had not wakened, that he might never have wakened; but he rose, and faced the day and its cares.

The morning papers brought the report of the fire, and the conjectured loss. The reporters somehow had found out the fact that the loss fell entirely upon Lapham; they lighted up the hackneyed character of their statements with the picturesque interest of the coincidence that the policy had expired only the week before; heaven knows how they knew it. They said that nothing remained of the building but the walls; and Lapham, on his way to business, walked up past the smoke-stained shell. The windows looked like the eye-sockets of a skull down upon the blackened and trampled snow of the street; the pavement was a sheet of ice, and the water from the engines had frozen, like streams of tears, down the face of the house, and hung in icy tags from the window-sills and copings.

He gathered himself up as well as he could, and went on to his office. The chance of retrieval that had flashed upon him, as he sat smoking by that ruined hearth the evening before, stood him in such stead now as a sole hope may; and he said to himself that, having resolved not to sell his house, he was no more crippled by its loss than he would have been by letting his money lie idle in it; what he might have raised by mortgage on it could be made up in some other way; and if they would sell, he could still buy out the whole business of that West Virginia company, mines, plant, stock on hand, good-will, and everything, and unite it with his own. He went early in the afternoon to see Bellingham, whose expressions of condolence for his loss he cut short with as much politeness as he knew how to throw into his impatience. Bellingham seemed at first a little dazzled with the splendid courage of his scheme; it was certainly fine in its way; but then he began to have his misgivings.

"I happen to know that they haven't got much money behind them," urged Lapham. "They'll jump at an offer."

Bellingham shook his head. "If they can show profit on the old manufacture, and prove they can make their paint still cheaper and better hereafter, they can have all the money they want. And it will be very difficult for you to raise it if you're threatened by them. With that competition, you know what your plant at Lapham would be worth, and what the shrinkage on your manufactured stock would be. Better sell out to them," he concluded, "if they will buy."

"There ain't money enough in this country to buy out my paint," said Lapham, buttoning up his coat in a quiver of resentment. "Good-afternoon, sir." Men are but grown-up boys, after all. Bellingham watched this perversely proud and obstinate child fling petulantly out of his door, and felt a sympathy for him which was as truly kind as it was helpless.

But Lapham was beginning to see through Bellingham, as he believed. Bellingham was, in his way, part of that conspiracy by which Lapham's creditors were trying to drive him to the wall. More than ever now he was glad that he had nothing to do with that cold-hearted, self-conceited race, and that the favors so far were all from his side. He was more than ever determined to show them, every one of them, high and low, that he and his children could get along without them, and prosper and triumph without them. He said to himself that if Penelope were engaged to Corey that very minute, he would make her break with him.

He knew what he should do now, and he was going to do it without loss of time. He was going on to New York to see those West Virginia people; they had their principal office there, and he intended to get at their ideas, and then he intended to make them an offer. He managed this business better than could possibly have been expected of a man in his impassioned mood. But when it came really to business, his practical instincts, alert and wary, came to his aid against the passions that lay in wait to betray after they ceased to dominate him. He found the West Virginians full of zeal and hope, but in ten minutes he knew that they had not yet tested their strength in the money market, and had not ascertained how much or how little capital they could command. Lapham himself, if he had had so much, would not have hesitated to put a million dollars into their business. He saw, as they did not see, that they had the game in their own hands, and that if they could raise the money to extend their business,

they could ruin him. It was only a question of time, and he was on
the ground first. He frankly proposed a union of their interests. He
admitted that they had a good thing, and that he should have to
fight them hard; but he meant to fight them to the death unless they
could come to some sort of terms. Now, the question was whether
they had better go on and make a heavy loss for both sides by competition, or whether they had better form a partnership to run both
paints and command the whole market. Lapham made them three
propositions, each of which was fair and open: to sell out to them
altogether; to buy them out altogether; to join facilities and forces
with them, and go on in an invulnerable alliance. Let them name
a figure at which they would buy, a figure at which they would sell,
a figure at which they would combine,—or, in other words, the
amount of capital they needed.

They talked all day, going out to lunch together at the Astor
House, and sitting with their knees against the counter on a row of
stools before it for fifteen minutes of reflection and deglutition,*
with their hats on, and then returning to the basement from which
they emerged. The West Virginia company's name was lettered in gilt
on the wide low window, and its paint, in the form of ore, burnt,
and mixed, formed a display on the window shelf. Lapham examined
it and praised it; from time to time they all recurred to it together;
they sent out for some of Lapham's paint and compared it, the West
Virginians admitting its former superiority. They were young fellows, and country persons, like Lapham, by origin, and they looked
out with the same amused, undaunted, provincial eyes at the myriad
metropolitan legs passing on the pavement above the level of their
window. He got on well with them. At last, they said what they
would do. They said it was nonsense to talk of buying Lapham out,
for they had not the money; and as for selling out, they would not
do it, for they knew they had a big thing. But they would as soon use
his capital to develop it as anybody else's, and if he could put in a certain sum for this purpose, they would go in with him. He should run
the works at Lapham and manage the business in Boston, and they
would run the works at Kanawha Falls and manage the business in
New York. The two brothers with whom Lapham talked named their

---

*Swallowing.

figure, subject to the approval of another brother at Kanawha Falls, to whom they would write, and who would telegraph his answer, so that Lapham could have it inside of three days. But they felt perfectly sure that he would approve; and Lapham started back on the eleven o' clock train with an elation that gradually left him as he drew near Boston, where the difficulties of raising this sum were to be overcome. It seemed to him, then, that those fellows had put it up on him pretty steep, but he owned to himself that they had a sure thing, and that they were right in believing they could raise the same sum elsewhere; it would take all of it, he admitted, to make their paint pay on the scale they had the right to expect. At their age, he would not have done differently; but when he emerged, old, sore, and sleep-broken, from the sleeping-car in the Albany depot at Boston, he wished with a pathetic self-pity that they knew how a man felt at his age. A year ago, six months ago, he would have laughed at the notion that it would be hard to raise the money. But he thought ruefully of that immense stock of paint on hand, which was now a drug in the market, of his losses by Rogers and by the failures of other men, of the fire that had licked up so many thousands in a few hours; he thought with bitterness of the tens of thousands that he had gambled away in stocks, and of the commissions that the brokers had pocketed whether he won or lost; and he could not think of any securities on which he could borrow, except his house in Nankeen Square, or the mine and works at Lapham. He set his teeth in helpless rage when he thought of that property out on the G. L. & P., that ought to be worth so much, and was worth so little if the road chose to say so.

He did not go home, but spent most of the day shinning round, as he would have expressed it, and trying to see if he could raise the money. But he found that people of whom he hoped to get it were in the conspiracy which had been formed to drive him to the wall. Somehow, there seemed a sense of his embarrassments abroad. Nobody wanted to lend money on the plant at Lapham without taking time to look into the state of the business; but Lapham had no time to give, and he knew that the state of the business would not bear looking into. He could raise fifteen thousand on his Nankeen Square house, and another fifteen on his Beacon street lot, and this was all that a man who was worth a million by rights could do! He said a million, and he said it in defiance of Bellingham, who had subjected

his figures to an analysis which wounded Lapham more than he
chose to show at the time, for it proved that he was not so rich and
not so wise as he had seemed. His hurt vanity forbade him to go to
Bellingham now for help or advice; and if he could have brought
himself to ask his brothers for money, it would have been useless; they
were simply well-to-do Western people, but not capitalists on the
scale he required.

Lapham stood in the isolation to which adversity so often seems
to bring men. When its test was applied, practically or theoretically,
to all those who had seemed his friends, there was none who bore
it; and he thought with bitter self-contempt of the people whom he
had befriended in their time of need. He said to himself that he had
been a fool for that; and he scorned himself for certain acts of
scrupulosity by which he had lost money in the past. Seeing the
moral forces all arrayed against him, Lapham said that he would
like to have the chance offered him to get even with them again; he
thought he should know how to look out for himself. As he understood it, he had several days to turn about in, and he did not let one
day's failure dishearten him. The morning after his return he had, in
fact, a gleam of luck that gave him the greatest encouragement for
the moment. A man came in to inquire about one of Rogers's wild-
cat patents,* as Lapham called them, and ended by buying it. He got
it, of course, for less than Lapham took it for, but Lapham was glad
to be rid of it for something, when he had thought it worth nothing; and when the transaction was closed, he asked the purchaser
rather eagerly if he knew where Rogers was; it was Lapham's secret
belief that Rogers had found there was money in the thing, and had
sent the man to buy it. But it appeared that this was a mistake; the
man had not come from Rogers, but had heard of the patent in another way; and Lapham was astonished in the afternoon, when his
boy came to tell him that Rogers was in the outer office, and wished
to speak with him.

"All right," said Lapham, and he could not command at once the
severity for the reception of Rogers which he would have liked to
use. He found himself, in fact, so much relaxed towards him by the

---

*Speculative patents on inventions unlikely to make money.

morning's touch of prosperity that he asked him to sit down, gruffly, of course, but distinctly; and when Rogers said in his lifeless way, and with the effect of keeping his appointment of a month before, "Those English parties are in town, and would like to talk with you in reference to the mills," Lapham did not turn him out-of-doors.

He sat looking at him, and trying to make out what Rogers was after; for he did not believe that the English parties, if they existed, had any notion of buying his mills.

"What if they are not for sale?" he asked. "You know that I've been expecting an offer from the G. L. & P."

"I've kept watch of that. They haven't made you any offer," said Rogers quietly.

"And did you think," demanded Lapham, firing up, "that I would turn them in on somebody else as you turned them in on me, when the chances are that they won't be worth ten cents on the dollar six months from now?"

"I didn't know what you would do," said Rogers, non-committally. "I've come here to tell you that these parties stand ready to take the mills off your hands at a fair valuation—at the value I put upon them when I turned them in."

"I don't believe you!" cried Lapham brutally, but a wild, predatory hope made his heart leap so that it seemed to turn over in his breast. "I don't believe there are any such parties to begin with; and in the next place, I don't believe they would buy at any such figure; unless—unless you've lied to them, as you've lied to me. Did you tell them about the G. L. & P.?"

Rogers looked compassionately at him, but he answered, with unvaried dryness, "I did not think that necessary."

Lapham had expected this answer, and he had expected or intended to break out in furious denunciation of Rogers when he got it; but he only found himself saying, in a sort of baffled gasp, "I wonder what your game is!"

Rogers did not reply categorically, but he answered, with his impartial calm, and as if Lapham had said nothing to indicate that he differed at all with him as to disposing of the property in the way he had suggested: "If we should succeed in selling, I should be able to repay you your loans, and should have a little capital for a scheme that I think of going into."

"And do you think that I am going to steal these men's money to help you plunder somebody in a new scheme?" answered Lapham. The sneer was on behalf of virtue, but it was still a sneer.

"I suppose the money would be useful to you too, just now."

"Why?"

"Because I know that you have been trying to borrow."

At this proof of wicked omniscience in Rogers, the question whether he had better not regard the affair as a fatality, and yield to his destiny, flashed upon Lapham; but he answered, "I shall want money a great deal worse than I've ever wanted it yet, before I go into such rascally business with you. Don't you know that we might as well knock these parties down on the street, and take the money out of their pockets?"

"They have come on," answered Rogers, "from Portland to see you. I expected them some weeks ago, but they disappointed me. They arrived on the *Circassian* last night; they expected to have got in five days ago, but the passage was very stormy."

"Where are they?" asked Lapham, with helpless irrelevance, and feeling himself somehow drifted from his moorings by Rogers's shipping intelligence.

"They are at Young's. I told them we would call upon them after dinner this evening; they dine late."

"Oh, you did, did you?" asked Lapham, trying to drop another anchor for a fresh clutch on his underlying principles. "Well, now, you go and tell them that I said I wouldn't come."

"Their stay is limited," remarked Rogers. "I mentioned this evening because they were not certain they could remain over another night. But if to-morrow would suit you better———"

"Tell 'em I sha'n't come at all," roared Lapham, as much in terror as defiance, for he felt his anchor dragging. "Tell 'em I sha'n't come at all! Do you understand that?"

"I don't see why you should stickle as to the matter of going to them," said Rogers; "but if you think it will be better to have them approach you, I suppose I can bring them to you."

"No, you can't! I sha'n't let you! I sha'n't see them! I sha'n't have anything to do with them. Now do you understand?"

"I inferred from our last interview," persisted Rogers, unmoved by all this violent demonstration of Lapham's, "that you wished to

meet these parties. You told me that you would give me time to produce them; and I have promised them that you would meet them; I
have committed myself."

It was true that Lapham had defied Rogers to bring on his men,
and had implied his willingness to negotiate with them. That was before he had talked the matter over with his wife, and perceived his
moral responsibility in it; even she had not seen this at once. He
could not enter into this explanation with Rogers; he could only say,
"I said I'd give you twenty-four hours to prove yourself a liar, and
you did it. I didn't say twenty-four days."

"I don't see the difference," returned Rogers. "The parties are
here now, and that proves that I was acting in good faith at the time.
There has been no change in the posture of affairs. You don't know
now any more than you knew then that the G. L. & P. is going to want
the property. If there's any difference, it's in favor of the Road's having changed its mind."

There was some sense in this, and Lapham felt it—felt it only too
eagerly, as he recognized the next instant.

Rogers went on quietly: "You're not obliged to sell to these parties when you meet them; but you've allowed me to commit myself
to them by the promise that you would talk with them."

" 'Twa'n't a promise," said Lapham.

"It was the same thing; they have come out from England on my
guaranty that there was such and such an opening for their capital;
and now what am I to say to them? It places me in a ridiculous position." Rogers urged his grievance calmly, almost impersonally, making his appeal to Lapham's sense of justice. "I *can't* go back to those
parties and tell them you won't see them. It's no answer to make.
They've got a right to know *why* you won't see them."

"Very well, then!" cried Lapham; "I'll come and *tell* them why.
Who shall I ask for? When shall I be there?"

"At eight o'clock, please," said Rogers, rising, without apparent
alarm at his threat, if it was a threat. "And ask for me; I've taken a
room at the hotel for the present."

"I won't keep you five minutes when I get there," said Lapham;
but he did not come away till ten o'clock.

It appeared to him as if the very devil was in it. The Englishmen
treated his downright refusal to sell as a piece of bluff, and talked on

as though it were merely the opening of the negotiation. When he became plain with them in his anger, and told them why he would not sell, they seemed to have been prepared for this as a stroke of business, and were ready to meet it.

"Has this fellow," he demanded, twisting his head in the direction of Rogers, but disdaining to notice him otherwise, "been telling you that it's part of my game to say this? Well, sir, I can tell you, on my side, that there isn't a slipperier rascal unhung in America than Milton K. Rogers!"

The Englishmen treated this as a piece of genuine American humor, and returned to the charge with unabated courage. They owned now, that a person interested with them had been out to look at the property, and that they were satisfied with the appearance of things. They developed further the fact that they were not acting solely, or even principally, in their own behalf, but were the agents of people in England who had projected the colonization of a sort of community on the spot, somewhat after the plan of other English dreamers, and that they were satisfied, from a careful inspection, that the resources and facilities were those best calculated to develop the energy and enterprise of the proposed community. They were prepared to meet Mr. Lapham—Colonel, they begged his pardon, at the instance of Rogers—at any reasonable figure, and were quite willing to assume the risks he had pointed out. Something in the eyes of these men, something that lurked at an infinite depth below their speech, and was not really in their eyes when Lapham looked again, had flashed through him a sense of treachery in them. He had thought them the dupes of Rogers; but in that brief instant he had seen them—or thought he had seen them—his accomplices, ready to betray the interests of which they went on to speak with a certain comfortable jocosity, and a certain incredulous slight of his show of integrity. It was a deeper game than Lapham was used to, and he sat looking with a sort of admiration from one Englishman to the other, and then to Rogers, who maintained an exterior of modest neutrality, and whose air said, "I have brought you gentlemen together as the friend of all parties, and I now leave you to settle it among yourselves. I ask nothing, and expect nothing, except the small sum which shall accrue to me after the discharge of my obligations to Colonel Lapham."

While Rogers's presence expressed this, one of the Englishmen was saying, "And if you have any scruple in allowin' us to assume this risk, Colonel Lapham, perhaps you can console yourself with the fact that the loss, if there is to be any, will fall upon people who are able to bear it—upon an association of rich and charitable people. But we're quite satisfied there will be no loss," he added savingly. "All you have to do is to name your price, and we will do our best to meet it."

There was nothing in the Englishman's sophistry very shocking to Lapham. It addressed itself in him to that easy-going, not evilly intentioned, potential immorality which regards common property as common prey, and gives us the most corrupt municipal governments under the sun—which makes the poorest voter, when he has tricked into place, as unscrupulous in regard to others' money as an hereditary prince. Lapham met the Englishman's eye, and with difficulty kept himself from winking. Then he looked away, and tried to find out where he stood, or what he wanted to do. He could hardly tell. He had expected to come into that room and unmask Rogers, and have it over. But he had unmasked Rogers without any effect whatever, and the play had only begun. He had a whimsical and sarcastic sense of its being very different from the plays at the theater. He could not get up and go away in silent contempt; he could not tell the Englishmen that he believed them a pair of scoundrels and should have nothing to do with them; he could no longer treat them as innocent dupes. He remained baffled and perplexed, and the one who had not spoken hitherto remarked:

"Of course we sha'n't 'aggle about a few pound, more or less. If Colonel Lapham's figure should be a little larger than ours, I've no doubt 'e'll not be too 'ard upon us in the end."

Lapham appreciated all the intent of this subtle suggestion, and understood as plainly as if it had been said in so many words, that if they paid him a larger price, it was to be expected that a certain portion of the purchase money was to return to their own hands. Still he could not move; and it seemed to him that he could not speak.

"Ring that bell, Mr. Rogers," said the Englishman who had last spoken, glancing at the annunciator button in the wall near Rogers's head, "and 'ave up something 'ot, can't you? I should like to wet me w'istle, as you say 'ere, and Colonel Lapham seems to find it rather dry work."

Lapham jumped to his feet, and buttoned his overcoat about him. He remembered with terror the dinner at Corey's where he had disgraced and betrayed himself, and if he went into this thing at all, he was going into it sober. "I can't stop," he said, "I must be going."

"But you haven't given us an answer yet, Mr. Lapham," said the first Englishman with a successful show of dignified surprise.

"The only answer I can give you now is, No," said Lapham. "If you want another, you must let me have time to think it over."

"But 'ow much time?" said the other Englishman. "We're pressed for time ourselves, and we hoped for an answer—'oped for a hanswer," he corrected himself, "at once. That was our understandin' with Mr. Rogers."

"I can't let you know till morning, anyway," said Lapham, and he went out, as his custom often was, without any parting salutation. He thought Rogers might try to detain him; but Rogers had remained seated when the others got to their feet, and paid no attention to his departure.

He walked out into the night air, every pulse throbbing with the strong temptation. He knew very well those men would wait, and gladly wait, till the morning, and that the whole affair was in his hands. It made him groan in spirit to think that it was. If he had hoped that some chance might take the decision from him, there was no such chance, in the present or future, that he could see. It was for him alone to commit this rascality—if it was a rascality—or not.

He walked all the way home, letting one car after another pass him on the street, now so empty of other passing, and it was almost eleven o'clock when he reached home. A carriage stood before his house, and when he let himself in with his key, he heard talking in the family-room. It came into his head that Irene had got back unexpectedly, and that the sight of her was somehow going to make it harder for him; then he thought it might be Corey, come upon some desperate pretext to see Penelope; but when he opened the door he saw, with a certain absence of surprise, that it was Rogers. He was standing with his back to the fire-place, talking to Mrs. Lapham, and he had been shedding tears; dry tears they seemed, and they had left a sort of sandy, glistening trace on his cheeks. Apparently he was not ashamed of them, for the expression with which he met Lapham was that of a man making a desperate appeal in his own cause, which was identical with that of humanity, if not that of justice.

"I some expected," began Rogers, "to find you here————"

"No, you didn't," interrupted Lapham; "you wanted to come here and make a poor mouth to Mrs. Lapham before I got home."

"I knew that Mrs. Lapham would know what was going on," said Rogers, more candidly, but not more virtuously, for that he could not, "and I wished her to understand a point that I hadn't put to you at the hotel, and that I want you should consider. And I want you should consider me a little in this business, too; you're not the only one that's concerned, I tell you, and I've been telling Mrs. Lapham that it's my one chance; that if you don't meet me on it, my wife and children will be reduced to beggary."

"So will mine," said Lapham, "or the next thing to it."

"Well, then, I want you to give me this chance to get on my feet again. You've no right to deprive me of it; it's unchristian. In our dealings with each other we should be guided by the Golden Rule, as I was saying to Mrs. Lapham before you came in. I told her that if I knew myself, I should in your place consider the circumstances of a man in mine, who had honorably endeavored to discharge his obligations to me, and had patiently borne my undeserved suspicions. I should consider that man's family, I told Mrs. Lapham."

"Did you tell her that if I went in with you and those fellows, I should be robbing the people who trusted them?"

"I don't see what you've got to do with the people that sent them here. They are rich people, and could bear it if it came to the worst. But there's no likelihood, now, that it will come to the worst; you can see yourself that the Road has changed its mind about buying. And here am I without a cent in the world; and my wife is an invalid. She needs comforts, she needs little luxuries, and she hasn't even the necessaries; and you want to sacrifice her to a mere idea! You don't know in the first place that the Road will ever want to buy; and if it does, the probability is that with a colony like that planted on its line, it would make very different terms from what it would with you or me. These agents are not afraid, and their principals are rich people; and if there was any loss, it would be divided up amongst them so that they wouldn't any of them feel it."

Lapham stole a troubled glance at his wife, and saw that there was

no help in her. Whether she was daunted and confused in her own
conscience by the outcome, so evil and disastrous, of the reparation
to Rogers which she had forced her husband to make, or whether her
perceptions had been blunted and darkened by the appeals which
Rogers had now used, it would be difficult to say. Probably there was
a mixture of both causes in the effect which her husband felt in her,
and from which he turned, girding himself anew, to Rogers.

"I have no wish to recur to the past," continued Rogers, with
growing superiority. "You have shown a proper spirit in regard to
that, and you have done what you could to wipe it out."

"I should think I had," said Lapham. "I've used up about a
hundred and fifty thousand dollars trying."

"Some of my enterprises," Rogers admitted, "have been unfortunate, seemingly; but I have hopes that they will yet turn out well—
in time. I can't understand why you should be so mindful of others
now, when you showed so little regard for me then. I had come to
your aid at a time when you needed help, and when you got on your
feet you kicked me out of the business. I don't complain, but that is
the fact; and I had to begin again, after I had supposed myself settled
in life, and establish myself elsewhere."

Lapham glanced again at his wife; her head had fallen; he could
see that she was so rooted in her old remorse for that questionable
act of his, amply and more than fully atoned for since, that she was
helpless, now in the crucial moment, when he had the utmost need
of her insight. He had counted upon her; he perceived now that
when he had thought it was for him alone to decide, he had counted
upon her just spirit to stay his own in its struggle to be just. He had
not forgotten how she held out against him only a little while ago,
when he asked her whether he might not rightfully sell in some such
contingency as this; and it was not now that she said or even looked
anything in favor of Rogers, but that she was silent against him,
which dismayed Lapham. He swallowed the lump that rose in his
throat, the self-pity, the pity for her, the despair, and said gently, "I
guess you better go to bed, Persis. It's pretty late."

She turned towards the door, when Rogers said, with the obvious intention of detaining her through her curiosity:

"But I let that pass. And I don't ask now that you should sell to
these men."

Mrs. Lapham paused, irresolute.

"What are you making this bother for, then?" demanded Lapham. "What *do* you want?"

"What I've been telling your wife here. I want you should sell to *me*. I don't say what I'm going to do with the property, and you will not have an iota of responsibility, whatever happens."

Lapham was staggered, and he saw his wife's face light up with eager question.

"I want that property," continued Rogers, "and I've got the money to buy it. What will you take for it? If it's the price you're standing out for———"

"Persis," said Lapham, "go to bed," and he gave her a look that meant obedience for her. She went out of the door, and left him with his tempter.

"If you think I'm going to help you whip the devil round the stump, you're mistaken in your man, Milton Rogers," said Lapham, lighting a cigar. "As soon as I sold to you, you would sell to that other pair of rascals. I smelt 'em out in half a minute."

"They are Christian gentlemen," said Rogers. "But I don't purpose defending them; and I don't purpose telling you what I shall or shall not do with the property when it is in my hands again. The question is, Will you sell, and, if so, what is your figure? You have got nothing whatever to do with it after you've sold."

It was perfectly true. Any lawyer would have told him the same. He could not help admiring Rogers for his ingenuity, and every selfish interest of his nature joined with many obvious duties to urge him to consent. He did not see why he should refuse. There was no longer a reason. He was standing out alone for nothing, any one else would say. He smoked on as if Rogers were not there, and Rogers remained before the fire as patient as the clock ticking behind his head on the mantel, and showing the gleam of its pendulum beyond his face on either side. But at last he said, "Well?"

"Well," answered Lapham, "you can't expect me to give you an answer to-night, any more than before. You know that what you've said now hasn't changed the thing a bit. I wish it had. The Lord knows, I want to be rid of the property fast enough."

"Then why don't you sell to me? Can't you see that you will not be responsible for what happens after you have sold?"

"No, I *can't* see that; but if I can by morning, I'll sell."

"Why do you expect to know any better by morning? You're wasting time for nothing!" cried Rogers, in his disappointment. "Why are you so particular? When you drove me out of the business you were not so very particular."

Lapham winced. It was certainly ridiculous for a man who had once so selfishly consulted his own interests to be stickling now about the rights of others.

"I guess nothing's going to happen over-night," he answered sullenly. "Anyway, I sha'n't say what I shall do till morning."

"What time can I see you in the morning?"

"Half-past nine."

Rogers buttoned his coat, and went out of the room without another word. Lapham followed him to close the street-door after him.

His wife called down to him from above as he approached the room again, "Well?"

"I've told him I'd let him know in the morning."

"Want I should come down and talk with you?"

"No," answered Lapham, in the proud bitterness which his isolation brought, "you couldn't do any good." He went in and shut the door, and by and by his wife heard him begin walking up and down; and then the rest of the night she lay awake and listened to him walking up and down. But when the first light whitened the window, the words of the Scripture came into her mind: "And there wrestled a man with him until the breaking of the day. . . . And he said, Let me go, for the day breaketh. And he said, I will not let thee go, except thou bless me."*

She could not ask him anything when they met, but he raised his dull eyes after the first silence and said, "I don't know what I'm going to say to Rogers."

She could not speak; she did not know what to say, and she saw her husband, when she followed him with her eyes from the window, drag heavily down toward the corner, where he was to take the horse-car.

He arrived rather later than usual at his office, and he found his

---

*Reference, from the Bible, to Jacob's nightlong wrestling with an angel until he receives its blessing (Genesis 32:24–29).

letters already on his table. There was one, long and official-looking, with a printed letter-heading on the outside, and Lapham had no need to open it in order to know that it was the offer of the Great Lacustrine & Polar Railroad for his mills. But he went mechanically through the verification of his prophetic fear, which was also his sole hope, and then sat looking blankly at it.

Rogers came promptly at the appointed time, and Lapham handed him the letter. He must have taken it all in at a glance, and seen the impossibility of negotiating any further now, even with victims so pliant and willing as those Englishmen.

"You've ruined me!" Rogers broke out. "I haven't a cent left in the world! God help my poor wife!"

He went out, and Lapham remained staring at the door which closed upon him. This was his reward for standing firm for right and justice to his own destruction: to feel like a thief and a murderer.

XXVI

Later in the forenoon came the dispatch from the West Virginians in New York, saying their brother assented to their agreement; and it now remained for Lapham to fulfill his part of it. He was ludicrously far from able to do this; and unless he could get some extension of time from them, he must lose this chance, his only chance, to retrieve himself. He spent the time in a desperate endeavor to raise the money, but he had not raised the half of it when the banks closed. With shame in his heart he went to Bellingham, from whom he had parted so haughtily, and laid his plan before him. He could not bring himself to ask Bellingham's help, but he told him what he proposed to do. Bellingham pointed out that the whole thing was an experiment, and that the price asked was enormous, unless a great success were morally certain. He advised delay, he advised prudence; he insisted that Lapham ought at least to go out to Kanawha Falls, and see the mines and works, before he put any such sum into the development of the enterprise.

"That's all well enough," cried Lapham; "but if I don't clinch this offer within twenty-four hours, they'll withdraw it, and go into the market; and then where am I?"

"Go on and see them again," said Bellingham. "They can't be so peremptory as that with you. They must give you time to look at what they want to sell. If it turns out what you hope, then—I'll see what can be done. But look into it thoroughly."

"Well!" cried Lapham, helplessly submitting. He took out his watch, and saw that he had forty minutes to catch the four o'clock train. He hurried back to his office, put together some papers preparatory to going, and dispatched a note by his boy to Mrs. Lapham saying that he was starting for New York, and did not know just when he should get back.

The early spring day was raw and cold. As he went out through the office he saw the clerks at work with their street coats and hats on; Miss Dewey had her jacket dragged up on her shoulders and looked particularly comfortless as she operated her machine with her red fingers. "What's up?" asked Lapham, stopping a moment.

"Seems to be something the matter with the steam," she answered, with the air of unmerited wrong habitual with so many pretty women who have to work for a living.

"Well, take your writer into my room; there's a fire in the stove there," said Lapham, passing out.

Half an hour later his wife came into the outer office. She had passed the day in a passion of self-reproach, gradually mounting from the mental numbness in which he had left her, and now she could wait no longer to tell him that she saw how she had forsaken him in his hour of trial and left him to bear it alone. She wondered at herself in shame and dismay; she wondered that she could have been so confused as to the real point by that old wretch of a Rogers, that she could have let him hoodwink her so, even for a moment. It astounded her that such a thing should have happened, for if there was any virtue upon which this good woman prided herself, in which she thought herself superior to her husband, it was her instant and steadfast perception of right and wrong, and the ability to choose the right to her own hurt. But she had now to confess, as each of us has had likewise to confess in his own case, that the very virtue on which she had prided herself was the thing that had played her false; that she had kept her mind so long upon that old wrong which she believed her husband had done this man that she could not detach it, but clung to the thought of reparation for it when she ought to have seen that he was proposing a piece of roguery as the means. The suffering which Lapham must inflict on him if he decided against him had been more to her apprehension than the harm he might do if he decided for him. But now she owned her limitations to herself, and above everything in the world she wished the man whom her conscience had roused and driven on whither her intelligence had not followed, to do right, to do what he felt to be right, and nothing else. She admired and revered him for going beyond her, and she wished to tell him that she did not know what he had determined to do about Rogers, but that she knew it was right, and would gladly abide the consequences with him, whatever they were.

She had not been near his place of business for nearly a year, and her heart smote her tenderly as she looked about her there, and thought of the early days when she knew as much about the paint as he did; she wished that those days were back again. She saw Corey at his desk, and she could not bear to speak to him; she dropped her veil that she need not recognize him, and pushed on to Lapham's room, and, opening the door without knocking, shut it behind her.

Then she became aware with intolerable disappointment that her husband was not there. Instead, a very pretty girl sat at his desk, operating a type-writer. She seemed quite at home, and she paid Mrs. Lapham the scant attention which such young women often bestow upon people not personally interesting to them. It vexed the wife that any one else should seem to be helping her husband about business that she had once been so intimate with; and she did not at all like the girl's indifference to her presence. Her hat and sack hung on a nail in one corner, and Lapham's office coat, looking intensely like him to his wife's familiar eye, hung on a nail in the other corner; and Mrs. Lapham liked even less than the girl's good looks this domestication of her garments in her husband's office. She began to ask herself exitedly why he should be away from his office when she happened to come; and she had not the strength at the moment to reason herself out of her unreasonableness.

"When will Colonel Lapham be in, do you suppose?" she sharply asked of the girl.

"I couldn't say exactly," replied the girl, without looking round.

"Has he been out long?"

"I don't know as I noticed," said the girl, looking up at the clock, without looking at Mrs. Lapham. She went on working her machine.

"Well, I can't wait any longer," said the wife abruptly. "When Colonel Lapham comes in, you please tell him Mrs. Lapham wants to see him."

The girl started to her feet and turned toward Mrs. Lapham with a red and startled face, which she did not lift to confront her. "Yes—yes—I will," she faltered.

The wife went home with a sense of defeat mixed with an irritation about this girl which she could not quell or account for. She found her husband's message, and it seemed intolerable that he should have gone to New York without seeing her; she asked herself in vain what the mysterious business could be that took him away so suddenly. She said to herself that he was neglecting her; he was leaving her out a little too much; and in demanding of herself why he had never mentioned that girl there in his office, she forgot how much she had left herself out of his business life. That was another curse of their prosperity. Well, she was glad the prosperity was going; it had never been happiness. After this she was going to know everything as she used.

She tried to dismiss the whole matter till Lapham returned; and if there had been anything for her to do in that miserable house, as she called it in her thought, she might have succeeded. But again the curse was on her; there was nothing to do; and the looks of that girl kept coming back to her vacancy, her disoccupation. She tried to make herself something to do, but that beauty, which she had not liked, followed her amid the work of overhauling the summer clothing, which Irene had seen to putting away in the fall. Who was the thing, anyway? It was very strange, her being there; why did she jump up in that frightened way when Mrs. Lapham had named herself?

After dark that evening, when the question had worn away its poignancy from mere iteration, a note for Mrs. Lapham was left at the door by a messenger who said there was no answer. "A note for me?" she said, staring at the unknown, and somehow artificial-looking, handwriting of the superscription. Then she opened it and read: "Ask your husband about his lady copying-clerk. A Friend and Well-wisher," who signed the note, gave no other name.

Mrs. Lapham sat helpless with it in her hand. Her brain reeled; she tried to fight the madness off; but before Lapham came back the second morning, it had become, with lessening intervals of sanity and release, a demoniacal possession. She passed the night without sleep, without rest, in the frenzy of the cruelest of the passions, which covers with shame the unhappy soul it possesses, and murderously lusts for the misery of its object. If she had known where to find her husband in New York, she would have followed him; she waited his return in an ecstasy of impatience. In the morning he came back, looking spent and haggard. She saw him drive up to the door, and she ran to let him in herself.

"Who is that girl you've got in your office, Silas Lapham?" she demanded, when her husband entered.

"Girl in my office?"

"Yes! Who is she? What is she doing there?"

"Why, what have you heard about her?"

"Never you mind what I've heard. Who is she? *Is it Mrs. M. that you gave that money to?* I want to know who she is! I want to know what a respectable man, with grown-up girls of his own, is doing with such a looking thing as that in his office! I want to know how long she's been there! I want to know what she's there at all for!"

He had mechanically pushed her before him into the long, darkened parlor, and he shut himself in there with her now, to keep the household from hearing her lifted voice. For a while he stood bewildered, and could not have answered if he would; and then he would not. He merely asked, "Have I ever accused you of anything wrong, Persis?"

"You no need to!" she answered furiously, placing herself against the closed door.

"Did you ever know me to do anything out of the way?"

"That isn't what I asked you."

"Well, I guess you may find out about that girl yourself. Get away from the door."

"I won't get away from the door."

She felt herself set lightly aside, and her husband opened the door and went out. "I will find out about her," she screamed after him. "I'll find out, and I'll disgrace you—I'll teach you how to treat me!"

The air blackened round her; she reeled to the sofa; and then she found herself waking from a faint. She did not know how long she had lain there; she did not care. In a moment her madness came whirling back upon her. She rushed up to his room; it was empty; the closet-doors stood ajar and the drawers were open; he must have packed a bag hastily and fled. She went out, and wandered crazily up and down till she found a hack. She gave the driver her husband's business address, and told him to drive there as fast as he could; and three times she lowered the window to put her head out and ask him if he could not hurry. A thousand things thronged into her mind to support her in her evil will. She remembered how glad and proud that man had been to marry her, and how everybody said she was marrying beneath her when she took him. She remembered how good she had always been to him, how perfectly devoted, slaving early and late to advance him, and looking out for his interests in all things, and sparing herself in nothing. If it had not been for her, he

might have been driving stage yet; and since their troubles had
begun, the troubles which his own folly and imprudence had
brought on them, her conduct had been that of a true and faithful
wife. Was he the sort of man to be allowed to play her false with impunity? She set her teeth and drew her breath sharply through them,
when she thought how willingly she had let him befool her and de-
lude her about that memorandum of payments to Mrs. M., because
she loved him so much, and pitied him for his cares and anxieties.
She recalled his confusion, his guilty looks.

She plunged out of the carriage so hastily when she reached the
office that she did not think of paying the driver; and he had to call
after her when she had got half-way up the stairs. Then she went
straight to Lapham's room, with outrage in her heart. There was
again no one there but that type-writer girl; she jumped to her feet
in a fright, as Mrs. Lapham dashed the door to behind her and flung
up her veil.

The two women confronted each other.

"Why, the good land!" cried Mrs. Lapham, "ain't you Zerrilla
Millon?"

"I—I'm married," faltered the girl. "My name's Dewey now."

"You're Jim Millon's daughter, anyway. How long have you been
here?"

"I haven't been here regularly; I've been here off and on ever
since last May."

"Where's your mother?"

"She's here—in Boston."

Mrs. Lapham kept her eyes on the girl, but she dropped, trembling, into her husband's chair, and a sort of amaze and curiosity
were in her voice instead of the fury she had meant to put there.

"The Colonel," continued Zerrilla, "he's been helping us, and
he's got me a type-writer, so that I can help myself a little. Mother's
doing pretty well now; and when Hen isn't around we can get
along."

"That your husband?"

"I never wanted to marry him; but he promised to try to get
something to do on shore; and mother was all for it, because he had
a little property then, and I thought maybe I'd better. But it's turned
out just as I said, and if he don't stay away long enough this time to

let me get the divorce,—he's agreed to it, time and again,—I don't know what we're going to do." Zerrilla's voice fell, and the trouble which she could keep out of her face usually, when she was comfortably warmed and fed and prettily dressed, clouded it in the presence of a sympathetic listener. "I saw it was you when you came in the other day," she went on; "but you didn't seem to know me. I suppose the Colonel's told you that there's a gentleman going to marry me— Mr. Wemmel's his name—as soon as I get the divorce; but sometimes I'm completely discouraged; it don't seem as if I ever could get it."

Mrs. Lapham would not let her know that she was ignorant of the fact attributed to her knowledge. She remained listening to Zerrilla, and piecing out the whole history of her presence there from the facts of the past, and the traits of her husband's character. One of the things she had always had to fight him about was that idea of his that he was bound to take care of Jim Millon's worthless wife and her child because Millon had got the bullet that was meant for him. It was a perfect superstition of his; she could not beat it out of him; but she had made him promise the last time he had done anything for that woman that it should be the last time. He had then got her a little house in one of the fishing ports, where she could take the sailors to board and wash for, and earn an honest living if she would keep straight. That was five or six years ago, and Mrs. Lapham had heard nothing of Mrs. Millon since; she had heard quite enough of her before, and had known her idle and baddish ever since she was the worst little girl at school in Lumberville, and all through her shameful girlhood, and the married days which she had made so miserable to the poor fellow who had given her his decent name and a chance to behave herself. Mrs. Lapham had no mercy on Moll Millon, and she had quarreled often enough with her husband for befriending her. As for the child, if the mother would put Zerrilla out with some respectable family, that would be one thing; but as long as she kept Zerrilla with her, she was against letting her husband do anything for either of them. He had done ten times as much for them now as he had any need to, and she had made him give her his solemn word that he would do no more. She saw now that she was wrong to make him give it, and that he must have broken it again and again for the reason that he had given when she once scolded him for throwing away his money on that hussy:

"When I think of Jim Millon, I've got to; that's all."

She recalled now that whenever she had brought up the subject of Mrs. Millon and her daughter, he had seemed shy of it, and had dropped it with some guess that they were getting along now. She wondered that she had not thought at once of Mrs. Millon when she saw that memorandum about Mrs. M.; but the woman had passed so entirely out of her life, that she had never dreamt of her in connection with it. Her husband had deceived her, yet her heart was no longer hot against him, but rather tenderly grateful that his deceit was in this sort, and not in that other. All cruel and shameful doubt of him went out of it. She looked at this beautiful girl, who had blossomed out of her knowledge since she saw her last, and she knew that she was only a blossomed weed, of the same worthless root as her mother, and saved, if saved, from the same evil destiny by the good of her father in her; but so far as the girl and her mother were concerned, Mrs. Lapham knew that her husband was to blame for nothing but his willful, wrong-headed kind-heartedness, which her own exactions had turned into deceit. She remained awhile, questioning the girl quietly about herself and her mother, and then, with a better mind towards Zerrilla, at least, than she had ever had before, she rose up and went out. There must have been some outer hint of the exhaustion in which the subsidence of her excitement had left her within, for before she had reached the head of the stairs, Corey came towards her.

"Can I be of any use to you, Mrs. Lapham? The Colonel was here just before you came in, on his way to the train."

"Yes,—yes. I didn't know—I thought perhaps I could catch him here. But it don't matter. I wish you would let someone go with me to get a carriage," she begged feebly.

"I'll go with you myself," said the young fellow, ignoring the strangeness in her manner. He offered her his arm in the twilight of the staircase, and she was glad to put her trembling hand through it, and keep it there till he helped her into a hack which he found for her. He gave the driver her direction, and stood looking a little anxiously at her.

"I thank you; I am all right now," she said, and he bade the man drive on.

When she reached home she went to bed, spent with the tumult

of her emotions and sick with shame and self-reproach. She understood now, as clearly as if he had told her in so many words, that if
he had befriended these worthless jades—the Millons characterized
themselves so, even to Mrs. Lapham's remorse—secretly and in defiance of her, it was because he dreaded her blame, which was so
sharp and bitter, for what he could not help doing. It consoled her
that he had defied her; deceived her; when he came back she should
tell him that; and then it flashed upon her that she did not know
where he was gone, or whether he would ever come again. If he
never came, it would be no more than she deserved; but she sent for
Penelope, and tried to give herself hopes of escape from this just
penalty.

Lapham had not told his daughter where he was going; she had
heard him packing his bag, and had offered to help him; but he had
said he could do it best, and had gone off, as he usually did, without
taking leave of any one.

"What were you talking about so loud, down in the parlor,"
she asked her mother, "just before he came up? Is there any new
trouble?"

"No; it was nothing."

"I couldn't tell. Once I thought you were laughing." She went
about, closing the curtains on account of her mother's headache, and
doing awkwardly and imperfectly the things that Irene would have
done so skillfully for her comfort.

The day wore away to nightfall, and then Mrs. Lapham said she
must know. Penelope said there was no one to ask; the clerks would
all be gone home; and her mother said yes, there was Mr. Corey; they
could send and ask him; he would know.

The girl hesitated. "Very well," she said then, scarcely above a
whisper, and she presently laughed huskily. "Mr. Corey seems fated
to come in somewhere. I guess it's a Providence, mother."

She sent off a note, inquiring whether he could tell her just
where her father had expected to be that night; and the answer came
quickly back that Corey did not know, but would look up the book-
keeper and inquire. This office brought him in person, an hour later,
to tell Penelope that the Colonel was to be at Lapham that night and
next day.

"He came in from New York in a great hurry, and rushed off as soon as he could pack his bag," Penelope explained, "and we hadn't a chance to ask him where he was to be to-night. And mother wasn't very well, and————"

"I thought she wasn't looking well when she was at the office today; and so I thought I would come rather than send," Corey explained, in his turn.

"Oh, thank you!"

"If there is anything I can do—telegraph Colonel Lapham, or anything?"

"Oh, no, thank you; mother's better now. She merely wanted to be sure where he was."

He did not offer to go upon this conclusion of his business, but hoped he was not keeping her from her mother. She thanked him once again, and said no, that her mother was much better since she had had a cup of tea; and then they looked at each other, and without any apparent exchange of intelligence he remained, and at eleven o'clock he was still there. He was honest in saying he did not know it was so late; but he made no pretense of being sorry, and she took the blame to herself.

"I oughtn't to have let you stay," she said. "But with father gone, and all that trouble hanging over us————"

She was allowing him to hold her hand a moment at the door, to which she had followed him.

"I'm so glad you could let me!" he said; "and I want to ask you now when I may come again. But if you need me, you'll————"

A sharp pull at the door-bell outside made them start asunder, and at a sign from Penelope, who knew that the maids were abed by this time, he opened it.

"Why, Irene!" shrieked the girl.

Irene entered, with the hackman, who had driven her unheard to the door, following with her small bags, and kissed her sister with resolute composure. "That's all," she said to the hackman. "I gave my checks to the expressman," she explained to Penelope.

Corey stood helpless. Irene turned upon him, and gave him her hand. "How do you do, Mr. Corey?" she said, with a courage that sent a thrill of admiring gratitude through him. "Where's mamma, Pen? Papa gone to bed?"

Penelope faltered out some reply embodying the facts, and Irene ran up the stairs to her mother's room. Mrs. Lapham started up in bed at her apparition.

"Irene Lapham!"

"Uncle William thought he ought to tell me the trouble papa was in; and did you think I was going to stay off there junketing, while you were going through all this at home, and Pen acting so silly too? You ought to have been ashamed to let me stay so long! I started just as soon as I could pack. Did you get my dispatch? I telegraphed from Springfield. But it don't matter now. Here I am. And I don't think I need have hurried on Pen's account," she added, with an accent prophetic of the sort of old maid she would become if she happened never to marry.

"Did you see him?" asked her mother. "It's the first time he's been here since she told him he mustn't come."

"I guess it isn't the last time, by the looks," said Irene; and before she took off her bonnet she began to undo some of Penelope's mistaken arrangements of the room.

At breakfast, where Corey and his mother met the next morning before his father and sisters came down, he told her, with embarrassment which told much more, that he wished now that she would go and call upon the Laphams.

Mrs. Corey turned a little pale, but shut her lips tight and mourned in silence whatever hopes she had lately permitted herself. She answered with Roman fortitude: "Of course, if there's anything between you and Miss Lapham, your family ought to recognize it."

"Yes," said Corey.

"You were reluctant to have me call at first, but now if the affair is going on————"

"It is! I hope—yes, it is!"

"Then I ought to go and see her, with your sisters; and she ought to come here and—we ought all to see her and make the matter public. We can't do so too soon. It will seem as if we were ashamed if we don't."

"Yes, you are quite right, mother," said the young man gratefully, "and I feel how kind and good you are. I have tried to consider you in this matter, though I don't seem to have done so; I know what your rights are, and I wish with all my heart that I were meeting even your tastes perfectly. But I know you will like her when you come to know her. It's been very hard for her every way,—about her sister,—and she's made a great sacrifice for me. She's acted nobly."

Mrs. Corey, whose thoughts cannot always be reported, said she was sure of it, and that all she desired was her son's happiness.

"She's been very unwilling to consider it an engagement on that account, and on account of Colonel Lapham's difficulties. I should like to have you go, now, for that very reason. I don't know just how serious the trouble is; but it isn't a time when we can seem indifferent."

The logic of this was not perhaps so apparent to the glasses of fifty as to the eyes of twenty-six; but Mrs. Corey, however she viewed it, could not allow herself to blench before the son whom she had taught that to want magnanimity was to be less than gentlemanly. She answered, with what composure she could, "I will take your sisters," and then she made some natural inquiries about Lapham's affairs.

"Oh, I hope it will come out all right," Corey said, with a lover's vague smile, and left her. When his father came down, rubbing his long hands together, and looking aloof from all the cares of the practical world, in an artistic withdrawal, from which his eye ranged over the breakfast-table before he sat down, Mrs. Corey told him what she and their son had been saying.

He laughed, with a delicate impersonal appreciation of the predicament. "Well, Anna, you can't say but if you ever were guilty of supposing yourself porcelain, this is a just punishment of your arrogance. Here you are bound by the very quality on which you've prided yourself to behave well to a bit of earthenware who is apparently in danger of losing the gilding that rendered her tolerable."

"We never cared for the money," said Mrs. Corey. "You know that."

"No; and now we can't seem to care for the loss of it. That would be still worse. Either horn of the dilemma gores us. Well, we still have the comfort we had in the beginning; we can't help ourselves, and we should only make bad worse by trying. Unless we can look to Tom's inamorata herself for help."

Mrs. Corey shook her head so gloomily that her husband broke off with another laugh. But at the continued trouble of her face he said, sympathetically: "My dear, I know it's a very disagreeable affair;

and I don't think either of us has failed to see that it was so from the beginning. I have had my way of expressing my sense of it, and you yours, but we have always been of the same mind about it. We would both have preferred to have Tom marry in his own set; the Laphams are about the last set we could have wished him to marry into. They *are* uncultivated people, and, so far as I have seen them, I'm not able to believe that poverty will improve them. Still, it may. Let us hope for the best, and let us behave as well as we know how. I'm sure *you* will behave well, and I shall try. I'm going with you to call on Miss Lapham. This is a thing that can't be done by halves!"

He cut his orange in the Neapolitan manner, and ate it in quarters.

XXVII

Irene did not leave her mother in any illusion concerning her cousin Will and herself. She said they had all been as nice to her as they could be, and when Mrs. Lapham hinted at what had been in her thoughts,—or her hopes, rather,—Irene severely snubbed the notion. She said that he was as good as engaged to a girl out there, and that he had never dreamt of her. Her mother wondered at her severity; in these few months the girl had toughened and hardened; she had lost all her babyish dependence and pliability; she was like iron; and here and there she was sharpened to a cutting edge. It had been a life and death struggle with her; she had conquered, but she had also necessarily lost much. Perhaps what she had lost was not worth keeping; but at any rate she had lost it.

She required from her mother a strict and accurate account of her father's affairs, so far as Mrs. Lapham knew them; and she showed a business-like quickness in comprehending them that Penelope had never pretended to. With her sister she ignored the past as completely as it was possible to do; and she treated both Corey and Penelope with the justice which their innocence of voluntary offense deserved. It was a difficult part, and she kept away from them as much as she could. She had been easily excused, on a plea of fatigue from her journey, when Mr. and Mrs. Corey had called the day after her arrival, and, Mrs. Lapham being still unwell, Penelope received them alone.

The girl had instinctively judged best that they should know the worst at once, and she let them have the full brunt of the drawing-room, while she was screwing her courage up to come down and see them. She was afterwards—months afterwards—able to report to Corey that when she entered the room his father was sitting with his hat on his knees, a little tilted away from the Emancipation group, as if he expected the Lincoln to hit him with that lifted hand of benediction; and that Mrs. Corey looked as if she were not sure but the Eagle pecked. But for the time being Penelope was as nearly crazed as might be by the complications of her position, and received her visitors with a piteous distraction which could not fail of touching Bromfield Corey's Italianized sympatheticism. He was very polite and tender with her at first, and ended by making a joke with her, to which Penelope responded in her sort. He said he hoped they parted friends, if not quite acquaintances; and she said she hoped they would be able to recognize each other if they ever met again.

"That is what I meant by her pertness," said Mrs. Corey, when they were driving away.

"Was it very pert?" he queried. "The child had to answer something."

"I would much rather she had answered nothing, under the circumstances," said Mrs. Corey. "However!" she added hopelessly.

"Oh, she's a merry little grig,* you can see that, and there's no harm in her. I can understand a little why a formal fellow like Tom should be taken with her. She hasn't the least reverence, I suppose, and joked with the young man from the beginning. You must remember, Anna, that there was a time when you liked my joking."

"It was a very different thing!"

"But that drawing-room!" pursued Corey; "really, I don't see how Tom stands that. Anna, a terrible thought occurs to me! Fancy Tom being married in front of that group, with a floral horse-shoe in tuberoses coming down on either side of it!"

"Bromfield!" cried his wife, "you are unmerciful."

"No, no, my dear," he argued; "merely imaginative. And I can even imagine that little thing finding Tom just the least bit slow at times, if it were not for his goodness. Tom is so kind that I'm convinced he sometimes feels your joke in his heart when his head isn't quite clear about it. Well, we will not despond, my dear."

"Your father seemed actually to like her," Mrs. Corey reported to her daughters, very much shaken in her own prejudices by the fact. If the girl were not so offensive to his fastidiousness, there might be some hope that she was not so offensive as Mrs. Corey had thought. "I wonder how she will strike you," she concluded, looking from one daughter to another, as if trying to decide which of them would like Penelope least.

Irene's return and the visit of the Coreys formed a distraction for the Laphams in which their impending troubles seemed to hang further aloof; but it was only one of those reliefs which mark the course

*Lively, bright person.

of adversity, and it was not one of the cheerful reliefs. At any other time, either incident would have been an anxiety and care for Mrs. Lapham which she would have found hard to bear; but now she almost welcomed them. At the end of three days Lapham returned, and his wife met him as if nothing unusual had marked their parting; she reserved her atonement for a fitter time; he would know now from the way she acted that she felt all right towards him. He took very little note of her manner, but met his family with an austere quiet that puzzled her, and a sort of pensive dignity that refined his rudeness to an effect that sometimes comes to such natures after long sickness, when the animal strength has been taxed and lowered. He sat silent with her at the table after their girls had left them alone; and seeing that he did not mean to speak, she began to explain why Irene had come home, and to praise her.

"Yes, she done right," said Lapham. "It was time for her to come," he added gently.

Then he was silent again, and his wife told him of Corey's having been there, and of his father's and mother's calling. "I guess Pen's concluded to make it up," she said.

"Well, we'll see about that," said Lapham; and now she could no longer forbear to ask him about his affairs.

"I don't know as I've got any right to know anything about it," she said humbly, with remote allusion to her treatment of him. "But I can't help wanting to know. How *are* things going, Si?"

"Bad," he said, pushing his plate from him, and tilting himself back in his chair. "Or they ain't going at all. They've stopped."

"What do you mean, Si?" she persisted tenderly.

"I've got to the end of my string. To-morrow I shall call a meeting of my creditors, and put myself in their hands. If there's enough left to satisfy them, I'm satisfied." His voice dropped in his throat; he swallowed once or twice, and then did not speak.

"Do you mean that it's all over with you?" she asked fearfully.

He bowed his big head, wrinkled and grizzled; and after a while he said, "It's hard to realize it; but I guess there ain't any doubt about it." He drew a long breath, and then he explained to her about the West Virginia people, and how he had got an extension of the first time they had given him, and had got a man to go up to Lapham with him and look at the works,—a man that had turned up in New

York, and wanted to put money in the business. His money would have enabled Lapham to close with the West Virginians. "The devil was in it, right straight along," said Lapham. "All I had to do was to keep quiet about that other company. It was Rogers and his property right over again. He liked the look of things, and he wanted to go into the business, and he had the money—plenty; it would have saved me with those West Virginia folks. But I had to tell him how I stood. I had to tell him all about it, and what I wanted to do. He began to back water in a minute, and the next morning I saw that it was up with him. He's gone back to New York. I've lost my last chance. Now all I've got to do is to save the pieces."

"Will—will—everything go?" she asked.

"I can't tell yet. But they shall have a chance at everything—every dollar, every cent. I'm sorry for you, Persis—and the girls."

"Oh, don't talk of us!" She was trying to realize that the simple, rude soul to which her heart clove in her youth, but which she had put to such cruel proof with her unsparing conscience and her unsparing tongue, had been equal to its ordeals, and had come out unscathed and unstained. He was able in his talk to make so little of them; he hardly seemed to see what they were; he was apparently not proud of them, and certainly not glad; if they were victories of any sort, he bore them with the patience of defeat. His wife wished to praise him, but she did not know how; so she offered him a little reproach, in which alone she touched the cause of her behavior at parting. "Silas," she asked after a long gaze at him, "why didn't you tell me you had Jim Millon's girl there?"

"I didn't suppose you'd like it, Persis," he answered. "I did intend to tell you at first, but then I put it off. I thought you'd come round some day, and find it out for yourself."

"I'm punished," said his wife, "for not taking enough interest in your business to even come near it. If we're brought back to the day of small things, I guess it's a lesson for me, Silas."

"Oh, I don't know about the lesson," he said wearily.

That night she showed him the anonymous scrawl which had kindled her fury against him. He turned it listlessly over in his hand. "I guess I know who it's from," he said, giving it back to her, "and I guess you do too, Persis."

"But how—how could he———"

"Mebbe he believed it," said Lapham, with patience that cut her more keenly than any reproach. "You did."

Perhaps because the process of his ruin had been so gradual, perhaps because the excitement of preceding events had exhausted their capacity for emotion, the actual consummation of his bankruptcy brought a relief, a repose to Lapham and his family, rather than a fresh sensation of calamity. In the shadow of his disaster they returned to something like their old, united life; they were at least all together again; and it will be intelligible to those whom life has blessed with vicissitude, that Lapham should come home the evening after he had given up everything to his creditors, and should sit down to his supper so cheerful that Penelope could joke him in the old way, and tell him that she thought from his looks they had concluded to pay him a hundred cents on every dollar he owed them.

As James Bellingham had taken so much interest in his troubles from the first, Lapham thought he ought to tell him, before taking the final step, just how things stood with him, and what he meant to do. Bellingham made some futile inquiries about his negotiations with the West Virginians, and Lapham told him they had come to nothing. He spoke of the New York man, and the chance that he might have sold out half his business to him. "But, of course, I had to let him know how it was about those fellows."

"Of course," said Bellingham, not seeing till afterwards the full significance of Lapham's action.

Lapham said nothing about Rogers and the Englishmen. He believed that he had acted right in that matter, and he was satisfied; but he did not care to have Bellingham, or anybody, perhaps think he had been a fool.

All those who were concerned in his affairs said he behaved well, and even more than well, when it came to the worst. The prudence, the good sense, which he had shown in the first years of his success, and of which his great prosperity seemed to have bereft him, came back; and these qualities, used in his own behalf, commended him as much to his creditors as the anxiety he showed that no one should suffer by him; this even made some of them doubtful of his sincerity. They gave him time, and there would have been no trouble in his resuming on the old basis, if the ground had not been cut from under him by the competition of the West Virginia

company. He saw himself that it was useless to try to go on in the old
way, and he preferred to go back and begin the world anew where
he had first begun it, in the hills at Lapham. He put the house at Nankeen Square, with everything else he had, into the payment of his
debts, and Mrs. Lapham found it easier to leave it for the old farm-
stead in Vermont than it would have been to go from that home of
many years to the new house on the water side of Beacon. This thing
and that is embittered to us, so that we may be willing to relinquish
it; the world, life itself, is embittered to most of us, so that we are
glad to have done with them at last; and this home was haunted with
such memories to each of those who abandoned it that to go was less
exile than escape. Mrs. Lapham could not look into Irene's room
without seeing the girl there before her glass, tearing the poor little keepsakes of her hapless fancy from their hiding-places to take
them and fling them in passionate renunciation upon her sister; she
could not come into the sitting-room, where her little ones had
grown up, without starting at the thought of her husband sitting
so many weary nights at his desk there, trying to fight his way back
to hope out of the ruin into which he was slipping. When she remembered that night when Rogers came, she hated the place. Irene
accepted her release from the house eagerly, and was glad to go
before and prepare for the family at Lapham. Penelope was always
ashamed of her engagement there; it must seem better somewhere
else, and she was glad to go too. No one but Lapham, in fact, felt
the pang of parting in all its keenness. Whatever regret the others
had was softened to them by the likeness of their flitting to many
of those removals for the summer which they made in the late
spring when they left Nankeen Square; they were going directly
into the country instead of to the sea-side first; but Lapham, who
usually remained in town long after they had gone, knew all the
difference. For his nerves there was no mechanical sense of coming back; this was as much the end of his proud, prosperous life as
death itself could have been. He was returning to begin life anew,
but he knew, as well as he knew that he should not find his van-
ished youth in his native hills, that it could never again be the
triumph that it had been. That was impossible, not only in his stiff-
ened and weakened forces, but in the very nature of things. He was
going back, by grace of the man whom he owed money, to make

what he could out of the one chance which his successful rivals had left him.

In one phase his paint had held its own against bad times and ruinous competition, and it was with the hope of doing still more with the Persis Brand that he now set himself to work. The West Virginia people confessed that they could not produce those fine grades, and they willingly left the field to him. A strange, not ignoble friendliness existed between Lapham and the three brothers; they had used him fairly; it was their facilities that had conquered him, not their ill-will; and he recognized in them without enmity the necessity to which he had yielded. If he succeeded in his efforts to develop his paint in this direction, it must be for a long time on a small scale compared with his former business, which it could never equal, and he brought to them the flagging energies of an elderly man. He was more broken than he knew by his failure; it did not kill, as it often does, but it weakened the spring once so strong and elastic. He lapsed more and more into acquiescence with his changed condition, and that bragging note of his was rarely sounded. He worked faithfully enough in his enterprise, but sometimes he failed to seize occasions that in his younger days he would have turned to golden account. His wife saw in him a daunted look that made her heart ache for him.

One result of his friendly relations with the West Virginia people was that Corey went in with them, and the fact that he did so solely upon Lapham's advice, and by means of his recommendation, was perhaps the Colonel's proudest consolation. Corey knew the business thoroughly, and after half a year at Kanawha Falls and in the office at New York, he went out to Mexico and Central America, to see what could be done for them upon the ground which he had theoretically studied with Lapham.

Before he went he came up to Vermont, and urged Penelope to go with him. He was to be first in the city of Mexico, and if his mission was successful he was to be kept there and in South America several years, watching the new railroad enterprises and the development of mechanical agriculture and whatever other undertakings offered an opening for the introduction of the paint. They were all young men together, and Corey, who had put his money into the company, had a proprietary interest in the success which they were eager to achieve.

"There's no more reason now and no less than ever there was," mused Penelope, in counsel with her mother, "why I should say Yes, or why I should say No. Everything else changes, but this is just where it was a year ago. It don't go backward, and it don't go forward. Mother, I believe I shall take the bit in my teeth—if anybody will put it there!"

"It isn't the same as it was," suggested her mother. "You can see that Irene's all over it."

"That's no credit to me," said Penelope. "I ought to be just as much ashamed as ever."

"You no need ever to be ashamed."

"That's true, too," said the girl. "And I can sneak off to Mexico with a good conscience if I could make up my mind to it." She laughed. "Well, if I could be *sentenced* to be married, or somebody would up and forbid the banns! I don't know what to do about it."

Her mother left her to carry her hesitation back to Corey, and she said now they had better go all over it and try to reason it out. "And I hope that whatever I do, it won't be for my own sake, but for—others!"

Corey said he was sure of that, and looked at her with eyes of patient tenderness.

"I don't say it is wrong," she proceeded, rather aimlessly, "but I can't make it seem right. I don't know whether I can make you understand, but the idea of being happy, when everybody else is so miserable, is more than I can endure. It makes me wretched."

"Then perhaps that's your share of the common suffering," suggested Corey, smiling.

"Oh, you know it isn't! You know it's nothing. Oh! One of the reasons is what I told you once before, that as long as father is in trouble I can't let you think of me. Now that he's lost everything————" She bent her eyes inquiringly upon him, as if for the effect of this argument.

"I don't think that's a very good reason," he answered seriously, but smiling still. "Do you believe me when I tell you that I love you?"

"Why, I suppose I must," she said, dropping her eyes.

"Then why shouldn't I think all the more of you on account of your father's loss? You didn't suppose I cared for you because he was prosperous?" There was a shade of reproach, ever so delicate and gentle, in his smiling question, which she felt.

"No, I couldn't think such a thing of you. I—I don't know what I meant. I meant that————" She could not go on and say that she had felt herself more worthy of him because of her father's money; it would not have been true; yet there was no other explanation. She stopped and cast a helpless glance at him.

He came to her aid. "I understand why you shouldn't wish me to suffer by your father's misfortunes."

"Yes, that was it; and there is too great a difference every way. We ought to look at that again. You mustn't pretend that you don't know it, for that wouldn't be true. Your mother will never like me, and perhaps—perhaps I shall not like her."

"Well," said Corey, a little daunted, "you won't have to marry my family."

"Ah, that isn't the point!"

"I know it," he admitted. "I won't pretend that I don't see what you mean; but I'm sure that all the differences would disappear when you came to know my family better. I'm not afraid but you and my mother will like each other—she can't help it!" he exclaimed, less judicially than he had hitherto spoken, and he went on to urge some points of doubtful tenability. "We have our ways, and you have yours; and while I don't say but what you and my mother and sisters would be a little strange together at first, it would soon wear off on both sides. There can't be anything hopelessly different in you all, and if there were it wouldn't be any difference to me."

"Do you think it would be pleasant to have you on my side against your mother?"

"There won't be any sides. Tell me just what it is you're afraid of."

"Afraid?"

"Thinking of, then."

"I don't know. It isn't anything they say or do," she explained, with her eyes intent on his. "It's what they are. I couldn't be natural with them, and if I can't be natural with people, I'm disagreeable."

"Can you be natural with me?"

"Oh, I'm not afraid of you. I never was. That was the trouble from the beginning."

"Well, then, that's all that's necessary. And it never was the least trouble to me!"

"It made me untrue to Irene."

"You mustn't say that! You were always true to her."

"She cared for you first."

"Well, but I never cared for her at all!" he besought her.

"She thought you did."

"That was nobody's fault, and I can't let you make it yours. My dear————"

"Wait. We must understand each other," said Penelope, rising from her seat to prevent an advance he was making from his; "I want you to realize the whole affair. Should you want a girl who hadn't a cent in the world, and felt different in your mother's company, and had cheated and betrayed her own sister?"

"I want you!"

"Very well, then, you can't have me. I should always despise myself. I ought to give you up for all these reasons. Yes, I must." She looked at him intently, and there was a tentative quality in her affirmations.

"Is this your answer?" he said. "I must submit. If I asked too much of you, I was wrong. And—good-bye."

He held out his hand, and she put hers in it. "You think I'm capricious and fickle!" she said. "I can't help it—I don't know myself. I can't keep to one thing for half a day at a time. But it's right for us to part—yes, it must be. It must be," she repeated; "and I shall try to remember that. Good-bye! I will try to keep that in my mind, and you will too—you won't care, very soon! I didn't mean that—no; I know how true you are; but you will soon look at me differently, and see that even if there hadn't been this about Irene, I was not the one for you. You do think so, don't you?" she pleaded, clinging to his hand. "I am not at all what they would like—your family; I felt that. I am little, and black, and homely, and they don't understand my way of talking, and now that we've lost everything————No, I'm not fit. Good-bye. You're quite right not to have patience with me any longer. I've tried you enough. I ought to be willing to marry you against their wishes if you want me to, but I can't make the sacrifice—I'm too selfish for that." All at once she flung herself on his breast. "I can't even give you up! I shall never dare look any one in the face again. Go, go! But take me with you! I tried to do without you! I gave it a fair trial, and it was a dead failure. Oh, poor Irene! How could she give you up?"

Corey went back to Boston immediately, and left Penelope, as he must, to tell her sister that they were to be married. She was spared from the first advance toward this by an accident or a misunderstanding. Irene came straight to her after Corey was gone, and demanded, "Penelope Lapham, have you been such a ninny as to send that man away on my account?"

Penelope recoiled from this terrible courage; she did not answer directly, and Irene went on, "Because if you did, I'll thank you to bring him back again. I'm not going to have him thinking that I'm dying for a man that never cared for me. It's insulting, and I'm not going to stand it. Now, you just send for him!"

"Oh, I will, 'Rene," gasped Penelope. And then she added, shamed out of her prevarication by Irene's haughty magnanimity, "I have. That is—he's coming back———"

Irene looked at her a moment, and then, whatever thought was in her mind, said fiercely, "Well!" and left her to her dismay—her dismay and her relief, for they both knew that this was the last time they should ever speak of that again.

The marriage came after so much sorrow and trouble, and the fact was received with so much misgiving for the past and future, that it brought Lapham none of the triumph in which he had once exulted at the thought of an alliance with the Coreys. Adversity had so far been his friend that it had taken from him all hope of the social success for which people crawl and truckle, and restored him, through failure and doubt and heartache, the manhood which his prosperity had so nearly stolen from him. Neither he nor his wife thought now that their daughter was marrying a Corey; they thought only that she was giving herself to the man who loved her, and their acquiescence was sobered still further by the presence of Irene. Their hearts were far more with her.

Again and again Mrs. Lapham said she did not see how she could go through it. "I can't make it seem right," she said.

"It is right," steadily answered the Colonel.

"Yes, I know. But it don't seem so."

It would be easy to point out traits in Penelope's character which finally reconciled all her husband's family and endeared her to them. These things continually happen in novels; and the Coreys, as they had always promised themselves to do, made the best, and not the worst, of Tom's marriage.

They were people who could value Lapham's behavior as Tom reported it to them. They were proud of him, and Bromfield Corey, who found a delicate, æsthetic pleasure in the heroism with which Lapham had withstood Rogers and his temptations,—something finely dramatic and unconsciously effective,—wrote him a letter which would once have flattered the rough soul almost to ecstasy, though now he affected to slight it in showing it. "It's all right if it makes it more comfortable for Pen," he said to his wife.

But the differences remained uneffaced, if not uneffaceable, between the Coreys and Tom Corey's wife. "If he had only married the Colonel!" subtly suggested Nanny Corey.

There was a brief season of civility and forbearance on both sides, when he brought her home before starting for Mexico, and her father-in-law made a sympathetic feint of liking Penelope's way of talking, but it is questionable if even he found it so delightful as her husband did. Lily Corey made a little, ineffectual sketch of her, which she put by with other studies to finish up some time, and found her rather picturesque in some ways. Nanny got on with her better than the rest, and saw possibilities for her in the country to which she was going. "As she's quite unformed socially," she explained to her mother, "there is a chance that she will form herself on the Spanish manner, if she stays there long enough, and that when she comes back she will have the charm of not olives, perhaps, but *tortillas*, whatever they are: something strange and foreign, even if it's borrowed. I'm glad she's going to Mexico. At that distance we can—correspond."

Her mother sighed, and said bravely that she was sure they all got on very pleasantly as it was, and that she was perfectly satisfied if Tom was.

There was, in fact, much truth in what she said of their harmony with Penelope. Having resolved, from the beginning, to make the best of the worst, it might almost be said that they were supported and consoled in their good intentions by a higher power. This marriage had not, thanks to an overruling Providence, brought the succession of Lapham teas upon Bromfield Corey which he had dreaded; the Laphams were far off in their native fastnesses, and neither Lily nor Nanny Corey was obliged to sacrifice herself to the conversation of Irene; they were not even called upon to make a social demonstration for Penelope at a time when, most people being still out of town, it would have been so easy; she and Tom had both begged that there might be nothing of that kind; and though none of the Coreys learned to know her very well in the week she spent with them, they did not find it hard to get on with her. There were even moments when Nanny Corey, like her father, had glimpses of what Tom had called her humor, but it was perhaps too unlike their own to be easily recognizable.

Whether Penelope, on her side, found it more difficult to harmonize, I cannot say. She had much more of the harmonizing to do, since they were four to one; but then she had gone through so much greater trials before. When the door of their carriage closed and it drove off with her and husband to the station, she fetched a long sigh.

"What is it?" asked Corey, who ought to have known better.

"Oh, nothing. I don't think I shall feel strange amongst the Mexicans now."

He looked at her with a puzzled smile, which grew a little graver, and then he put his arm round her and drew her closer to him. This made her cry on his shoulder. "I only meant that I should have you all to myself." There is no proof that she meant more, but it is certain that our manners and customs go for more in life than our qualities. The price that we pay for civilization is the fine yet impassable differentiation of these. Perhaps we pay too much; but it will not be possible to persuade those who have the difference in their favor that this is so. They may be right; and at any rate the blank misgiving, the recurring sense of disappointment to which the young people's departure left the Coreys is to be considered. That was the end of their son and brother for them; they felt that; and they were not mean or unamiable people.

He remained three years away. Some changes took place in that time. One of these was the purchase by the Kanawha Falls Company of the mines and works at Lapham. The transfer relieved Lapham of the load of debt which he was still laboring under, and gave him an interest in the vaster enterprise of the younger men, which he had once vainly hoped to grasp all in his own hand. He began to tell of this coincidence as something very striking; and pushing on more actively the special branch of the business left to him, he bragged, quite in his old way, of its enormous extension. His son-in-law, he said, was pushing it in Mexico and Central America: an idea that they had originally had in common. Well, young blood was what was wanted in a thing of that kind. Now, those fellows out in West Virginia: all young, and a perfect team!

For himself, he owned that he had made mistakes; he could see just where the mistakes were—put his finger right on them. But one thing he could say: he had been no man's enemy but his own; every dollar, every cent had gone to pay his debts; he had come out with clean hands. He said all this, and much more, to Mr. Sewell the summer after he sold out, when the minister and his wife stopped at Lapham on their way across from the White Mountains to Lake Champlain; Lapham had found them on the cars, and pressed them to stop off.

There were times when Mrs. Lapham had as great pride in the clean-handedness with which Lapham had come out as he had himself, but her satisfaction was not so constant. At those times, knowing the temptations he had resisted, she thought him the noblest and grandest of men; but no woman could endure to live in the same house with a perfect hero, and there were other times when she reminded him that if he had kept his word to her about speculating in stocks, and had looked after the insurance of his property half as carefully as he had looked after a couple of worthless women who had no earthly claim on him, they would not be where they were now. He humbly admitted it all, and left her to think of Rogers herself. She did not fail to do so, and the thought did not fail to restore him to her tenderness again.

I do not know how it is that clergymen and physicians keep from telling their wives the secrets confided to them; perhaps they can trust their wives to find them out for themselves whenever they wish. Sewell had laid before his wife the case of the Laphams after they came to consult with him about Corey's proposal to Penelope, for he wished to be confirmed in his belief that he had advised them soundly; but he had not given her their names, and he had not known Corey's himself. Now he had no compunctions in talking the affair over with her without the veil of ignorance which she had hitherto assumed, for she declared that as soon as she heard of Corey's engagement to Penelope, the whole thing had flashed upon her. "And that night at dinner, I could have told the child that he was in love with her sister by the way he talked about her; I heard him; and if she had not been so blindly in love with him herself, she would have known it too. I must say, I can't help feeling a sort of contempt for her sister."

"Oh, but you must not!" cried Sewell. "That is wrong, cruelly wrong. I'm sure that's out of your novel-reading, my dear, and not out of your heart. Come! it grieves me to hear you say such a thing as that."

"Oh, I dare say this pretty thing has got over it—how much character she has got!—and I suppose she'll see somebody else."

Sewell had to content himself with this partial concession. As a matter of fact, unless it was the young West Virginian who had come on to arrange the purchase of the Works, Irene had not yet seen any one, and whether there was ever anything between them is a fact that would need a separate inquiry. It is certain that at the end of five years after the disappointment which she met so bravely, she was still unmarried. But she was even then still very young, and her life at Lapham had been varied by visits to the West. It had also been varied by an invitation, made with the politest resolution by Mrs. Corey, to visit in Boston, which the girl was equal to refusing in the same spirit.

Sewell was intensely interested in the moral spectacle which Lapham presented under his changed conditions. The Colonel, who was more the Colonel in those hills than he could ever have been on the Back Bay, kept him and Mrs. Sewell over night at his house; and he showed the minister minutely round the Works and drove him all over his farm. For this expedition he employed a lively colt which had not yet come of age, and an open buggy long past its prime, and was no more ashamed of his turnout than of the finest he had ever driven on the Milldam. He was rather shabby and slovenly in dress, and he had fallen unkempt, after the country fashion, as to his hair and beard and boots. The house was plain, and was furnished with the simpler movables out of the house in Nankeen Square. There were certainly all the necessaries, but no luxuries, unless the statues of Prayer and Faith might be so considered. The Laphams now burned kerosene, of course, and they had no furnace in the winter; these were the only hardships the Colonel complained of; but he said that as soon as the company got to paying dividends again,— he was evidently proud of the outlays that for the present prevented this,—he should put in steam-heat and naphtha-gas. He spoke freely of his failure, and with a confidence that seemed inspired by his former trust in Sewell, whom, indeed, he treated like an intimate friend, rather than an acquaintance of two or three meetings. He went back to his first connection with Rogers, and he put before Sewell hypothetically his own conclusions in regard to the matter.

"Sometimes," he said, "I get to thinking it all over, and it seems to me I done wrong about Rogers in the first place; that the whole trouble came from that. It was just like starting a row of bricks. I tried to catch up, and stop 'em from going, but they all tumbled, one after another. It wa'n't in the nature of things that they could be stopped till the last brick went. I don't talk much with my wife any more about it; but I should like to know how it strikes you."

"We can trace the operation of evil in the physical world," replied the minister, "but I'm more and more puzzled about it in the moral world. There its course is often so very obscure; and often it seems to involve, so far as we can see, no penalty whatever. And in your own case, as I understand, you don't admit—you don't feel sure—that you ever actually did wrong this man."

"Well, no; I don't. That is to say————"

He did not continue, and after a while Sewell said, with that subtle kindness of his, "I should be inclined to think—nothing can be thrown quite away; and it can't be that our sins only weaken us— that your fear of having possibly behaved selfishly toward this man kept you on your guard, and strengthened you when you were brought face to face with a greater"—he was going to say temptation, but he saved Lapham's pride, and said—"emergency."

"Do you think so?"

"I think that there may be truth in what I suggest."

"Well, I don't know what it was," said Lapham; "all I know is that when it came to the point, although I could see that I'd got to go under unless I did it, that I couldn't sell out to those Englishmen, and I couldn't let that man put his money into my business without I told him just how things stood."

As Sewell afterwards told his wife, he could see that the loss of his fortune had been a terrible trial to Lapham, just because his prosperity had been so gross and palpable; and he had now a burning desire to know exactly how, at the bottom of his heart, Lapham still felt. "And do you ever have any regrets?" he delicately inquired of him.

"About what I done? Well, it don't always seem as if I done it," replied Lapham. "Seems sometimes as if it was a hole opened for me, and I crept out of it. I don't know," he added thoughtfully, biting the corner of his stiff mustache—"I don't know as I should always say it paid; but if I done it, and the thing was to do over again, right in the same way, I guess I should have to do it."

THE END

ENDNOTES

1. (p. 10) *Back Bay!*: This section of Boston, west of the Boston Commons and newly fashionable at the time, is where Lapham is building his new house. It was created by filling in the muddy tidal flats of the Charles River and hence was called the New Land.

2. (p. 12) *his troubles with Marcia had seriously begun*: Howells's earlier novel *A Modern Instance* (1882) centered on the marriage, the growing discord, and finally the divorce of Bartley Hubbard and his wife, Marcia. The present novel, set in the late 1870s, precedes this bitter outcome.

3. (p. 19) *Daisy Millerism*: Henry James's highly popular short novel *Daisy Miller* (1878) led to a controversy about its portrayal of a headstrong, independent-minded young American girl touring Rome, who dies after contracting a fever amid the ruins of the Roman Forum.

4. (p. 25) *the novel point of view which they were acquiring*: Following this sentence in the serial version in *Century* magazine, there is a passage in which the Laphams discuss whether, as she has heard (from Tom Corey), the value of their property has declined because wealthy Jews have moved into the neighborhood. This raised objections from Jewish readers, such as Cyrus L. Sulzberger, the editor of the *American Hebrew*, who felt that it contributed to prejudice. Howells responded that he had already cut the passage from the book version (after hearing other objections) but thought he deserved an apology, since he had intended it as a *rebuke* to prejudice. "My irony seems to have fallen short of the mark," he wrote. "So far short that you are not the first Hebrew to accuse me of 'pandering' to the stupid and cruel feeling against your race and religion. . . . I merely recognized to rebuke it, the existence of a feeling which civilized men should be ashamed of." The lines removed read as follows:

> It was something that Mrs. Lapham especially submitted to her husband when they got home; she asked him if it were true, and if it made any difference.

"It makes a difference in the price of property," replied the Colonel, promptly. "But as long as we don't want to sell, it don't matter."

"Why, Silas Lapham," said his wife, "do you mean to tell me that this house is worth less than we gave for it?"

"It's worth a good deal less. You see, they *have* got in— and pretty thick, too—it's no use denying it. And when they get in, they send down the price of the property. Of course, there ain't any sense in it; I think it's all dumn foolishness. It's cruel, and folks ought to be ashamed. But there it is. You tell folks that the Savior himself was one, and the twelve apostles, and all the prophets,—I don't know but what Adam was— guess, he *was*,—and it don't make a bit of difference. They send down the price of real estate. Prices begin to shade when the first one gets in.

Mrs. Lapham thought the facts over a few moments. "Well, what do we care, so long as we're comfortable in our home? And they're just as nice and as good neighbors as can be."

"Oh, it's all right as far as I'm concerned," said Lapham. "Who did you say those people were who stirred you up about it?"

Mrs. Lapham repeated their name.

The best discussion of these revisions and their significance is by Kermit Vanderbilt, *William Dean Howells: A Reinterpretation*, pp. 116–126 (see "For Further Reading"). Howells's exchange of letters with Cyrus L. Sulzberger can be found in *The Rise of Silas Lapham*, edited by Don L. Cook, pp. 342–344.

5. (p. 29) *"They say it's unhealthy over there"*: There were rumors that the once-swampy landfill where Lapham was building his new home was an unhealthy place, though it was becoming quite fashionable. In the serial version in *Century* magazine this exchange was even stronger. Mrs. Lapham says: "Where is your lot? In the Diphtheria District?" Silas replies: "No, it ain't in the Diphtheria District . . . and I guess there's more diphtheria in the name than anything else, anyway." Perhaps Howells toned this down to avoid alarming or offending the residents of Back Bay.

6. (p. 30) *The Colonel . . . instilled into her mind:* This sentence replaced a second passage about Jews that was cut after appearing in the serial version. Mrs. Lapham is speaking:

> "A Mr. Liliengarten has bought the Gordon house across the square," she said, thoughtfully.
> "Well, I'm agreeable. I suppose he's got the money to pay for it."
> "Oh, yes, they've all got money," sighed Mrs. Lapham.

7. (p. 181) *applying dynamite:* The editor and publisher of *Century* magazine, where the novel was first serialized, strongly objected to this reference, which they associated with anarchism, terrorism, and threats to private property. The phrase was changed to "personally affronting" in the *Century* version but slightly strengthened to "offering personal violence" in the book version, which was how it read until the original text was restored in 1971.

INSPIRED BY
THE RISE OF SILAS LAPHAM

In *The Rise of Silas Lapham* (1885), William Dean Howells captured the essence of the self-made businessman at a time when such men and their families were rising in prominence in American society. Nineteenth-century America, unencumbered by a titled aristocracy and invigorated by the notion that all men are created equal, was a fertile ground for plucky upstarts trying to transcend modest economic origins. In the March 1917 issue of the *Atlantic Monthly*, Wilson and Helen Thomas Follett heralded Silas Lapham as the prototypical self-made man:

> *The Rise of Silas Lapham*, our first and best analysis of a self-made man and of the social implications of his money, is a tragedy whose significance reaches nearly the whole of self-made America. Written at the nexus of so many tendencies and interests, the novel remains to-day as poignantly contemporary as ever, a drama of transitions not yet more than half accomplished. We clamor still for 'the great American novel'? Why, we have been reading it these thirty years and more.

Since *Silas Lapham*'s publication, the novel of the self-made businessman—chronicling his rise and frequently his fall—has become a staple of American letters. As America continues to dominate the global economy, the novel of the self-made businessman stands firm as a representative national genre.

The self-made man had a place in American literature before Howells's Lapham codified the type. Following the Civil War, Horatio Alger achieved staggering success with his novel *Ragged Dick* (1868), the story of an orphaned bootblack who rises to great material prosperity. Though a mediocre writer at best, Alger authored more than one hundred novels. He was immensely popular and influential in America and sold some twenty million copies of his books. Another early novel of society featuring a businessman as its protagonist is Henry James's The American (1877), though it operates on a different plane of shrewdness and sophistication. The American uses the world of commerce as a backdrop rather than as its primary material, as the fabulously wealthy and good-natured Christopher Newman retires from business, and from America, to seek a wife among the idle nobility in Europe.

A new generation of business-oriented novels appeared in America as the twentieth century began. Booth Tarkington's The Magnificent Ambersons (1918) traces the fortunes of the richest family in a growing midwestern town, focusing on the life of George Amberson Minafer, gentleman and grandson of a man who made an immense fortune in land speculation. Woefully oblivious to the changes industrialization has set in motion, Minafer allows the Amberson legacy to decline precipitously. Tarkington's novel, a best-seller in its day, won the Pulitzer Prize in Literature in 1919 and was adapted into a vivid and appealing film by Orson Welles in 1942.

Sinclair Lewis railed against the staleness of middle-class values in Babbitt (1922), his novel about a successful real-estate agent and respected member of the community in the midwestern town of Zenith. When the title character's only friend is arrested for shooting his wife, Babbitt begins to question his own pattern of conformity. He flirts with rebellion, has an extramarital affair, and declines to join the Good Citizen's League, but a fear of ostracism causes him to repent his brief indiscretions. Scared into submission himself, Babbitt encourages his son to lead a full and independent life.

Eight years after the Folletts called Howells's book the representative text of the self-made businessman, F. Scott Fitzgerald published The Great Gatsby (1925), a work often cited as "the great American novel." The tender, elegiac novel follows the strangely dispassionate Nick Carraway as he cautiously befriends his new neighbor, a disconcerting millionaire named Jay Gatsby. Having amassed a fortune through mysterious and possibly illicit means, Gatsby throws lavish get-togethers every weekend at his Long Island mansion in an attempt to impress the girl who once spurned him.

No discussion of the perils of success would be complete without mention of Citizen Kane (1941), Orson Welles's masterful, innovative directorial debut, in which Welles also starred. Loosely based on the life of newspaper magnate William Randolph Hearst, Citizen Kane probes the personality of the megalomaniac Charles Foster Kane, who has risen from humble beginnings to rule a media empire yet is nagged by a sense of emptiness. Kane is not strictly a self-made man, since he inherits his fortune, but wealth tempts him to exert control over everyone around him. The iconic opening scene features Kane on his deathbed, a snow globe tumbling from his hand as he utters his mysterious dying word: "Rosebud." The movie, stunning in its technical achievements, has influenced generations of film-makers. In 1998 the American Film Institute rated Citizen Kane number one on its list of greatest American movies of all time.

COMMENTS & QUESTIONS

In this section, we aim to provide the reader with an array of perspectives on the text, as well as questions that challenge those perspectives. The commentary has been culled from sources as diverse as reviews contemporaneous with the work, letters written by the author, literary criticism of later generations, and appreciations written throughout the work's history. Following the commentary, a series of questions seeks to filter The Rise of Silas Lapham *through a variety of points of view and bring about a richer understanding of this enduring work.*

Comments

LITERARY WORLD

The extraordinary impression made by Mr. Howells's history of *The Rise of Silas Lapham* as it appeared from month to month in serial form is more than justified now that we have it before us in its entirety, and are better able to analyze the sources of its unmistakable strength. That its artistic merit rises above any previous work of the author is indisputable. It has the fresh, unsparing, almost pitiless realism of *A Modern Instance*, but it touches throughout a higher plane. In tracing the career of this typical "self-made" American, Mr. Howells omits nothing. All that is crude, hard, and forbidding in his surroundings is portrayed with a fidelity that never wavers; his physical unattractiveness is always insisted on; none of his rude ancestral traits and native awkwardness of body, speech, and thought are glossed over. Uncouth, self-assertive, endowed with a primitive energy of purpose akin to the forces of nature, eager to get and to spend, careless about the minor morals, but with an underlying stratum of honesty in his character able to sustain him in great emergencies, Silas Lapham stands before us a definite creation, a specialized example of a widely existent type. There is no superficial portraiture in this the finest of Mr. Howells's *dramatis personae*—no working from the outside. This keen, far-reaching insight never wavers; every motive is laid bare; all the hesitations, the struggles, the obstinate determinations,

are revealed in the mirror-like text, with an accompanying glow of
humor that brings out clearly every line and mark—that grim, fatal-
istic humor latent in every Yankee, but which no other novelist has
ever succeeded in transferring to his pages undimmed.

But Silas Lapham is something more than the leading personage
in a cleverly contrived story. He is the protagonist in a great moral
drama as impressive in its inevitableness as a Greek tragedy. And here
is the real strength of the book. It discerns and emphasizes the moral
element which exists in every phase of poor humanity. It recognizes
that innate desire, weak in some but never wholly wanting, the desire "to do better," the yearning, often vague and unexpressed, yet
still a germ of possible effort, to place its possessor on the side of
what makes for righteousness. It is this discernment and expression
of the truth that art of vital and permanent value can only be attained
by a recognition of the underlying moral forces, that constitutes
Mr. Howells's triumph. . . .

We have spoken of Mr. Howells's humor, and if in closing we
refer to it once more, it is because of that most delightful of persons
Bromfield Corey, who at the other extreme from Silas Lapham is a no
less accurate synthesis, emphasizing the range of the author's art. If
we denominated Mr. Howells's method as almost pitiless, we did so
having in mind its fidelity. The pitilessness is there, but there is another essential element, the "beneficent quality," as a French man of
letters has described it, "the beneficent quality of charity." Humanity
with its faults and foibles, Mr. Howells delineates as he sees it, with
never a touch of unkindly satire to mar the faithfulness of the representation. The sympathy of genius is in what he writes, the sympathy that says, I also am one of you. How much nobler an inspiration
this is than the spirit of detraction and caricature, one has only to
compare The Rise of Silas Lapham with the work of some other novelists
of the day to be convinced. Art that is based on a sympathetic appreciation of its subject-matter may be of greater or lesser moment according to the capacity of the artist, but it alone is the art that
endures.   —September 5, 1885

WASHINGTON POST
Take it all together, [The Rise of Silas Lapham] is a book to read with a
great deal of pleasure and to be laid down, after being read, with

much disappointment. It can hardly, with propriety, be called a novel, for it has so slight a story. It is really a series of suggestions for character and social studies, bound together by an attenuated narrative.

—September 6, 1885

NEW YORK TIMES

With his usual skill Mr. Howells has put his hand on a typical American business man of the New England variety. Silas Lapham in his crudeness and shrewdness, his good-heartedness in the family relation, and his cruelty in business relations; in his ostentation and secret fear of defect from a lack of early advantages, gathers up in himself the traits of many self-made men of our cities and towns.

—September 27, 1885

HJALMAR HJORTH BOYESEN

Literature is the autobiography of the race, and that part of it which is not autobiographic in the sense of being contemporary is of inferior value.

It is the contemporaneousness of Howells which constitutes one of his chief charms. He sees life as we all see it, and he wears no obscuring or embellishing literary spectacles. That good-natured disrespect toward the past, that humorous tolerance of amusing shams, that large-hearted sympathy and kindliness toward all humanity, which are the most characteristic qualities of the American people, have never before found so typical a representative in American literature. The temperamental keynote which sounds through the score of novels that bear his name is a very sweet one. He has the courage of his convictions, and can fight for them right valiantly when occasion demands. But his critical savagery, though full of ardor, is without hate. He has thrown off the last fetters of intellectual allegiance which marked and yet marks our provincial relation to England; and he has spoken frankly and bravely what hundreds of us have thought, but have not dared to say. However much the English may resent his candor, we, as Americans, ought to be grateful to him for it. For surely, if we could realize how this undue respect for British models and British opinion hampers our artistic and literary progress, we would assert our intellectual enfranchisement as vigorously as we are maintaining our political independence. We are a vast, composite nation, and though we owe much to England we are no longer in any real sense merely a transplanted sprout of the British race. Accordingly, English traditions and English judgments become, year by year, less applicable with us, and it is only a question of time when we shall have nothing but the language in common, and even that in modified form. What a delightful gallery of truly American character heads Mr. Howells' novels do contain! First and foremost comes Silas Lapham, than whom I know no more American figure in American literature. His sanguine temper, his indefatigable enterprise, his social insecurity, his ambition and his generosity are but the rudimentary outlines of a portrait which is most beautifully realized and finished with the most delicate modelling. Where in American fiction do we find more exquisite workmanship than is displayed in the portraits of Lydia Blood in The Lady of Aroostook, Mrs. Vervain, Florida Vervain and Don Ippolito in A Foregone Conclusion, or in that beautiful specimen of sweet, generous but raw girlhood, Imogene in An Indian Summer.

It is needless to multiply examples. Our memory is crowded with characters equally vivid, all individualized with that delicate distinctness which is the mark of a high and mature art. It is not to be expected, of course, that this verdict will be accepted by the many who yet clamor for the heroic and demand of the novelist that he shall give them something better and more "elevating" than the "sordid" and familiar reality which surrounds them. Mr. Howells does not believe that any man can invent anything which is better and more elevating than reality, if studied and interpreted with a conscientious desire to arrive at the truth. He does not appeal to the crude appetite for wonder tales. He does not arouse what Mr. Henry James calls "the pleasure of surprise" but "the pleasure of recognition." And to our mind the latter is the nobler, maturer and more enduring pleasure.   —from Cosmopolitan (February 1892)

AMBROSE BIERCE
The master of this detestable school of literature [that is, realism] is Mr. Howells. Absolutely destitute of that supreme and sufficient literary endowment, imagination, he does not what he would but what he can; takes notes with his eyes and ears, and writes them up as does any other reporter.

He can tell nothing that he has not seen or heard, and in his personal progress through rectangular streets and between trim hedges of Philistia, with lettered old maids of his acquaintance courtesying from doorways, he has seen and heard nothing worth telling.

—from the *New York Times* (May 23, 1892)

BRANDER MATTHEWS
Mr. Howells's plea and protest was straightforward and plain spoken. The novelist should deal truthfully with his material, which is human life in all its breadth and in all its depth. He should not sophisticate it nor should he in any wise attempt to idealize it. He is to be a witness sworn to tell the truth, the whole truth, and nothing but the truth. "The object of a novel should be to charm through a faithful representation of human actions and human passions, and to create by this fidelity to nature a beautiful work"—according to the pertinent dictum which Mr. Howells translated from Señor Valera. The novelist should deal with the mean of human life, and not with the exceptional, the abnormal, the monstrous, or else he will surely violate just proportion and present but a distorted vision of the world as it really is.

Above all, he will set up no false ideas of self-sacrifice, of heroism, of strength, of passion; for who is the novelist that he shall presume to improve upon human nature as it is? It was Emerson who said with his pithy shrewdness that "the foolish man wonders at the unusual, but the wise man at the usual"; and Carlyle it was who declared that for grown persons reality was the only genuine romance. The novelist must beware of begetting high-strung and supersensitive ideals of life which falsify the simpler and saner ideals. He must refrain from the wild, the visionary, the exaggerated, the freakish. He must deal with man as he sees him and with woman as he sees her; observing carefully, with whatever insight and imagination he may have, and then recording faithfully the things of good report and the things of evil report. He must keep his pages free from the hectic flush, which follows when passion is exalted above principle. Though he must needs show sin and sorrow and suffering, he can never palter with the everlasting standards of right and wrong.

—from *Forum* (January 1902)

MARK TWAIN

For forty years [Howells's] English has been to me a continual delight and astonishment. In the sustained exhibition of certain great
qualities—clearness, compression, verbal exactness, and unforced
and seemingly unconscious felicity of phrasing—he is, in my belief,
without his peer in the English-writing world.

—from *Harper's Monthly* (July 1906)

VAN WYCK BROOKS

Mr. William Dean Howells has never surprised anybody, thrilled anybody, shocked anybody. His career and his works alike seem devoid
of inspired moments. He has never written a bad sentence, never
struck a false note. To great numbers of people, he is simply "unin-
teresting." Nevertheless, there is a curious paradox in his position.
The very people who would be first to call his work mediocre are
those who instinctively recognize in him a unique distinction. He is,
in fact, a very great and very choice artist—"one of the chief honors
of our literature,"—Lowell called him. His light is the light of common day. He has pictured nothing remote, fantastic, tragic. It is only
rare minds who are impressed by common things. Ordinary people
are not interested in ferry-boats and office-desks and knitting-needles,
and yet these are really the true, immediate, actual things that make up
life. Mr. Howells is interested in these things, and, therefore, his audience is small. But it is picked, constant.

—from *World's Work* (May 1909)

HENRY JAMES

It was impossible, I think, to be in more instinctive and informed
possession of the general truth of your subject than you happily
found yourself. The *real* affair of the American case and character, as
it met your view and brushed your sensibility, that was what inspired
and attached you, and, heedless of foolish flurries from other quarters, of all wild or weak slashings of the air and wavings in the void,
you gave yourself to it with an incorruptible faith. You saw your field
with a rare lucidity: you say all it had to give in the way of the
romance of the real and the interest and the thrill and the charm of
the common, as one may put it; the character and the comedy, the
point, the pathos, the tragedy, the particular homegrown humanity

under your eyes and your hand and with which the life all about you was closely interknitted. Your hand reached out to these things with a fondness that was in itself a literary gift and played with them as the artist only and always can play: freely, quaintly, incalculably, with all the assurance of his fancy and his irony, and yet with that fine taste for the truth and the pity and the meaning of the matter which keeps the temper of the observation both sharp and sweet.

—from a letter to Howells, printed in the
North American Review (April 1912)

JOHN A. MACY

If in his many books Mr. Howells has not had a great deal to say that is significant, he has said everything he meant in an unimprovable manner.   —from The Spirit of American Literature (1913)

H. L. MENCKEN

The profound dread and agony of life, the surge of passion and aspiration, the grand crash and glitter of things, the tragedy that runs eternally under the surface—all this the critic of the future will seek in vain in Dr. Howells' elegant and shallow volumes. And seeking it in vain, he will probably dismiss all of them together with fewer words than he gives to "Huckleberry Finn."

Already, indeed, the Howells legend tends to become a mere legend, and empty of all genuine significance. Who actually reads Howells' novels? Who even remembers their names? "The Minister's Charge," "An Imperative Duty," "The Unexpected Guests," "Out of the Question," "No Love Lost"—these titles are already as meaningless as a roll of Sumerian kings. Perhaps "The Rise of Silas Lapham" survives—but go read it if you would tumble downstairs. The truth about Howells is that he really has nothing to say, for all the charm he gets into saying it. His psychology is superficial, amateurish, often nonsensical; his irony is scarcely more than a polite facetiousness; his characters simply refuse to live. No figure even remotely comparable to Norris' McTeague or Dreiser's Frank Cowperwood is to be encountered in his novels. He is quite unequal to any such evocation of the race-spirit, of the essential conflict of forces among us, of the peculiar drift and color of American life. The world he moves in is suburban, caged, flabby. He could no more have written the last

chapters of "Lord Jim" than he could have written the Book of
Mark. . . .

Somehow, he seems blissfully ignorant that life is a serious business, and full of mystery; it is a sort of college town *Weltanschauung*
that one finds in him. . . . If he actually tries, like Conrad, "to make
you hear, to make you feel—before all, to make you *see*," then he fails
almost completely. One often suspects, indeed, that he doesn't really
feel or see himself.   —From *Prejudices: First Series* (1919)

C. HARTLEY GRATTAN
Though [Howells] was vaguely disquieted both by his personal
position and by social conditions, he never clearly analyzed either.
He accepted the tolerance of a society he could not, in his more
thoughtful moments, respect, and won success by conformance to its
attitudes and prejudices. He never cut through the surface and became a true portrayer of human life as it appeared in the United
States.   —from the *American Mercury* (May 1930)

NEWTON ARVIN
With all his deficiencies, Howells is one of the decisive figures in the
development of our literary culture. The meaning of his career it is
no longer possible to neglect or belittle: he was the first of our important imaginative writers thoughtfully to consider and intelligently
to comprehend what was happening to the form and quality of
American life as it moved away from the simplicity, the social fluid-
ity, the relative freedoms, of the mid-century towards the ugly
disharmonies of monopolism and empire.
                    —from *The New Republic* (June 30, 1937)

Questions

1. H. L. Mencken wrote, "The truth about Howells is that he really
has nothing to say." And Ambrose Bierce wrote, "The master of this
detestable school of literature [that is, realism] is Mr. Howells. Absolutely destitute of that supreme and sufficient literary endowment,
imagination, he does not what he would but what he can; takes notes

with his eyes and ears, and writes them up as does any other reporter." Is this fair? Is Howells truly just a reporter? Do you think a novelist is saying something by the way in which he depicts what his characters do and say, how they look, how they dress? Do readers really want authors to insert essays into their novels that comment on the state of the world and their characters' morals?

2. On the other hand, is this novel weakened in its effect by the apparent lack of overt judgment, of evaluation? Does Howells seem bland to you? Are there events or situations in his own novel that should have made even Howells angry, or that should have been depicted by the author so as to make the reader angry?

3. How do you define the word "realism" in literature? Is a work informed by the methods of realism necessarily realistic? Does Howells's reticence about bodily matters and sex diminish the novel's realism? Compare *Silas Lapham* with any *naturalistic* novel you know—such as Stephen Crane's *Maggie: A Girl of the Streets* or most of Émile Zola's novels.

4. Consider the famous dinner scene in this book. Which character or characters do you sympathize with most? Could such a scene still occur in today's world? If so, in what setting and among which types of Americans?

FOR FURTHER READING

Howells and American Realism

Barrish, Phillip. *American Literary Realism: Critical Theory and Intellectual Prestige, 1880–1995*. New York: Cambridge University Press, 2001. Shifting critical understanding and judgments of American realism.

Bell, Michael Davitt. *The Problem of American Realism: Studies in the Cultural History of a Literary Idea*. Chicago: University of Chicago Press, 1993. An essential study of American realism.

Borus, Daniel. *Writing Realism: Howells, James, and Norris in the Mass Market*. Chapel Hill: University of North Carolina Press, 1989. The realist in the literary marketplace.

Carter, Everett. *Howells and the Age of Realism*. Philadelphia, PA: J. B. Lippincott, 1954. Pioneering critical study of Howells's realism. Still valuable.

Kaplan, Amy. *The Social Construction of American Realism*. Chicago: University of Chicago Press, 1988. The best of the new historical studies, brilliant and provocative.

Kazin, Alfred. *On Native Grounds: An Interpretation of Modern American Prose Literature*. New York: Reynal and Hitchcock, 1942. The classic work on the struggle for realism, beginning with Howells's symbolic move from Boston to New York.

Martin, Jay. *Harvests of Change: American Literature, 1865–1914*. Englewood Cliffs, NJ: Prentice-Hall, 1967. Valuable literary history.

Shi, David E. *Facing Facts: Realism in American Thought and Culture, 1850–1920*. New York: Oxford University Press, 1995. Accessible and wide-ranging study, including the visual arts.

Thomas, Brook. *American Literary Realism and the Failed Promise of Contract*. Berkeley: University of California Press, 1997. Includes searching essay on the moral economy of *The Rise of Silas Lapham*.

Biographies

Cady, Edwin H. *The Road to Realism: The Early Years, 1837–1885, of William Dean Howells* and *The Realist at War: The Mature Years, 1885–1920, of William Dean Howells.* Syracuse, NY: Syracuse University Press, 1956, 1958. The first comprehensive biography, by a leading Howells scholar.

Goodman, Susan, and Carl Dawson. *William Dean Howells: A Writer's Life.* Berkeley: University of California Press, 2005. Shrewd, readable, and engrossing biography.

Lynn, Kenneth S. *William Dean Howells: An American Life.* New York: Harcourt Brace Jovanovich, 1971. Keen psychological portrait, especially good on *A Modern Instance.*

Critical Studies

Cady, Edwin H., and Norma W. Cady, eds. *Critical Essays on W. D. Howells, 1866–1920.* Boston: G. K. Hall, 1983. Wide selection of reviews and essays published in Howells's lifetime.

Cawelti, John G. *Apostles of the Self-Made Man.* Chicago: University of Chicago Press, 1965. Provides relevant context.

Eble, Kenneth E., ed. *Howells: A Century of Criticism.* Dallas, TX: Southern Methodist University Press, 1962. Good selection of Howells criticism through the 1950s.

Gibson, William M. "Introduction." In William Dean Howells, *A Modern Instance,* edited by William M. Gibson. Boston: Houghton Mifflin, 1957. Insightful introduction to a well-edited text of one of Howells's key novels.

————. *William D. Howells.* Minneapolis: University of Minnesota Press, 1967. Good brief introduction to Howells's life and work.

McMurray, William. *The Literary Realism of William Dean Howells.* Carbondale: Southern Illinois University Press, 1967.

Pease, Donald E., ed. *New Essays on "The Rise of Silas Lapham."* Cambridge: Cambridge University Press, 1991. Challenging, sometimes controversial essays situating Howells's novel in various economic and social contexts.

Trilling, Lionel. "William Dean Howells and the Roots of Modern Taste." 1951.

————. *The Opposing Self: Nine Essays in Criticism.* New York: Viking Press, 1955. Eloquent evocation of Howells's social imagination, contrasting it with aspects of the modern sensibility.

Vanderbilt, Kermit. *The Achievement of William Dean Howells: A Reinterpretation.* Princeton, NJ: Princeton University Press, 1968. Valuable discussions of four outstanding Howells's novels.

Howells as Critic

Cady, Edwin H., ed. *W. D. Howells as Critic.* London: Routledge and Kegan Paul, 1973. A choice selection of Howells's important critical writings.

Other Works Cited in the Introduction

Howells, William Dean. *A Hazard of New Fortunes.* 1890. New York: Signet, 1965.

————. *Howells Novels, 1886–1888: The Minister's Charge/April Hopes/Annie Kilburn.* Library of America edition; edited by Don L. Cook. New York: Literary Classics of the United States, 1989.

————. *The Rise of Silas Lapham.* 1885. Norton Critical Edition; edited by Don L. Cook. New York: W. W. Norton, 1982.

————. *A Modern Instance.* 1882. Edited by William M. Gibson. Boston: Houghton Mifflin, 1957.

TIMELESS WORKS. NEW SCHOLARSHIP. EXTRAORDINARY VALUE.

Look for the following titles, available now and forthcoming from
BARNES & NOBLE CLASSICS.

Visit your local bookstore for these fine titles.

Adventures of Huckleberry Finn	Mark Twain	1-59308-000-X	$4.95
The Adventures of Tom Sawyer	Mark Twain	1-59308-068-9	$4.95
The Age of Innocence	Edith Wharton	1-59308-143-X	$5.95
Alice's Adventures in Wonderland and Through the Looking-Glass	Lewis Carroll	1-59308-015-8	$5.95
Anna Karenina	Leo Tolstoy	1-59308-027-1	$8.95
The Art of War	Sun Tzu	1-59308-017-4	$7.95
The Awakening and Selected Short Fiction	Kate Chopin	1-59308-001-8	$4.95
The Brothers Karamazov	Fyodor Dostoevsky	1-59308-045-X	$9.95
The Call of the Wild and White Fang	Jack London	1-59308-200-2	$5.95
Candide	Voltaire	1-59308-028-X	$4.95
A Christmas Carol, The Chimes and The Cricket on the Hearth	Charles Dickens	1-59308-033-6	$5.95
The Collected Poems of Emily Dickinson		1-59308-050-6	$5.95
The Complete Sherlock Holmes, Vol. I	Sir Arthur Conan Doyle	1-59308-034-4	$7.95
The Complete Sherlock Holmes, Vol. II	Sir Arthur Conan Doyle	1-59308-040-9	$7.95
The Count of Monte Cristo	Alexandre Dumas	1-59308-151-0	$7.95
Daniel Deronda	George Eliot	1-59308-290-8	$8.95
David Copperfield	Charles Dickens	1-59308-063-8	$7.95
The Death of Ivan Ilych and Other Stories	Leo Tolstoy	1-59308-069-7	$7.95
Don Quixote	Miguel de Cervantes	1-59308-046-8	$9.95
Dracula	Bram Stoker	1-59308-114-6	$6.95
Emma	Jane Austen	1-59308-089-1	$4.95
Essays and Poems by Ralph Waldo Emerson		1-59308-076-X	$6.95
The Essential Tales and Poems of Edgar Allan Poe		1-59308-064-6	$7.95
Frankenstein	Mary Shelley	1-59308-115-4	$4.95
Great American Short Stories: from Hawthorne to Hemingway		1-59308-086-7	$7.95
Great Expectations	Charles Dickens	1-59308-006-9	$4.95
Gulliver's Travels	Jonathan Swift	1-59308-132-4	$5.95
Hard Times	Charles Dickens	1-59308-156-1	$5.95
Heart of Darkness and Selected Short Fiction	Joseph Conrad	1-59308-021-2	$4.95
The Histories	Herodotus	1-59308-102-2	$6.95
The House of Mirth	Edith Wharton	1-59308-153-7	$6.95
Howards End	E. M. Forster	1-59308-022-0	$6.95
The Hunchback of Notre Dame	Victor Hugo	1-59308-047-6	$5.95
The Idiot	Fyodor Dostoevsky	1-59308-058-1	$7.95
The Importance of Being Earnest and Four Other Plays	Oscar Wilde	1-59308-059-X	$6.95
The Inferno	Dante Alighieri	1-59308-051-4	$6.95
Jane Eyre	Charlotte Brontë	1-59308-007-7	$4.95
Jude the Obscure	Thomas Hardy	1-59308-035-2	$6.95
The Jungle Books	Rudyard Kipling	1-59308-109-X	$5.95
The Jungle	Upton Sinclair	1-59308-008-5	$4.95
The Last of the Mohicans	James Fenimore Cooper	1-59308-137-5	$5.95
Leaves of Grass: First and "Death-bed" Editions	Walt Whitman	1-59308-083-2	$9.95
Les Misérables	Victor Hugo	1-59308-066-2	$9.95
Little Women	Louisa May Alcott	1-59308-108-1	$6.95

(continued)

Main Street	Sinclair Lewis	1-59308-036-0	$5.95
Mansfield Park	Jane Austen	1-59308-154-5	$5.95
The Metamorphosis and Other Stories	Franz Kafka	1-59308-029-8	$6.95
Moby-Dick	Herman Melville	1-59308-018-2	$9.95
My Ántonia	Willa Cather	1-59308-202-9	$5.95
Narrative of the Life of Frederick Douglass, an American Slave		1-59308-041-7	$4.95
Notes From Underground, The Double and Other Stories	Fyodor Dostoevsky	1-59308-037-9	$4.95
O Pioneers!	Willa Cather	1-59308-205-3	$5.95
The Odyssey	Homer	1-59308-009-3	$5.95
Oliver Twist	Charles Dickens	1-59308-206-1	$6.95
The Origin of Species	Charles Darwin	1-59308-077-8	$7.95
Paradise Lost	John Milton	1-59308-095-6	$7.95
Persuasion	Jane Austen	1-59308-130-8	$5.95
The Picture of Dorian Gray	Oscar Wilde	1-59308-025-5	$4.95
The Portrait of a Lady	Henry James	1-59308-096-4	$7.95
A Portrait of the Artist as a Young Man and Dubliners	James Joyce	1-59308-031-X	$6.95
Pride and Prejudice	Jane Austen	1-59308-201-0	$5.95
The Prince and Other Writings	Niccolò Machiavelli	1-59308-060-3	$5.95
The Red Badge of Courage and Selected Short Fiction	Stephen Crane	1-59308-119-7	$4.95
Republic	Plato	1-59308-097-2	$6.95
Robinson Crusoe	Daniel Defoe	1-59308-360-2	$5.95
The Scarlet Letter	Nathaniel Hawthorne	1-59308-207-X	$4.95
Sense and Sensibility	Jane Austen	1-59308-125-1	$5.95
Sons and Lovers	D. H. Lawrence	1-59308-013-1	$7.95
The Souls of Black Folk	W. E. B. Du Bois	1-59308-014-X	$5.95
The Strange Case of Dr. Jekyll and Mr. Hyde and Other Stories	Robert Louis Stevenson	1-59308-131-6	$4.95
A Tale of Two Cities	Charles Dickens	1-59308-138-3	$5.95
Tao Te Ching	Lao Tzu	1-59308-256-8	$5.95
The Three Musketeers	Alexandre Dumas	1-59308-148-0	$8.95
The Time Machine and The Invisible Man	H. G. Wells	1-59308-032-8	$4.95
Tom Jones	Henry Fielding	1-59308-070-0	$8.95
Treasure Island	Robert Louis Stevenson	1-59308-247-9	$4.95
The Turn of the Screw, The Aspern Papers and Two Stories	Henry James	1-59308-043-3	$5.95
Twenty Thousand Leagues Under the Sea	Jules Verne	1-59308-302-5	$5.95
Uncle Tom's Cabin	Harriet Beecher Stowe	1-59308-121-9	$7.95
Vanity Fair	William Makepeace Thackeray	1-59308-071-9	$7.95
Villette	Charlotte Brontë	1-59308-316-5	$7.95
The Voyage Out	Virginia Woolf	1-59308-229-0	$6.95
Walden and Civil Disobedience	Henry David Thoreau	1-59308-208-8	$5.95
The War of the Worlds	H. G. Wells	1-59308-085-9	$3.95
Wuthering Heights	Emily Brontë	1-59308-044-1	$4.95

BARNES & NOBLE CLASSICS

If you are an educator and would like to receive an
Examination or Desk Copy of a Barnes & Noble Classic edition,
please refer to Academic Resources on our website at
WWW.BN.COM/CLASSICS
or contact us at
B&NCLASSICS@BN.COM.

All prices are subject to change.